Malcolm McDonald

Writing from the Outskirts of Hope

Chapbook Press

Chapbook Press
Schuler Books
2660 28th Street SE
Grand Rapids, MI 49512
(616) 942-7330
www.schulerbooks.com

Printed at Schuler Books in Grand Rapids, MI on the Espresso Book Machine®

Printed in the United States of America
Publisher's Note
This is a work of fiction. With the exception of the Maria Colwell case, names, characters, and incidents are the product of the author's imagination or are used fictitiously, and any resemblance to actual persons, living or dead, business and educational establishments, or events is entirely coincidental.

ISBN 13: 978-1-936243-09-9
ISBN 10: 01-936243-09-1

For Barb

'The miserable have no other medicine

But only hope.'

William Shakespeare

Measure for Measure

1.

Resolution

The call of the goose pierced the evening mist, raising the ghosts of autumns past and causing McDermott to halt his business at the woodpile. Wiping his brow, he scanned the drab shroud of a sky and listened. Northwest Michigan in early October; soon the twilight of each day would be heralded by the same call multiplied a thousandfold, as the great V formations swept in from the north to overnight on their journey south. For now, though, only a few plaintive cries echoed that initial honking: the first he'd heard of the season's migration.

He sauntered round the side of his cabin to the top of the river bank. As Connor joined him, black nose twitching and sniffing the air, he watched a pair of the big birds circle back on themselves before feathering their wings and gliding down on to one of the many bayous. It was a scene he had thought never to tire of: a pastoral picture that invariably raised within him a feeling of being at one with the Earth. On the far side of the river, the Potawatomi marshland spread out before him in the enveloping mist: over a thousand acres of tributaries and bayous, grasses and reeds that effectively constituted his backyard. It should have lifted his spirits that great, sprawling view, but instead he found himself dwelling on the thought that he was witnessing another first: one more marker in the wasteland that was her absence.

Sighing, he sat on the old stone bench at the top of the river steps and, hunched over, hands thrust deeply into his pockets, observed a pair of the Canada geese gliding around, rippling the water and honking satisfaction with their day's achievement. The sight, the sounds and the accompanying smell of the river led him easily into a maudlin reflection of the myriad 'firsts' that had colored the two hundred and fifteen days since she'd left him: those perennial events, the continuation of which they'd taken so innocently for granted.

The most difficult had been the noisy arrival of the red-winged blackbirds – she'd missed those favorites of hers by a mere week. Then there'd been their anniversary, her birthday, and not long thereafter the return of her beloved orioles with their flash, orange breasts. The hummingbirds had followed within a couple of days, and shortly afterwards the annual procession of the turtles up from the river to lay their gooey eggs – laying waste to her carefully laid-out garden in the process. On and on they marched, those markers: the first Memorial Day, July 4th, Labour Day, and now the geese – the same birds that had almost finished their leaving when she'd completed hers. Were they actually the same? Could the pair paddling around before him have been present that day?

It was getting cold. Unfolding his frame from the bench, he turned back toward the cabin, inhaling the earthy tang of fall with its hints of dying leaves, damp earth and riparian silt. It was a pungency that pressed the play button on an autumnal highlight reel featuring mulled wine sipped by log fires, burning leaves on fading afternoons, and intimate walks along paths hidden beneath the red and gold detritus of Michigan falls.

Was it the intensity of his nostalgic broodings that occasioned her appearance at that moment? Whatever the reason, she materialized in front of the main deck, kneeling over her flower pots, prepping them as she always did for the winter. He took in the outrageous dimensions of the old, floppy hat she invariably wore while gardening, and the faint smile on her lips as she worked. As if sensing his presence, she turned her head toward him and her smile widened. Then she was gone.

Engulfed again in his own private morass of grief, he turned back toward the river allowing the tears their freedom and, squinting through the colors of their refracted light, he stood, shoulders stooped, and watched, without seeing, the unconcerned bobbing of the geese. It wasn't the first appearance she'd put in since her departure, and he hoped to hell it wouldn't be the last, but those sudden sightings of her had the effect of sucking the air from him and hurling him back to that cold February night when she'd closed her eyes on him for the last time. He drew in great drafts of the damp air and slowly exhaled. Connor stood beside him, tongue lolling from the corner of his mouth, his big warm body pressing against his master's legs.

Writing from the Outskirts of Hope

After dinner that night, McDermott banked up the porch fire, cracked open the windows and leaned back in his chair with a glass of The Glenrothes, his favorite Scotch. The glass was brimming, but what the hell; at this stage in his life, he had little time for moderation. He listened to the sounds of the marsh: the splashing of the giant carp, the honking of the geese, the accompaniment of ducks, the prehistoric calls of sandhill cranes, even the chatter of a few remaining tree frogs. He looked over to the log bookshelves and Jean's collection of bird and animal books, books that had been relentlessly thumbed by those long tapering fingers and scanned by her luminous brown eyes. More melancholia . . . It was high time he got a grip on his life; time to decide what the hell he was going to do with whatever he had left. Perhaps he should move. At least it would give him something to do. Something to do . . . His eyes strayed to the file boxes in the far corner of the room. Eighteen months ago he'd thought the notes and recordings within those boxes central to what he'd be doing for the rest of his life.

Barbara A. Staniforth had appeared as a gift from writers' heaven when she'd called asking for a meeting to discuss his writing of her biography. The retired CEO of the largest electronics company in the world and the most famous of the new breed of female super executives, Ms. Staniforth, a resident of Harbor Springs, had heard of him through her association with a U.S. Senator for whom he'd written a number of speeches. And her story was a potential blockbuster, no doubt about that. During the course of a spellbinding initial meeting, she'd sketched out the story of a meteoric rise from obscurity as an entry-level engineer, to fame as one of the most powerful corporate executives on Earth. It was a story that would have been gripping had she been a man; as a female it was the stuff of fantasy. The charismatic woman had not merely broken the glass ceiling, she'd vaporized it – and in a notoriously male-oriented world where she'd been subjected to every form of sexual harassment. Some of the anecdotes she'd related he couldn't have invented, and he'd known instinctively that he had within his grasp, a golden writing opportunity that could form the basis for a new career as a respected biographer. It was exactly what he'd been looking for. He'd always believed that if he was going to develop a writing career, the genre on which he should concentrate was biography, since it most closely paralleled the type of writing through which he'd made his living for so long. It was writing that depended upon the skills he'd honed over the years: the ability to form relationships quickly, research and interviewing expertise, the easy inspiration of trust in one's subjects.

And God, he'd needed something. After receiving an unsolicited offer for his small Training and Communications Company ten years ago, he'd pocketed what he'd reckoned to be the outrageous sum of ten million dollars and imagined a carefree life from there on in. Except it hadn't worked out that way. Yes, he and Jean had become wealthy, but in the process he'd lost his identity and a fair portion of his self-esteem. With no more deadlines to meet, no clients to impress, an absence of projects to be created and sold, he'd fallen into a depressive haze from which volunteerism and a brief flirtation with art photography had provided only temporary relief.

So the elegant Ms. Staniforth had seemed a godsend when she'd arrived on the scene. She'd taken to him from the beginning, had enthused over his portfolio, and offered a contract giving him 10% of any profits the book might make. A strict regimen of recorded daily interviews had followed and his excitement had mounted as he'd learned more of the woman's stirring climb to executive prominence. Although he was previously unpublished, he'd been confident of the book's commercial value and had told Jean on more than one occasion, a bidding war for the rights was not out of the question.

He'd had around thirty hours recorded when it had all gone pear-shaped. It had become obvious to him that her former employer would be less than thrilled over her revelations and he'd thought it his duty to bring up the issue at the end of one of their sessions.

'You do realize do you, Barbara, that you're going to seriously piss off some important people with this book?'

'Well, the thought had occurred to me,' she'd said. 'Perhaps I should get my attorney's input before we go much further. There was an awful lot of paperwork I never bothered to read when I received my severance package; maybe I should have him cast an eye over it.'

One hour. That was what it took the attorney to find the clause in Barbara's severance agreement, the clause pursuant to which, any public utterances or publications that could be construed as being injurious to the company's image, would result in the loss of that part of her pension deemed 'discretionary.' Since that figure was in excess of $1,000,000 per year, she'd had no choice. He'd understood her position, of course he had: he couldn't see himself giving up that kind of cash to publish a biography. Nevertheless, it had been a blow – but then, within a couple of weeks, Jean had been diagnosed, and writing had become the least of his concerns.

McDermott contemplated the bottom of his glass and heaved himself up; damned drink had evaporated on him again. One more, he promised himself as he poured The Glenrothes, one more and then bed. He rearranged the glowing logs, closed the windows against the cool night air and eased back into his chair. Closing his eyes and savoring the distinctive taste of Scotland's Speyside, it occurred to him again that the mere act of moving somewhere else would be a creative project that might help him move forward. They'd talked about it toward the end. Jean had urged him to consider returning to England and, despite his denials, he had entertained the notion: not England exactly, maybe the West coast of Scotland, perhaps up around Skye. But then, as the days passed after the funeral and he'd struggled with the empty reality of her never-ending absence, he'd realized that memories were what he needed and they were more easily savored in their birthplace. And so he'd decided to stay. He would stay because he had to stay. Now here he was again, second guessing himself.

One thing was for sure, he had no one to worry about but himself. Hell, when he thought about it, there was no one *left* to worry about. No one left to worry about – it wasn't the first time that thought had intruded over the past few months. Jesus Christ, who'd have thought it? Who'd have picked him as the lone survivor? Not many; certainly not twenty-five years ago when he'd had his heart attack. He took another sip of Scotch, held up the heavy crystal glass against the light of the lamp, and eyed the amber liquid as the surgeon's words came back. 'A myocardial infarction to the posterior of the heart . . . least effect on the pumping action . . . least effect on longevity . . . lucky.' McDermott allowed himself a wry smile: lucky –

well, he supposed he had been. That little episode had led to a change in his lifestyle including the cessation of smoking, the adoption of a heart-healthy diet and a daily exercise routine. Meanwhile he'd watched a succession of friends and relatives die from cancer of this and that, Parkinson's, Alzheimer's, Multiple Sclerosis and God knew what else. Still, maybe being the last one was its own disease. Ah, the hell with it: too much theorizing for one night. Levering himself up, he checked the fire screen, turned off the lamp, deposited his glass in the kitchen and went to bed. Only when Connor jumped up into Jean's place did he remember he'd not let the retriever out, and he stumbled back out to the deck. As the dog sniffed around, he looked up at the stars – the air had cleared now – and smiled as he thought how Jean would have scolded him for thinking there was no one left to worry about. In her eyes, animals were the most important ones to worry about and of those, Connor was paramount.

It was close to twenty years since McDermott had slept through an entire night, so he was surprised when he awoke the next morning to see it was seven thirty. Connor, feeling his movement, was on him immediately, sniffing and snuffling in his face, anxious to begin the day. McDermott shrugged on his robe, pulled open the door to the bedroom deck and watched the dog rush past him. As Connor explored the scents laid down by the night's visitors, he looked out over the river. Day 216 and another fine day brewing from the look of the dawn – all he had to do was figure out how to fill it. That thought took him back to his ruminations of the previous evening on the subject of finding something to do.

He was still wrestling with the issue an hour later as he regarded his wet, shaven face in the bathroom mirror. There was little hair left on his head; just the shaved fringe of silver round the back and sides, but although his neck was going to flab beneath his chin, he had few wrinkles. His body was in decent shape too, thanks to his daily work-out regimen. Even his pale blue eyes remained clear, although the sockets were darkened, testament to the torment of the past few months. Toweling his face dry, he smiled as the self-assessment of his body took him back to his first date with Jean when, for some reason, he'd seen fit to give her a full, unsolicited report on the general state of his health. She'd taken great delight in making the story her party-piece over the years, exaggerating the details a little more with each telling.

It was the hairpiece he'd been wearing at the time that had started the thing off, he recalled. He'd always liked to be up front about that with new dates, because the fact was, despite all the advertising blurb about it acting like 'real hair' and its 'security,' the bloody thing did move during sex, and on one occasion it had finished up over his eyes. Anyway that's how his rambling 'confession' had begun during their first dinner together. Gesturing upwards with his eyes, he'd said, 'By the way, this isn't real.'

Jean, nonplussed, had stopped chewing, regarded him quizzically, and said, 'What's not real?'

To be fair to her, she'd kept a straight face at first, but then he'd moved on to the souvenirs his soccer playing days had left him: his dodgy knees, the absence of elasticity in his ankle ligaments, and the small scar on his left ear. When he'd concluded with how cross country running on English winter days had caused the intermittent rheumatism in his shoulders, and the problem with the right hip, Jean had carefully laid down her knife and fork, and with raised eyebrows, politely asked, 'Is everything else in working order?' They'd started laughing at that point and they'd been laughing together ever since until . . . Goddamnit! Why her? Why now? If she'd stopped smoking when he had, perhaps . . . McDermott threw on his workout gear and stormed out of the cabin, Connor by his side.

Pounding along the hard sand by the lake's edge for five miles had its customary effect of lowering his angst in direct proportion to the elevation of his heart rate, and following a shower upon his return, he felt ready to face the day. The bright sun and fresh morning air demanded he find outdoor chores to occupy his time and he elected first to check out the condition of the cabin exterior. Normally around this time of year Jean, who'd always been in charge of 'maintenance and grounds' as she'd put it, would perform this task, informing 'Sam the Cabin Man' their log expert, of any staining requirements. Now the regular inspection was his responsibility alone.

He circled the cabin, found nothing he felt couldn't wait until the spring and was about to go back in through the garage, when he paused to admire the interlocking ends of the massive twelve inch logs on the south east corner of the house. He slapped the ends with his hands as he often did, marveled at the star patterns of sawn-through knots, and laid his face against the wood, smelling its primitive essence. A mix of lodge-pole pine and Englewood spruce, the logs had been trucked the fifteen hundred miles from Montana nineteen years ago when he'd sold the business and he and Jean had wanted to build their own shrine to Jenny Lake and the Tetons. Every year of their marriage they'd made the pilgrimage to the Teton National Park during the first week in October when the tourists had left and the trails were quiet. They'd hiked the switchback trails, ridden horses through meadows lit by golden aspens, and revisited their favorite spots: Lupine Meadows, Leigh Lake, Jenny Lake, Signal Mountain, Inspiration Point . . . The names flowed easily back, one more avalanche of recollections, and he wondered anew whether the associated pain might ever dissipate.

Later in the morning after splitting half a cord of wood, he took his second shower of the day, made more coffee and retired to his den. Sitting before the open windows, Connor at his feet, he resolved again to focus his attention on the future and what it might hold for him. The dawn's early promise had been fulfilled and the river reflected just a few white clouds in a deep blue sky. A muskrat pushed a V of water as it moved toward its lodge, and he spotted a great blue heron standing on the far bank, a study in stillness. Wallowing in the tranquility, he relived the unlikely journey he and Jean had made to find this place.

McDermott had grown up in an English fishing port and the nearest beach had been a mere ten mile bike ride away. The magic of the sea and sands had always attracted him and thus the lake had been a logical choice when he and Jean had begun their search for a retirement home. Finding a suitable lot had proved easier said than done, however, and a number of trips to the area had proved fruitless. Their real estate agent had pushed the idea of the river, but they'd been determined to find a lot on the Lake, until that is, McDermott had made the mistake with the book.

Dressing for work one morning, he'd been vaguely listening to a morning news show when the words, 'midlife crisis' had focused his attention on the T.V. Howell Raines a newspaper editor, had written a book called 'Fly Fishing Through the Midlife Crisis.' The book had appeared to McDermott, judging from the interview with the author, to be about the vicissitudes of life, and targeted at men like him-although, at fifty, 'midlife' might have been a tad optimistic. He'd bought the book only to discover that the damned thing was actually about fly fishing, a subject in which he had no interest whatsoever. Nevertheless the book had given him pause, Raines pointing out the beauty of rivers, their ever-changing aspects and the vast numbers of species to be discovered in and around them. It had been enough to persuade him and Jean that river banks as a potential home site merited more consideration, one thing had led to another and they'd found their dream spot.

McDermott grimaced: back in the past again. Where had he been? Oh yes, his future. He turned and allowed his eyes to play over the familiar interior of the den: the packed bookshelves, the rough pine desk, the computer station still flanked by his photographic printers. It was a room that said a lot about him, but the details were all Jean: the arrow shaped handles on the drawers; the lamps with the subtle hints of the Great Northwoods on their shades; the table waterfall crowded with rocks they'd gathered from the banks of the Snake, and the shores of Superior and Michigan. The photographs crowding the walls caught his attention. He studied the nudes he'd shot with Kim Weston out in California. Maybe he should get back into photography, he could – No, who was he kidding? He'd been there and done that. Enjoyable? Yes. A potential late career? No. Although he'd enjoyed the creative charge and the cerebral challenges involved in the new digital age of photography, he had no interest in doing the necessary marketing to sell his work. No, he needed a new challenge, something that would grip him, take him by the balls and return him to the single mindedness he'd possessed when he was running his business. Obsession, Jean had called it, and she'd been right. A total ability to shut out the rest of the world he'd had then, and he needed it back now. He'd actually rediscovered that particular gift during his brief work with Barbara Staniforth – only to have it snatched away again.

His thoughts turned idly back to the thrill he'd felt in being involved once more in the writing process. The writing process; the phrase sent him over to his bookshelves and his collection of books on that very subject – not an extensive selection, but one he enjoyed dipping into from time to time. His eyes swept over the titles: Norman Mailer's 'The Spooky Art,' Stephen King's 'On Writing,' a couple of volumes of the New York Times' series of 'Writers on Writing,' Jon Winokur's, 'Advice to Writers,' Lamont's, 'bird by bird,' and . . . what was this? McDermott withdrew from the shelf, still encased in its cellophane wrapper, a thick CD case, and recalled as he read the title and took in the British Library logo, that he'd ordered the double CD collection shortly before Jean's diagnosis. Its delivery would have passed virtually unnoticed amid the tumult of those early days of her illness, and he must have simply filed it away on the shelves. He opened the case and read the accompanying booklet. The CDs contained extracts from interviews with British authors from the Library's, 'Authors' Lives' project launched in 2007. The list of authors was impressive and he slipped the first disc into his computer and settled back to listen. It wasn't long before he was pausing the recording and making notes. When he'd listened to both discs he replayed them.

Only when he laid down his pen and switched off the computer, did he realize he'd missed lunch and the day was drawing to a close. He rose and stretched, went through to the porch and poured himself a Scotch. Ambling over to the windows, he gazed out over the river and played back the comments of some of the authors in his mind: Michael Morpurgo's approach of simply letting the words flow – just writing and worrying about mistakes later; Philip Hensher's comments on making sure there are enough 'drops in the bowl' before you start; Michael Holroyd's words on the real happiness of discovering something on the page that works; P.D. James saying that, yes there will be times of regret, disappointment; Ian Rankin admitting that on some days, when he found writing like 'digging coal,' he did 'fuck-all.'

Connor's insistent brushing against his leg accompanied by heavy panting – a sure sign the dog believed it time to eat – interrupted his thoughts, but later, while preparing his own dinner, he continued his analysis of what he'd heard those great authors say. He understood that at some level he'd found their words motivational; he just wasn't sure in what way.

It was following dinner and his third playing of the discs, when he identified the effect the writers were having upon him. They were enabling him, they were intimating that he had the freedom to write – in any genre, on any subject and in any way he wanted. Everything else was irrelevant: the writing was all. Many of the authors said the same thing in different ways, but the words of Hilary Mantel and Beryl Bainbridge he found especially inspirational.

Here was Hilary Mantel: '. . . *writing is not about status and if status is what you seek, you're better off taking up any profession that will allow you to hang your certificates on the wall and to have the obvious trappings of success. . . . My considered opinion is this: That there is nothing you have to do, no task, except to watch the curve of your own development as an artist.*'

And Beryl Bainbridge: '*I don't write for readers. I don't think many writers do. I only write for myself . . . I think I'd have written books whether they were published or not. I just like writing.*'

It was a thoughtful McDermott who went to bed that night, a restless one too, and eschewing sleep, his mind ran over the possibility that embarking on a new writing project might effectively bring some purpose into what he knew at that moment, to be an aimless, empty life. He pondered again the obvious choice of biography as a genre. The problem as he saw it was not so much his ability, but of finding someone notable and interesting enough, willing to entrust the story of their life to a previously unpublished writer. Opportunities such as Barbara Staniforth, he knew, came along once in a lifetime if you were lucky. He considered Samuel Giddons, Vanguard Motor Company's ex-vice president for corporate relations. He might be a possibility; McDermott had met him a few times during his work with Vanguard and the IBAW, and the story of what Giddons had accomplished in developing a union-company relationship was remarkable. But then, even if he were to be successful in seeing the man and acquiring his assent – both big ifs – the amount of travel involved would be horrendous, and travel was something McDermott had no interest in. Indeed – and he had no idea why this fact hadn't occurred to him before – the whole concept of biography as a genre was a non-starter if he was not prepared to leave the river and the marsh for long periods. It was with that realization that he fell asleep.

Despite the negative conclusion to the previous evening, McDermott was upbeat during his run the next morning. He put aside the issue of what to write, comforted himself with his decision to actually have a go at something – whatever that might be – and determined to concentrate on developing a foundation of facts about the writing life that he'd have to understand and accept in order to proceed. Those facts could be gleaned from what he'd heard the previous day as he'd listened to 'The Writing Life' and, following his return to the cabin, he spent the rest of the morning listening again and making notes. Not long after lunch, he had a list of facts – verities perhaps – the acceptance of which he believed to be key if he was to persevere through the challenge ahead. He read them over.

> 1. Whatever I write will almost certainly not be published; indeed there is a high probability no one will ever read it, but that is irrelevant since I will be writing for myself.

> 2. Although my efforts may leave a good deal to be desired, the important thing to remember is that this is about the process not the product.

> 3. It will be a long, hard slog accompanied by frustrations, disappointments and moments of despair. Nevertheless, I will draw strength from the fact that I will be sharing those experiences with writers a good deal more accomplished than me.

> 4. I should follow Morpurgo's advice and write, write, write. Errors I will address later during the editing process.

> 5. My work will require numerous revisions: perhaps as many as ten before I'm likely to be satisfied with the end product.

He might have to add a few things later, but for now he felt those points covered the essentials. He still had no bloody idea what he was going to write, and was well aware that having the freedom to write about anything posed its own challenges. Back in the day, when he'd been on the lecture circuit, he'd constantly advised young teachers: 'Don't tell kids to write about anything they want to write about: it's the hardest subject in the world.' Now he was setting himself that same incredibly difficult task.

McDermott spent the rest of the afternoon, to Connor's delight, roaming the beach and thinking. He was happy with his decision to write, accepting of the potential pitfalls, and was conscious of a reawakening of the excitement inherent in the beginnings of a new project. It was the direction in which he should proceed that continued to evade him. Fiction seemed the logical choice: if he was going to test himself, embrace the freedom of writing, why not go the whole hog? According to more than one author he'd listened to over the past couple of days, the best preparation for writing fiction was reading it, and if that was true, he was better prepared than most. He'd been an avid reader of fiction all his life and his personal library contained more than a couple of thousand volumes. Having said that, at what genre should he try his hand? His mind roamed over his favorite 'page-turners,' for although he loved literary novels, he was sensible enough to know he had a ways to go before he tested himself in that direction.

Crime came to mind, and with it the writers he and Jean had shared a love for: Rankin, Hoag, Reichs, Johannson, Nesbo, Larrson, and Sandford. Sandford; when you thought Sandford you thought Davenport, the tough cop, and when you thought Davenport you thought serial killer. Now there was a possibility. Questions raced through his mind. What about the 'Lolita Complex? Missing kids? The killer's predilections? Trophies? He saw a vague figure lying in bed in a room papered with famous posters of fairies. A killer with a taste for young girls? Why? What was the trigger that set him off? McDermott hurried home.

Three hours later, he sat slumped over his desk, the top of which was littered with printouts from the internet of statistics and photographs of missing kids. The figures were staggering, the faces heartbreaking, and he knew he couldn't do it. He was incapable of delving into the twisted psyches of people who killed for pleasure: couldn't face up to the savagery inherent in the subject. So – no serial killer book.

McDermott had, on numerous occasions throughout his life, lauded the calming and refreshing qualities of The Glenrothes, but he'd never ascribed the power of inspiration to the famous Scotch. Nevertheless, it was as he was gazing into the golden depths of his glass later in the evening, that something Beryl Bainbridge had said tickled the roots of his memory. Setting down his drink, he went over to his computer and, using the table of contents for the CDs as a guide, he played back her contributions. It didn't take him long and for the second time that day he set himself to transcribing from the discs. There were two relevant statements by Bainbridge, both on the first disc. It was the word 'biography' in the first statement that intrigued him and started him thinking.

When I'm writing a novel, I'm writing about my own life. I'm writing a biography; almost always. And to make it into a novel I either have a murder or a death at the end.'

The second statement by the famous writer took McDermott to the next level and effectively jumpstarted his fiction writing career – if a career it was going to be.

The only reason I wanted to write was to write down my childhood: to write down about the things I knew, the people I knew. I don't believe anybody makes anything up. There's no such thing as the imagination. I mean, people may say they don't know where the story comes from, but they must do. You can't . . . there's nothing you can make up. In general, you're recalling memories I think.'

It was those bold, controversial words from the five-time Booker award nominee that sent McDermott scurrying over to the bookshelf where he stored all the material he'd ever written. He pulled down the notes he'd made for his autobiography when he'd retired, notes he'd never got around to using, and began to read. As he journeyed back through his past, the concept began to form. What if he took –? He needed to do more thinking.

He grabbed a windbreaker; called Connor – who couldn't believe his luck – piled into Jean's old SUV, and drove back out to the beach. He rarely walked at night but the moon was full in a clear sky and provided enough light for someone as familiar with the lakeshore as he.

The wind had come up on the shoreline and breakers were rolling in from the northwest. Body bent against the wind, he walked by the water's edge as Connor raced back and forth checking out the same dead fish and gulls he'd sniffed earlier. In the few moments he had before the great waves of ideas, potential plots and schemes cascaded into his mind, McDermott registered the perfection of the conditions for creative thought: air sharp enough to color cheeks and clear sinuses, the susurration of the wind in the shoreline trees, the rasp of the shingle as the froth of the lake retreated, and the damp scent of sand meeting the tang of pine. The irony of such rusticity providing the backdrop for his journey back to the crowded, concrete setting forming in his brain, was lost on him as he gave himself up to his memories and the book he thought might work.

It was remarkable how clearly it had come to him once he'd begun to read those old notes of his; no hard thinking involved at all really – it was just there: Cracker's story and his relationship with McDermott. Whether the saga would constitute a short story, a novella or a novel, he was unsure, but it would certainly cover the whole concept of friendship: its beginnings, its evolution, its complexities, its vulnerability to the changing circumstances of life. Sweeping clouds of times and places rolled through his memory as he weighed the directions in which he might go. There was no doubt he had a lot of material and some interesting stories, but did he have enough? And did he have the skill to play around with the raw material, to change the characters, to juxtapose incidents, to enhance the comedy, the drama: to push out from the biographical facts into fiction? Did he have the ability to bring the characters to life on the page, and most important of all, could he do justice to the icon that Cracker became? There was also one other, more difficult and emotionally taxing question to address: Was it possible that revisiting the endings of old relationships could seriously exacerbate the very condition from which he hoped the exercise of writing would rescue him? Could old grief reignite the new?

There was only one way to definitively answer that question and that was to press ahead.

By the time he arrived back at the cabin, the thoughts were coming thick and fast, and midnight found him still scribbling furiously as his pen struggled to keep pace with his brain. When he'd finally exhausted his initial thoughts – during which he'd realized the genre he was getting into was general fiction – he turned off the lamp and lay on his back for a while watching shafts of moonlight play on the wood ceiling. He'd made some progress. The book would lean heavily upon actual events, especially those related to Cracker, but where necessary he'd deviate from the truth, introduce fictional characters and move around times and places; have some fun with the thing. When he'd been a child, his mother had always called him a little romancer; now he'd discover whether he had the ability to be a big one – although, considering the life Cracker had led, and the unlikely relationship they'd shared, he wasn't sure much romancing would be required. He had a momentary frisson of fear. Was this really something he should be considering? Did he have what it would take? What if he found it was beyond him? Ah, the hell with it, he thought, just think of the freedom, and the truth behind those words of Vonnegut:

The primary goal of practicing any art whether well or badly is that it enables the soul to grow.'

That was the kind of positive thinking he should be concentrating on, that and his list of verities. And the freedom too. During his entire career in the training business he'd written what clients had paid him to write: manuals, pamphlets, handbooks, promotional pieces, industrial video scripts, speeches – the whole bloody gamut of communications in corporate America. So okay, yes, he'd written some decent poetry since he'd retired, but fiction he'd always felt beyond him. Now though, he would have a go; after all, what was the downside? Depression if he failed to finish what he started? He was going down that road anyway if he didn't pull his finger out.

Cracker. At so many critical junctures in McDermott's life, Cracker had been there like some grand conductor, directing him this way and that, and now here he was again. McDermott drifted back to sleep, visions of his old friend and the turbulent times they'd shared together playing in his mind.

It was early the next morning, the sun still below the horizon, when he began to write. Philip Hensher had likened the emotions he felt prior to starting a new book to the feeling of being in a shuddering airplane at the end of the runway prior to takeoff. McDermott felt more as a runner might feel before the ten thousand meters in the Olympic Games: highly strung, nervous, excited, and full of expectation. He supposed he faced the same kind of possible outcomes too: winning in a blaze of glory, lumbering along in the middle of the pack or quitting half way.   He knew he should be planning, drawing up time-lines, coming up with an overall structure, maybe a synopsis – and he would get to those things – but today he had to write. Because, he thought to himself, as he wrote those opening eight words, he first had to determine whether he actually could.

2.

Roots

Alastair James McCracken was a friend of mine. He wasn't perfect, being rather too fond of using his fists and other men's wives for that, but he was special. Although baptized Alastair James, I rarely heard him referred to by names other than those bearing only the most tenuous connection to such splendid appellations. To his mam, he was 'Our Ally' when he was behaving well (which was rarely), and 'You Little Sod,' when he was in the shit (which was often). To his father he remained largely anonymous, being to the big man little more than an inconvenience for whom the title, 'you' was deemed more than adequate. To the cane-wielding teachers of our youth, not in the habit of using given names, he was 'McCracken,' the formal surname usually spat out with a theatrical drum roll of the 'r,' and a whiplash emphasis on the central syllable. To me, and all the other kids on the streets of our childhood, he was always 'Cracker,' a sobriquet whose origin, in the nature of such things, was obscure, but in perfect harmony with his persona.

The two of us were born during World War II on the same day, in the same city, in the same building. While the identical date of birth was coincidental, the city, Gainsborough in the County of Lincoln, and the building, Gateburton Hall, were present on our birth certificates as a result of the wartime evacuation of our mothers from the port city of Kingstown which was, throughout the war, a primary target of the German Luftwaffe.

Once returned to our homes, we spent the first eleven years of our lives on the same street, a circumstance that ensured we grew up with innumerable things in common – not the least of which was the city's damp, malodorous environment.

Dimly lit and often fouled by dogs or the brewery's dray horses, our street comprised two facing rows of houses of the 'two-up-two-down' Victorian design spawned by the industrial revolution to provide low cost housing for the masses. Comprised, as the name suggests, of two rooms on the ground floor (sitting room and kitchen), and two bedrooms on the upper floor, these tiny dwellings had no bathroom and no hot water. The toilet, known as the 'lav,' was situated next to the 'coalhouse' in the small, concrete backyard, the door of which led out into a shared 'back passage' separating one line of houses from another. Like the crosses on Flanders fields, these houses of our childhood stretched row on regimented row, staring blankly out at the usually wet streets they lined.

While the physical nature of our childhood environment was less than inspiring, the air we breathed was almost certainly hazardous. The chimneys of the paint factory at the end of the street spewed out dark smoke reeking of lead-based paint, while round the corner the tan yard produced the mephitic odours concomitant with the tanning industry. Augmenting this farrago of industrial fumes and gases, depending on the time of day and the prevailing wind, were the odours of the dock-side fish processing plants; the fermenting hops from Kingstown Brewery; and the stench of Queensferry, the site of rendering plants and the city's gasworks.

Although we shared the same environment – only the width of a mere four houses separated Cracker's home from mine – our families occupied vastly different rungs on the working class ladder of postwar England. Cracker hailed from the lowest level of that ladder, a level populated by the truly poverty-stricken, direct descendants of the Victorian working class whose families had been unable to escape the degradation of a life in which high levels of disease and malnutrition were endemic. Often subsisting on handouts from the State, a large percentage of which would find its way into liquid relief at the local pub, these folk had little concern for cleanliness and no time at all for godliness. My parents in contrast, by virtue of dad's position in the Transport and General Workers Union on the docks, had reached the upper echelons of the working class. While we had few material possessions, cleanliness and churchgoing were imperatives, and education was revered. We lived, my mam said, according to 'good Christian values,' and both she and dad ensured I was 'well dressed' before they considered clothing purchases for themselves.

Even as a child I was not impervious to the divide between Cracker's life and my own. I puzzled over the use in his house of cupboard doors, floorboards, and even steps from the stairs, as firewood. I studiously avoided using my comb and handkerchief in his presence, knowing he possessed neither, and never passed comment on his bedraggled appearance, or the occasional shearing of his head ordered by the school nurse to rid him of the head lice that were the bane of his existence. Despite our differences, I loved spending time in Cracker's house – although I knew I would not like to live there. The battered, brown doors, both front and back, were open to anyone whenever Big Jim McCracken was absent, and the standard rules that applied in my house relating to climbing on furniture, wiping your feet on entry, and generally behaving in a civilized manner, appeared to be non-existent in that wonderful free-for-all playground that was Cracker's home. The missing floorboards and steps on the stairs provided a wealth of grist for our imaginative mills, while the great piles of dirty dishes in the kitchen and the odour of old mashed potatoes and gravy mixed with stale cigarette smoke, added a chaotic cachet to the whole experience.

In the absence of Big Jim, the daily comings and goings of Cracker's family were presided over by his mother, Doris, a huge woman with a doughy face and greasy hair, who rarely moved from the confines of the shabby old armchair from which she squinted out at the world through her cigarette smoke. She was a woman with a big heart but a heavy hand – a hand she would use to mete out arbitrary punishment to anyone who became too rambunctious, and was careless enough to stray within range.

Apart from Cracker and his mam and dad, the house, with its two small bedrooms, was also home to his teenage sisters, Janice and Brenda, and little Audrey, a six year old who had been a late, surprise addition to the fold. All three girls shared a bedroom with Cracker – a circumstance no doubt instrumental in his becoming an expert in the facts of life years before the rest of us.

The master of the house, Big Jim McCracken was a hulk of a man over six feet in height, with the massive shoulders and muscular forearms common to the labourers on the city's docks where he made a tenuous living. His weathered skin was stretched tightly over the angles and planes of his raw face from which his eyes, the only small aspect of his countenance, gave the impression of regarding life as something to be fought. He was, in common with many of his ilk at that time, a consummate bully who thought nothing of using his fists on any member of his family, particularly Doris if she was ever less than prompt in having his evening meal on the table. Whenever he judged misdemeanors on the part of his children to warrant more severe punishment, he would take considerable pleasure in using 'Old Shiner,' his wide, highly polished leather belt, on the bare buttocks and thighs of the offending miscreant. Fortunately for his family, other than when he was eating or sleeping, Big Jim spent little time at home. Whenever he was off-shift or on strike, he could be found at the Bull, the local hostelry, where a regular evening's input would routinely comprise eight pints of Kingstown Brewery's best bitter – twelve pints a night being the norm on a weekend. The family lived in daily fear of him as did the rest of us, and we were always safely back in our own homes before the scrape of his hobnailed boots down the back passage heralded his return from work.

In contrast to the cowboy and Indian country that was Cracker's house, my home was a study in good housekeeping. Mam scrubbed it clean on a regular basis, the windows and curtains were regularly washed, and the front door step (the outward measure of a house's cleanliness in those days), glowed daily with the yellow evidence of mam's close attention with a pumice stone. Throughout the house too, there hung, depending on the day of the week, the tang of disinfectant, the smell of furniture polish, or the scent of newly ironed laundry.

If the difference between Cracker's home life and my own, and the disparate values of our parents were enough to make our friendship implausible, the contrast in our individual characteristics was sufficient to make it downright improbable. I was quiet, cautious and skinny, with an almost slavish respect for authority, while Cracker was a loud, fearless, stocky kid who never met a rule he wasn't prepared to break. If that was not enough, I was soft, sensible and steady, while Cracker was a hard, mischievous risk taker.

So from where did our childhood affinity spring? Proximity and convenience were certainly primary elements, while the quid pro quo of childhood friendship – the complementing of one's weaknesses by the other's strengths — must assuredly have played a part. My prudence tempered his audacity, while my intellect balanced his physical prowess. His house provided me an indoor playground, while the quiet orderliness of my home gave him a respite from the chaos that was his. He protected me from the bullies that roamed the school playground and the streets; I helped him in more cerebral ways, when the complexities of new language or mathematical concepts proved too much for him. We also had much in common: an Arthurian belief in loyalty, a quick sense of humour, a vivid imagination, and a hatred of injustice.

Cracker took his role as my protector seriously and was, in this respect, capable of a raw violence that was frightening to behold. One of the more memorable examples of his ferocious interventions occurred on a warm Thursday evening in the ninth year of our lives. I know it was a Thursday evening for the incident occurred on our swimming night. Cracker and I were already accomplished swimmers by the time we were nine and were enthusiastic members of Kingstown Swimming Club. We were in the process of leaving after our swim, and looking forward to a threepenny bag of chips from the local chippy, when Jackie Wales, our swimming coach, called Cracker over to him. I told Cracker I'd wait outside, passed through the doors — and straight into trouble.

I was halfway down the steps of the swimming baths to the street, my threepenny piece clutched in my hand, before I saw Knocker Brentwood and his mate, Tadge Tyler leaning against the pillars at the bottom of the stone stairway. The Brentwood family was notorious in our area for both theft and violence, and I'd heard mam say Knocker's father and two brothers were in Kingstown high security prison. Knocker was a twelve-year-old thug who'd acquired his nickname through an ability to bang his head against brick walls without apparently feeling pain. Tyler was an abject sycophant, classified as educationally sub-normal in school, who blindly followed Brentwood's bidding.

Whether it was simply nerves or the certain knowledge they would not let me pass, I don't know, but as I approached them, I lost my footing on the bottom step and sprawled onto the pavement, cossie and towel flying one way and my threepenny piece the other. Brentwood had the money in his hand before I could get up.

''Ere, look what I've found Gobby Robbie,' he said, brandishing the coin in the air. 'Must be my lucky day.'

The pain from my scraped knees allied to fear and frustration brought forth tears and a choked response. 'Give me that back. It's mine,'

'Cor blimey, look at this Tadge. Poor little sod's crying. What's up little Robbie? Want yer mammy do yer?'

Infuriated by his taunting, I hurled myself at him stretching for the threepenny piece held aloft in his hand. 'You give that back right now, you, you bloody thief,' I shouted through my tears.

'Or what, Gobby Robbie?'

'Or I'm going to have to make you,' came a quiet voice from the swimming pool steps.

Coming from anyone else, the words in the context of the situation would have been laughable, for the nine year old boy on the steps was a good three inches shorter and ten pounds lighter than Brentwood. The boy on the steps, however, was Cracker McCracken and he wasn't pretending to be John Wayne or some other matinee hero; he was serious.

'Oh yeah? You and whose army McCracken?'

As if from nowhere, a crowd formed around us and I could hear the whispered word, 'fight' drifting from the gathering mob. Cracker put down his wet roll of cossie and towel and slowly walked up to the taller and heavier Brentwood. As if taking their cue from him, the crowd hushed.

It began with something as simple as a glance. As Cracker stopped in front of Brentwood he suddenly looked to his right. Brentwood followed Cracker's eyes and before his slow mind could register the feint, Cracker's right boot thudded into Brentwood's groin. As his adversary cried out and doubled up in agony, Cracker's boot swung again catching Brentwood flush on the chin and sending him to the ground. There followed a scene of such savagery – Cracker alternately banging Brentwood's head against the pavement and punching him in the face – that I was beginning to fear for the older boy's life, when the muscular arms of Jackie Wales appeared as if from nowhere, and hauled Cracker to his feet.

Cracker was lucky, for although Knocker Brentwood spent three days in the hospital receiving treatment for his injuries, his mother was so ashamed of his beating at the hands of a nine-year-old she refused to press charges. I never forgot that night: the wait for Nobby Clarke, our local bobby; the ambulance arriving for Brentwood; and the concern of mam and dad when I arrived home late. But my prevalent memory is of the expression on Cracker's face as he systematically set about destroying another human being; it was devoid of all feeling.

Cracker's toughness and easy willingness to use it in inflicting bodily harm on others made him, in the parlance of the streets, a hard case, and earned him a level of respect from kids two and three years older. For me, though, it was his fearlessness that made him so remarkable – and never more so than when he led a raid on the garden of the local witch.

The episode began as a childish prank but set in motion a chain of events that would alter Cracker's life forever. There were four of us involved: Smigger Smith, a spotty-faced kid whose parents ran the corner shop at the end of our street; Chaz Wardrobe, who lived in the street behind us; Cracker; and me. We'd been lounging around in Cracker's backyard for want of anything better to do, when Smigger threw out a dare that carried with it such perilous implications that the atmosphere in the yard immediately changed from carefree to serious. Cracker, however, paused only for a moment before smiling that lop-sided grin of his, and waving us on behind him as he led the way toward Madrigal Gardens, one of two small culs-de-sac that relieved the uniformity of our street.

As the name implied, the homes in the small terrace differed from ours in that each house had a tiny square of garden between the pavement and the front door. Our target was the only house boasting a privet hedge, the presence of which had the effect of casting the house into the shade, making it a dark, forbidding place; an impression enhanced by the house's dirty windows and ragged grey curtains. To us it was the consummate witch's house and, as we knew, a witch did actually live there. She was a crinkly faced crone with a hunchback, called Mrs. Ling, whose screeched harangues whenever children played in her vicinity convinced us she was straight out of Hansel and Gretel. The woman's obvious connection with witchcraft was at the heart of the dare, of course, since without the very real danger of encountering evil, stealing the one perfect geranium bloom from the center of her postage stamp of a garden, would have been no dare at all.

It was a typical Kingstown kind of day that saw us creep Indian style toward the witch's hedge. The wind was off the river blanketing the City with the stink of fish, while limited sun cast only a pale yellow hue over our surroundings. Even that light dimmed as we approached our objective, and I began to have grave misgivings – despite my relatively tame role as an observer. Cracker, for his part, appeared as cocky and self-assured as ever, and I watched him admiringly as he squeezed through a gap in the privet and slithered on his stomach toward that beckoning flower. Given the distance he had to travel was less than six feet, it can't have taken him long, his attempt to mimic Hiawatha notwithstanding, but it felt an age before he reached out and broke the flower's stem. It was at that point, as Cracker turned with the bloom in his hand and a triumphant grin on his face, that the door of the dark house flew open and the old biddy was out and clutching Cracker's arm in her claw-like fingers.

"Got you, you nasty little bugger,' shouted the old woman. 'I know who you are: you're McCracken's kid aren't you?'

My attention was diverted for a moment as Smigger's strangled cry of 'Run,' heralded the abrupt departure of him and Chaz from the scene. I remained – paralyzed with fear. Only when the writhing Cracker bellowed his fourth or fifth 'Gerroff,' and hit the Ling witch in the face causing her to lose her grip, did I turn tail and run, Cracker close on my heels. The old lady's screams followed us threatening the vengeance of Job – a vengeance I fervently hoped would not include mam and dad hearing of my part in the caper. I peeled off from Cracker to hide in our backyard toilet, while he continued on to his house. Only when the pangs of hunger intimated it might be tea time, did I emerge from my refuge.

Apart from mam asking me why I was so quiet, tea passed without incident, and by the time I went to bed I was daring to think that perhaps Job's intervention had been put on hold. It was only when mam, about to pull down my bedroom window blind said, 'That's strange,' that I instinctively knew trouble was brewing.

'What?' I said.

'Mrs. Ling just walked by with Nobby Clarke. It looks as if . . .' She placed her head sideways on to the window to follow their progress. 'They are. They're going to the McCracken's. I wonder what that's all about.'

Nobby Clarke, who already knew Cracker well, was the old-school type of cop absent from the streets these days. Red faced with an impressive paunch, he was more likely to mete out a clip round the ear to any child he found committing a minor misdemeanor, than take official action. Only when he viewed something as serious was he known to visit someone's house.

Feigning ignorance, I said goodnight to mam, huddled under my bedclothes, and spent what felt like hours hoping to hell there'd be no knocks on our front door from Nobby Clarke. I was ashamed to realize later that my concerns were strictly selfish and never once had I given a thought to Cracker.

Our usual meeting place, where most kids from the street congregated, was the 'bonnie,' the graveyard of what had once been a block of houses, flattened by a German bomb during the war, and where the street held its bonfires every November 5th. It was in this location, with its dirt-covered mounds and scrubby weeds, that we first set eyes on Cracker a couple of days following our foray into Madrigal Gardens, and none of us, not even the usually garrulous Smigger, knew what to say. We'd seen Cracker after previous beatings at the hands of his father, but nothing like this. His face, from which his swollen eyes peered like slits, was more blue than white; he was limping heavily, and the backs of his legs were covered with welts, courtesy of 'Old Shiner.'

The way Cracker told it, it had not been his theft of the flower, or his punching of Mrs. Ling that had enraged Big Jim, but the fact that his actions had brought the law to the McCracken door. We were as bemused as Cracker as to why mere embarrassment should occasion such a vicious attack on his son, but Big Jim had always been capricious, and our immediate concern for Cracker overrode any inclinations we may have had to contemplate any deeper motives.

'Why don't you run away?' I asked him, horrified at the brutality visited upon him.

'Not worth it Robbie,' he said. 'Last time I only got as far as Sculcoates Lane before the bastard caught me and gave me another dose.'

'But you can't let him keep doing this to you,' I said. 'He's going to put you in the hospital.'

Cracker smiled. 'Don't you worry, Robbie,' he said, 'he'll be in the bloody hospital before me, and when he comes out – if he comes out – he won't be laying so much as a finger on me ever again – and not on mam or our lasses either.'

For once his bravado did not impress me, for while Cracker was a well built lad for a nine-year-old, and inarguably tough, he was still a young boy, whereas Big Jim was a bruiser of a man with a dispassionate approach to inflicting pain, and I worried over what the future might have in store. That worry blossomed into fear on the Saturday night at the end of that week, when the screech of a siren pierced my dreams, and I awoke to see from my bedroom window, an ambulance illuminated by its own flashing blue light, parked outside Cracker's house. As mam and dad joined me, I watched as the back doors of the ambulance opened, and a stretcher with the familiar red blankets was borne through Cracker's front door. Almost immediately a police car arrived and braked to a halt behind the ambulance.

It was at that point I knew for certain my fears for Cracker's safety had been well founded and I was out of my bedroom and halfway down the stairs before dad's shout brought me to a momentary halt. 'You stop right there, young man. It's none of our damned business.'

'It is. It is,' I shouted, continuing down the stairs. 'He's killed Cracker. I knew he would, the bastard.' The shock of using that word in front of mam and dad stopped me in my tracks, and in the time it took to clamp my hand over my mouth in a reflex action of horror, dad was upon me and had me in his grip.

'You use language like that again in this house, you little bugger, and they'll be sending a bloody ambulance for you. Just calm down. Somebody's probably fallen ill, that's all. Now, let's have you back in that bed.'

Once back in my room they both relented a little and allowed me to follow the rest of the drama with them from my window. It wasn't long before the uniformed ambulance men emerged from Cracker's front door with the stretcher, now weighed down by a red swaddled bundle. They loaded it gingerly into the ambulance, slammed the doors and within moments, the blue light and siren were fading into the distance.

There was no consoling me the next morning. I'd spent the remainder of the night in a state of near hysteria punctuated by frequent trips to the toilet, where I repeatedly deposited the contents of both my stomach and bowels until I had nothing left to evacuate. Dreams came and went featuring coffins, holes in the ground, and any number of visions of an eviscerated Cracker stumbling through misty graveyards. Mam tried to coax me down for breakfast, but the thought of food was as abhorrent to me as the idea of a future without my friend. I eventually withdrew from the nightmare by falling into a deep sleep.

When Cracker woke me with a teeth-rattling shake and I opened my eyes to find him grinning down at me, I thought at first I too had died and was in some sort of ante-room to whatever came next. Only when he spoke did I realize that I was awake and Cracker's lop sided grin and shock of wiry, blond hair were real. Mam served us breakfast as Cracker related his story.

Big Jim had stumbled home from his regular evening booze-up at the Bull, and passed out next to Doris in his customary drunken stupor. Awakened in the middle of the night by the need to rid himself of the evening's gargantuan, liquid intake, it appeared that he'd been attempting to navigate his way down the unlit stairs to the backyard toilet when the location of the missing steps had eluded him. He'd been found broken and unconscious at the bottom of the stairs by Doris – alerted by the sounds of his fall. The trauma to his head had been of such a severe nature as to have sent him into a coma. The police meanwhile, having responded as a matter of routine to the ambulance call, were delighted to discover in a deep space beneath the bottom steps, cases of cigarettes and whiskey all of which, based upon the customs labels affixed to them, had been purloined from the docks. Should Big Jim ever wake from his coma, he was going to be facing some serious charges.

While the police discovery explained the real reason for Big Jim's rage and subsequent savage beating of his son following the flower incident, I remained puzzled by subsequent rumours concerning the stairs having been missing almost every other step. I'd played on those stairs a number of times that week and had never noticed more steps missing than the three we were all accustomed to. And there was something else: since it was the middle of the summer and there was no need for a fire to heat the house, why would Big Jim have removed them? Cracker's shrug and accompanying comment, 'Who knows what the old bastard was playing at?' never did answer my questions, but as a young boy might be expected to do, I soon forgot the conundrum and moved on to more important things.

As September and our tenth birthdays approached, Cracker was already beginning to take on the physical attributes that would forever elicit admiration from his peers. His square head, featuring that wiry, blond hair, piercing blue eyes and sculpted lips, sat atop broad shoulders and a barrel chest that belied the poor diet on which I knew he existed. He'd actually seemed to grow in stature following the hospitalization of Big Jim, while his happy-go-lucky demeanor had become even more pronounced. Certainly, the fact that his father was lying in hospital in a coma did not appear to concern him, and even when Big Jim passed away without regaining consciousness, Cracker exhibited no overt signs of grief.

Big Jim's funeral was memorable for me, not because of the novel presence of a hearse on the street, but rather the absence of flowers, and tears. Although I'd never previously seen a funeral cortege, I knew from books what was supposed to occur and thus was well aware of the significance of the absence of the usual conventions: Big Jim would not be mourned.

Whatever happened behind the scenes in the McCracken household following Big Jim's demise was kept from me and, as far as I could discern, from Cracker, and we concentrated on making the most of the last week of our holidays. It was a week marked by Cracker's decision to educate me in the mysteries of the female form, an education he effected with the assistance of Maggie Turner.

Maggie Turner was a pretty, blue-eyed kid with straggly blond hair from Fenchurch Terrace, whose Aunt Florry lived on our street, and it was not uncommon on Maggie's visits to her aunt's, for us to award her temporary membership in our gang. She was every bit as daring as the rest of us, and God help any boy who had the temerity to brand her as 'just a girl.' She'd once laid open the lip of Smigger when he'd mentioned the lowly position of girls in the scheme of things, and we'd all watched in awe on a famous day in her history when she'd scratched, kicked and punched her way to an incredible victory over the notorious neighbourhood bully, Victor Rodmell.

On the day Cracker chose for my sexual awakening, the three of us had been playing hopscotch at the end of our back passage, when Cracker's oldest sister, Brenda walked by and our conversation drifted into a discussion of the new sleeping arrangements at the McCracken house in the absence of Big Jim. Cracker told us that Audrey was now sleeping with Doris while Brenda and Janice continued to share a bed with him.

'Bloody 'ell, Cracker,' said Maggie to whom the overcrowded reality of Cracker's life was obviously news, 'that means you must have seen their slits and everything.'

Slits? What the hell was she talking about? 'What do you mean, slits?' I blurted out.

'Jesus Christ, Robbie,' said Cracker, grinning at Maggie, 'are you kidding? You don't know?'

'Know what?' I said, realizing too late I was exposing an ignorance that was, perhaps, best kept quiet.

'Why don't you show him Maggie?' said Cracker.

'Bugger off, you dirty sod,' said Maggie, although the cheeky grin on her face belied her affected antipathy to the idea.

'Aw, come on Maggie. I'll tell you what; you let him feel yours and he'll let you feel his. Won't you, Robbie?'

My eyes widened and I could feel the heat rushing to my face as it slowly dawned on me what was being discussed.

'You wanna do it Robbie?' said Maggie, a funny look on her face.

'You mean – '

She didn't let me finish. She just lifted up her short dress, pulled the elastic of her green knickers away from her belly, and said, 'Look, Robbie; you just put your hand down here and feel mine, and then I'll put my hand down your trousers and feel yours.'

I stood there dumbstruck for a moment before my obvious reticence galvanized Cracker.

'Oh, come on Robbie; don't bugger about,' he said. 'You'll like it. Honest.'

Affecting a nonchalance I did not feel, I said, 'Oh, go on then,' and tentatively insinuated my grubby hand down Maggie's knickers. As sexual awakenings go, the following few seconds were both puzzling and frustrating. I couldn't find anything – a task naturally made more difficult by my ignorance of what I was supposed to be looking for. I stared wide-eyed and panic stricken at Cracker as I unsuccessfully rummaged around between Maggie's legs, before the lass decided it was time to move things along.

'OK. That's enough, Robbie. Now it's my turn,' she said, and without any hesitation at all, she began to slide her hand down the front of my trousers.

Until this point I'd felt nothing but the annoyance of having been cheated, and was tempted to withdraw from the exercise altogether, but as those enquiring fingers closed upon their objective, my irritation melted away, and I felt for the first time the delicious thrill that only the innocent can experience. Although girls may not have anything between their legs, I decided at that moment, they still had an awful lot to recommend them. Had we been left alone to pursue this game I would, no doubt, have grown up a cocky and sexually precocious stud like Cracker, but it was then that my mother, who was engaged at the time in washing the bedroom windows – a task that gave her an uninterrupted view of the street – elected to glance our way. The scream, when it came, was piercing, potentially sex-life-ending, and icily inquiring.

'You Robbie!' it went, 'What are you doing?'

If I'd learned in the few previous moments how fast the male body could react to the caresses of the female hand, I now learned how quickly the reverse could occur in response to the female voice. The experiment was over – not to be repeated for many years, and regretfully, never again with the delectable Maggie.

A few days later, Cracker and I returned to school for the final year of our primary education. It was a period that would prove pivotal to our future lives, for it was during that year our joint desire to become teachers was born, and we faced the first hurdle to the achievement of that goal.

Our enthusiasm for the teaching profession was kindled during a visit to Kingstown Training College arranged through the auspices of a student teacher, Miss Fisher, with whom we were both hopelessly infatuated. A slim brunette with hazel eyes and a dazzling smile, she was the first female to teach us since our infant days: not surprising then that the two of us responded with enthusiasm when she asked for volunteers to help her on a college project relating to 'inner city kids.' The incentive she offered was tea at her college on the outskirts of the city.

Memories of 'the project' are vague, but not of the college visit. So many amazing things were revealed to us during that tea with Miss Fisher. Her room, a veritable palace in our terms, featured a large desk, a reading lamp, and a built-in wardrobe, while a huge bay window, looked out upon a grass quadrangle. It was another world, a way of living way beyond our experience; a world to which we both aspired from that day on. Such a small, incidental part of our school lives that visit, but one whose effect was such as to constitute for Cracker and me, what psychiatrists today would label a significant traumatic event. We had no concept at that time of the arduous road down which we would have to travel in order to join the teaching profession, or of how the odds were stacked against kids from our background achieving such lofty heights. What we did understand was that unless we could pass the scholarship examination that was fast approaching, we could forget the whole thing.

The scholarship examination, established in 1944, comprised tests in English, arithmetic and 'intelligence,' and was used to select the nation's 25% brightest children. Those so labeled were awarded places in 'grammar' schools where success in further exams could lead to a university education. The remaining 75% were sent to 'secondary' schools from which the doors to higher education were effectively closed. The examination was nothing less than a future-defining fork in the road for the country's children. We sat the exam in the early summer and our results arrived in the mail a few weeks later. The level of joy I felt at my success was matched only by that of my misery over Cracker's failure. We were to be separated for the first time in our lives. I would be attending Bricknall Grange High School on the other side of the City, while Cracker would go to Wilberforce High, the local secondary school. I would spend my days in a highly respected institution of higher learning surrounded by playing fields, Cracker in a larger version of the gloomy, Victorian structure in which we'd spent our previous seven years. The educational system had succeeded where differing family values and even class had failed: it had effectively placed us upon roads heading in opposite directions.

'Well, we'll still be together at nights, weekends and holidays,' I said. 'When you think on, it's only at school we won't be seeing each other.'

'I don't know, Robbie,' muttered Cracker. 'The way I see it, you'll get to that fancy school and meet all them hoity-toity kids and maybe I won't be good enough for you anymore.'

'Don't be bloody daft,' I said. 'We'll still be on the bonnie every night just like always.'

As things turned out, it was a promise that would not be kept. Two weeks later, mam and dad informed me we were leaving Nickerson Street, their application for one of the new council houses on the city outskirts having been finally approved after nine years on the waiting list. The educational system had parted Cracker and me intellectually and now we were to be separated geographically. I cried, I pleaded, I sulked. I had no interest in a real bathroom with hot and cold running water, and I couldn't care less about the advantages of an inside toilet and an extra bedroom: Cracker would be two bus rides away and I could not visualize a future without him. My pleas were ignored, and shortly after the summer holidays began, mam, dad and I took up residence on Langston Estate on the city's northern side.

Cracker visited numerous times that summer and was suitably awed by the change in my family's circumstances. We roamed the nearby river bank, chased cows in the adjacent fields, trespassed on the public golf course down the road, and climbed the myriad trees available, but once the new school year began, our new schools brought new friendships and the time between visits grew lengthier.

3.

Reconsideration

Day 226. McDermott was floundering in the black pools again. It was research that had done it: just a wee bit of poking around in a place best left the hell alone. He'd been rooting about in his strongbox for school reports and found instead the order of service for Jean's funeral. The formality of the cover with its date and time, Jean's photograph, and the numbers spelling out the length of her days, had drained his enthusiasm for writing as effectively as a hot sun sucking rain from tarmac. Through the open window of his den, he could hear the honking of the geese punctuated by the prehistoric calls of the sandhill cranes as twilight settled over the marsh. A mere year ago he and Jean would have listened and watched; their books momentarily forgotten on their laps, grateful for the paradise in which they lived. Now . . . McDermott glanced again at the order of service and recalled the day of the funeral, the memory of which he'd fervently wished to bury along with the remains of his wife.

Being both a pragmatist and a staunch Methodist, Jean had planned the funeral with her customary attention to detail. Comprising four hymns, three readings, and a eulogy written and delivered by McDermott himself, the only non-traditional element had been in her choice of hymns, a deviation from the norm that had not gone unnoticed by the church's Abide-With-Me-Brigade. Rather than dwelling on the sad and austere, Jean had opted for bright uplifting music reflecting her love of life, and had accordingly plumped for 'All Things Bright and Beautiful,' 'Hills of the North Rejoice,' 'I Vow To Thee My Country' and, to finish, the rousing, 'When A Knight Won His Spurs.'

McDermott had taken some satisfaction from the raised eyebrows and quizzical looks exchanged among the elders of the church as the organist had belted out the stirring music. There'd been no pleasure at all though, in his delivery of the eulogy; only loyalty to his wife and respect for her beliefs, had enabled him to follow the agreed upon script. McDermott would rather have used the pulpit, to ask some serious questions of the 'almighty' God who had seen fit to visit upon his wife the horrors of her final months.

He pushed himself up, pulled the curtains on the encroaching darkness and poured himself another Scotch. Connor raised his head and regarded McDermott gravely, as if disapproving of his master's new nightly ritual. Drink replenished, McDermott settled back down, closed his eyes and played out the remainder of that dark day in his mind: the procession down the aisle; the short drive to the cemetery; the hearse bearing the mahogany casket with its flower arrangements; the limousines; and then, that final insult.

He'd remained sitting in front of her coffin after the mourners had left, wanting to eke out the last few moments with her alone, when the error had leaped out at him, destroying his affected stoicism. He'd collapsed then, helpless in his grief, while the gravediggers stood laconically back, waiting for him to bugger off so they could finish the job and get home for their dinner.

They'd omitted the 'e.' 'Jean Anne McDermott,' the brass plaque on the side of the casket should have read, instead of which the inscribed letters had spelled out, 'Jean Ann McDermott.' And she'd been so particular about that 'e,' even though few people knew her full name was actually Jean Anne. All her life, whenever she'd been required to give her full name, she'd always added, 'and it's Anne with an 'e.'' He didn't know for how long he'd sat and cried; could not recall much of the wake in the church basement. He had vague memories of the obligatory potato salad, luncheon meats, sandwiches, coffee, faces looming before him offering condolences, but nothing of consequence until he'd returned on his own to the dark cabin and Connor's welcoming softness. There, in the quietude of the March evening, one hand stroking his dog's velvet head, the other caressing a heavy crystal tumbler of Scotch, he'd given vent to the grief he'd been nursing since Jean had first been diagnosed and the death sentence pronounced.

When he awoke it was well past midnight. With an effort, he regained something of his equilibrium, and managed to work through his nightly routine of dog, fire, locks, ablutions and lights, before retiring to bed and the place that only Scotch seemed able to take him.

Locking up the cabin after breakfast the next morning, he took off with Connor for the beach. As usual at this time of year they encountered few other people, and ran swiftly and unhindered along the wild shoreline, McDermott pushing himself to a speed beyond his regular six miles per hour. It was not a bright day; the lake and sky merged into one milky whole to the west, and dark grey clouds hung off to the east. The previous day's depression still clung to him like the sticky strands of some black spider's web, and McDermott was now questioning both the merit of his writing project and his literary ability. He'd been going hard at it for almost a couple of weeks now, alternating between writing character and chapter synopses and working on the manuscript itself, and still the doubts would intermittently assail him, crawling around his brain like hungry ants over a sugar cube. Was it any good? Was it worth it? Why was he working so hard for almost certainly no monetary return? He'd made more money than most authors during his career, writing to order for the IBAW and Vanguard; if he wanted to write why not return to that? Why put himself through this daily purgatory? The questions led him to a reconsideration of his reasons for writing: the need for a focus to his life, and his desire for a new challenge. He recalled the motivational effects of the British Library CDs, particularly the words of Mantel and Bainbridge, and attempted to mentally review his list of verities. Perhaps he should revisit that list. To Connor's evident relief, he turned on his heel and retraced his steps.

By the time he emerged from the shower and took his seat at his desk, the sun was out over the marsh and the threatening skies of the earlier morning hours had moved on. He read through his list of verities and replayed the thoughts of P.D. James from her British Library interview: *There are times of boredom, there are times of regret, there are times of disappointment and there are times of it's just hard work, and times when you wonder if you'll go on today.'* The words provided enough encouragement to force his head back down and to read once more what he'd already written.

Almost three hours had passed by the time he meandered through to the kitchen to make some lunch. In general he felt pleased with his effort so far, although he agreed with John Fuller's words on his CD that an author is not necessarily the best judge of his work, having a tendency to be either over-fond or over-critical. He supposed himself to be the latter if the amount of red ink he'd left on the pages was indicative, but the story so far had engaged him and he felt he'd achieved a decent balance between reality and fiction.

He reflected on the lot of the kids who'd been left behind because of the insane scholarship system. Not Cracker – his situation was eventually addressed – but Chaz, Smigger; all those kids he'd shared his infant and junior school years with. Condemned to a secondary education in both name and quality, and thereby to a life on the bins, behind a shop counter, or to any one of a thousand basic service jobs, they'd been branded as failures before their adolescence had begun. And now, based upon what he'd read in the newspapers, they were returning to the same antediluvian system over there. Would they never learn?

He dwelled on memories of Cracker for a while and the central role his friend had played throughout McDermott's formative years in the area of sex. Even at the 'you-show-me-yours-and-I'll-show-you-mine' stage of development, Cracker had been omnipresent – and it hadn't stopped there.

He'd been surprised to discover, while editing, that he'd been writing in Anglo English, rather than American English. It was as if putting himself back there had tripped something in his brain: spelling, vocabulary, colloquialisms, the whole lexicon of his childhood had returned unbidden. He rather liked the idea, he decided, and would leave it as it was.

While eating his lunch, he considered again those early days of his childhood with Cracker. How two kids so different could have become so close still baffled him. He understood the quid pro quo thing, but even so, the huge chasm between his parents' values and those of Doris and Big Jim was such that the relationship between he and Cracker had been atypical to say the least. Would such a relationship have been sustainable in the America of Jean's childhood – when the affluence of the working classes had afforded kids the mobility of bicycles and their parents the luxury of cars? Whatever the case, he felt himself fortunate to have been raised in what most people today, on either side of the Atlantic, would regard as a slum. The experience had taught him the importance of education, the power of fortitude, the humanizing force of compassion, and the value of money: lessons that had enhanced his appreciation of the privileged lifestyle he'd come to enjoy.

Washing his dishes, he imagined the life he might have had without Cracker's protection. He recalled the Rodmell brothers, Brentwood, and the Barker boys, and even some of the hard lasses he'd had to watch out for when Cracker wasn't around: the Hunt sisters, Molly Wixford, and 'Tits' Tollerton. Yes, Cracker had seen him through those bully-infested years with his mix of street smarts and his own brand of hardness; without him, McDermott's childhood would have involved a great deal more running and hiding.

Returning to his desk with a reawakened enthusiasm, he decided to spend the rest of the day on those character synopses that still awaited development. He enjoyed thinking up 'models' from real life on whom to base physical and intellectual characteristics, and he'd been fascinated to see how characters could drive the direction and very structure of the plot.

The work went well, with new characters giving birth to new ideas, and by the time he stopped for dinner, the gremlins of the preceding forty-eight hours had receded.

His mood change was much in evidence as he cooked his dinner that evening. For the previous couple of days he'd lived on sandwiches, but now he set to work on Jean's special salad featuring a plethora of ingredients including oven fries. It was one of many dishes Jean had insisted upon him mastering during the first days following her diagnosis. While they'd always cooked together, McDermott had been very much the sous-chef, following directions and helping out with the wine drinking without worrying too much about the more cerebral aspects of the process. It had not simply been the cooking Jean had prepared him for either, he mused, as he mixed the dressing.

Jean had organized everything in preparation for his aloneness. With consummate zeal and her usual attention to detail, she'd simplified the garden, ensured their financial affairs were in order, and reorganized the house, stripping away anything extraneous to simple living. She'd concluded her preparations for his life without her, by having the whole place re-stained. She'd wanted to clear our her clothing and personal effects too, but he'd drawn the line at that – as he had with her attempt to remove the big 20x30 canvas he'd made from their wedding portrait. He glanced across the kitchen to the great room wall where it hung and took in Jean's three quarter profile. Her beauty still caused him to shake his head in wonder: the huge, brown eyes; the close cropped blond hair; the model figure; and most of all, that enigmatic smile playing around her full lips – the smile she'd been wearing when he'd first seen her. He returned to reality and his dinner. Tonight he would toast her with a fine bottle of wine, concentrate on his good fortune in having had the time he'd had with her, and tomorrow he would begin work on his next chapter.

4.

Reunion

Bricknall Grange High School with its ivy covered walls, marbled staircases and wainscoted classrooms, exuded an aura of tradition and scholarship as alien to me as the culture of its pupils, who appeared to hail from a different planet. Immaculately uniformed and coiffed, they lived in private homes, spoke with cut-glass accents, rode the best bicycles and were possessed of a *savoir-faire* I could only marvel at. I was equally intimidated by the sight of stern-faced masters and mistresses, their black, academic gowns billowing behind them, sweeping down the school's wide corridors like yachts under full sail. I was overawed, lonely, and longed for the reassuring presence of Cracker.

I was placed in form 1B where the school's more rigorous intellectual standards were quickly brought home to me – as was the fight for places on sports teams where I managed to make only sporadic appearances for the Under Twelve football team. As that initial year wore on, however, I assimilated the culture of my new school with its higher scholastic demands and authoritarian regimen, and also developed two new circles of friends; one group of kids at school, and another in my more working-class neighbourhood. Thus it was that when Cracker made his reappearance, I had all but forgotten my initial misgivings over the move from Nickerson, and the bitter wrench of our parting.

When Cracker appeared at our back door at the beginning of the summer holidays following my first year at Bricknall, the change in his appearance was as dramatic as that of his circumstances. He'd always been a big lad, but now, though approaching only his twelfth birthday, his broad shoulders and barrel chest were those of a fifteen year old, while the sideburns he'd affected with his newly swept back hair hinted of leanings toward the 'teddy-boy' image that was fast becoming the rage. Even more startling than his physical maturation, was the news that not only had his academic performance at Wilberforce High earned him a rare transfer to Bricknall, but thanks to the condemning of our old street by the Kingstown Council, the McCracken family was being re-housed a mere mile from our

41

house on Langston. It was marvelous news for Cracker and his family, but even as I enthused over their good fortune, I worried over the ramifications. During the past year I'd formed new relationships and developed interests far removed from the inner city life Cracker and I had shared; how would they be affected by Cracker's return? Was Cracker ready for the middle-class, academic environment of Bricknall Grange? And, more pertinently, was it ready for him?

Fortunately, Cracker had the luxury of the summer holidays to tackle the local scene before braving the new environment of Bricknall, and he eased into it within a matter of days, quickly becoming friends with my local mates who were more than ready to accept him as their leader. I must admit to having had some feelings of resentment as he effortlessly assumed the leadership role in a world it had taken me a year to adapt to. It was the first time I'd ever borne any type of animosity toward Cracker and I should have known then that storm clouds were on the horizon.

Prior to Cracker's appearance on the scene, I'd invested a good deal of time in my pursuit of Janet Maybury, a chorister and youth club member at St. Michael-and-all-Angels, the local church. A year older than me, with dark hair, brown eyes and interesting bumps beneath her school sweater, I had, for her sake, suffered through innumerable obfuscatory sermons, agonized over the foreign cadences of the Magnificat and Nunc Dimittis, and knelt in prayer for hours on sagging hassocks. My total return from those tortuous Sundays had been one dance with the pubescent Janet at a youth club social. Thus when Cracker exploded upon the youth club dance scene and selected the girl of my dreams as his partner in a stunning demonstration of jiving to Bill Haley's 'Rock Around The Clock,' I was less than impressed and stormed home alone resolving never to speak to Cracker again.

The truth was, I had yet to accept that as handsome, athletic and charismatic as Cracker was, I would necessarily be spending a good deal of time in his shadow if I wished to be his friend; that was part of the deal. It would also be some time before I understood that, as far as girls were concerned, my naivety was always going to be sucking hind-tit to his precocity. Accordingly I was less than congenial the following day when Cracker came calling.

'What's up with you then?' he said, as we set out for the local playing field, pushing a football along between us.

'You're bloody joking aren't you?' I snapped.

'What are you on about?'

'Have a good time with Janet Maybury last night did you?'

'Jesus Christ, Robbie. Is that what you've got a cob on for; because I danced with Janet bloody Maybury?'

'I've been after her for months, Cracker and you know it,' I said.

'Well, you know what Robbie? You can keep on after her. I don't bloody want her; she's not my type anyway. Go ahead; help yourself.'

And just like that I was defeated. I knew in my heart that Cracker or no Cracker, Janet Maybury was out of my league anyway, and so did my friend. He did at least leave me a graceful exit.

'Mind you,' he said, 'I wouldn't bother if it was me.'

'Why not?' I asked, knowing instinctively there was a punch line coming.

'Well, think about it, Robbie. You're not going to get anything there are you: a bleeding choirgirl? And he took off laughing down the road as I belted the football after him.

The remainder of the summer flew by, and it was soon time for Cracker to introduce himself to the world of Bricknall Grange where yet more extraneous circumstances contrived to separate us. I had impressed enough in my first year to be assigned to the top academic stream, while Cracker, as a transfer, had been placed in a lower form. Thus although we were in the same building, our paths rarely crossed during school hours, and our social circles naturally tended to centre on our classmates.

Cracker adapted well to life behind the ivy covered walls, thereby confirming what his teachers at Dunswell and I had known all along: although Cracker was a hard case, he was also intellectually bright, an unusual combination that would confound many throughout his life. That being said, it was not too long into his Bricknall career before Cracker's new peers came to appreciate the raw, physical power behind his affable exterior.

Brian Ramsbottom was the kind of bully one read about in schoolboy books in the 1950s: big for his age, raw-boned, with dull, flat eyes, he wore a perpetual sneer which he used to good effect in frightening smaller kids. Like most bullies, he was scorned by his peers, a circumstance that exacerbated his anger toward the world in general and younger, more delicate children in particular. Three years older than me, his name was legion in a school that, in truth, contained few of his type, and from which he had once been infamously suspended for smashing a basketball into the face of a smaller opponent during a physical education lesson. Throughout my time in the first form, I'd managed to stay well clear of Ramsarse, as he was known, but one day early in my second year, I found him barring my path as I wandered back to afternoon classes from the sweet shop across Pearson Park. He gestured toward the tube of fruit gums in my hand as he swaggered toward me, tut-tutting and shaking his head.

'Oh dear, oh dear, oh dear,' he said. 'Don't you know the school rules about having sweets in school? You'd better give them to me, sunshine before you get yourself into trouble.'

'Sod off Ramsarse!' I responded, and began running, something I knew how to do well, having proved myself to be one of the fastest sprinters in the lower school. Running fast successfully, however, is best accomplished with both shoelaces tied, a lesson painfully learned as I fell to the ground only a couple of yards beyond my antagonist. He was on me in a second, his knee in the middle of my back, as he twisted my arm with the apparent intention of tearing it from its socket.

'What did you call me, you little bastard?' he hissed in my ear.

Throughout my early years I'd been known as a stubborn little bugger: someone to whom easy acquiescence did not come easily, and such was the case at that moment.

'Ramsarse,' I groaned, and then screamed as he exerted more upward pressure on my arm.

Adolescents have an extraordinary ability to scent a fight, and by now I could sense the gathering of a crowd around us. That they were in my corner was evident from their shouts:

'Get off him! He's half your size!'

'Leave him alone you great bully!'

'Yeah, why don't you pick on somebody your own size?'

The calls quickly became a chorus, but no one seemed anxious to intervene until, just as I thought Ramsarse would indeed break my arm, there came through the shouts and jeers a voice I knew well, and one that carried compelling authority.

'Let go of his arm now Ramsarse and then stand up, because I'm going to bash your ugly mush in and I don't want you saying I didn't give you a fair chance,' said Cracker, in tones that left no doubt as to his intentions.

I felt the grip on my arm released and the pressure on my back relaxed as, spluttering with rage, Ramsarse got to his feet and confronted Cracker. Since Cracker was new to both the school and the area, he was unknown to the majority of the school population, and certainly to Ramsarse, whose look of incredulity upon facing a second year kid who'd had the audacity to threaten him, underlined his ignorance.

'Say that again if you dare you little git,' said Ramsarse, advancing upon Cracker.

'I'm going to bash your ugly mush in,' repeated Cracker cheerfully to the muted 'Oohs' of the surrounding observers.

Ramsarse was nonplussed: he couldn't grasp the concept of a smaller kid standing up to him. Then again, he had no way of knowing where Cracker had come from or what he was physically capable of.

'Come on, Ramsarse; let's get this over with shall we? We don't want to be late for school. Or should I call you Sheepshagger? That might be a better name for you come to think about it.'

That was enough for Ramsarse; goaded beyond his limits, he rushed headlong at Cracker who responded exactly as I expected by swinging his right foot unerringly into the testicles of the bigger boy. Ramsarse went down in a heap, clutching his groin and screaming something about rules. The crowd, being largely of a middle class background and ignorant of real violence, imagined, as Ramsarse must have done, that the fight was over at that point. I knew better, and didn't attempt to intervene as Cracker knelt upon the shoulders of Ramsarse, and calmly headbutted him with a sickening crack to the nose.

'You see, Sheepshagger,' said Cracker, as the blood flowed from what looked suspiciously like a broken nose, 'this is what it feels like: painful isn't it? And you know what, you cowardly prat? If I ever see you bullying anybody again, I'm going to *really* hurt you,' and with that Cracker headbutted the bloodied face again, eliciting one more scream of agony from the thoroughly beaten Ramsarse.

We walked back to school in front of an awed, I think somewhat horrified, crowd of uniformed boys and girls, all of whom now knew of the existence of Cracker: a new second year kid who appeared to be a hardened street fighter with a total disregard of such niceties as the Queensbury rules.

At Bricknall Grange, violence was not tolerated and offenders could normally expect a suspension if not outright expulsion, but the resulting inquiry, led by the headmaster, Mr. Leslie Chatsworth, and which involved personal interviews with a number of bystanders, as well as Ramsarse, Cracker and me, resulted in nothing more serious than censure. Ramsarse was given a final warning regarding his persistent bullying, while Cracker was admonished for the tactics he'd employed in subduing his opponent. For my part, gratitude for Cracker's intervention was tempered by concern that his easy embrace of no-holds-barred brutality in physical confrontations would one day land him in serious trouble. As it was, it became common knowledge throughout the school that only the headmaster's intervention prevented the parents of Ramsarse from bringing criminal charges: an intervention that leaned heavily upon their son's bullying background in general and his assault on me in particular. There was too, the difference in age and size between Cracker and Ramsarse and, a quiet satisfaction, I believed, on the part of Mr. Chatsworth, that Brian Ramsbottom had received his just deserts.

The remainder of that school year passed uneventfully, with Cracker forming new friendships and, as usual, playing his role as leader with all the aplomb that came so naturally to him. Not only did he make the Under-Thirteen football team but by the end of the season he'd been installed as captain, displaying a vision and ball ability way beyond his years. Moreover, his heroics as a member of the Colts cricket team allied to his feats with the javelin and shot put, served notice that a natural athlete had arrived at Bricknall Grange, while his acceptance, a year earlier than the norm, into the school's Taekwondo club made him a celebrity among the more pugnacious of his peers. Meanwhile I enjoyed the new academic challenges that membership in the top form brought with it, and I too formed new relationships with other kids. Cracker and I saw each other at playtimes when we played football, and continued our close relationship on Langston at weekends and during school holidays. It was a looser relationship than we'd enjoyed on Nickerson Street, but it remained special nevertheless – due in no small part to our history and a delicate balance: Whereas Cracker was way ahead of me physically, I still, by virtue of my membership in a higher form, had the edge on him intellectually. It was a balance we never mentioned, but we felt it certainly, and it provided my ego with a necessary fillip during that period of our lives when Cracker's skills and charisma were the subjects of universal admiration on the part of our mutual friends.

One area in which Cracker continued to be my mentor was that of sex, and thus it was, with considerable enthusiasm, that he informed me one sunny morning during the summer holiday, of a 'deal' he'd set up for that afternoon with Brassieres Braintree, a fifteen-year-old neighbor of his. Brassieres, so called because of the impressive conical nature of her breasts, was what mam referred to as a 'common' girl who attended a local girls secondary school, infamous for the high number of pregnancies occurring among its pupils each year. The deal, as Cracker described it, was both tempting and expensive.

'She says she'll do it for a tanner, Robbie,' he said. 'Just sixpence and she'll show us her tits.'

'Bloody hell Cracker! A tanner? That's a lot of money just for a look.'

'Come on, Robbie, how many tits have you seen in your life?' He knew the answer without having to wait for it, and burbled on excitedly about the prospects. 'Two o' clock under Salterness Road Bridge. She's bringing Molly Atkinson with her. Maybe she'll show us hers as well. And look, I've borrowed this from mam's sewing box.' Cracker pulled a dressmaker's tape from his pocket. 'Maybe they'll let us measure them.'

Even though sixpence represented half of a full week's pocket money, I found my prurient interests outweighing my pecuniary concerns, and by ten minutes to two that afternoon, I was loitering with Cracker on the river bank beneath the bridge, anxiously awaiting a moment I had long fantasized over. The two older girls were a good ten minutes late and we were about to give up and leave, when they appeared round the buttress at the base of the bridge. As they made their way toward us with Brassieres in the lead, I found myself staring helplessly at her breasts straining against a yellow blouse.

'Hiya, Brassieres,' said Cracker nodding to her friend Molly. 'This is Robbie.'

'Right,' said Brassieres, barely acknowledging me. 'Well, you got the money then or what?'

''Course we have,' said Cracker. 'Show her Robbie.'

I held up the sixpence, and almost dropped it, as without hesitation she began unbuttoning her blouse.

'Cracker says you've never seen any o' these before. Is that right, Robbie?' she grinned.

'Yeah,' I croaked as I registered the grubby state of her once white bra beneath the blouse.

'Well, feast yer eyes on these then, Robbie boy, 'cos these are as good as they get,' she said.

With that she reached her hands behind her and, with what at the time looked to me like a conjuring trick, revealed the most majestic sight I'd ever seen. Jutting straight out as if rendered by an artist for a comic book heroine, the alabaster cones were relieved in their creaminess by two erect pink nipples that hypnotized me.

'What d'yer think then, Robbie? Are they worth a tanner or what?' she said, thrusting them toward me. 'No, no, no,' she admonished, as I involuntarily reached out toward those magnificent orbs, 'Touching's extra. Let's see the tanner first, then maybe for another one I'll let you have a feel.'

As I handed her the sixpence with a hand that was visibly shaking, Cracker chimed in.

'Okay then Brassieres, I'll tell you what. One more tanner; but we both get a feel, and we want to measure them as well.' With that Cracker pulled the tape measure from his pocket.

'Sodding hell, that's worth at least a bob,' said Molly.

'Take it or leave it Brassieres,' said Cracker ignoring Molly as I continued to gaze adoringly at Brassieres' still exposed breasts.

'Oh sod it! Go on then,' said Brassieres, pushing herself forward again.

'Everything off first,' said Cracker. 'We need to do this right.'

'Bloody 'ell, yer don't want much do yer?' said Brassieres who nevertheless removed her blouse and hanging bra with a practiced flourish.

'Me first,' said Cracker, and brushing past me, cupped her breasts in his hands and rubbed his thumbs over the nipples which rose even more to his touch.

''Ere, none o' that,' said Brassieres. 'That is definitely extra.'

'Oh, give over, you know you like it,' said Cracker. 'Come on, Robbie; your turn.'

As I'd realized years before with Maggie Turner, the first time for any level of sexual experience provides a unique moment rarely forgotten, but as I fondled those smooth, pale breasts, I believed myself to have attained the zenith of what life had to offer. I also learned the limited life span of such episodes when purchased, for I'd no sooner felt the incredibly soft skin on those firm, young tits than they were withdrawn.

'Alright, Cracker; that's it, let's 'ave the other tanner,' said Brassieres.

'Just a minute; got to measure them yet, remember,' said Cracker. 'Here Robbie, you take this end,' he said, handing me one end of the tape measure. 'You hold that there,' he said, placing the knuckles of my right hand atop one rosy nipple, 'and I'll come round this way.'

'Yer a cheeky bastard, Cracker,' said Brassieres realizing that my crafty friend had set us up for an extra feel. ''Ow big are they anyway?'

'Thirty seven and a half,' said Cracker. 'What about if I measure the circumference?'

'The what? Sod off, Cracker. You'll want me to throw in a shag next. Let's 'ave the money.'

Grinning, Cracker handed over his sixpence and we both watched wistfully as Brassieres dressed and left us with a flighty wave over her shoulder.

'Nice doing business with yer,' she called as she and Molly retreated along the river bank. 'Bring another couple of bob next time and we'll 'elp yer get rid of them stiff things in yer pants.'

Cracker and I looked down at the fronts of our trousers and Cracker joined in the laughter of the two departing girls, as I felt the fire of a blush suffuse my body.

5.

Confrontation

It was the evening of Day 236, a Saturday, when McDermott made the decision, and the following morning when he acted upon it. It was a course of action, he'd delayed for close to a quarter of a century, and why the conviction to act gripped him at that particular time, he could not say. Was it the primeval aspects of the great rolls of thunder and sky-splitting shards of lightening sweeping across the marsh that evening, or the accompanying bitterness over his lot in life that had returned, seemingly on the wings of the storm? Whatever the catalyst, he'd been gripped by a compulsion to bring closure to his concerns over the eternal issues of existence, and here he was: on his way to curtail a relationship that had commenced shortly after his birth.

Joining the line of cars edging into the church's parking lot, McDermott cast his mind back over the highlights of his affiliation with an organization that had been so integral to his early life. There'd been Sunday school, the Junior Missionary Association and Cub Scouts; his temporary conversion from Methodist to C. of E. in order to pursue a girl; and the years as a Presbyterian for the Sea Scouts, youth clubs, and football teams. Years of spasmodic attendance had followed college – as a Methodist again – when Easter and Christmas services or, more likely, the associated music, had revived his faith for short periods, and then his real involvement here, thanks to Jean.

He waited in the car until the last moment before slipping through the doors of the church, accepting the order of service from Mary Ann and Jim Rollins, the ushers, and proceeding to what had been Jean's preferred location in the right corner of the back pew, on the right side of the aisle. He nodded politely to a young couple to his left who scooted up to make space for him, and as the strains of Bach filled the air, he bowed his head in the semblance of prayer, and asked himself why he'd elected to attend one more service. He'd called Pastor Dan the evening before to request a meeting following the morning worship; he could have simply – The triumphant climax of the organ music cut into his thoughts and he looked up as Pastor Dan made his way to the pulpit.

'Good morning! And what a wonderful day on which to . . .'

It wasn't, he supposed, a bad service, although the goddamned sermon set his teeth on edge, and he found dark irony in the words of one of the hymns. Still, it was his last time so what the hell? McDermott remained in place as the congregation drifted out, his head bowed once more as if in prayer, the posture insurance against unwanted conversations with well-wishers. Why had he thought it necessary to have this meeting at all? He could, after all, have simply continued to stay away as he had since burying Jean. But then, based on the number of phone calls he'd already received from Pastor Dan and other 'concerned' members of the congregation, he supposed a definitive, official break was necessary. He also accepted that he owed the pastor and the church members this final courtesy: they'd not only been of great importance to Jean, they'd been of infinite comfort to her during her last weeks.

The church was almost empty now, a few muted conversations by the door the only sounds. McDermott raised his head and stared at the massive suspended cross above the pulpit. He'd helped hoist that cross into position and heard the Oohs and Aahs of the congregation when it had made its Good Friday debut with the purple shroud. And the pulpit. How many times had he preached from there, looking out over the rapt faces as he captivated them with his speaking skills and 'cute' English accent? He'd spent a lot of time here one way or another: as a Steven minister, member of the finance and fundraising committees, and helping out with the annual spring and fall cleanups in the grounds. A regular church stalwart he'd – A gentle hand on his shoulder brought him back to the present.

'You want to come on back, Robbie?' Dan Dodgson, the senior pastor and old friend, had the kind of mellifluous voice that could make even an invitation to his office sound special.

'Sure, thanks Dan,' said McDermott, and rose to follow the pastor. The church had the deserted feel that to McDermott always seemed to settle upon the place after the congregation had left. It was an atmosphere enhanced by the peculiar hollow silence that was unique, he thought, to an empty sanctuary.

Usually Dan Dodgson would be chatting away by now, but he led the way in silence and McDermott wondered whether the pastor had somehow defined the reason for this rare, post-service meeting. He studied the pastor's broad shoulders and shock of white hair from behind, picking up the familiar sweet scent of pipe tobacco. Dodgson was a good pastor, he thought, and a fine man. He and his wife had played a critical role in helping him and Jean cope with the horror of impending death and McDermott felt a momentary sense of betrayal.

'Have a seat Robbie,' said the pastor as they entered his office, gesturing to one of two armchairs facing each other in front of the big oak desk.

McDermott had always loved this room. While the building was late seventies contemporary, Dodgson had somehow contrived to make his study nineteenth century Cambridge. Floor to ceiling bookshelves obscured each wall; piles of books covered every surface – including part of the floor; the desk itself was awash in a sea of files and papers; and the omnipresent aroma of Dutch, pipe tobacco somehow evoked warmth rather than pollution.

'So,' said the pastor as he settled opposite McDermott and commenced his pipe filling ritual, 'to what do I owe the pleasure, Robbie? More important, how are you doing?'

'Fine,' said McDermott. 'Look, Dan, I want to thank you for seeing me now. I know Kate is waiting lunch on you, and I promise I won't take up too much of your time, but it's just that . . . Well, I've been thinking a good deal about this, and I need to have done with it.'

'Jeez, Robbie; sounds serious,' said Dodgson. 'What's up?'

'Well, Dan,' McDermott paused and he wasn't sure why. Was he having second thoughts? Even now? The hell he was. He plunged on. 'I'm leaving, and I wanted you to be the first to know.'

'You're leaving? I thought you'd decided to stick around?' Dodgson's face, behind the screen of smoke from his pipe, was puzzled.

'No, I'm sorry, Dan; I didn't put that well. I'm not leaving the area, I'm leaving the church. I'm done with it all: the whole father, son and Holy Ghost, come to Jesus and be saved, religious bullshit. Sorry, I shouldn't have said that.'

'Oh, I've heard worse,' said the pastor. 'As for your decision to leave the church, I suppose I'll surprise you if I tell you I understand.'

'No, you wouldn't surprise me, but you do not understand. You think I'm angry at God because of Jean and that eventually I'll come to accept and so on and so forth. I've heard all that stuff. Hell, I've even helped you try and get it across to bereaved folks. But no, I'm not angry at God, I've passed that stage, although I won't deny I didn't go through it. I simply no longer believe in His existence.

'Oh, come now, Robbie,' said Dodgson, 'that's a bit extreme isn't it? You know enough – '

'No, I'm sorry Dan, but let me try and explain this to you. And first, I must apologize, because I understand that in saying what I'm about to say, I'll be calling into question who you are and everything that you've devoted your life to, and I feel bad about that. Your support and guidance over the past few years have been critical to me, and to Jean too before she died, but I just can't go on pretending, so please, let me try and elucidate. Okay?'

'Okay, fine, go right ahead,' said Dodgson as he relit his pipe.

McDermott gathered himself for a moment and then began. 'I guess my doubts first surfaced with dad's death in '88. I watched this big, powerful man, my first hero, slowly reduced to a skeletal parody of what he'd been, and I couldn't help but question where God was in the whole equation. By the time dad's carers were obliged to lift him with a hoist to get him to the bathroom so they could change his diaper, wipe his ass and bathe him, I'd come up with some serious questions about your friend,

God. But you know what I did, Dan? I put them on the old backburner: too many other things going on in my life, I suppose. Oh, I didn't attend church anymore, but I didn't really go in search of the answers either. Then Jean came along and a strange thing happened when her mother was diagnosed with ovarian cancer; you know what that was, don't you Dan?'

'Yes, I remember perfectly,' the pastor said, relighting his pipe yet again and taking his time about it. 'Jean, in her time of need, reached out for the comfort of the church, and you, being a good husband came along with her.'

'That's right, Dan: the suffering Jean's mother went through had a diametrically opposite effect on Jean's belief system than my dad's had on mine, and religion became important to her again. And yes, I felt it incumbent on me to support her.'

'So are you saying you came along strictly for the ride, Robbie? Because if you are, I have to tell you I have difficulty with that. The man I've listened to preaching from that pulpit in the sanctuary out there wasn't simply pretending.'

'Oh no, you're correct there, Dan. I was sucked back in again – hook, line and sinker. Honestly, I believe I became one of those 'sentimental Christians,' seduced by the inspirational music and language.'

'And then Jean was diagnosed.' The pastor regarded McDermott sadly.

'And then Jean was diagnosed,' McDermott repeated, nodding. 'And that's when the questions resurfaced, Dan. Except this time I went looking for answers. Jean didn't know of course. I wouldn't have done anything to question her faith: it was all she had left in the end except me – and I wasn't a hell of a lot of help. But I read – Dawkins, Hitchens, Barker, Russell – and the more I read, the more convinced I became of the non-existence of the Almighty.'

'Well, that's not really surprising, Robbie, is it? Considering the theories of those particular gentlemen.'

'Oh, come on, Dan, you're not suggesting that merely reading a few books guarantees the reader's agreement with the hypotheses of the writers are you? And remember – '

The pastor suddenly cut him off. 'Yes, okay, I understand your position, Robbie. Well look, I can see that right now you're pretty well set on this course of action and any argument from me will be a waste of time, but I would like you to promise three things before you leave here: First, I want you to remember that the door of the church is always open to you; second, Kate and I have been your friends for what, fifteen years? I'd like to think we can remain so; and third, I'd like you to think about meeting with Greta VanDamm.'

'Aw, Jeez Dan.'

'I know, I know: you think counseling is a bunch of B.S. and you don't need it, but listen to me, Robbie,' Dodgson leaned forward and looked deep into McDermott's eyes. 'I've been keeping tabs on you since Jean passed, and you worry me. This has nothing to do with religion: it's about your health. You've cut yourself off from everyone from what I've heard: nobody sees you around town, you're not answering your telephone, and e-mails go unanswered. I've been doing this job for over thirty-five years, Robbie; buried more people than I care to think about. I know what grief can do, and believe me, my friend, you need help. So I'll do you a deal: I won't bug you about your faith issues if you'll give Greta a try. What do you say?'

McDermott heaved a sigh. Maybe he owed the pastor at least this. 'Okay. I'll talk to her, but I'm not promising anything regular. And, Dan, needless to say, our friendship is a given as far as I'm concerned.'

'Great, I'll have Greta give you a call.'

'Yeah, but you'd better warn her she'll probably have to leave a message. I'm not answering the phone because I'm doing some writing, but I will return her call.'

'Writing, Robbie? That's interesting; what are you writing?'

'It's a bit early to talk about yet,' McDermott said. 'Probably a load of rubbish, but we'll see.' McDermott got to his feet the same time as Dodgson, and the two men eyed each other for a moment before grasping each other in an awkward hug.

'Thanks for hearing me out, Dan,' said McDermott. 'And I'm sorry about . . . Well, you know.'

'Don't worry about it, Robbie: you're not my first dropout, and I'm inclined to believe you won't be the last. And who knows? You may change your mind at some point – that's been known to happen too.'

McDermott smiled and took his leave. The pastor remained at his desk deep in thought for a few minutes before packing his briefcase and heading home for his Sunday lunch.

McDermott recalled, as he drove home, that there'd been a hint of a knowing smile playing around Dodgson's mouth as he'd spoken those parting words. Goddamnit! Did the pastor really doubt his sincerity? He believed he'd been pretty forceful, maybe even over the top, and yet Dan had not really argued with him, tried to put forward 'The Case for Christ,' or even attempted to dissuade him. In fact he'd cut off the meeting pretty damned quick. Perhaps that's what they taught pastors: 'Don't argue, they'll come around in the end.' Well, here was one guy who wouldn't be coming around anytime soon. He thought about Greta VanDamm. The church's volunteer grief counselor, Greta had a flourishing psychiatric practice down in Traverse City and had given freely of her time and expertise to the church since she'd first moved to Westwood ten years previously. Now in her late sixties, Greta nevertheless retained the stately posture and classical features of a once-beautiful woman. She would be more accurately described as handsome now, but still . . . Around five feet ten, she peered out at the world through dark eyes, set in an oval face wreathed by thick, wavy, gray hair that in its styling put him in mind of Jane Russell in her early days.

Writing from the Outskirts of Hope

McDermott was pulling into his driveway before he remembered there was nothing to eat in the house and he'd intended to do some shopping after his meeting. Shit, he thought, I'm getting old. Reversing out of his driveway, he pondered over how big a part his thoughts of Greta VanDamm had played in his forgetfulness because, if he was honest, he'd been entertaining lascivious thoughts of what the lady must have been like when she was young. Now what the hell was that all about? He hadn't had a sexual thought in close to a year: hadn't had any interest once Jean had reached the point where . . . Jesus, and here he was damn near drooling over a woman who, as attractive as she might have been once upon a time, he still perceived as a warm-hearted grandmother – despite their similarity in ages.

He and Jean had laughed and joked in their early days together about what they'd do for sex when one or the other of them passed on. She believed he'd get married again and fast. Bollocks, he'd said, he'd just pay for it: find a high class hooker – in Chicago maybe – and make a monthly pilgrimage. Jean had laughed at that; said based on her experience with him that once a month wouldn't hack it. God, they'd had a great sex life: tried every position known to man and some that weren't. And in almost thirty years, he mused, it had never got stale: they'd always been comfortable with each other, always been ready to say what worked and what didn't, and they'd laughed a lot too . . .

McDermott pulled into the IGA parking lot, dragged his mind back to the grim present, and focused on food. The interior of the store appeared cold beneath fluorescent lighting that also served to accentuate the bored expressions of the idle checkout staff. The whole scene brought to his mind Johnny Cash's 'Sunday Morning Coming Down,' a song that to him had always conveyed the implicit sadness of Sundays, and he found himself mentally singing the haunting words. He trudged round the aisles, picking up this and that and thought how pathetic the few items appeared in the big shopping cart. He had a sudden flashback to grocery shopping with his mother shortly before she died: he'd been looking for tomatoes or something, she'd shuffled on ahead, and when he'd caught her up she was slowly pushing her cart along with one lemon in the bottom of it.

He'd never had to shop much for groceries: Jean had always taken care of that side of things, which was good, since he'd always been of the opinion that taking a good beating was preferable to shopping – unless a bookstore was involved. And now, here he was, not only shopping, but shopping on a Sunday for Christ's sake; if ever there was a recipe for melancholy, this was it. He thought back to his early life in England when the Sunday trading laws were still in effect and the only stuff you could buy on a Sunday were newspapers, sweets and ice cream. There was something so bloody civilized about that – why the hell couldn't shops close for just one day a week? And it wasn't about religion and the Sabbath, it was simply the logical notion that families should have one day a week during which they might gather, eat and play as a family unit.

McDermott's mood, which hitherto this day had run the gamut from anger through sorrow and depression and back to anger, was not improved as he observed the desultory manner in which the obese cashier at the checkout moved his items through her scanner. For Christ's sake, he fumed, this woman with her couldn't-give-a-shit attitude, wouldn't have lasted five minutes in a grocery store in 1950s Britain. What the hell was going on in the world?

By the time he returned to the cabin, McDermott was ready for a drink, despite the fact it was still early in the day, and once he'd let Connor out for his midday 'sniff and whizz' as Jean used to call it, he poured himself a healthy Glenrothes which he sipped as he put away his groceries and made himself a sandwich. The fact that he was drinking earlier each day and consuming ever increasing quantities, failed to register, as he mulled over the planning he would do that afternoon in order to get an early start on his writing the next morning.

After lunch and another Scotch or two, he decided he'd begin by re-reading the last section he'd written, since that practice invariably led to editing, which in turn had the effect of pulling him back into the flow of the narrative. Once he'd re-immersed himself, he'd outline the way ahead. Only he didn't do any of that: he had a conversation with Jean instead.

He was sitting in front of the big wedding portrait when he did it: when he told her what he'd done and why. The half empty bottle of Scotch on the floor beside him, tumbler in hand, he regarded the image of his dead wife solemnly. 'So that was the last time today Jeanie: last bloody service for me and a fucking good job too based on what I had to listen to. Strange when you think about it: how pissed off you can get with hymns and sermons when you realize it's all a bunch of bullshit. I mean, take "The King of Love My Shepherd Is." What about that? Remember that Jeanie?' McDermott began to sing raucously. 'The King of Love my shepherd is, whose goodness faileth never – Well it fucking failed for you didn't it love? Not a lot of goodness around for you when you were curled up and screaming with the pain was there? Bloody extra morphine was the best you could hope for. Why don't you ask our good shepherd about that Jeanie? Ask him where his bastard love and goodness were when they took half your lung out, or when they found the lesions on your brain. And while you're at it, ask him how come we had half the sodding town praying for you, and he heard fuck-all. In fact, Jeanie, if you can find him, which I seriously doubt, you might just ask him what the fuck he's doing up there.

'Course, it wasn't just the bloody hymns: the fucking sermon wasn't far behind when it came to the old bullshit quotient. "God as the Caregiver" was Dan's contribution today. God as the bleeding caregiver! Well, you got as much useful care from him as from all those fucking doctors didn't you Jeanie? The pulmonologist and radiologist, the neurologist and the fucking oncologist; not one of them could do anything but tell you, "Six months without chemo and maybe ten months with," and "Oh, by the way, it's your own fucking fault for smoking."'

McDermott paused for a moment to search for the bottle and refill his glass. 'Mind you, Jeanie; they did have a point didn't they? I mean, you didn't exactly help yourself smoking those bastard cancer sticks for twenty-seven years did you? What was it that cardiologist said? "You just don't get it do you Mrs. McDermott?" Well, at least he got that one right, because you bloody didn't did you? Jesus! It pisses me off when I think about it. I mean it wasn't as if you didn't have any warnings or anything was it Jeanie? How long ago was it when they took those nodules from your throat? Fifteen years? Remember how fucking frightened you were when they found them? "Dear God, just let them be benign," you said, "and I promise I'll never smoke again." And how long did that attempt last? Six weeks, that's how long. About the same as you managed when I quit. Six bloody weeks and you were back puffing away to beat the bastard band. "I'll just keep it to ten a day," you said, and then it was fifteen, and in no time you were right back where you fucking started.

'And you always had a clever answer didn't you? Always had some silly bloody statistics to quote at folk about how many people died of cancer without ever smoking or some such fucking rubbish. And by God, you were quick with the rationalizations as well weren't you love? Especially the one about the old feller we saw on the telly, the one who was ninety-three and started smoking when he was twelve or something. Jumped all over that one didn't you eh? Used that one for fucking years. Told every bugger who'd listen about that old lad. You just figured if he could roll the dice and win, then so could you. Except you bloody lost didn't you Jeanie old love? Even after all the fucking chemo and the radiation shit.

'And that's another thing Jeanie. Why the hell did you let the bastards put you through that? You could have had maybe six decent months, but what you got was six months and four bloody days of vomiting and hair loss and feeling like shit. And we knew Jeanie, we fucking knew. We'd talked about it; said if it happened to us, we'd tell them to go fuck themselves with their chemo. I mean, how many people had we watched go through that shit Jeanie? And you know what the worst thing is? I never said a fucking word: I just sat there and went along with it. I –' McDermott choked and began to retch.

When he awoke he was curled on the floor beside the chair, vomit clinging to his face and shirt. His head felt as if half a dozen elves with giant hammers were attempting to exit from just above his eyes, and his mouth felt as if it had been glued shut – with fish glue from the taste of it. Connor lay next to him, with what he imagined for a moment, to be a look of disdain on his face.

It was after lunchtime the following day before McDermott managed to clean up the living room, and felt sufficiently recovered to begin the planning he'd intended to do the day before. He had little memory of the tirade he'd subjected Jean's photograph to, merely a vague recollection of tremendous rage and sorrow. As for his drinking, he felt nothing but shame, and promised himself he'd get a handle on that before it got out of control. For now, he went through to his den to start work. He read through the previous chapter, made a number of grammatical corrections, changed a couple of sentences and then laid the book down with a sigh. Way too many words he thought: too loose, he needed to tighten things up. Was it Stephen King who'd opined that an original manuscript minus ten percent equaled a first draft? McDermott reckoned in his case the figure might be closer to twenty percent, and picking up his red pen, he commenced to attack each sentence again.

It was a few hours later before he felt satisfied. He made a note to check the entire manuscript for manifestations of his evident love for the passive voice, and then thought how he might pick up the narrative. It was time, he thought, for Cracker to impact the future life of his protagonist in some way. He began to piece together a scenario and in doing so, thought of his own days in grammar school and the sacrifices they'd necessitated on the part of his parents.

His mother had passed her scholarship, but had not been able to take her place at the prestigious girls' school she'd qualified for, because her widowed mother couldn't afford the uniform. She'd been determined that her son would be given the opportunity denied her. His father had had the same attitude: compelled to leave school at fourteen, he'd had a hell of a tough start in life. McDermott could still hear his dad telling him about his early life on the docks, where, as a young boy, he'd been obliged to work on ship repair, handing white hot rivets to the riveters –   a job that often required walking across the open tops of deep holds of ships on slippery planks of wood. He could still see the bitterness in his dad's eyes as he'd related the mixed emotions of hope, rage and embarrassment he'd felt, standing before the closed dock gates, under the appraising gaze of the gaffers who decided who would work a ship and who would not. 'We were nowt so much as slabs of meat to those bastards,' his dad had said. God, he'd had it easy in comparison, thought McDermott. His biggest problems during his early teens had been competing with cheap, loosely strung,

Pakistani tennis racquets against kids with the best Slazengers that money could buy; wearing his uniform maybe one year longer than its sell-by date; playing football in the old clodhopping style boots when most kids were into the new, low-cut 'continental' style; having to stay at home when his friends were going on school trips to Germany and France.

'You didn't have it so bad,' his dad had said to him before he died, and he was right: he bloody didn't. He thought back to some of the kids he'd known who'd never gone to a grammar school, and wondered what had happened to the girl on whom he'd based the character of Brassieres Braintree. He'd seen her a couple of years before he'd left for college. She was pushing a baby in a battered old pram with one hand and dragging along another kid with the other. She would have been around eighteen he supposed, her future already nailed down: striving to get by from week to week on government handouts, with the odd Saturday night down the pub providing the high spot of her days. She hadn't recognized him – he'd been six feet tall by then and decked out in a suit: a long way from the boy who'd last seen her going upstairs giggling with a kid at some party. He'd almost failed to recognize her. A good twenty pounds heavier with breasts already pointing south beneath a stained pink sweater, her face wore the tired, careworn expression of a much older woman, while her once chestnut hair had been dyed a lifeless, matte black. Would her life have been different had she passed her scholarship? Would an advanced education have offset her physical precocity, her probable minimal nurturing at home? Not necessarily, he concluded: he'd seen more than one privileged girl from Bricknall go down the same route.

It was almost four o'clock when he rose from his desk, the notes for the next day's writing completed to his satisfaction, and he wandered through to the porch to check out the marsh. It was the middle of October now and the fall color was reaching its peak: while the oaks still clung to their fading green, the maples and beeches, the birches and willows on the far side of the marsh were a mass of reds, gold and yellows beneath a sun that was still warm. Enough daylight remaining for a run, thought McDermott, and with Connor prancing beside him, he picked up his keys and headed for the garage.

Driving to the beach, he reflected on what Dan Dodgson had said about his isolating himself. It was true: he'd done a pretty good job of cutting off contact with most people. He never checked for e-mail messages, scorned Facebook and other such social networks, and rarely returned telephone messages. He'd quietly resigned from volunteer positions on a number of local boards, and had been eminently successful in severing ties with the numerous couples he and Jean had once socialized with. He felt somewhat guilty about that, but on those few occasions he'd accepted lunch or dinner invitations, he'd been so overcome by nostalgia, grief and jealousy, he'd found it difficult to communicate.

When they returned from their run, Connor slumped with a thud before his water bowl and lapped away with great slurps, while McDermott opened the refrigerator and mulled over what he might prepare for dinner. He was invigorated by his exercise and thought he might try putting a chicken wellington together, with perhaps some roast potatoes in pesto. He assembled the necessary ingredients on the counter top, thought about a Scotch to help in the cooking process, decided that wine was a better option in the light of the previous day's debacle, and moved over to the built-in wine cooler. Only then did he notice the telephone answering machine was flashing. He knew before he pressed the playback button whose voice he would hear, and as Greta VanDamm's throaty voice echoed from the speaker, he grimaced at his powers of intuition. Still, a promise was a promise, and thinking the sooner he got it over with the better, McDermott picked up the receiver. A few minutes later he had his appointment; for Halloween, he noted wryly – exactly one week away. Time enough for another chapter if he pushed it.

6.

Dramatics

Prior to our third form year at Bricknall, Cracker had been my friend, confidante, and protector. They were key roles, but in truth their influence on my life had been largely peripheral. That changed with Cracker's insistence that I tread the boards.

The Dramatic Society at Bricknall was serious business: membership had traditionally been reserved for pupils in the fourth year and above, and its high standards of production were renowned throughout the city. I certainly had no aspirations in that direction: although I'd enjoyed playing parts in class dramatizations in my junior school, appearing on a real stage at Bricknall before hundreds of people held no appeal for me – until, that is, Cracker decided I should rethink my position.

'Here, have you heard Robbie?' he shouted, as he spilled out of the school onto the playground one morning.

'Heard what?'

'The Dramatic Society's doing 'The Rose and the Ring' and they need young kids, so they're letting third years have a go.'

'So?'

'So we need to get our names down for auditions.'

'Don't be so bloody daft, Cracker. There's no way you're getting me into that.'

'Aw, come on, Robbie. Remember when you were Prince Pip at Dunswell Road? And what about that haunted house thing we did at Sea Scouts? It'll be bloody great. Come on! Let's do it!'

'Listen Cracker, you silly pillock. I was Prince Pip in our classroom with a bunch of kids watching, and we did the haunted house thing for about twenty parents. This is the Bricknall Grange Dramatic Society you're talking about – audiences of seven hundred plus. Even if we could get parts, which I doubt, it'd scare the hell out of me.'

'Aw, bloody hell, Robbie, what's up with you?' Cracker said, putting his arm round my shoulder. 'Look at it this way, Anita Black is bound to be the star; think of all the rehearsals you'll get to spend with her.'

Cracker was, in truth, a clever young bastard: by invoking those two magical words, Anita Black, he had found my weakness and he knew it. I idolized her. A sixth former and rumoured to be heading for drama school, Anita Black was tall, stately, possessed of a superb voice, and was the perennial star of the school's dramatic productions. I promised Cracker I would audition.

'The Rose and the Ring,' William Thackeray's 'Fireside Pantomime for Great and Small Children,' does indeed call for a number of young children in the cast and Cracker and I were successful in landing parts. I was given the role of 'First Child,' in a production that was, for me, memorable in three ways: I had the smallest part, I bore the responsibility of the opening line, and the first performance proved to be a personal disaster. My biggest problem was with that opening line – 'I think that mummy's voice is much sweeter than a piano.' As a working-class kid, bringing even a small measure of conviction to words such as 'mummy,' and 'sweeter' was a tall order, and I was aghast at the potential reaction among my teenage peers when they heard me deliver such a mawkish line. My semantic concerns and fears of emasculatory embarrassment aside, however, Cracker and I had a good time at the rehearsals where the presence of Anita Black added immeasurably to my own enjoyment of the experience.

It was with the arrival of opening night that the magnitude of what I had signed up for hit me. Shortly before the opening curtain, in the gloom of the unlit stage, Cracker and I and a couple of other kids took up our positions stage centre, arranged on the floor around our 'mother's' knees. Beyond the stage curtain, we could hear the hubbub of the sold-out house – around seven hundred people. It sounded to me as if the whole world awaited my appearance, and my bowels and throat constricted in tandem.

'Stage lights up!' With the producer's order the hot stage lights washed over us.

'House lights down!' The sound of the audience died like the chatter of birds sensing the presence of a hawk.

'Curtain!' The curtains parted with a rasp of rings and soft swish of velvet. It was then, as sweat streamed from my face, I committed the cardinal sin. Ignoring the constant warnings from Ollie Holloway, our teacher-producer and my own, oft repeated vows, I looked directly into the audience. Except it didn't look like an audience. It looked like thousands of disembodied white faces all staring at me as if saying, 'Well, come on then, you prat. Say something!'

'Ah – ah – ah' I uttered a strangled croak.

'Ah – ah – ah' Cracker and the rest of the cast stared at me intently, willing me on, while backstage, the prompter slowly came to terms with the fact that her services were urgently required although the play had yet to begin.

'I think . . .' the prompter's theatrical whisper jolted me out of my mesmerized state.

'Ithinkthatmummy'svoiceismuchsweeterthanapiano.' I spat the words out fast and flat, wanting nothing more in the world than to get off that stage. The audience heaved a collective sigh of relief and the play began. Things went only marginally better at the following performances, and as we left the stage after the final curtain-call on the closing night, I vowed to Cracker: 'Never again!'

Despite my pledge, 'The Rose and the Ring' proved to be the first of five occasions on which I would appear in school productions. Although my inability, during five years of Dramatic Society membership, to secure a part that actually merited a *name* was disappointing, it was more than compensated for a few years later, when my brief forays on to that school stage played a pivotal part in not only my career but in the rest of my life. Unknowingly, Cracker had, with his prodding and prompting on the playground that day in the third form, set me forth on a path that would stretch for years into the future.

It would have been reasonable to expect, given Cracker's fierce independence and general disregard for authoritarian figures, that he would have difficulty living within the strictures of life at Bricknall, and yet, with the exception of the Ramsbottom affair, he stayed out of trouble – until we entered the fourth form.

The staff at the school, while demanding and unfailingly strict, were fair, decent people devoted to their profession and the interests of their pupils – with one exception. Albert Kenworth was a tall, spare individual with cadaverous features, thinning black hair and a perpetual frown. Although his official subject was mathematics, his real talent resided in his uncanny ability to identify the weakest, most vulnerable pupils whom he would bully unmercifully through a combination of biting sarcasm and scorn. He notoriously reserved the most withering of his verbal attacks for any child who had the temerity to seek permission to use the toilet during his lessons. I went through my school career without making his acquaintance, but Cracker's fourth form class was on Kenworth's teaching schedule, and a confrontation between a boy like Cracker and a man like Kenworth was always going to happen. It was not long in arriving.

I knew nothing of Derek Witherspoon, a small, bespectacled youth in Cracker's class, other than what I'd been told. A quiet, studious boy with a slight stammer he had few close friends but was accepted by his classmates who had adopted him as something of a class mascot. It was Derek's mauling by Albert Kenworth that landed Cracker back in the headmaster's study. He related the story to me later in the day of the event, when I inquired as to the veracity of the rumours of his having received a caning at the hands of old Chatsworth.

'The poor little sod only wanted to have a piss,' Cracker said.

'So what happened exactly?' I said.

'Well, old Withers put his hand up and asked to be excused, and instead of just giving him the nod like any other teacher would, that bastard, Kenworth started in on him with this great long performance.'

'In what way?'

'Oh, you know: "I beg your pardon, boy? Why didn't you go at the correct time like everyone else?" Then he called him out to the front of the class where he could really show him up and let go at him. "Do you consider yourself to be special, or do you merely have a weak bladder?" All that kind of crap. 'Course, old Withers was standing there almost crossing his legs by that time, and when Kenworth asked him to speak up, his stammer came back. That's when I lost it.'

'Oh, Christ,' I said. 'What do you mean, "lost it?"'

'Well, Kenworth asked Withers whether it was beyond his ability to wait to the end of the lesson and Withers tried like hell to say it was, but all that came out was, "Y – y – y – ." Bastard Kenworth laughed and said, "Y – y – y – . What on earth does that mean, boy? Come on, dogsbody, spit it out." That's when I stood up and said it.'

'Said what?'

'I just said, "Sir, why don't you stop being such a prat and just let him go to the toilet?"'

'Bloody hell, Cracker; and then what?'

Cracker laughed. 'The old bugger went into orbit: came roaring toward me and tried to hit me. I just reacted: stopped him with my left, hit him in the gut with my right and he went down like a sack of spuds. I told Withers to get moving and I just tootled down to Chatsworth's office. I knew I'd be sent there anyway so I thought I'd get my five penn'orth in first.'

'So what did Chatsworth say?'

'He was okay. I told him what had happened and he had me wait while he went off to see Kenworth and then, when he came back, he prattled on about teachers sometimes overstepping the mark, but that was no justification for assault blah, blah, blah. Rabbited on about expulsion being the usual punishment for striking a teacher, but in the circumstances, blah, blah, blah. And then he gave me three on each hand.' Cracker held out his hands and showed me the welts across his palms.

'Sodding hell, Cracker; you could have been history.'

'Yeah, I know,' he said, 'but you can't let bullies get away with that kind of crap. And you know what, Robbie? I bet that bugger, Kenworth won't piss about with me again – or anyone else in my class either. And not only that, but I reckon old Chatsworth was on my side; he just couldn't say so.'

Cracker's reputation was considerably enhanced by the incident, but he knew how fortunate he'd been in escaping expulsion, and he stayed out of Chatsworth's office for the remainder of his school career. In the meantime, my friend's quixotic approach to life, allied to his charisma and dashing good looks, contrived to separate us a little more through their magnetic effect on the opposite sex.

Cracker had already had a number of liaisons with Bricknall girls, but until he took up with Jennifer Topliss, none of them had interfered unduly with the time we spent together outside of school. This relationship proved to be different and I found myself increasingly alone on Friday and Saturday evenings, as Cracker and Jen, in the company of two or three other couples in steady relationships took off for the back row of the Astoria, our local cinema.

Cracker's infatuation was understandable, Jen being probably the most attractive girl in the school. With green eyes and dazzling white teeth, she seemed to sport a perpetual tan, and with her shock of black, glossy hair, she turned heads wherever she went. At five feet three inches, she was a good deal shorter than Cracker, but she more than made up for her lack of height with a trim figure and shapely legs – showed off to good effect by her pushing of the school's limits on acceptable skirt length. The only surprising aspect of Jen and Cracker's courtship was the disparity in their socio-economic circumstances: while Cracker's background was lower working class, Jen was the pony-riding daughter of a wealthy landowner who lived in a fancy country house. Nevertheless it turned out to be a long relationship; one from which Cracker learned a good deal. For me, the advent of Jen Topliss in Cracker's life marked another fork in the road of our friendship.

Our fifth form year at Bricknall brought the trauma of O Level examinations, success in which was mandatory if we were to continue on into the sixth form – a requirement for eventual college entrance – and the promise of the traditional post-exam visit to France. The exams proved to be less of a memorable event than the French trip, thanks to Cracker and his part in an incident that was as serious as any the school had had to face in over thirty years of excursions abroad.

Cracker and I saw little of each other during the period leading up to the exams. Socially he became more closely involved than ever with Jen, while along with the rest of our classmates wishing to pursue further education, we focused on cramming our brains with memorized blocks of data for regurgitation on the appointed examination days. Once the exams were over with Adam Faith's, 'Poor Me,' and the Everly Brothers,' 'Cathy's Clown,' dominating playing time at our celebratory parties, and Cracker belting out Johnny Preston's, 'Running Bear' at every opportunity, we prepared for our trip to France.

Cracker and I were enthusiastic over our first trip abroad, and looked forward to living cheek by jowl with our peers in a foreign country – a scenario that promised plenty of laughs. I was secretly pleased too, that Jen Topliss would not be accompanying us, having qualified for some National Gymkhana or other that was to be held while we were away.

Our destination was Annemonde in the Haute-Savoie region of France, close to the Swiss border, where we lodged at 'Le Grand Hotel de France.' 'Grand' it wasn't, but the accommodations were comfortable enough for kids such as Cracker and I who had, not so long ago, been strangers to indoor plumbing. The pair of us shared a room with two classmates of Cracker's, and the four of us rarely stopped laughing, as we enjoyed the freedom of raucous teenage nights without the interference of adults.

The school magazine article that later summarized the trip included the statement: 'Someone found a small café where the majority spent their evenings.' What the magazine failed to mention was that the 'small café' was a licensed brasserie where our girls made eyes at the local men, a few idiots drank themselves into a nightly stupor, and Cracker made school history.

The invasion of a small town such as Annemonde by a group of adolescent English schoolgirls, was sure to excite the hormones of the local male population, and the sight of youths attempting to scale the walls of our hotel late at night became commonplace, as did the spectacle of Bricknall girls being ferried around on the pillions of motor scooters driven by tanned local youths. Trouble was bound to occur sooner or later and the only real surprise was that it took so long. When the incident occurred, Cracker and I were at the back of the brasserie in question, engaged in a game of fussball with a pair of French kids, and thus we had no idea of the drama unfolding across the room until a sudden silence fell over the place.

Accounts of the events leading up to the confrontation varied in the aftermath, but the consensus seemed to be that a local French thug had taken more than a passing interest in Maureen Evans, an attractive member of our party, and upon having his advances rejected, had turned nasty. It was when he moved from verbal abuse to physically pawing Maureen that Mally Binns, a classmate of mine, had stepped forward in a courageous attempt to play the knight in shining armour. At that point the Frenchman had drawn a knife and thus the sudden silence that had alerted Cracker and me to the imbroglio.

The great John Huston, at the height of his directorial prowess, could not have set a dramatic scene more perfectly: the smoke filled bar; the rich aroma of Galloises; the neon lights in the window; and the absolute stillness of the crowd, transfixed by the gleaming blade. The eyes of every Bricknall student focused upon Cracker as he moved away from our game and walked slowly, but with a determined step, toward the man with the knife. Even now, the scene remains surreal: this was a school trip for Christ's sake. We were a bunch of English high school kids in search of French culture, and here was Cracker making like Steve McQueen with a grown, armed man. And make no mistake – this knife-wielding prat *was* a man. He was not some school bully or playground lout, he was a swarthy, nasty-looking individual whose frantic eyes, as they swept over the approaching Cracker, scared the hell out of me.

'Move away Mally,' said Cracker as he walked almost nonchalantly toward the stand-off.

Mally Binns was more than happy to oblige, and he backed away as Cracker moved past him and stopped a few feet in front of the Frenchman.

'Donnez-moi le knife s'il vous plait monsewer,' said Cracker, in his less than perfect French, holding out his hand.

The response was a torrent of French which only the transfixed French patrons could understand, and the man began to circle Cracker waving the knife in a threatening circle and gesturing Cracker onwards with his left hand. Cracker did not disappoint him, moving toward the man in what I recognized as his basic Taekwondo stance. When the expected lunge came from the Frenchman, it was effortlessly brushed aside as, with astonishing speed, Cracker's left hand struck the man's forearm and the outside of his right foot smashed into the interior side of the hoodlum's left knee. It was at that moment, as the man fell to the floor with a scream that two baton-wielding gendarmes, responding to a call from the bartender, burst through the open door of the brasserie.

The rest of the evening passed as one might expect: the arrest and subsequent removal of the knife-wielding Frenchman; long, arduous interviews between the gendarmes, who spoke little English, and we who spoke even less French; and the eventual arrival of our French teacher, 'Ollie' Holloway, whose face reflected the level of anxiety and shock one might expect of someone in his situation. It was Ollie who sorted things out with the gendarmes and who prevented the arrest of Cracker with the ready assistance of the bartender and some customers who had witnessed the whole thing.

The following day found those of us who had been present at the brasserie that evening involved in a long post mortem with the Bricknall Grange staff team. The outcome was as predictable as I suppose it was sensible: the entire school party was confined to the hotel for the remaining two evenings of our stay.

I continue to have questions concerning that incident. How many understood that Cracker could have been killed that night – or indeed could have killed? (I learned later that the Taekwondo move employed by my friend is known as a Front Snap Kick, which is capable of causing death from cardiac arrest.) How did the whole episode escape the attention of the local newspapers when we arrived home, when every Bricknall pupil and teacher must have known of the incident within days of our arrival back in England?

Although the memory of Cracker's final violent act of his schoolboy days remained with everyone present that night – it being the one that made him a hero in the eyes of the staff as well as pupils – other memories of the trip soon faded into insignificance as the summer holidays rolled on and we awaited our exam results. We need not have worried: the two of us passed all of our eight subjects, and we were set for two more years at school and an opportunity, if we could pass our advanced level GCEs, to go to college. Our dream of becoming teachers, born six years previously, was one step closer to being realized.

7.

Therapy

Day 245. McDermott turned into the parking lot of the Professional Plaza on the bay side of U.S. 31, chose a parking spot facing the water, and cut the engine. Prime piece of real estate for an office building, he thought, as he looked across at the fall colors on the Mission Peninsula. Probably not surprising though: how much did a psychotherapist with Greta VanDamm's qualifications pull down these days? $120 an hour? $150? And therapists were probably at the low end of the trough in comparison to the other doctors practicing in the three-story stone and glass edifice reflected in his rear view mirror. He studied it. How many similar buildings had he entered during Jean's illness, and how much money had it taken from how many people – many of them now dead – to pay for them? Enough; he picked up his briefcase, and with one last look at the wind-ruffled surface of the bay, eased himself out of the sleek XJ. Walking toward the office entrance in the morning breeze, he speculated as to the place of his briefcase and the Jag in the morning's proceedings. There was nothing in the former except his glasses and a book, and he hadn't used the latter for weeks, preferring the SUV for local driving. So, why? Image? For who? Jesus, he thought, I'm analyzing myself before I give her the chance.

He followed VanDamm's directions and located her office on the second floor of the building. A small brass plaque by the doorway bore the imprint:

G. VANDAMM, M.D. Ph.D. LIFE COACH AND COUNSELOR

The door opened into a small waiting room with no windows. The only light came from two table lamps, and soft music issued from hidden speakers. He was ten minutes early, so he took out his glasses with the intention of reading for a while. His current book was a biography of Big Jack Charlton, and the craggy face of the retired, English football player with his flat, tweed cap, on the cover of the book put him in mind of his father. He smiled as he thought of how the old man might have reacted to his imminent appointment.

'You're going to see a what? A trick, bloody cyclist? What the hell for? What the hell's up with you? I've bloody heard everything now. I never thought I'd see a son of mine – '

McDermott's reverie was interrupted as the door to the inner office opened and the tall, stately figure of Greta VanDamm advanced toward him, hand outstretched.

'Hello, Robbie,' she said. 'Come on through why don't you,' and she turned to lead him into her office. She was wearing a dark, pin-striped business suit, the jacket tucked at the waist, emphasizing the slim figure she still clearly took pride in. Following her, he recalled Jean's words about the therapist. 'She might look matriarchal now, Robbie,' she'd said, 'but I'll bet that once upon a time, Greta VanDamm was a hot-looking broad.'

Inside the office, he took in the clean, contemporary lines: the cherry desk with its Aeron chair; the credenza mounted computer station; and, directly across from VanDamm's leather armchair, the ubiquitous couch and matching chair from which he knew patients were expected to choose. He plumped for the corner of the sofa next to the coffee table with its box of Kleenex, not that he thought for a moment he would be availing himself of the tissues: it would be a cold day in hell before he opened up to that extent. He was, he reminded himself, going through the motions because he'd promised Pastor Dan. He had little faith in the efficacy of therapy in solving personal problems of any kind. Where he came from, you were expected to handle these things yourself, and that, by God, what was what he would do.

VanDamm folded her tall frame into her armchair, perched a pair of half – moon glasses on her nose, and regarded McDermott thoughtfully. 'So, Robbie, why don't I begin by telling you what I know about why you're here, and then you can fill me in on the details. Does that sound like a plan?'

'Sure,' McDermott said.

'Well, the extent of my knowledge right now, Robbie, is that Dan Dodgson thinks you could use some help with the grieving process. He's concerned about what he believes to be problems you may be having with anger and loneliness? Maybe a little depression? And he thinks I may be able to help. So, here we are. Oh, and by the way, before we begin, I should emphasize that although I'm seeing you in my capacity as volunteer grief counselor for the church, standard practices apply: whatever is said in this room stays in this room. Okay?'

'Sure, that's fine.'

'You don't have any concerns about confidentiality?'

'No, none. I'm sure you're completely professional.' McDermott was beginning to wish she'd get on with it.

'Okay then, Robbie. Would you like to begin by sharing with me the reasons you believe you're here?'

McDermott was honest: as much as he was tempted to tell the woman what he thought she would like to hear, he knew he owed her the truth. He recounted his promise to the pastor, his own ambivalent views of a therapeutic approach to resolving personal problems, and his belief that grief was best dealt with by the person doing the grieving.

If he'd expected to put her on the back foot; to shock her; to make her realize what a waste of time the whole thing was, then he was sorely disappointed.

'Sort of, "Real men take care of themselves," Robbie. Is that what you're saying?'

'Well, something like that I suppose.'

As a matching of wills, he thought, driving home later, it had been no contest. He recalled how she'd dissected his beliefs, with the cool efficiency of a vivisectionist, gently disabused him of his outdated convictions, and convinced him of her ability to assist in his healing. She was, he had to admit, bloody good at her job, and he let his thoughts range over the pertinent points she'd made.

'So, if I understand you correctly, Robbie,' she'd said in that smoky voice of hers, 'you're saying that the only reason you're here is that you made a promise to Dan Dodgson, and you think that coming here to get some support during this difficult time in your life, means that you're weak in some way; that you can take care of your own problems. Is that a fair summation?'

Given his concurrence with her succinct analysis, she'd wasted no time in getting down to business and doing it in the most effective way.

'May I ask you a question about the relationship between you and Jean, Robbie? Did you feel as if either of you were weak when you supported each other through your years together? Or did you feel you were strong?'

No argument there. McDermott had had to agree: he and Jean had been strong in supporting each other – despite the arguments toward the end.

'So,' Greta had continued (interesting, he thought, how he was now thinking of her by her first name), 'you agree you were strong. Now, I'm not going to change your belief system in one session, but I will challenge it often if it doesn't serve you well. When you're here and when you leave here, I want you to think about that. I want you to remember that in the past, it has been strength that has allowed you to call upon someone you trust to help you; not weakness. So when you begin to think, "I'm weak because I'm seeing a therapist," I want you to play back this moment. Are you willing to do that? Because otherwise, when it gets difficult, you're going to latch on to that misconception of "If I can't handle this on my own, I'm weak," and it's going to make the journey more difficult.'

Her cool logic, allied to the straightforward nature of her delivery, had so impressed him he'd forgotten much of the remainder of the session, but she'd certainly made him feel better and less alone, and it had come as no surprise when he'd agreed to see her again in a couple of weeks.

So engrossed was he in his thoughts, he was entering Westwood before he knew it. Now how the hell had that happened? He'd steered clear of the town since Jean's funeral, and here he was cruising up Main. Well, what the hell, it was close to lunchtime; he might as well call in at Bridie's for a bite. He rolled north up Main, past the cemetery at the top of the hill, past the Fellowship Hall, over the junction with 2nd where Main separated the elementary school from the middle-high school campus, and pulled into the vacant lot opposite Bridie's Diner. He had no doubt his presence in the town would be widely reported within hours, despite the few people around, but, he reflected happily, as he pushed through the door into Bridie's, he couldn't really give a shit.

At 11:30, the place was kind of between breakfast and lunch, and was relatively quiet. McDermott walked past the long line of red leatherette booths to the back, nodding at young Tiffany Atkins who was cashing out a customer at the till. Poor Tiffany, he thought, as he slid into his customary rear booth that gave him a view of the whole diner. Tiff was the archetypical high school dropout in small town rural America: pregnant at seventeen, reluctant husband gone by eighteen, now living with her child and her thirty-something mother who'd done the whole thing the same way eighteen years earlier. He watched the girl as she approached, menu in one hand, coffee jug in the other. He could still see the cute cheerleader behind the tired eyes and the bottle blond, big hair, but the once athletic body was already showing signs of softness, and her smile was no longer the same ear-to-ear, spontaneous statement of joy she'd once possessed.

'Hello, Mr. McDermott. Coffee?'

'Please, Tiff. Thanks.'

'You know what you want, Mr. McDermott, or shall I give you a couple of minutes?'

'Just give me a moment or two would you Tiff?'

'Sure thing Mr. McDermott.'

He studied her back as she walked toward the counter and shook his head at the waste. Everyone tended to think of America's inner cities when the subject of high school dropout rates came up, but he knew from his previous years on the Westwood School Board, that rural America had massive problems too. Almost 70% of Westwood's children had been classified as 'at risk' during his last year on the board. That translated into seven out of ten kids on the 'free or reduced lunch' program, with most of them living with single parents and little hope of ever breaking free of the perpetual loop of poverty. McDermott sighed and began to skip through the menu.

'Holy shit! Well what do you know? If it aint the squire of Westwood himself.'

McDermott laughed the first honest laugh he'd allowed himself in a long time, and looked up into the cornflower-blue eyes of Bridie Donovan.

'Hey,' he said. 'How're you doing, Bridie?'

'How am I doing? How am I doing? I'll tell you how I'm doing, Robbie McDermott: I'm doing a whole lot better than you will be if you don't get off your ass and give me a fucking great hug.'

McDermott slid out laughing from the booth and complied, knowing there was significantly more depth to Bridie's demand than her colorful language implied. Owner of the only diner in the town, chief booster of the Westwood Lancers, the schools sports teams, and prime mover behind Westwood's volunteer food bank and resale shop, Bridie had been a close friend since he and Jean had arrived in the neighborhood. She was also the only person to whom Jean and McDermott would ever entrust the care of Connor whenever they travelled: like them, Bridie was a consummate animal lover.

'You want some company, old man, or just peace and quiet?'

'Hey, passing some time with you is just what I need. Have a seat,' said McDermott. 'Let's just have a bit less of the 'old man' shit, eh?'

'Yeah, yeah. Well, you know, if it looks old, sounds old – '

McDermott threw his napkin at her, dodged her return throw, and leveled his eyes at her. 'Seriously though, Bridie; bullshit aside, it is good to see you.'

'Likewise,' she said, 'Thought maybe we'd lost you there for a while. You doing okay?'

'Yeah, I guess. Good days and bad days you know,' McDermott picked at the corner of his menu as he avoided her eyes.

Bridie reached out and covered his hand with hers. 'It's gonna take a while, Robbie. I know it's not the same, but when my old man pissed off, I was hurting for a long time. And you went through worse than that. But you know what? You can't lock yourself away over there like some fucking hermit: you have to get out – Robbie, are you listening to me?'

McDermott was studying her tanned hand with its turquoise ringed fingers lying on top of his own hand, and thinking that this was the first physical, human contact he'd had since Jean died. He placed his other hand over hers and gave it a squeeze. 'Yeah, I'm sorry love; I kinda drift off now and then. You were saying?'

'Mrs. Donovan,' Tiffany appeared at the end of the booth, 'George said can you come quick, he's – '

'That goddamn George,' Bridie said, 'I leave that kitchen for one fucking minute! Listen, you get something to eat Robbie and I'll see you in a few, okay?' She hurried off after Tiffany.

McDermott got himself a BLT and as he ate, he thought about Bridie Donovan. He knew she was fifty-four, but she was still a damned attractive woman, and she had that kind of knowing look that told you she knew it. It was a look somehow enhanced by her tanned, leathery skin with its deeply etched grooves and laugh lines and the faint grin that constantly played around her mouth. Around five nine, she was big: 'well upholstered' his dad would have said, but she remained well proportioned, and her breasts were a talking point for most of the men in the area. She regularly dressed in plain Levis and denim shirts except for her evenings at the

Golden Nugget, Westwood's only bar, when she sported fancier jeans with sequins on the pockets, and figure hugging sleeveless tops. Rounding the outfit off with a short denim jacket, high heeled cowboy boots, and a Stetson, she'd sit at the end of the Nugget's polished pine bar shooting the shit with Rory Brennan, the proprietor.

Not much of a life for an attractive, intelligent woman, thought McDermott. And she was intelligent – despite her raunchy language. She was a voracious reader of almost every genre, a political activist for the local Democratic Party, and had been in the middle of veterinarian studies at MSU when her parents met a truck coming toward them on the wrong side of U.S. 31. They were both gone now, but Bridie had left college to care for them and taken over the running of their diner. As far as he knew, she'd done only one really stupid thing in her life, and that was marrying Mickey Shanahan, a Westwood High School football star who'd failed to make it in the college ranks and had carried a chip on his shoulder from that moment on. He'd left Bridie and their twin boys twenty-five years ago and had never been heard from since. How the hell Bridie had managed her parents and the twins, while simultaneously running the diner, was beyond him, but one thing was for sure: she was as tough as she was good looking and intelligent. There'd been a rumor around town for a long time that she was a lesbian – the legacy of a long friendship with a female boarder she'd once taken in. That woman was long gone now, but the rumors persisted, given credence, perhaps, by there having been no significant man in her life since Mickey, and her constant rebuffing of offers from the many males both local and tourist that frequented the Nugget. Gay or straight, McDermott thought the woman bloody marvelous and –

'Hey, Handsome; a penny for 'em.' Bridie slid back across from him.

McDermott grinned. 'You don't want to know. Everything okay in the kitchen?'

'Yeah, yeah. That fucking George; I don't know why I keep him on. One burner goes out and he thinks it's the frigging Apocalypse. Anyway, enough of that old fart; how's Connor?'

'Doing great thanks, Bridie; in fact I need to be getting back for him. He'll be wanting his lunchtime whizz.'

'Yeah, and I need to get my ass in gear too: twenty minutes from now this place is gonna be like church on Easter Sunday. Hey, before you go. You heard about Steve and Holly?'

'Steve and Holly? No. What?'

Bridie glanced around and lowered her voice. 'They're splitting.'

'What? The Kosinskys?' McDermott was incredulous: if there was such a thing as a perfect family, Steve and Holly Kosinsky and their two girls were it. As owners of the Belvedere, a Michelin two-star rated restaurant that was a major tourist attraction in the area, Steve and Holly were pillars of the community, devout Episcopalians, and devoted parents. McDermott and Jean had stayed with them on many weekends while their cabin was being built, and the two couples had become close friends. And they were splitting? Suddenly McDermott realized how long he'd spent away from the community he and Jean had been such an integral part of.

'But, but – Why? – I mean – What the hell –?' McDermott was lost for words.

'Well, you know Steve's been in rehab down in Traverse since he got his new knee?'

McDermott nodded.

'Well, according to Rory Brennan, who got it from his wife who got it from Holly, turns out Steve's got a thing going with a receptionist at the hospital. Seems his knee isn't the only joint he's been getting exercised.'

'Jesus Christ,' said McDermott,' the stupid, fucking idiot.'

'Tell me about it,' Bridie said. 'Anyway, the whole thing is one big clusterfuck from the sound of it. Holly's living up at the house with the girls and won't let Steve near the place – he's staying at this broad's apartment. Holly's found herself a chef and she's running the restaurant on her own.

'How are the girls doing?' said McDermott.

'Well, at seventeen and fifteen, they're old enough to know the score, but – '

'I'm sorry, Mrs. Donovan, but George – '

Bridie whirled around to face Tiffany. 'What? What? Jesus H. Christ. I will rip that man a new fucking asshole!' She turned back to McDermott. 'Sorry hon, I'll have to go and sort that sad sack out. But, hey, don't be a stranger eh?'

'I won't, Bridie, and thanks for the info.' McDermott picked up his bill and followed her down the aisle.

Bridie paused at the entry to the kitchen, waited for him to catch up and snatched the bill out of his hand. 'This one's on the house Robbie: that way I know you'll be back.'

'No, come on – '

'No, forget it, Robbie. Just one thing though.'

'What's that?'

'You need any help or anything, you give me a call. Okay?'

'Yeah, sure. Thanks love.'

'You're welcome hon,' Bridie said, and gave him a quick hug before she disappeared into the kitchen.

McDermott slipped Tiffany five bucks on the way out and walked slowly across to his car. Steve and Holly? He couldn't get his head around it. And where had he been when all this was happening? Well, daft question; he'd been locked away contemplating his own problems.

By the time he rolled into the cabin driveway, the temperature had dropped another five degrees and he guessed the leading edge of the promised cold front had arrived out of northern Wisconsin. The clouds had darkened too, so he wasted no time once Connor had sprinkled, in changing his clothes, bundling his dog into the SUV and taking off for the lakeshore.

As usual, the sound of the breaking waves and the wind skittering through the trees on the shoreline cleared his head, and with Connor patrolling ahead of him, he went over the events of the morning.

They represented, he sensed, an important stage in whatever the hell kind of journey he was engaged upon. The appointment with Greta had provided a kind of catharsis, while seeing Bridie again had stirred his sense of humour for the first time in months. He acknowledged too, that the very act of speaking with other people had lifted his mood. So: a day of discovery. He'd found in Greta VanDamm a talented woman who could potentially help him, he'd been reminded that he had a real friend in Bridie Donovan, and getting out and about had not been the big deal he'd envisioned.

His thoughts turned to the Kosinskys. As sad as that situation was, it served as a valuable reminder: he was not the only poor sod suffering in the world; not the only lost soul grieving; and, selfish as it was, that sobering thought gave him some comfort. He cast his mind back over the dinners and wild times he and Jean had shared with Steve and Holly: the confirmations of the girls, Loren and Mandy; the hundreds of nights at the Westwood high school gym, cheering the kids on in basketball and volleyball games; the holidays on Mackinaw Island . . . Goddamnit, they were such a perfect family; what the hell was Steve playing at? And Holly? Jesus; she must be hurting like McDermott himself. After all, what was the difference between mourning the loss of a spouse to death, and mourning the loss of a spouse to a stranger? Was there a difference? What was it? He worried the issue. Yes, he thought, there was a difference: the little matter of betrayal in Steve and Holly's case. Having said that, there were an awful lot of common denominators too: loss, grief, absence, loneliness, despair, depression. Suffering, he supposed, was the one word that encompassed all of those dark feelings. . . . A sudden strengthening in the wind alerted him to an imminent change in the weather, and hailing Connor, he turned back, noticing as he did so rain falling out on the lake's horizon. Fall was almost done in this part of the country: soon the white stuff would be falling, bringing with it the first Thanksgiving and then the first Christmas since . . . As he bent his head against the wind, he felt his mood begin to darken with the skies, and quickened his pace.

It was raining hard by the time he arrived back at the cabin, and determined to fight the onset of another depressive episode, he lit a majority of the cabin's lights, made a pot of coffee and immersed himself back in his book.

He finished reading one hour and a lot of red ink later, and laying aside the manuscript and his notes for the morning, he removed his glasses, pinched the bridge of his nose, and gave himself up to what he hoped was a blunt appraisal. As usual he'd been way too verbose and was concerned about his vocabulary. He knew there was almost a canon of the faith in the publishing world pursuant to which 'simple' was preferable to 'fancy' in one's choice of words. Indeed, Jean had joined many of his clients in criticizing his use of 'million-dollar words' as she called them. McDermott though, while he was not given to combing the OCED for esoteric words, did believe in accuracy of word choice, and when he felt the need for a specific word, he used it.

If there was one positive he felt good about, it was the evolving development of his ability to push the envelope on the fiction side; to take a fact and embellish it to the point of creating a story. The French trip was a good example. Of course, financial circumstances had precluded the presence of both he and Cracker on that excursion, but he felt he'd done a workmanlike job of taking the few facts he'd gleaned from friends and fashioning them into a story. He knew a knife had been pulled by a Frenchman on one of the school party, and that the incident had been hushed up, but other than that it had been all his. On the negative side, he was concerned about the remaining plotting of his story, because at the present time, he was approaching the thing in the same way as Ian Rankin — with no real idea of how he would arrive at the end. For an established author with a lifetime's experience behind him, and a detective's mind to boot, that might work, but McDermott was a rookie and beginning to feel more and more that P.D. James's model of charting the direction of the plot might be more appropriate for him. He needed to take some time off from the actual writing soon and work on that.

Should he have spent more time on the issue of corporal punishment? Old Chatsworth and his cane . . . Today they'd lock him up and throw away the key. . . . In the end he decided against pushing the issue: the book, after all, was primarily concerned with Cracker; not with his own beliefs on the merits or otherwise of a variety of social issues. Still, it was a bloody crazy educational world now, he reflected as he went through to the kitchen to mix Connor's kibble: no cane – fair enough – but to have no acceptance on the part of school district authorities of any kind of discipline other than suspension was nonsensical. Well, thank God he was out of it – although he shuddered at the thought of what lay ahead for the nation's schools.

To celebrate what he thought had been his best day for many weeks, his brief dalliance with pain and suffering notwithstanding, McDermott built a postprandial fire in the porch and treated himself to a healthy measure of The Glenrothes. As he relished the taste of the Highlands and studied the flames, he thought again of the Kosinskys. What should he do there? He and Jean had faced this question before with a professor friend and his wife. As the parents of three vivacious and well-mannered children, the couple had presented to the world a picture of the model family, a picture that was shattered when the wife suddenly left for the arms of a hedge fund manager. With a daughter in her sophomore year at Penn State University and two sons in high school, their friend had been left to ponder over the smoking remains of a twenty-five year marriage. Friends of couples in such situations are invariably obliged to lean one way or the other with their affections, and Jean and McDermott had stuck with the husband, feeling that as the injured party, he was more deserving of their support.

McDermott was wise enough to know that only the two principals in a marriage knew the real story behind any breakup, but based on the facts as he knew them, it was Holly who'd been betrayed and thus was the one to whom he should reach out. That decision, however, presented a conundrum: he was a widowed, single male, and Holly a separated, single female. Might she see his overtures of friendship for something other than what they were? What of the people of Westwood? Would they jump to conclusions? Well, some would, and some wouldn't – that was about the size of it – but since it was none of their business and since he couldn't really give a damn, he'd do what he believed to be right, and without further hesitation he picked up the phone and dialed the Kosinskys' number. He felt bad for Steve, he thought, as he listened to the dial tone, but the hell with it, he had little time for people who cheated on their marital partners.

'Hi, you've reached Holly Freeman. Please leave a message.'

Put off his stroke a little by Holly's use of what he presumed had been her maiden name, McDermott left a simple request for Holly to call him back and hung up. He smiled as he resumed his seat: typical of Holly to have already ditched the name Steve had given her. Knowing her, everything else of Steve's would have found its way on to the front lawn within moments of her hearing of his infidelity. She'd always been a spitfire, packing into her five foot, well-toned body, an energy that literally crackled. She was a natural for the restaurant business where her easy banter and love of gossip made her popular with female guests, while her impish face beneath spiky, black hair and her jocular, flirtatious manner delighted the male customers. What in God's name was Steve thinking about?

Falling asleep that night became an exercise in frustration as McDermott's mind tangled with a plethora of images and soundbites from a day that had represented a coming-out of sorts for him. He'd travelled further, seen more people, and engaged in more conversation than on any other day since the funeral. It was as if a portal had opened on the world and he'd wandered tentatively through it. A bit like Alice, he thought. Did it indicate a new beginning, or was it merely a brief interlude in his grief? And what about his writing? What would happen to that if he started venturing out into the world? It was the central paradox of the writing life: on the one hand he believed his writing was helping him stave off the ever-present specter of depression, but on the other the process demanded solitude, and solitude . . . Sleep came.

'Oh God! Yes, Yes! Oh Jesus! Yes! Like that! Like that! Oh my God!' A twenty –year-old version of Greta VanDamm, feet hooked around McDermott's neck, lay backward on her desk, resting on her forearms, her head up watching him, as he plunged in and out of her. Her smart, pin-striped jacket lay open exposing impressive breasts that shuddered with each of his thrusts. Her nipples . . . Now he was in a hotel desperately searching for a toilet. If he didn't find one soon, he was going to . . . Yes! He burst through a pair of saloon- type doors and confronted a disgusting mess, the contents of the toilet bowl overflowing on to a floor strewn with feces. He turned and ran, his bowels bursting, up steps and down grand staircases, as people stared, and toilet after toilet appeared as smeared and stinking rooms that were unusable. In desperation he pushed through metal swinging doors into what appeared to be the nineteenth-century kitchen of an English pub.

'Hello, Robbie, you old bugger,' said Bridie Donovan. 'Looking for the john are you? Over there in the corner darlin.' He backed toward a door labeled 'Knaves' as he tried to make sense of her appearance. She looked to be dressed as Nell Gwynn, her ample breasts spilling from an emerald-green, stringed corset, as she turned what appeared to be a huge mangle from which some kind of red meat was oozing. . . . He emerged from the toilet in a hospital gown, pushing a portable IV drip. He could feel the eyes of other patients on his ass – stupid, bloody hospital gowns – but he ignored them as he approached his bed. Why was the curtain drawn around it? He pulled it back to find Holly Kosinsky lying there. She was dressed in the old fashioned blue and white starched nurse's uniform of 1950s England complete with black stockings and white hat.

'Well, there you are,' she said, getting off the bed. 'You should be in here Robbie. Come on love, let me help you.'

McDermott was bemused as to why Holly was speaking in a broad Yorkshire accent as she helped him into the bed.

'Why don't we get rid of all these tubes?' she said, unhooking him from the IVs attached to both his arms and his neck. 'There we are love, you don't want those nasty things in you do you? Now, what about a nice shag, because I don't know about you, but I'm gagging for it.' And she commenced to slowly unbutton her uniform. . . .

McDermott awoke with an erection, a full bladder and a sense of being cheated. Sitting on the cold toilet seat, it occurred to him that the celibate life he'd been leading was finally affecting him. First those thoughts about Greta VanDamm, now weird dreams. The toilet thing had to be an anxiety thing, but anxiety about what? And the hospital? The sex? How long was it since he'd had a sexually oriented dream? Even when he'd had them they'd invariably involved Jean rather than anyone else. In fact, they'd both laughed at how he had to be the only guy who dreamed about sex with his wife. Jean; what would she tell him to do now? He suspected that she would, in her own blunt way, be perfectly logical about it. 'Go get your ashes hauled,' she'd say, 'and stop pissing about.'

Back in his bed with Connor snoring beside him, McDermott let his thoughts drift over Bridie Donovan and Holly Kosinsky. Ironic really, that of the two women in the area around Westwood he found to be remotely interesting, one was gay and the other far too young for an old goat like him. Goat; why was it that when it came to the subject of sex, young males were likened to studs, stallions, rams and bulls, whereas the older generation drew the use of that word, goat? Unable to come up with an answer he returned to his thoughts of the women he'd been considering. Not only were they too young for him, he mused, sex with either of them, even were it on offer, would carry an unspoken promise of a relationship, something he did not believe himself to be ready for: not with Jean only eight months gone. Thinking of sex and Jean led his thoughts to the Chicago option they'd laughed about. Could he do that? How did you do it? He'd read about concierges at the big hotels knowing the score, but did they really? And how the hell did you go about broaching the subject? He thought about the Yellow Pages; would they . . . ? He started to laugh. 'It's 2011 you silly sod,' he said aloud. 'Look on the bloody internet!' He got up, put on his dressing gown and went to his den, leaving a bemused Connor watching his departure from the bed.

'Holy shit!' McDermott's eyes widened in astonishment: all he'd had to do was Google, 'Escort Agencies in Chicago' and he was looking at

778,000 results: company after company offering the services of men, women, impersonators, bored husbands and housewives; the list went on and on. What he was looking at represented a world he was ignorant of: certainly a long way from the table-dancers at the shabby Detroit joints his clients had dragged him to.

Aware that what he was about to do would likely result in a number of unwanted ads, and/or e-mails appearing on his computer screen in the future, McDermott clicked on the 'Royal Russian Agency' which advertised itself as the 'Most Prestigious Agency in Chicago.' The screen showed an entry page featuring a beautiful, scantily clad model and the amusing disclaimer:

'In no way should the contents of this site be viewed as an offer for prostitution. Any money paid to our Russian Princesses is for companionship only. Other transactions that may be conducted are the private business of two or more consenting adults over the age of 18.'

A click on the 'Enter' icon introduced McDermott to an array of photographs featuring ten 'Russian Princesses' with such authentic sounding names as Aleksi, Katyenka, Danya, Lanya and Pashanka. A further click on any one of the pictures brought up the chosen Princess in a provocative pose, overlaid by personal details including vital statistics. McDermott reviewed each one with a mixture of awe, fascination and, although he hated to admit it, sexual excitement. Each 'Princess' appeared to be stunningly beautiful, and when he clicked on the 'rates' label on the main menu, he was not surprised to find prices ranging from $400 for half an hour to $1500 for two hours. Finally, he navigated to 'Contact' and found that a simple telephone call to 'Tsarina' Agrafina was all that was required to schedule an appointment. Noting down the number, McDermott pushed himself away a little from the screen and thought. Should he? Shouldn't he? Good idea or bad? The money certainly wasn't an issue. What would Jean advise? Jean. What the hell was he doing? He switched off the computer and slunk back to his bed.

Eight hours later, following a morning that had seen him produce less than three hundred words of useable copy, McDermott was back in front of the parade of 'Russian Princesses.' He studied each individual picture again before selecting 'Princess Grisha', a twenty-five-year old brunette, described as being five feet one, weighing 115 pounds, and boasting vital statistics of 34B-26-34. She also had the advantage, McDermott thought, of appearing to have natural breasts, and an intelligent countenance, although why the latter should be of any consequence considering the nature of their proposed relationship, he could not say.

Within twenty minutes, he had an appointment with Princess Grisha for two hours on the coming Saturday (address to be provided when he confirmed – which should be forty-eight hours prior to his appointment). He also had a room at the Peninsula Hotel for the Saturday and Sunday evenings, and two nights at 'camp' booked for Connor with Bridie Donovan. Jean, he had decided, would have wished him all the luck in the world.

8.

Rehabilitation

Day 247. McDermott had three days before he set out for Chicago: three days during which the ability to concentrate deserted him. On the Thursday morning he let Connor out for his early morning pee and forgot about him until the dog's whining drew his attention. The following day, he burned out a saucepan while attempting to boil eggs, left his wallet at the Westwood Farmers Exchange, and prior to calling the 'Tsarina' to confirm his appointment, allowed the sink to overflow in the kitchen.

Fortunately his powers of concentration returned on the Saturday morning and the drive to Chicago passed without incident. Connor was housed at Bridie's place with her German shepherds, Lance and Shep, and the cabin was safely locked – McDermott having checked every door and window twice prior to his departure. Other than his mounting trepidation over what the evening had in store, there were only two small clouds hanging over him as he pulled into the Peninsula forecourt: the necessary lie he'd told Bridie (a bank meeting he'd said), and the fact that Holly Kosinsky had not returned his call. Still, he thought, as the Jaguar was converged upon by the usual hotel welcoming committee, what Bridie didn't know couldn't hurt her, and he'd call Holly again when he returned on Monday.

McDermott had planned the trip with the same meticulous care he employed in constructing new chapters of his book, and once checked into his suite, he began to methodically work the plan. He had the bellman bring him ice after dropping off his luggage, and sipped a leisurely Jameson's as he ran the Jacuzzi and hung his clothes. His appointment was at seven and it was currently three-thirty. He intended to follow a soak in the big tub with afternoon tea in The Lobby and a stroll down the Magnificent Mile. He'd return to the hotel at six, have a hot shower, dress and leave for his appointment by cab at six-thirty. Based upon the information provided by 'Tsarina' Agrafina, he should arrive at the house on Drayton Street in Lincoln Park around six-fifty. The up-market address had surprised him, but then, he reasoned, considering the rates charged for the services provided, one would expect something more than a third rate walk-up on Rush Street.

Apart from a detectable increase in his heart rate, he felt good as he left the cab in front of the imposing townhouse. He'd dressed in a double-breasted blazer over a black polo sweater with cavalry twill slacks and black and tan loafers. Ian Fleming's James Bond would have approved, he thought, as he depressed the brass doorbell. James Bond would also have been a comforting presence, for the huge man who opened the door in a military-looking uniform bore a marked similarity to Mr. Big from Fleming's book, Live and Let Die. Not someone to argue with then. Thankfully his manner was as expansive as his frame, and having confirmed McDermott's name and appointment, the giant ushered him into a small well-appointed bar area that apart from the bar itself resembled a library in an old English manor house. An impression of leather, mahogany and brass buttons registered upon McDermott as the doorman left him with the invitation to help himself to a drink, and the information that Princess Grisha would join him directly. The Glenrothes not being in evidence, he poured a small Glenlivet and wandered over to a bookcase to see what books were all the rage in whorehouses these days.

It was the complex musk of her perfume rather than the opening of the cleverly hidden elevator door that announced the arrival of his 'Princess,' but the shock to his taut nerves was still sufficient to cause him to spill some of his drink as he whirled around.

'Aw shit! I'm sorry,' he managed to get out.

'Hey, don't worry about it,' she laughed. 'You want a refill?'

'Um . . . No thanks,' McDermott said. 'I'll just finish this off. Thanks anyway.'

'Well, I think I'll join you,' she said, pouring a small Di Saronno. 'Come on, have a seat.' She patted the bar stool beside her. 'Your name's Robbie, right? Mine's Grisha, you can drop the princess crap in here.'

The internet pictures did not do her credit, he thought: the camera had softened her image to the extent her athletic build had been lost. In fact this woman was not only beautiful, she was built in a way that suggested serious time spent in a gym. Broad shoulders tapered to a narrow waist, while her arms and legs had the definition of the true fitness aficionado. Despite the ample breasts and sublimely rounded buttocks, he estimated her body mass index below ten.

With the introductions out of the way, there followed a brief period of small talk that reminded McDermott of the chats he'd had with nude models he'd photographed: a 'put-you-at-ease' conversation designed to facilitate an easier transition to the real purpose of the meeting. Just as McDermott was calculating the cost of these minutes, Grisha moved into a more professional mode.

'Okay, Robbie, why don't we get the business stuff out of the way and then we can relax.'

McDermott could not help thinking that relaxing was going to come difficult with this young woman. The loose fitting, red shift she wore clung to her whenever she moved, and its diaphanous nature left no doubt as to the absence of underwear. Bright green eyes looked out at him from beneath a chic hair arrangement and her full lips, immaculately painted like the rest of her face, made him think of Goldie Hawn.

'You ordered the two hours straight. No specials. Right, Robbie?'

'Um . . . Yeah,' said McDermott.

'You sure about the specials hon? I do a great nurse, a fantastic lawyer and I'm told my strict teacher is one of the best around.'

McDermott laughed. 'No, honestly, I just need . . . you know.'

'You just want to fuck. Well, that's fine too. Okay, Robbie, you know it's $1500 cash, right?'

'Yeah,' McDermott said, and handed over the money.

Grisha placed the cash on the bar, pressed a button beside it, and said, 'Okay, hon, why don't we go up?' She held out her hand for McDermott's, and led him to the elevator. Before they entered the small cage, 'Mr. Big' was at the bar collecting the money.

'Two hours straight,' Grisha called out to him as the elevator doors closed.

With that final reference to the business end of the transaction, Grisha focused her entire attention on McDermott. By the time they entered her room, an impressive suite of white and gold furniture, the fifty milligrams of Viagra he'd popped before he left the hotel, allied to the effects of her subtle but sensual ministrations in the elevator, had him close to bursting.

'Hey,' she breathed into his ear as she eased him gently away, 'slow down, big guy: there's lots of time. What about a little massage to relax you hmm? How would that be?'

'Sure,' croaked McDermott, wishing she'd get on with it.

'Okay, darling, why don't we start by ridding you of all these clothes? You just lay back on the bed there, and I'll take care of that. Okay?'

McDermott lay back on the gold, silk duvet and watched in a giant overhead mirror, as Grisha slowly divested him of his clothing. She murmured compliments about his body as she slowly revealed it, taking every opportunity to brush her lush breasts against him, and by the time she left him naked 'just for a moment' he was seriously concerned that he might ejaculate before any actual sex occurred. That possibility increased when she suddenly reappeared in the nude, and began to slowly rub a lemon-scented lotion in long gentle strokes into his skin beginning with his face. She straddled him as she smoothed the emollient in, and his eyes moved from her face and breasts above him to the view of the parted cleft of her ass in the overhead mirror as she worked her way down his body. Finally, there came a moment when her shaved pubis brushed the swollen glans of his cock and he could take no more.

'Now,' he said, and relieving her of the jar, he reared up, turned her on to her back and entered her hard and fast.

'Jesus,' she said, as her legs wrapped around his waist. You always like this?'

'Shh,' he said, as he got into his rhythm and took charge of the situation for the first time in the evening.

He'd worried on his journey down to the city that his performance would be hampered: by guilt; by images of Jean; by imagining the hooker as someone's daughter; by thoughts of the men who'd been with his 'Princess' before him, and those who'd follow him. But as he moved in and out of this beautiful creature, and her cries mingled with the slapping of their coming together, all extraneous thoughts receded and everything was concentrated into an exquisiteness he'd not felt for over a year. When he finally came, it was as if he'd ejaculated a pent-up lava of anger, pain and frustration that had been struggling for release for a lifetime.

'Holy shit,' said Grisha. 'How old are you?'

'Sixty-seven,' said McDermott, studying his reflection in the mirror overhead and wondering how he came to be wearing a condom.

'Well, I want to tell you,' she said, dropping a box of Kleenex on his chest, 'you fuck like a thirty-year-old. And I know. Give me a few minutes okay?' And she hopped off the bed and went into what he presumed was a bathroom.

Where the hell had the condom come from? As he listened to the sounds of a shower, McDermott shook his head in amazement. He'd heard of sleight of hand, but –

'Hey,' Grisha, her tanned body dripping, beckoned him from the bathroom door, 'you wanna join me in this shower?'

'Aw jeez, I don't think – '

She padded across to him, water dripping from her young face and grasped his cock which amazingly began to stir. 'You don't think what?' she grinned, and led him by his rapidly recovering member into the bathroom.

Afterwards, when they were dried off and Grisha had produced a passable, if cheap, bottle of wine, they lay propped up against the bed's pillows and swapped a few personal details. He learned she was from Iowa, had a bachelor's degree in sports management, a master's in physical therapy and was only a dissertation away from a doctorate in sports medicine. Now that was a surprise, and McDermott turned to her, puzzled.

She held up her hand. 'I know, I know. You want to know how come I'm working as a hooker when I've actually got brains. Right?'

'Yeah, something like that.'

'Well, it's like this, Robbie. My hometown has a population of 200,000 and no gym, health club, nothing. I've already had a marketing survey done that shows a demand for a good health club, and in two years time I intend to open one. I've already bought the land and I figure in a couple of years I'll have made what I need to get it done, and I'll have my doctorate. There's only one way I could make that kind of money that fast and it's doing what I do.' She turned to him with a grin, 'And you've got to admit, I am fucking good at it.'

McDermott kept his story brief, not wanting to get into a long conversation about Jean, in a hooker's bed, no matter how personable and attractive he found her. Even so, the few details he shared elicited genuine empathy from the woman beside him, who elected to show it in the one way she knew how. Glancing at the clock, she stretched and said, 'Well, hon, you've got thirty minutes left, how about you let me chase a few of those dark clouds away before you leave?'

McDermott laughed. 'Listen,' he said, 'as far as I can recall, the last time I had sex more than twice in one session, I was in my thirties or something. There is absolutely no way – '

'Oh I think there is.' Grisha pushed back the duvet that had been covering them and jumped up to stand over him, legs apart, one foot on either side of his head. The provocative pose and the view it offered him of the glistening lips of her vagina parted in a pink grin, were, as it happened, enough to stir him again.

'Jesus Christ,' he said, 'I – '

'See what I mean, Robbie? Now, this time it's my way. You just relax and let me take care of things. Okay?'

The ensuing half an hour featured a farrago of sexual sensations, the like of which he'd never been previously subjected to: hardened nipples brushing his face, chest and cock; the stubble of her pubis teasing his mouth; the tight suction of those pouting lips as she slowly sucked him; the lightening flicks of her tongue in his mouth, his ears, around his scrotum; and, finally, a long, slow ride as she sat astride him, dictating the pace until, sensing his urgency, she leaned forward offering her breasts to his mouth, and pumped faster and faster until his hips heaved her upwards in his climax.

He'd promised her, on parting, he would return, but later, as he watched the streets of Chicago slipping by the windows of his cab, he thought it unlikely. The experience had been all he'd hoped it would be: a catharsis that both his body and mind had been ready for, but it was almost certainly a one-off. It was the only time in his life he'd paid for sex and it would be the last. He thought Jean had probably known that would be the case but, in her quiet way, had understood it was something he would have to discover for himself. Oh, Jean, Jean, Jean; he gazed at the slow moving crowds on Michigan Avenue attempting to focus on the present, but Jean's face smiled back at him from the cab window, and the lights beyond blurred as the tears came.

He devoted the entire Sunday to Jean and their favorite Chicago haunts: not out of any guilt over his Saturday evening's activity – which, contrary to his fears, had elicited no such feelings – but because Chicago had been special to them and provided such a fund of cherished memories. So he breakfasted at the little coffee shop round the corner from the hotel, before strolling down to Border's where he picked up the New York Times, and did the crossword puzzle over a cappuccino in the upstairs café. In the afternoon, after a light lunch at what had been Jean's favorite Italian restaurant, he walked the length of the Mile to Millennium Park and back. The city was bathed in sunlight and he reveled in the stiff, fall breeze and the recollections of the early Christmas shopping expeditions it evoked.

He finished the day in his suite drifting in and out of consciousness as the Bears and the Packers went at it on TV. That evening he had a couple of drinks in the bar prior to taking a late dinner in the hotel's excellent Avenues dining room, where he requested, and was given, the table he and Jean had always preferred. Finally, as he drifted off into sleep that night, McDermott relived the first time he and Jean had visited the Peninsula when she'd inadvertently revealed herself in all her glory to a mesmerized room-service waiter.

They'd returned to the hotel from a wedding and Jean, a little tipsy, had been in one of her mischievous moods. She'd come grinding her way out of the bathroom, stark naked, swinging her brief, black panties around her head and belting out 'The Stripper' as she advanced on McDermott. What she hadn't known was that McDermott had ordered drinks and a little snack which the room service waiter was in the process of laying out in the room behind her. He'd never been able to decide which expression had been the most amusing: that on the waiter's face, or that on Jean's when he'd gestured behind her and she'd whirled around and seen the waiter. By God, she'd fair scorched a trail in the carpet getting back into the bathroom. They'd laughed about that for years. McDermott was still smiling as he fell asleep.

By the time he hit the road the following morning, he felt a peace he'd not known for some time and which, if he was honest about it, hadn't expected to find on this trip. He'd taken big risks during the weekend, risks that had involved riding his emotional luck, but apart from a few tearful episodes here and there, he believed he'd exorcised a few demons. Now he was looking forward to getting back and picking up on his writing, and as he turned north onto U.S. 31 from I-94, his thoughts returned to Cracker and where he was in the story.

As always, Connor's reaction to McDermott's return was to lie down and pee all over himself before attempting to knock his master over with repeated leaps against his body. Bridie's shepherds regarded the display in silent befuddlement while Bridie eyed McDermott speculatively.

'Looks like that bank meeting did you some good,' she said.

'Oh yeah? How's that?' said McDermott.

'Well, you kinda look like the cat that got the fucking cream or something. I dunno, you just look kinda . . . kinda . . . Shit, I don't know, kinda *fitter*.'

'Well, I had a good weekend; a good rest,' said McDermott. 'Visited a lot of places Jean and I used to go to, you know?'

'Oh, well, that's good I guess,' Bridie said, as he covered the back seat of the Jag with Connor's dog blanket. 'So, we gonna see you down at the diner again this side of Christmas?'

He laughed as he hugged her goodbye, 'Yeah. I think so Bridie. Anyway, love, thanks for looking after my boy. See you soon, okay?' As McDermott closed the door and started the engine, Bridie knocked on his driver's window and he slid it down.

'These banker people of yours,' she said. 'They always work Saturdays do they?' She was smiling.

'Um . . . No, not usually; but they made an exception for me: me living all the way up here and all.'

'Oh, right. Yeah, I guess they would. Well, you take care, Robbie, and make sure we see you now and again. No more of that hermit shit. Okay?'

'Don't you worry, Bridie; a good-looking woman like you, how could I stay away?'

'Cheeky bastard,' she called after him cheerfully as he moved off, but McDermott didn't miss the thoughtful expression on her face.

Goddamnit, he thought, as he pulled on to the main road, she thinks I've got something going in Chicago. Then he smiled to himself: ever since he'd known Bridie, he'd allowed her colorful language to lull him into forgetting how smart she was. She hadn't swallowed that banking story for a moment.

He was pleased to find a message from Holly Kosinsky waiting for him when he got back to the cabin and, after a quick lunch of baked beans on toast, an English habit he'd never lost, he called her back. Ten minutes later, McDermott had his first lunch date with a single female in many years – solely though, he cautioned himself, to offer his avuncular support to a friend in need. Banishing the uneasy suspicion he wasn't being up front with himself, he picked up his manuscript and began to read the last couple of chapters. He'd slowed down considerably prior to his Chicago trip – only around a dozen pages completed in eight days – and then there'd been the little matter of his furlough. It was going to take some time to get back into it.

9.

Drifting

As we embarked upon our final two years of high school, Cracker and I found ourselves on divergent paths both academically and socially. Academically, while we both remained intent on becoming teachers, I'd determined to go to university and become a grammar school teacher of English, while Cracker had decided to teach primary school kids and thus would go the college of education route. For my advanced level course of study I opted for English, German and French; Cracker chose history, geography and German. Thus not only had our ambitions changed, our chosen means of achieving them had undergone a reassessment. Socially, thanks to the time-consuming demands of increased academic study and Cracker's deepening relationship with Jen, time spent out of school together was minimal. Even so, we might have remained closer had it not been for the rejection by Cracker of my first steady girlfriend, Caroline Dunham.

Caroline was a tall, attractive girl with masses of back-combed auburn hair, and almond-shaped hazel eyes that gazed out onto the world with a wide-eyed innocence I found bewitching. One year my senior, Caroline represented something of a novelty in that she was already working for a living, having left Englewood High with qualifications in shorthand and typing which she employed as a secretary in a firm of accountants. We shared a similar sense of humor, a love of music, many of the same values, and she was, in my opinion, the perfect match for me. It was not an opinion shared by Cracker.

'So what do you think?' I said, as we made our way to the ubiquitous cider keg at a Saturday night party. It was Caroline's first exposure to the Bricknall in-crowd, and its acceptance of her was important to me.

'She's okay,' Cracker said.

'Okay? What the hell is that supposed to mean?'

'Well, I don't think she's your type, Robbie, that's all,' said Cracker, pushing his way through a throng of dancers all singing along with Elvis's 'Latest Flame.'

'Oh yeah? So why exactly isn't she my type?' I could see Caroline's eyes on us across the room as she hovered self-consciously on the fringes of Jen's group of friends.

'Well, let's face it, Robbie, she's not going to be knocking on the door at Oxford or Cambridge any time soon, is she?'

'Oh, and you are eh?' I was getting hotter by the second.

'Oh bugger off, Robbie; you know what I'm saying. I mean, she thought Magna Carta was a bleeding rock band for Christ's sake.'

'Okay, so she's not a historian,' I said. 'So what? How many words can you type a minute, and how's your shorthand?'

'Oh, this is bloody ridiculous,' said Cracker. 'Look, Robbie, if you like her, fine. You go right ahead.'

'Thanks a bunch, Cracker, and you know what? I will.' Turning on my heel I returned to Caroline, and a few minutes later we left. It wasn't a friendship-ending argument, but from that night, my out of school social life revolved around Caroline's friends, and we left the school in-crowd to their own devices.

Although the relationship between Cracker and me at that point might have been more accurately described as an acquaintanceship rather than a friendship, we still saw each other from time to time out of school and away from our respective girlfriends. It was on one such occasion I was treated to a classic display of Cracker's considerable talent for dissembling. It occurred on a rare Saturday night alone together not long before our A level examinations. We were queuing to watch 'Lawrence of Arabia' outside the Regal Cinema in the city centre, when Cracker was approached by a girl who appeared to be a prostitute. Grinning beneath a huge, stiff, back-combed mass of bottle-blond hair, she tottered up on stiletto heels of spectacular height, and peering at Cracker from the shadows of her heavily mascaraed eyes, she let out a squeal of excitement and began to speak.

'Ello there! How are yer?'

To my amazement Cracker flashed one of his most winning smiles, and speaking as if he'd just been reunited with his long lost sister, said, 'Hello! I'm fine. How are you? What have you been doing with yourself? I haven't seen you for ages. In fact, where was it?'

'It was that party at Liz Strickland's wasn't it?' she said.

'Do you know,' said Cracker, 'I think you're right. How is Liz anyway?'

'Ooh, didn't you 'ear? She's pregnant poor lass: to that tosser, Willy Tasker.'

'Yeah? Well, he always was one for putting it about a bit, wasn't he?' said Cracker.

'You can say that again: the bugger tried it on with me once, the cheeky sod. And that mate of 'is, Jackie Beaumont: he's another randy git.'

'Yeah, I think I heard something about him myself,' said Cracker.

'You probably 'eard about 'im trying to get in Marge Thompson's knickers down the Roxy: back row of the fucking pictures for Christ's sake.'

'Yeah, that was it,' said Cracker. 'Didn't she . . .'

The conversation went on and on as the queue slowly shuffled forward, until suddenly the girl squealed again and said, 'Ooh! There's me boyfriend. I'll 'ave to go. It's been really nice seeing you again. Tarrah!' And with that she disappeared into the milling crowds.

'Bloody hell, Cracker,' I said. 'Who was that?'

'Haven't got a bleeding clue,' he said.

Writing from the Outskirts of Hope

'And Wally Tasker and Jackie whoever?'

'No bloody idea.'

Such brief memories of Cracker from our final two years of school are indicative of how little we saw of one another and of how tenuous our relationship had become. Certainly, as our A-level examinations were completed and we drifted off into holiday employment, I don't believe either of us expected our friendship to ever regain the intensity it had once possessed. Cracker was set to go to the Lady MacManus College of Education at Oakham in Rutland, should he acquire two A-level passes, whereas I had hopes of studying English at Queens College, London, if I could make two Bs and a C. We were both successful and at the end of the summer, following a couple of 'till we meet again' parties, I left for the Capital and Cracker for the rather more rural pastures of Rutland. Jen departed for Manchester where she was to read Divinity with, Cracker assured me, his guarantee of fidelity. It was a guarantee that would last as long as my university career which, as it turned out, was not very long at all.

My experience in London proved to be the darkest period of my young life. I hated the city, found the people cold and indifferent, and discovered university study to be little different from the A-level cramming I thought I'd escaped from. I was, moreover, living in lodgings far from the 'university experience,' ruled over by a draconian landlady whose knowledge of the culinary arts was on a par with my own. I also found it difficult to be away from Caroline.

Within the course of a few weeks, I'd begun to favour table tennis over lectures, and by the end of November, according to my doctor, I was clinically depressed. What to do? I dreaded speaking to my parents, for not only had they sacrificed a good deal to get me to university, they were, I knew, immensely proud that I was the first in the family to enter the halls of academe, and would have taken pains to boast of their son's achievement to friends and relatives alike. I did speak over the phone with Caroline of my dilemma, but as someone who'd left school at sixteen, there was, in reality, little chance she could offer sage advice on how I might salvage my academic future. Finally, in desperation, I turned to the only person I thought may be of assistance. I called Cracker.

Cracker arrived in London on a Friday evening within two days of my call, and by the time I bade him farewell on the Sunday afternoon, my way forward had been settled. We had many conversations that weekend, but that conducted over a few pints on the Friday evening, was when my decision was made. Cracker's patience as I laid out my problems was impressive with nary a word's intervention to halt my flow, but when I confided that I'd entertained thoughts of suicide, he stopped me in my tracks.

'Okay, okay. Hold it right there for a minute, Robbie, because this is some serious shit you're talking here. I'm no trick-cyclist, but you know, and I know, that even having those kinds of thoughts is not a good thing.' He paused to down more of his beer, but did not take his eyes off me as he drank. Setting down his pint, he began to summarize my predicament.

'Let me see if I've got this right, old son,' he said. He used his fingers to enumerate his points. 'One, you don't like London. Two, you hate the digs. Three, you aren't keen on the people down here. Four, you can't stand the thought of another three years of note taking and examination crap. And five, the whole fucking mess has made you so unhappy, you've actually thought of topping yourself. Is that a reasonable summary?' He watched me closely as he awaited my reply.

'Well, yeah,' I said, 'but – '

'No buts, Robbie; have I got it right or haven't I?'

I was embarrassed to realize that my eyes were misting up as I said, 'Yeah, that about sums it up.'

'Well, sup that pint up then, lad, and I'll get another couple in before I tell you what you're going to do,' and with that, Cracker gulped down his remaining beer, took my hurriedly emptied glass, and headed to the bar.

While he was gone, I gazed around the crowded room, taking in the romantic couples, the raucous parties, the domino playing groups of older men, and the loud darts game in the far corner. What was it about these people that made them so different from those in my home town? Certainly they spoke with a different accent, but it was more than that; they appeared inward-looking somehow. Even here, in this crowded saloon bar, each group of folk, no matter how animated and close to other tables around them, seemed to be an island unto themselves. There was none of that interplay between strangers that would have been present in a Kingstown pub. This kind of isolation was even more discernible in the mornings on my bus and tube journeys, when everyone buried their heads in the morning newspaper, avoiding at all costs any contact with those around them.

My thoughts were interrupted by Cracker slamming down two more foaming pints on to the table.

'Okay, sunshine, get some of this down your neck and listen to your Uncle Cracker.' He lit another cigarette, exhaled, and looked at me reflectively, his eyes screwed up against the smoke.

'First of all, let's look on the bright side,' he said. 'We know what the problem is. In simple terms, you fucked up and now you're in the wrong place doing the wrong thing for the wrong reasons. That's the problem; all we have to do is come up with a solution and from where I'm sitting, that's pretty straightforward. You have to leave.'

'Jesus Christ, Cracker,' I said, 'what about – '

I was given no time to voice the obvious objections. Cracker had already figured them out. 'Yeah, I know: you're going to disappoint your mam and dad; you don't know whether you'll have to pay your college grant back; you won't get your precious degree, at least not here; and what the hell will you do next? Does that about cover it?'

I nodded, not trusting myself to speak, as I contemplated the enormity of my misery and the abject failure I felt myself to be.

'Well, here's the plan: As soon as we've supped up, you're going to call your mam and dad and tell them what you're going to do and why. I'll talk to them too if you want, but think on, Robbie: don't you think they'd rather have their son – degree or no degree – than a suicidal depressive?' He didn't wait for an answer. 'Next, we'll swan over to Kings Cross in the morning and get you a ticket home for, let's say, next Friday: that'll give you time to sort out your landlady and the college. Once you're back in Kingstown, you can go down to the education authority and find out about the grant situation. Any questions so far?'

I shook my head, both in answer to my friend's question and in admiration at the ease with which he'd removed so much of the burden from my shoulders.

'Okay, now we've got that sorted,' Cracker said, 'I've got some advice for you to think about. When you get back, you're going to be too late to go to any other college until next year, so you'll need a job. When you go down the education authority, ask if they hire temporary assistant masters. A mate of mine at Lady Mac had one of those jobs in Wyvern last year and he said it was great. They actually hired him to teach in a primary school as a backup kind of thing, and he had a bloody great time.'

'Aw shit, Cracker,' I said, 'I – '

'I know, I know, you want to teach high school kids, but think about it, Robbie. It's a job, it pays a decent wage, and it'll help you in your application to wherever you decide to go. And speaking of that,' Cracker halted mid-sentence to down a healthy portion of his pint, 'apply to Lady Mac, Robbie: the place is fucking fantastic. Apart from –'

'Cracker,' I interjected, 'I want to – '

'Yeah, yeah, I know: you want a degree and Lady Mac just does teaching diplomas. But think about it. No matter where you go, to get a degree you're going to have to do three more years of that memorize and regurgitate shit. Lady Mac is an assessment college: no exams – pass or fail only; all coursework taken into account; and you learn about kids and how to teach, instead of jamming more subject matter into your skull. I'm telling you Robbie, I love the place. I live in a fabulous hall of residence out in the country with its own bar and dining room, and after A-levels, the work is a piece of piss. And not only that; there's three women for every male on a seven hundred and fifty person campus. Think about those odds.'

Despite the gravity of my position and the tough hurdles ahead, or perhaps because of them, the incongruity of Cracker's last words broke a dam in me and I started to laugh uncontrollably.

'What?' Cracker was bemused by my reaction.

'Bloody hell, Cracker, you are something else; you know that? Here I am, my whole fucking college career – no, my entire future on the line – and you're suggesting the number of birds available as being a rationale for my next move.'

Cracker grinned, 'Well, you know what they say, Robbie: a well rounded person makes a good teacher. I just happen to believe that being well rounded involves plenty of healthy interaction with the opposite sex.'

'What about Jen then?' I was seriously interested here: only three months before, Cracker had been contemplating marriage after a steady relationship of almost four years.

'Yeah, well, I'm still thinking about that. I mean, we're still close and everything, but I'm of the opinion that maybe we should play the field a bit, see other people if we want to. You know, kind of test the waters of our relationship, and make sure we're right for each other.'

'And what does she think about that?'

'Yeah, well, I haven't exactly passed on my feelings to her yet, Robbie. You see – '

My laughter cut him short. 'You are so full of shit Cracker,' I sputtered. 'Face it, you bugger, you are a randy prat.'

'Yeah, well, maybe. But I tell you, Robbie, if you get into Lady Mac, you might find being faithful to Caroline a bit more than you can handle.'

'Not a chance, old love,' I said. 'Not a chance.'

Cracker simply smiled and looked me in the eyes again as he drained his pint, before bringing our evening to a close – and me back to reality – with his final words in the pub that night. 'Okay, Robbie. Let's go and call your mam and dad.'

There remained a good deal to be done, but in essence, another seminal moment in the life of Robbie McDermott had just been produced and directed by Alastair James McCracken. That trumpets and the tinkle of champagne glasses were absent was of little consequence to me: the buzz and clamour of a saloon bar and the clanking of dimpled pint pots was entirely appropriate. That an eighteen year old boy, albeit one mature beyond his years, should have the ability to divine and solve what were, to me, overwhelming issues of both a psychological and practical nature, appears in retrospect to be astounding. And yet it was to me, at the time, and in the months that followed – as my life unfolded more or less as Cracker had ordained it –perfectly natural.

Mam and dad were disappointed in my decision, but after numerous questions of the 'Are you sure?' and 'It isn't just homesickness is it?' variety, they pledged their absolute support as I should have known they would. Dad even volunteered to go down to the education authority office on the following Monday and sort out the grant situation. As I wiped a few tears from my eyes, and replaced the receiver in that public telephone box before rejoining an inquiring Cracker, I knew with certainty that my old friend had saved my life, not literally perhaps, but certainly from an emotional and intellectual point of view. As subsequent events would prove, thanks once again to Cracker, I'd just taken a new fork on the road of life, a fork that would lead me in directions I'd never dreamed of.

10.

Nadir

The morning of Saturday, November 12th dawned with all the promise of a bright, fall Michigan day. The sun rose big and red at precisely 7:19 and thirty minutes later McDermott was pounding the trails of Fisherman's Island, Connor panting along beside him. It was, he knew, Day 257. His cabin was situated a mere dozen miles north of the forty-fifth parallel – midway between the equator and the North Pole – and despite the unseasonal warmth, the signs of approaching winter were everywhere. Where only a few weeks ago, the ferns of the forest floor had been a mass of yellows and rusts, brown and black predominated now, and while a few oaks stubbornly held on to remnants of their greenery, the leaves of the maples were gone, the pools of curling, spotted leaves around their bases the only reminder of what had been. He was running well, glorying in the exercise, the rich scent of damp earth and pine needles in his nostrils, shafts of sun slicing through the woods around him, and he allowed his thoughts the freedom to roam over the lunch he'd shared with Holly Freeman the previous day.

He'd found it a difficult meeting at first. They'd met in a small restaurant on a quiet side street in Traverse, a venue arrived at through some unspoken agreement that discretion might be in order, and yet that mutual understanding itself, allied to the intimacy of the restaurant had, he felt, leant a slightly clandestine atmosphere to what, after all was a simple lunch. He'd also felt an awkwardness, borne of a number of other factors, not the least of which was the profound sense of loss they shared. He'd also been somewhat taken aback by her choice of attire. Apart from fancy dinners or local benefit events, he had difficulty recalling Holly wearing anything but flannel or denim shirts with jeans in the winter, or T-shirts and shorts in the summer. For their lunch, however, she'd chosen a short flowery dress with a scooped neck that had shown off her small, taut breasts to advantage, especially when she leaned forward, which was often. She was a good looking woman, more than making up for her lack of height with that hard, muscular body. Jean had always said that with her spiky, short black hair and perpetual tan she would have been a great, sexy female Ariel in Shakespeare's 'The Tempest. He'd found the intensity of her startling blue eyes particularly arresting over lunch and he'd worried it had showed. Still, it had gone pleasantly enough he supposed. A bottle of good Chardonnay had helped loosen their initial wariness, and once each had made all the correct noises concerning the others misfortunes, they'd talked a little about future plans, even managing laughter now and then.

Holly was unclear as to what would happen to the Belvedere or what the final divorce settlement would bring, but her lawyer was confident she'd be fine since it had been her money that had financed the original purchase. Both the girls, she thought, were in her corner, though she was concerned about their reactions. Loren, the eldest, was exhibiting vociferous anger at her father, while Mandy refused to talk about either her father or the separation. Holly said little about the exact circumstances of the split, but one thing she did say shocked and angered McDermott.

'You know, his infidelity was one thing, Robbie, but it was his last words to me that hurt more than anything. He said, "I always felt I should never have married you in the first place." It was like the last twenty years of my life had been flushed down the toilet.'

Swallowing his anger and limiting his response to expressions of sympathy, not wishing to get too involved, McDermott had gone on to speak of his difficulty relating to other people since Jean's death, and his resulting loneliness. He took care to stay away from his separation from the church, being well aware of Holly's Episcopalian beliefs, and as far as the future was concerned, he fudged a little, saying only that he intended to stick around for a while.

There was one thing about the lunch he'd found particularly disconcerting: it had occurred outside the restaurant as they'd prepared to go their separate ways. They'd hugged each other in farewell as they'd done on any number of occasions in the past, but Holly's idea of a friendly hug had apparently changed: rather than adopting the platonic upper-body forward, lower-body back position, she'd pressed her entire body against him, holding him closer and longer than usual. At least, that's how it had felt to McDermott. Could he have imagined it? He thought not, and yet there had been nothing of a suggestive nature in their lunch conversation, nor anything but the hand of friendship in Holly's invitation to join her and the girls for dinner on the following Saturday evening.

Back in the park's lot, he reached in the car for Connor's canvas water bowl, poured the thirsty animal a drink, and as Connor greedily lapped at the liquid, McDermott went through his stretching exercises with the thought that perhaps his imagination was getting the better of him in the matter of Holly Freeman. When he got home, he'd put all that stuff on the backburner where it belonged, take a long shower, have a quick breakfast and pitch back into his writing.

Day 259. Like the clouds rolling over the marsh, McDermott's memories eddied and swirled: misty tendrils curling around his limbs, tugging him back into the darkness which he'd thought was behind him.

The day had begun well enough despite the rain sweeping in off the lake: a brisk run with Connor, a breakfast fry-up, and an examination of what he'd written during the previous couple of days. And then, quite spontaneously he'd made The Decision.

He'd always known it was ahead of him and indeed, Greta VanDamm had mentioned its inevitability. Sooner or later, she'd warned, he would have to decide when and how to dispose of Jean's belongings. Moreover, she'd stressed the critical importance of his taking care of things himself.

'It's not a job for friends or some odd-job outfit, Robbie,' she'd said. 'It has to be you and you alone.'

Still, that the moment arrived when it did came as a decided shock. He'd had no intention of climbing that particular mountain until sometime in the distant future. Nevertheless he found himself driving, almost unthinkingly, out to the local U-Haul office in Charlevoix from which, after much consideration of how many boxes it took to remove a life, he emerged with enough cartons of varying sizes and types to fill the SUV. On his return he plunged into the task with the stoic determination he'd always called upon when confronting daunting situations.

He should have known that neither stoicism nor determination could furnish him the necessary strength required for such a monumental undertaking. Now, as he sat, shoulders slumped, on the bed he and Jean had shared for so many years, he surveyed the piles of slacks and tops, sweaters and dresses, evening gowns and robes, jeans and underwear, hats and socks, belts and purses, and gave in to the misery that had been whispering ever more insistently into his ear from the moment he'd begun. It commenced, as these things do, with silent tears; gathered momentum with sobs born deep in his diaphragm; gathered pace and ferocity with convulsions that wracked his upper body; and gave way ultimately, to an unrestrained howling that was animalistic in its primeval expression of loneliness and loss. Had McDermott possessed either the inclination or talent to paint a picture of his grief, he would have employed crimson and scarlet in depicting a raw wound, a jagged gash of opened flesh, so wide and deep as to be beyond any hope of healing. Only when exhaustion overcame him did he curl up amid the textures, colors and scents, and fall into a troubled sleep.

He had a cruel awakening, the dreamlike promise of Jean's perfume in his nostrils replaced by the stark reality of what he saw as his eyes opened, and the memory of the previous few hours. When he'd begun the task, he'd entertained thoughts of suspending his emotions until he was finished, and at first he'd succeeded. He'd started in the master bathroom, systematically moving from drawer to drawer and from cupboard to cupboard, boxing up hairsprays, lipsticks, moisturizers, nail varnishes, conditioners of this and that: all the mysterious paraphernalia of a woman's bathroom. It was stressful work, but he'd managed to retain his focus and restrict his tears to a minimum, and soon the drawers lay empty and the cupboards bare, their contents consigned to anonymous boxes. It was when he'd moved into the master closet and begun to remove Jean's clothes that he'd run into trouble, for it was then it had occurred to him that he was not so much removing Jean's belongings from their home, as excising her from his life. Each jacket, each suit, each dress, had acted like a stimulus in a creative writing class, evoking memories happy and sad, funny and serious, private and public. He'd even found the rust-colored dress she'd been wearing when he'd first set eyes upon her. . . .

He'd been in the hospitality suite of a Governor's conference on education, engaged in conversation with a professor from Western University, his back to the suite's entrance, when the young professor had said, 'Don't look now, but in a moment, have a look behind you at the door.' Naturally, he'd turned immediately and seen her across the room, leaning idly against the doorway, Bacall-style, in that dress. She was nursing a drink and surveying the assembled throng with the amused, almost haughty smile she'd always employed to such good effect.

'Now that,' the professor had said, 'is class.'

McDermott roused himself. Suddenly it was important to find that dress. He wandered around the bed scanning each tottering pile until he found it. He unfolded it, held it up before him and buried his face in the material. Little of Jean's scent remained now: drained away by the years as Jean's life had been extinguished by the cancer, but the memory of his first sight of her in that dress was as vivid as ever. He clenched the dress in his hands and recalled the less than propitious circumstances of their first meeting.

He'd insulted her while exhibiting a boorishness of embarrassing proportions. No doubt his alcohol intake had played a part in his behavior, but he still cringed at the memory of the first words he'd said to her. The hospitality bar had provided a prelude to a welcome dance for the conferees and toward the latter part of the evening, as she'd walked by his table on the way to the dance floor with some guy in tow, he'd reached out, grabbed her hand, and said, 'If you're real lucky, I'll save the last dance for you tonight.' Jean, displaying the equanimity he would, in future years, come to delight in, had not missed a beat: treating him to one of her cooler stares, she'd shot back, 'If you're real lucky, I'll still be here.' And amazingly, she had been. Their first date had occurred the following Saturday night during which – apart from his ridiculous monologue about the state of his body – they'd discovered each other to be divorced and adamant about never marrying again. So much for convictions: She'd cooked dinner for him the next evening, and the one after that and they'd married six months later. They'd spoken often of that first meeting but McDermott, knowing her as he did, continued to be baffled as to why she'd not treated his opening line with the contempt it had deserved. She said she'd been impressed at his persistence in the face of her retort, but still . . . Now the dress she'd worn at the beginning of everything was empty and hung lifeless from his hands. He folded it gently and laid it back down.

Although he had no desire to eat, he trudged through to the kitchen, knowing if he was to get through the remainder of the afternoon, he had to get something into his stomach. Only as he was finishing up a bowl of tinned soup did he register Connor's absence. He frowned: Connor's absence from his side at any time was rare, but he'd never known it to occur at mealtimes, the dog having a Micawberish faith that something would turn up whenever his master sat down to eat. Calling the dog's name, he began to move quickly through the cabin. Had he left him outside again after a whizz? Had he inadvertently locked him in a room? Was he lying sick somewhere?

McDermott's anxiety monitor swung from mild concern to outright panic quickly when it came to Connor's wellbeing, and it was with relief that he found the golden back in the master bedroom. The big retriever was laid on the bed amidst his missing mistress's clothes, his great head, ears splayed, resting upon a pile of Jean's underpants, his soft mouth clutching a red bra. McDermott's heart and eyes filled again as Connor regarded him sadly from one big, brown eye, and crawling on to the bed, he laid his head upon the dog's flanks and stroked its soft belly. 'You and me against the world, big guy,' he whispered in Connor's ear, 'You and me against the world.' Helen Reddy had sung that song he mused: one of Jean's favorites. Moving to kiss Connor's long nose, he looked at the pile of underwear the dog had adopted as his pillow. Those items of clothing too carried memories: passionate reunions following his business trips; long discussions, punctuated with laughter, about the male love of black and red in intimate garments; McDermott's fondness for stockings as opposed to panty hose . . .

He forced himself to his feet, walked through to his den and stared out at the marsh. The rain had stopped, but gray rugs of clouds continued to envelop the bayous and he turned the lights on. It occurred to him he should push on: at least finish off the closet, box up the stuff and get it into one of the guest bedrooms. Alternatively he could work on his book for a while, perhaps take his mind off things. In the end he simply sat in his den and attempted to find solace in the scent of peat and the taste of the Highlands.

It was past six when he awoke. Outside, the light had gone and Connor, well aware of the hour in relation to his gastronomic requirements, was panting as he eyed his master from the floor beside him. Feeding the dog and nibbling at a grilled cheese sandwich were as much as McDermott could manage and he retired early, hoping the soporific effects of the Scotch would be enough to take him under. Possessing neither the physical nor the emotional fortitude to face removing Jean's clothing from the bed in the master suite, he bedded down in the lakeside guestroom with a bemused Connor settling down with a loud sigh beside him.

His first thought upon waking the following morning, was that he'd never slept in one of the guestrooms before; his second was that the coming hours would bring the same challenges to his psyche he'd endured before he'd fallen asleep. Nevertheless he arose quickly, and set out from the cabin for his run, resolving to plunge back into his clearing-out project with renewed vigor upon his return. He would not engage in reminiscing, would not allow himself to be side-tracked: he would, as they said in his native Yorkshire, just get on with it.

He accomplished the shower and breakfast components of his plan admirably. He even contrived to box up Jean's clothing from the master suite and get the numerous boxes into one of the spare bedrooms. It was the remainder of the closet's contents that stalled him. He began with the shoes. Arranged on eight shelves, each six feet in length, they covered the gamut of female footwear with every shade of the color spectrum represented, in materials ranging from straw and canvas through plastic and vinyl to the finest leather. It was as he was taping up the final box he broke down, and it was the sight of the empty shelves rather than the packed boxes of shoes that did it. Dusty, bare, bereft of what had filled them since their birth, there was, about them, a dull void that sang of finality. Jean was leaving again, he thought. She'd left him originally, encased in fine, polished mahogany and here she was, slipping away once more, in a growing mountain of innocuous cardboard containers. He thought, through his tears, of unpacking the shoes and replacing them on the shelves – it wasn't as if he needed the space – but he knew if he didn't get through the job in the next few days, he'd never be able to let her rest in peace. And wasn't that what this was all about? It was all so ironic. Jean's doctor, David Kramer, and Pastor Dan had told him on that final day, how important it was for him to give Jean permission to leave. Now he had to give himself permission to let her go.

Jean's hats and purses that matched in volume, material and style, all of her shoes and more, filled the remaining boxes he had, and he took a break for another trip to the U-Haul depot to replenish his supply before he tackled her jewelry.

When he opened the first jewelry box, the one he'd found her in Seattle while on some business trip, his day came to a halt, the present fled and the past flooded the closet like a North Sea tide submerging a Yorkshire cove in January. There, in two gold loops, was the night of their silver wedding anniversary; lying in their individual nests beside them were the diamond studs from their first transatlantic crossing on the QE 2; grinning at him from the lower left corner were the silver crescents from their Cairo trip. . . McDermott slammed the cedar lid down. He could not do this; any of it. He possessed neither the mental fortitude nor the motivational will to re-live those special moments, and he'd be damned if he'd give her jewelry away. No, it had to stay; perhaps when he'd healed a little, he'd spend some time with it all, allowing the individual pieces to take him back. For now, he arranged the boxes carefully on the empty shoe shelves, and turned to the cupboards in the deepest recesses of Jean's part of the closet. He took a deep breath. This was strictly Jean's territory. That had always been her admonition whenever he'd asked what the hell she was collecting back there, and accordingly he had no idea what he might find.

What he found was an Aladdin's cave dedicated to what might have been, for there, on shelf after shelf in each cupboard, was a nursery's worth of books and toys waiting for the little people he and Jean had never been able to provide. McDermott slid to the floor as he tasted, yet again, the salty phlegm of tears. When had she started? For how long had she collected these things? Why had she kept them a secret? Why had she hung on to them? The questions roared through his brain with the clatter and speed of a night express.

When they'd first married, despite their deep involvement in the development and education of young children, they'd decided not to have kids. Part of their thinking had been Jean's age. She was in her early thirties then, and at that time, the risks of such relatively late pregnancies had been viewed as significant. There was too, a shared reticence between them resulting from the disasters of their previous marriages, none of which had produced children – something they'd been thankful for. And then things had changed: bearing children had suddenly become of paramount importance, and they'd set about the procreation business with a will.

He thought back to that difficult period of their lives as he surveyed the stuffed animals staring wide-eyed at him from the shelves, and breathed in the odor of printer's ink coming off the thick-paged books. There'd been the initial surprise over their long wait for a result; the trips to first the doctor and then the specialists; the tests and the pre-intercourse temperature taking; the trotted out statistics; and finally the verdict, delivered in a white, sterile room. Jean, it was agreed, had a Robertsonian translocation, some form of chromosomal rearrangement that could cause complete infertility, spontaneous abortions or the birth of a child with Down's syndrome. They'd accepted the situation with a *que sera* attitude and indeed, considering what could have occurred, had felt somewhat fortunate. His vasectomy had followed as a matter of course. Adoption had been something they'd considered for a while but in the end they'd found a more than satisfying outlet for their parental instincts in a succession of golden retrievers. At least McDermott thought they had, but if that had been the case, what were all these toys and books about? He closed his eyes and focused on the timeline of their procreative efforts. Was it a year? Two?

Yes, he supposed, from start to finish it could have been, and all that time Jean had . . .

He reached into the first cupboard from his position on the floor and pulled out a large yellow volume. It was 'Brown Bear,' the classic book for pre-readers by Bill Martin Junior. He opened the book, taking in the beautiful illustrations, and began to chant the familiar words before he stopped. I could write something for me like this, he thought, and began to aimlessly recite to himself: 'Rob-bie, Rob-bie, what do you see? I see a Dark Cloud looking at me. Dark Cloud, Dark Cloud, what do you see? I see a –' Jesus Christ! He closed the book, got to his feet and proceeded to load the contents of the cupboards into boxes. He'd take this stuff over to Pastor Dan for the Angel Tree at Christmas. That thought led him to think about how he would dispose of Jean's clothes. He'd been thinking about the re-sale shop in Westwood, but the possibility of bumping into someone in the town wearing something of Jean's occurred to him now for the first time, and he realized that idea was a non-starter. Maybe someplace down in Traverse. He'd ask the pastor when he dropped off the books and toys: perhaps he'd know of somewhere. In the meantime he needed to tackle the basement.

The lower level of the cabin with its vast store of ornaments and vases, table setting paraphernalia and candles, platters and china, brought its own particular brand of whispers from the past, and returning a few hours later to the main level of the cabin, he was surprised to find the cabin in total darkness. His own appetite was non-existent, a consequence, he vaguely thought of the emotional stress of the previous hours, but as he watched Connor greedily slurp up his kibble he saw no reason why he should not have a wee Scotch. If ever he deserved one, it was now.

He should have eaten, he should not have started in on the Scotch, and he definitely should have left Jean's bedside table alone. Had there been a third party present to point out the common sense intrinsic in such advice, McDermott would likely have heeded it, but he was alone: the only third party around was the ghost of his wife, and she was mute.

Opening Jean's bedside cabinet was, to the slightly inebriated McDermott, akin to Bram Stoker's Mina or Lucy opening the window for Count Dracula. He invited the monster in; welcomed back the nightmare; embraced pain. He stared, horror-stricken at the contents of the top drawer, at the array of plastic bottles: large ones, small ones, fat ones, narrow ones: orange predominantly, but a few somehow ominously small and white. McDermott began to scrabble through them, before commencing to fling them on to the bed. They were all there: the ones she'd tried and had to quit, those she'd still been taking before the hospital had finally taken her: the Emend and Anzemet, the Kytril, Zofran and Aloxi, the Compazine and Phenagen. He wanted all the bastards out of his house. He emptied the drawer and cupboard beneath it, the red mist before his eyes deepening in intensity until, ultimately, he was left with one blue, plastic container bearing Jean's name scrawled on a piece of masking tape. He snatched it from the floor of the cupboard and tore off the lid. More fucking pills? And then, as the contents of the container were revealed, he stopped dead and slid to the floor for the second time that day. There was a label from the funeral home and three additional items: Jean's plastic, hospital I.D. bracelet; her wedding ring; and the eternity ring he'd bought her – mere weeks before she'd been diagnosed. He must have hidden the box away here in the confusion and agony of those days surrounding her death. McDermott clenched his eyes shut and let it all come seeping back, over and through the barriers he had pathetically thought he'd erected against its invasion.

It had started with a simple dry cough: nothing particularly unpleasant or threatening, they'd thought, for otherwise Jean had looked and felt perfectly healthy. 'Probably some allergy thing,' she'd said, 'I'll go and see Allan. I'm behind on my shots anyway.' Allan was Jean's allergist as well as being a good family friend, and Jean had been receiving allergy shots for some six years. Allan had been concerned with both the cough and the sound of Jean's lungs through his stethoscope and had sent her post-haste to a pulmonologist friend in the same medical complex for a breathing test. Jean's poor test results had led the pulmonologist to call for an immediate CT scan, and within a matter of hours from arriving at Allan's office with what they'd thought to be nothing more than a minor irritation, they'd sat in stunned silence as their friend gave them the diagnosis and prognosis.

123

Metastasized primary lung cancer with evidence of the cancer in the bones and the brain as well as the lungs. Given no treatment at all, Jean might expect another six months of life: should she opt for chemo and radiation therapy, there was a possibility of buying her a further four to six months.

That's when it had all begun, the whole fucking circus: exhausting trips from one specialist to another in a vain quest for a second opinion of a more positive nature; the long discussions of treatment pros and cons, potential side-effects and what the oncologist euphemistically referred to as 'quality of life considerations;' and then the seemingly unending schedule of treatments, and seminars to help deal with the treatments. Worst of all had been the bloody arguments, the gut-wrenching fights over the best course of action at each stage of the process that had often lasted long into the night. They had been arguments fuelled by tears, shouting and recriminations, their futility only acknowledged when, exhausted, they fell into each other's arms, their tears intermingling. Most of the confrontations had occurred at the beginning when they were both fragile and battling the magnitude of what lay ahead. That was when they'd had to make the most significant decision of all: acceptance or rejection of the chemo and radiation paths outlined for Jean by Doctor Pallister, the oncologist.

McDermott's anger had arisen from his bewilderment when Jean had intimated she was leaning toward electing treatment and buying as many days as she could get. They'd previously spoken hypothetically on the subject – often when friends or acquaintances had been faced with the same agonizing choice – and Jean had always been as adamant as he that when it came to one's last days, quality not quantity was the sensible option. Jean could not, for her part, understand why McDermott could not appreciate the difference between hypothesis and reality, or why he was not as intent as she on her living as long as possible. In the end it was a *fait accompli*. 'My life, my decision,' Jean had declared bluntly, and with that the big top had been open for business.

The chronology of it all was blurred now, the whole experience reduced to a muddled collage of vague images and impressions in which the brief moments of elation and happiness – usually brought about by false remission messages – occupied the tiniest, peripheral edges, while the countless treatments, their devastating side-effects and the ever present looming spectre of death occupied the center of the canvas. He saw again the succession of waiting rooms with their gurgling water coolers and paper cups; the coffee machines with caramelized coffee; the outdated magazines; and most of all, the dizzying parade of receptionists behind their sliding glass windows. It was the puzzling standard operating procedure of these scrub-suited office sentinels that provided McDermott the only light relief he ever experienced while he awaited Jean's reappearance from the treatment rooms. Whenever anyone approached their window, the first thing the receptionists would require of the customer was his or her parking ticket in order that they could stamp it, thus saving the lucky person a few bucks on the way out. Only then would they continue on with the more medically oriented part of their script: 'And your primary care physician is . . . ? And you're here to see Doctor . . . ? And your insurance carrier is . . . ?' Had no one ever noticed the incongruity there? It was a nice touch to provide free parking, but was there not something wrong with the order of priority? He'd become used to the question, but he thought it must come as a shock to new patients recently diagnosed with a terminal disease to be first asked for their parking ticket.

Outside the waiting rooms, there'd been the seeming miles of antiseptic corridors with their attendant features: the satellite cafeterias with their smiling servers; the volunteer 'gardeners,' wandering the indoor gardens with their watering cans; and the proliferation of signs carrying words as frightening to the uninitiated as they were helpful to the knowledgeable. Jean had received much of her treatment at the Lofthouse-Slocum Cancer Center in Traverse, and such was the esoteric language of the signage in the place, McDermott had once walked around the facility making notes in order to feature the words in some poetic piece. He particularly remembered 'Behavioral Oncology' and his initial shock when Googling the phrase to find eight million three hundred thousand responses – for a phrase he'd never come across before. In the end, of course, he and Jean had learned firsthand what that was all about. In fact, in retrospect, he believed they'd spent as much time in receiving counseling as Jean had spent in treatment.

He recalled the succession of 'patient education' classrooms – small bright places with clean lines of matching chairs and desks, ruled over by a succession of unctuous nursing specialists or therapists of one type or another. And then there were the 'students,' half of them with jaundiced faces and hollow eyes filled with resignation. McDermott could even recall some of the classes. There'd been 'Taking Time,' – dealing with cancer diagnosis; 'Chemo Brain,' about side effects; 'Chemotherapy and You;' and finally, 'Radiation Therapy and You.' Jean had about had it with the whole thing by that point. As helpful as the sessions had been, they'd both been well versed by then in the real-world lessons of the bedside bucket and the commode when it came to cancer treatments and their side effects.

Sitting there in the dim light between the wall and the bed, the pill bottles lying on the coverlet where he'd hurled them, McDermott perceived the whole sequence of Jean's demise as a carefully choreographed theatrical production: Directed by the oncologist with production services provided by radiologists and other specialists, backstage assistance had came courtesy of nurse practitioners. Certainly the treatment had followed a well rehearsed course – as had Jean in the end. He'd watched as her movement had deteriorated from athletic walk, through the shuffling stage, to the wheelchair. He'd cried quietly in the bathroom over the loss of her beautiful, blond hair, the slowly dying light in her eyes, and the inexorable advance of the jaundice. All of it had been pre-ordained, with the only intangible, as far as McDermott could ascertain, being the extent of the debilitating side effects: the nausea and the vomiting; the skin crusts resulting from desquamation; the hoarseness and coughing; the relentless diarrhea; and, through it all, the fatigue and depression.

It was as the end approached that the most soul destroying aspect of Jean's losing battle affected them, and despite himself, McDermott allowed his mind to dwell again on the misery it had brought to the final weeks of their lives together. Their arguments over treatment options during the early days of her illness had been bad enough, but as Jean's time grew ever shorter, an all encompassing anger had settled over their relationship like a dark bird of prey, its talons clutching them in an unrelenting grip while its great wings fanned their discord. It was both normal and inevitable the doctors had said: the logical outcome of a bitter cocktail of fear, frustration, fatigue, depression and helplessness that each of them imbibed each day. Normal or not, Jean's constant demands and increasingly irrational accusations whenever he was obliged to leave her, for even the shortest periods, allied to McDermott's despair and lack of sleep, resulted in a number of confrontations that led to ever deeper troughs of remorse.

And now, here he was. Why? What for? What was the point? He looked at Connor sleeping soundly beside him. 'If it wasn't for you big feller,' he whispered, and then, pulling himself up, he roused the slumbering dog and took him out for the final whizz of the day.

It struck McDermott the following morning, the morning of Day 261, as he struggled vainly to find a way into the next chapter of his book, that his 'grieving process' was not proceeding according to any logical pattern. He was well aware from his research, of the Kubler-Ross model and the five stages of grief. He knew too, that not everyone necessarily progressed through each stage, and that the stages had no particular order, but nothing he'd read explained what he appeared to be going through. He seemed to be not so much on a roller-coaster, as on a particularly nasty mountain stage in the Tour de France. He got up and wandered through the cabin. Jean would not be a happy camper if she could see the state in which he was living, he thought. Boxes of her belongings spilled out of the guestrooms and were everywhere, dirty dishes were piled in the sink, books and magazines littered the working tops, and dirty clothes lay around his unmade bed. Room after room provided further evidence, if any were needed, of the telltale signs of serious depression. All this shit just wasn't like him, and yet he was totally incapable of summoning up the energy to get it sorted.

It was the dark thoughts of the previous night though, that concerned him the most. He appeared to have gone back to square one – as if Jean had passed away just yesterday. In spite of the fog within which his brain was evidently operating, he was still aware enough to know he was teetering on an edge and needed help. Time for another session with Greta

VanDamm, he thought, if he could find the balls to call her. He'd cancelled what would have been his second appointment at very short notice – he'd been having one of his 'up' days – and she hadn't sounded too thrilled. Still, she'd told him to call whenever he needed her. He picked up the phone and dialed.

'Greta VanDamm.' Her voice was as smoky as ever.

'Uh, morning, Greta. It's Robbie. Robbie McDermott.

'Hello, Robbie. How are you?' She sounded friendly enough.

'Well, erm, I thought perhaps I might be able to make an appointment.'

'Of course you can, Robbie. When would you like to come in?'

'Well, as soon as possible, I guess.'

'This isn't an emergency or anything is it, Robbie?' She sounded concerned.

'No, no, no. It's . . . Well, I just know I need to see you.'

'Okay, what about . . . Let's see . . .' he could hear the sound of pages turning, 'Say, three o'clock next Tuesday, the twenty-second?'

'That's fine, Greta. Thanks a lot. I'll see you then.'

'No problem, Robbie. Look forward to seeing you. Bye.'

Strange, McDermott thought as he replaced the receiver, but he already felt better. Now why the hell was that? Whatever the reason, there was a little more purpose in his walk as he went through to his den, intent on recommencing his writing. The thought even fleetingly occurred to him that he might do a little house cleaning, but he banished it quickly. Two days and nights had elapsed since he'd read the previous chapter, he needed to put his role as an artist first.

It did not take him long, making notes here and there, correcting grammar, and cutting words, to become engrossed, and soon he was laying the manuscript back down and reflecting on what he'd read. He judged the flow to be reasonable but remained concerned over a few issues: his use of a phrase when one word would suffice; his continued repetition of certain words – 'apparently,' 'however,' 'nevertheless,' and 'seemed,' sprang immediately to mind; and he fretted over his use of what the dictionary referred to as 'vulgar slang' – the shits and the sods, the buggers and the bloodys, but mostly, the fucks and the fuckings, words he and his peers seemed to have mysteriously adopted at the beginning of their college years. 'Foul,' his mother would have called this kind of language; while 'industrial' might have been his father's more balanced take. He found it interesting that despite his own personal use of such words in everyday speech, he had, by virtue of never having written them before, broken some kind of taboo in committing them to paper. He had vague memories of coming to realize during early childhood what he'd been more formerly taught during his teacher-training days: that all children possessed and used different languages based upon location. There was a language of the schoolroom and of the playground, of the home and of the street. When he'd first started using such words as a kid, he'd worried that he might get mixed up somehow and let loose the wrong words at home or in the classroom. As it happened, the one time he'd slipped up had been as the result of ignorance rather than of any slip of the tongue. He'd heard a friend call somebody a cunt, and liking the sound and the feel of it rolling off his tongue, had merrily confided to his mother that he thought a new teacher at his school was a right cunt. He could not be exact about his age at that time, but he'd never forgotten his mother's reaction: It was the only time she'd ever hit him hard enough to knock him off his feet.

Smiling at the memory, he returned to the present and imagined the reactions such language in his book might elicit in people like Pastor Dan and his wife, the elders of the church and many of his older friends in front of whom he would carefully refrain from using such language. They would, he supposed, be appalled, but the language of his characters was as integral to their identities as his language was to his own, and he reckoned he owed it to himself as a writer to follow his instincts in that regard. He placed his notes in his 'Considerations' file and, picking up his pen, began to flow-chart the next part of the book's development..

11.

Transition

Cracker's role as conductor of my life's affairs was by no means completed with his rescue of me from my London misery, but my deliverance remains, I believe, the most critical operation he ever pulled off. From the moment I arrived back in Kingstown, my fortunes turned. My Uncle Fred, a director of a local cut - price grocery shop chain, Happy Sam's, gave me a job as an assistant in the company's Dock Road shop, and the Kingstown Education Authority (which had forgiven me the majority of my grant), appointed me as a temporary assistant master for the spring and summer terms of the following year. In the meantime, after speaking with my old English teacher at Bricknall, I took Cracker's advice and applied for admission to the Lady MacManus College of Education in the following autumn. While I waited to hear from Lady Mac, I settled into my job at Happy Sam's supervising the biscuit counter, and resumed my courtship of Caroline who had been delighted by my return. I did not have long to wait for word from Lady Mac, being invited for an interview at the beginning of December.

It was the college's practice to have prospective students spend a night on the college campus prior to attending their interviews, and after meeting me at the Oakham railway station, Cracker escorted me to the College campus where he spent the remainder of the day showing me around. The college appeared to be everything he had promised and more: modern buildings, extensive facilities, acres of playing fields, an impressive student union building, a large yet cozy college bar, and an overwhelming number of female students. By the time Cracker left me that evening, I'd seen and heard enough to know I wanted nothing more in the world than to attend that educational establishment.

My day of interviews did not begin well. I'd applied to study English and was stunned to hear from the college principal during the day's first interview, that he believed the English course to be full. My mood darkened further during my interview with the College's senior English tutor who confirmed the principal's belief. 'What the hell am I doing here,'

I wanted to ask, 'if there are no places available?' It was at that point that things began to look up.

The tutor, a Mrs. Livingstone, who had been flicking through my school reports, said, 'I see you were in a lot of school plays.'

'That's right,' I said, puzzling over what this had to do with my applying for a course that was full.

'Read this to me,' she said, thrusting a page of D.H. Lawrence's 'The Rainbow' into my hand.

I scanned the page and then read it, after which Mrs. Livingstone removed her spectacles, regarded me thoughtfully, and said, 'Have you thought of studying drama?'

'I, er, didn't know that was an option,' I said.

'It's a brand new course starting next year. Look, why don't you wait outside a moment while I have a word with Mrs. Lowell, the lecturer in charge of the course.'

From that moment things progressed fast, and when I left the college that afternoon, I'd been offered a place on the new drama course based upon those few small parts I'd played with the Bricknall Dramatic Society. The only downside was a requirement that I study 'dance' for a minimum of one year as part of the drama program. Since I'd always been a hopeless dancer, and had no idea of what the subject entailed, it was a concern I shared with Cracker as we waited on the platform at the railway station. His response was to dissolve into laughter.

'What? What?' I said. When Cracker laughed like that, I knew something was wrong. It took him a while to stop laughing and answer.

'Oh, fucking hell, Robbie; did they tell you about the leotard?' he gasped, and commenced to laugh again.

'The what? Piss off Cracker: that's what ballet dancers wear.'

'Well, that's kind of what this dance shit is,' said Cracker, and he began to hop around on one foot with his arms out wide like Rudolph bloody Nureyev.

'Sod off,' I said. 'You're taking the piss.'

'No, no, I'm serious, Robbie. They have a studio with mirrored walls, a barre and everything. Don't worry though, if you can get some muscles on those skinny legs of yours, I think you'll look fucking great; his laughter peeled once more around the station.

Despite my anxiety over the dance thing, I felt enthusiastic over the future as I journeyed back to Kingstown. I was looking forward to my teaching job that would commence after Christmas; I'd landed a college place to study drama, a subject I'd always looked upon as fun; I'd be at an assessment college with no exams to dread; and, for a couple of years at least, Cracker and I would be together again. Cracker. I had to smile as I reflected how Cracker's insistence that I join Bricknall's dramatic society, had turned out to be so instrumental in my landing a college place. Even then, however, I had no idea just how critical drama in general, and dance in particular, would be to my future career.

Returning to the humdrum life of the biscuit counter at Happy Sam's after the excitement of my interviews was difficult, but the boredom was more than relieved, when I was able to again prevail upon the good graces of my Uncle Fred, and secure a Christmas holiday job for Cracker in the same Dock Road shop as me. We had a lot of laughs in that job. We enjoyed good natured banter with the female staff, and the customers themselves provided more than their fair share of entertainment. Dock Road ran the entire length of the fish docks and was home to the toughest element of Kingstown's population. While most of the men worked on the docks, or on the hazardous decks of the City's deep sea trawlers, the majority of the women made a hard living in the fish processing factories. It was one of those women who, thanks to Cracker's wicked sense of humour and love of practical jokes, provided me with the most embarrassing moment of my teenage years.

It was a wet, blustery day, and the reek of the fish docks was borne into the shop on the wet clothes of the clientele. It wasn't long, though, before the smell in the air was the least of my problems. With the Christmas holiday round the corner, it was busy in the shop as a whole, and particularly hectic at the biscuit counter. As I eyed the line that stretched to the door, I called for Cracker to top up the depleted stocks of Custard Creams and Fig Newtons as I completed another order.

'There you are love, one pound of Nice, and another of Ginger Snaps. Change out of a ten-bob note? There you go; thank you pet.' As one more satisfied customer turned to push her way through the crowd to the exit, I was confronted by the next woman in line, a huge specimen of the fishwife breed that Dock Road, was famous for.

'Give us a packet o' them paper 'ankies please luv,' she said, pointing to the shelf high over our array of biscuits. It was the first time I'd ever been asked for anything off that shelf, but as it happened there was quite a display up there, and I asked the woman which she would prefer.

'Them purple uns'll do,' she said.

I turned to lift the box down and froze in consternation, just as Cracker reentered the space behind the counter bearing more biscuit tins. There were no purple-boxed paper handkerchiefs to be seen: the only purple box up there bore the name of a well known brand of tampons.

'I'm sorry love, but they're not paper-hankies.'

Behind the customer, a line of similar looking women obviously aware of my predicament, grinned broadly along with Cracker, while I was powerless to halt the instant flow of blood to my face.

'What d'you mean, not paper 'ankies? What the 'ell are they then?'

Her strident voice had now captured the attention of everyone in the shop, all of whom were observing my crimson face with a mixture of pity and delight. I looked pleadingly at Cracker who leaned forward and whispered something to the woman.

Writing from the Outskirts of Hope

My tormentor's face lit up as understanding dawned, and in a voice calculated to ensure that no one in the shop or its immediate environs would miss the humor of the situation, she said, 'Ooh, I am sorry luv: did I embarrass you? Give us that blue box o' Kleenex then.'

Since the floor obstinately refused to open and swallow me, I acceded to her request while noticing for the first time that my shirt was sticking to my back. Only later did I learn that the presence of the tampons alongside the tissues had been contrived by Cracker in the hopes of creating just such a moment. I believe he lunched off that story for the rest of his life.

That Christmas saw 'Little Miss Dynamite,' Brenda Lee, rocking around the Christmas tree, Cracker breaking things off with Jen, and Caroline and I arguing interminably over becoming engaged. Jen refused categorically to go along with Cracker's 'relationship testing' concept, and while Caroline was eager to put things on a more formal basis, I saw no sense in committing to a marriage that would not be feasible until I finished college.

Thus it was that as the holiday season drew to a close, Cracker was eager to return to the fertile grazing grounds of Lady Mac and I was anxious to take my place before a class of children for the first time.

The Kingstown Education Authority had assigned me to Dagger Lane Primary School, close to the City's timber docks, and two bus journeys from my home. Other than the name and address I knew nothing of the school, but looking over the stark, Victorian exterior as I approached it on my first day, I heard again the advice of my interviewer after I'd been given the job. 'Don't let the little buggers get away with anything,' he'd said, 'or they'll kill you.' Reflecting that those words represented the extent of my training for whatever lay ahead; I gripped my new briefcase a little tighter, and pushed open the green, steel gates.

I retain many fond memories of my two terms at the school, but that first day remains the most vivid. It was a full hour prior to the morning bell when I arrived, and only the caretaker was around. He ushered me into the staffroom and left me alone with the information it would be at least a further half hour before the school's teachers arrived. I remember walking across to a window and lighting a cigarette, as I gazed out over the wet slate roof of the school toilets, to the hunched Victorian row houses beyond. The school looked and smelled the same as Dunswell Road: late nineteenth century architecture featuring massive paned windows and huge, wooden doors, and uneven, planked floors smelling of disinfectant and spilled milk.

As I took in the surroundings, my thoughts turned to the circuitous path that had led me there and the role Cracker had played. Would I have remained an unhappy student at Queens without his intervention? Would I have acquired a place at Lady Mac? Would I be standing in that Dagger Lane primary school staffroom? I was still engrossed in the whole question of Cracker's influence when the staffroom door opened to the gossiping, and laughing of my first teaching colleagues, and I was plunged into the world of primary school education.

As a back-up teacher, I 'taught' every age group from five to eleven at that school. I taught 'bright' kids, 'average' kids and 'slow' kids; I taught clean kids and dirty kids; kids from happy homes, and kids from broken homes. But whatever their age, intellect or home situation, they had one thing in common: they hailed from the same social spectrum as me – the working class of England – and I loved them all.

Such was the positive nature of my first teaching experience, that had I been called upon to do so, I would have taught those kids for free. As it was, by the time the autumn of 1963 arrived and I left home for Lady Mac, I was convinced my future lay in primary education. I'd learned that teaching all subjects to younger children offered me far more creativity than the repetitive teaching of a set curriculum in high school English, and primary education provided me the opportunity of dealing with the development of the whole child. Accordingly, on arrival at Lady Mac, I became one of the few men at the college to specialize in infant-junior education. My life's direction had altered – thanks once again to a suggestion from Cracker.

I arrived for my three day orientation period at Lady Mac in both considerable discomfort and reflected glory, courtesy of riding in Cracker's newly acquired Austin A35 van. It was an old banger with a top speed of forty-five miles per hour, purchased with the proceeds of his summer earnings as a labourer on Kingstown's docks. Nevertheless it was one of only four vehicles owned by the residents of the Gables hall of residence, and as such its advantages were considerable. Since the Gables was five miles from the college campus, with the rigidly scheduled college bus the only alternative form of transportation, a car carried not only cachet but power. It was also clear to me, as we were met in the small car park of the Gables by a crowd of whooping and cheering students, that the old car's image was burnished to a large extent by virtue of its owner being Cracker.

I should have known, of course, that the leadership qualities exhibited throughout his life would have carried over into his college years. He was, by now, a good six feet two inches tall, and his handsome features and athletic build – augmented by his continued practice of Taekwondo (He was, by then, a third-degree black belt) – along with his quick sense of humour and natural charisma, inspired both devotion and respect, which in turn, led to his acceptance as one of the 'big men' on campus. The benefits of being his old friend from home were not lost on me – although I was a mere freshman, my *entré* into the college in-crowd was assured.

The Gables, which I'd requested as my hall of residence, was all that Cracker had promised. Each of the forty-five residents had his own room, cleaned each morning by a private cleaning crew; we had our own refectory providing excellent meals; and with a bar organized and run by ourselves, along with a comfortable common room, we wanted for nothing. The warden of the hall, George Cavendish, was a kind, slightly disheveled man in his early fifties, who believed in self-discipline and self governance, and accordingly left us to ourselves. His attempt to have condom dispensers installed in the hall's lobby was shot down by the College Board, but we loved him for the attempt.

Cracker's description of the work involved at Lady Mac as being 'a piece of piss after A-levels' also proved correct, and with the exception of dance, I eased my way through that first year picking up As and Bs without ever moving out of second gear. Not only were there no examinations at the college, but since I was studying Drama, most of my main course work involved acting, producing, and learning the arts of make-up and lighting. Thus, while many of my peers were writing essays, I was learning lines for my next performance. Such a relatively easy regimen left me with plenty of time for sports and social events.

Dance proved to be my only real difficulty. The drama course was split 50-50 between drama and dance for the first year, after which one was free to choose 'pure' drama or 'pure' dance. Based upon the teachings of Rudolph Laban, Modern Dance was the coming thing according to our two dance lecturers, and was, in fact, soon to become a requirement for physical education teachers. I was slow to see its benefits at the time, and even slower to achieve any level of success in its practice. Saddled, as I was, with the dread of being perceived effeminate, and possessing a singular lack of rhythm, my efforts in the dance studio were more comical than inspiring, and the very real possibility of failing the course often kept me awake at night.

I saw little of Cracker during college hours by virtue of our being in different year groups, but we moved in the same social circle back in hall, played football for the College, and from time to time, had the opportunity to partake in college trips together. One such excursion provided us with one of the funnier moments of our college careers and underlined, once again, Cracker's willingness to break the rules and walk his own path, a trait that in later years would have a significant effect on his success.

Cracker was studying History as his main subject, and it was his history tutor, legendary for her knowledge of local church architecture, who organized a trip around nearby Rutland villages to familiarize students with the local churches and their history. The outing was mandatory for Cracker while purely voluntary for me, but Cracker prevailed upon me to take one of the spare seats in the coach, and we set off from the college campus on a pleasant September evening, with the famous Edith Farleigh, historian, author and inveterate chain smoker, holding forth on the bus's microphone.

The woman was good, I could see that, and it was easy to understand why she was held in such high regard by her students, despite her baritone voice, the smoke that constantly wreathed her, and the comical habit she had of referring to students as 'my loves.' Nevertheless, even allowing for Edith's incredible knowledge and entertaining delivery, after three hours, when we pulled up outside yet another village church, Cracker had had enough, and as he eyed the pub across the road, he said, 'Fuck this Robbie, I'm parched. Why don't we just nip in that pub for a pint while they're doing the tour?'

'Okay with me,' I said, 'I'm just along for the ride, but what about you? Won't you –?'

'Shit, no. Old Edith's so excited about this stuff, she won't even notice. Let's go.'

Because the local pub, as in many English villages, was directly across the road from the church, we were able to observe our peers entering the ancient building as the landlord pulled our pints.

'You two with that lot over there me ducks?' he said.

'Yeah,' said Cracker, lifting his pint. 'History tour.'

'Well, they'll find plenty of history in St. Wilfred's,' said the landlord. 'Place goes back to Norman times, and there's a sixteenth century minstrel's gallery hidden away at the back of the sanctuary that's still got a couple of the original instruments.'

'Is that right?' said Cracker, 'Know a lot about the church then do you?'

'Oh yeah, I'm a deacon over there,' said the landlord. 'I know more about that place than I do about this pub if I'm honest. Mind you, they were both actually built around the same time. As a matter of fact . . .'

For the next fifteen minutes, the landlord leant on his beer pumps and gave us chapter and verse on the history of the church, the pub and most of the buildings in the village. We were draining our second pints by the time we saw the first of our fellow students straggling out of the church; with a farewell thanks to the landlord, we scuttled out of the pub to rejoin the tour.

As they boarded the bus, those of our friends who knew where we'd been, made a number of ribald comments to Cracker regarding his 'peasant' background while laughing at his bravado. Their laughter soon died. Edith had the habit of walking down the bus's centre aisle after each stop chatting to students about what they'd observed; this stop was no exception. As she approached Cracker she grinned her gap-toothed smile, and said, 'Well, my love, what did you think to St. Wilfred's?'

'Oh, I thought it was fascinating, Miss Fairleigh,' said Cracker. 'Especially that minstrel's gallery and the instruments. I thought –'

'Minstrel's gallery? Instruments, my love?' exclaimed Edith, 'But where were they?'

'Well, said Cracker, 'if you go through that little door at the rear of the sanctuary – '

'My loves,' cried Edith, 'Everybody off the bus! We have more to see thanks to our observant Mr. McCracken here.'

The looks and comments directed at Cracker as his fellow history students wearily filed past us on their way off the bus, were significantly less good natured than those he had received just moments before.

The Fairleigh trip was but the first episode of my college years to demonstrate that Cracker had lost nothing of his ability to assume centre stage in whatever he undertook. Even the relatively serious business of teaching practice was treated by him as merely another opportunity to embrace the lighter side of life, and it came as no surprise to hear of his being at the heart of memorable teaching moments.

One such Cracker classic occurred when he was exposed, for the first time, to the teaching of five-year-olds. It was Lady Mac policy to have students experience the challenges inherent in teaching every age level regardless of the student's chosen education course, and thus, although Cracker was a Junior-Secondary specialist, he was required, for a fixed number of hours, to face classrooms of children aged five to seven. It was during a morning spent in an inner city infant school in Wyvern, with his education tutor observing, that Cracker was confronted by the 'boy with the ship' as the child would become known in Lady Mac lore.

Cracker was feeling pretty good about the way things were going: he'd prepared an arts and crafts lesson, and all thirty-five youngsters in the classroom were busily engaged in a variety of projects. He was speaking to his tutor while surveying the classroom activities, when an insistent finger poked him in the rear.

'Mister, Mister,' a voice called, and Cracker turned to face a young, snotty-nosed kid dressed in the kind of hand-me-down clothes that Cracker himself had once worn. The boy was clutching a small piece of rectangular wood into which he'd hammered a row of three nails, and his eyes shone with pride. 'Mister,' he said again, holding his creation up for Cracker's inspection, 'do you like my ship?'

Cracker, with no experience of engaging such young children, reacted in the simplistic way that any parent might opt for. 'That's very nice,' he said to the obvious consternation of both his tutor and the boy.

'Nice? Nice?' said the child incredulously, 'Nice? It's fucking fantastic!'

Cracker collapsed in laughter, another clear negative in the eyes of both members of his audience, one of whom walked off in a huff, while the other took considerable pains to explain to Mr. McCracken the teaching opportunity he'd missed, and the potentially harmful aspects of laughing at a child.

Cracker's teacher rating suffered another blow that could well have had more serious ramifications for his college career, when he was called upon one day to substitute for a secondary school mathematics teacher who was taken ill. Once again, Cracker's education tutor was in attendance. Cracker was a history specialist taking subsidiary physical education and while he could have made a reasonable stab at giving a lesson in any number of subjects, mathematics was not one of them. His brief was to teach percentages to a class of twelve-year-olds. Believing that an example in which he would show how 10% of 100 is 10 would prove to be a straightforward approach to the concept, Cracker picked up his chalk with confidence, and commenced to expound to the class as he scribbled away furiously on the blackboard.

As he explained later, he wasn't exactly sure where he took a wrong turn (although the glazed look on the face of his tutor might have alerted him), but after filling three blackboards with an impressive array of computations, he had somehow proved that 10% of 100 was 120.His tutor took over the lesson in short order, and attempted to undo the damage my friend may have done to the scholastic futures of his pupils. Cracker's embarrassment was considerable – as was his discomfort during the post-lesson review delivered in scathing terms by his tutor.

That Cracker could emerge from such episodes and successfully maintain a B+ practical teaching average, speaks volumes of how accomplished an educator he was in his chosen field of history. As his final teaching practice report would attest, he was a natural born history teacher: his love of the subject, his empathy for kids (especially those from difficult socio-economic backgrounds), and his easy ability to inspire those around him, taken together, ensured that a distinguished future in education was assured.

It is sobering, in the light of his accomplishments, to record that it was during this period I first perceived aspects of Cracker's character that were less than honourable. While he had always had a short fuse and a capacity for violence, there had always been, in my experience, logical reasons for him to exhibit the former and employ the latter. During those two years I spent in his company at Lady Mac, however, I watched him demonstrate both a cynical wielding of power, and a lack of compassion that were as disconcerting as they were disappointing.

It was during a card game in Cracker's room early in my first year that I first saw his despotic side. Sessions of three card brag were a regular evening pursuit in Cracker's room, and games could continue into the early hours of the morning. The stakes were relatively low, but a pot could build up into a significant amount on occasion, and it was possible to lose a whole week's allowance if one were not careful. On the night in question, Paul Davies, a regular member of our group, who had lost far more than was usual, decided at around two o'clock in the morning that he'd had enough and got up to leave. Cracker, who was also deep in the red, and therefore not in the best of moods, squinted through the smoke from his cigarette as he shuffled the cards and said, 'So where are you going then?'

'Bed,' said Paul. 'I'm broke and I'm knackered.'

'Oh yeah?' said Cracker, 'And how are you getting in to college in the morning?'

Although I didn't want to believe it, the words were clearly an implied threat. Paul was accustomed, as were the rest of us in Cracker's in-crowd, to riding in to college in Cracker's van, thus allowing us the luxury of arising later than those who were obliged to ride in on the 8.00a.m. College bus. It was sad to watch Paul, never the most forceful of individuals, stand there awkwardly in Cracker's room, as he gamely attempted to make light of the cheap intimidation.

'Well, er, with you, in the van, aren't I?'

'Not if you don't sit your arse down and get your money out,' said Cracker, exhaling a plume of smoke as an exclamation point.

Paul sat.

If Cracker's use of his van to coerce his closest friends in such a way was tacky, his utilization of it as part of his seduction process with women was repugnant. He thought nothing of picking up a woman at a party on the college campus, ferrying her back to Gables 'for a coffee,' and then refusing her return transportation until the following morning. Since by that time the City's buses had stopped running, the woman faced the option of staying in Cracker's room – which meant sharing his bed – or embarking upon a five mile walk back to the campus on unlit country roads.

I'd revered Cracker all of my life – at the young age of nineteen I already owed him an extraordinary amount – and to observe such behaviour was unsettling. And yet, I did nothing about it: along with the rest of Cracker's cohorts, I swallowed my objections and laughed at his autocratic antics. I am ashamed to admit too, that my abject acceptance of the baser aspects of his character, extended to his total rejection of compassion as an honourable trait.

In retrospect, I should have known that in the light of Cracker's appetite for violence, compassion was unlikely to comprise a significant part of his emotional make-up, and yet, perhaps, because of the empathy I observed in his nature during his mid teens – defending Derek Witherspoon from the antics of Albert Kenworth for example – I'd assumed this part of his character had developed accordingly. His treatment of poor George Aloysius Pendleton proved otherwise.

George Aloysius, as everyone referred to him, was one of those unfortunate individuals destined to go through life unappreciated, unhappy and unloved. Other than being a mathematical genius, he had little to recommend him, and the entire student body was perplexed as to how he had gained College admission. An ungainly individual with a woeful lack of hand-eye coordination, George Aloysius was around six feet tall, with a stooping posture and long hanging arms. His black hair was wild and frizzy and stood out from his head as if recently exposed to an electric charge of considerable voltage. Apart from his Cro-Magnon appearance and unfortunate name (why, oh why, did he ever allow 'Aloysius' to become public knowledge?), he smelled abominably – for what reason we were never able to ascertain – and it was his odour more than anything else that was responsible for the contempt in which he was held, and the derision heaped upon him.

By the time I was elected Gables domestic liaison officer, George Aloysius had already been the recipient of numerous 'gifts' of soap and detergent thrown over the wall of his bathroom cubicle, and had been subjected to more than one forced 'deodorizing' of his room by long suffering students who shared his corridor and therefore his odour. When the daily cleaning crew ultimately refused to clean his room, our warden, George Cavendish became involved. Summoning me to his office in my role as DLO (a post that hitherto had been devoted to the issue of hall food alone), George handed me a two gallon can of industrial strength disinfectant with directions to deliver it to George Aloysius along with a quiet word about personal hygiene. When the contents of the can mysteriously disappeared within a week with no discernible improvement in the air around either George Aloysius or his room, Cracker decided a more direct approach was called for.

The raw cruelty of which children are notoriously capable may be excused, to some extent, by ignorance and a primitive desire to act in packs against one of their weaker brethren. There could be no such excuse for the humiliation visited upon George Aloysius, by Cracker and four handpicked heavyweights, on 'the night of the perfumed bath.'

Immediately following dinner on that infamous evening, Cracker asked George Aloysius if he'd like to join a game of cards in his room later. Since only a privileged few were included in our card games, the invitation alone should have served as a warning to someone who was routinely shunned, but ever anxious to be accepted, and thinking, no doubt, his prayers had been answered, the unsuspecting and eager George Aloysius hurried along to Cracker's room at the appointed hour.

Once inside the room, he was manhandled on to the bed and stripped of his clothes, while being subjected to exaggerated howls of disgust over the stink his body emitted. Stripped naked, he was then carried down the corridor to the bathroom, accompanied by the cheers of the majority of the hall's residents who, alerted to the planned 'entertainment,' had assembled to watch. The hot bath had already been prepared, and the sweet, sickening smell of the added cheap, Woolworths perfume floated from the bathroom and down the corridor, leaving no doubt in the mind of the struggling George Aloysius as to what awaited him. He was deposited unceremoniously into the bath to the loudest cheers of the evening, and before he could rise from the steaming water, hands appeared from everywhere armed with tins of talcum powder. As a now sobbing George Aloysius attempted to shield himself against the white clouds of talculm, I glimpsed Cracker through the mist of that crowded bathroom, and saw the same cold, dispassionate eyes I'd observed in his childhood, when he was administering merciless beatings to Knocker Brentwood and Ramsarse Ramsbottom.

It was a cruel, vile thing to do, and it could have had incalculable consequences. Neither I nor anyone else who stood by and watched could be described as innocent bystanders: we all bore part of the shame. It was later that evening, when Cracker's dispassion in particular was brought home to me. We were having a pint in the Gables bar when I mentioned how sorry I felt for the hapless George Aloysius. Cracker's response was as illuminating as it was brief.

'You can't afford sympathy for someone like that,' he said.

Paradoxically, George Aloysius gained a small measure of respect that night. The mephitic odour surrounding him and his room never went away, but neither did he, and the mere fact that he stayed, allied perhaps to the number of people feeling a measure of guilt over the incident, afforded him at least the minimal comfort of being left alone from that point on. What became of him following graduation I have no idea, but I do know that suicides have resulted from treatment less humiliating than that handed out to him that night, and everyone present, Cracker especially, was fortunate that George Aloysius survived.

It became evident soon after my arrival at Lady Mac, that during the previous year, despite his relationship with Jen, Cracker had acquired a reputation as a swordsman. To hear his friends tell it, his room had seen a veritable parade of attractive young women arrive in the late evening and leave the following morning – and that was before he had the van with which to make an overnight stay a *fait accompli*. It was not surprising then, considering our previous history that Cracker should take more than a passing interest in my sexual welfare, especially when he discovered that female visitations to my room were of no more than a platonic nature. It was a week following our nineteenth birthdays and three weeks before a party at Gables to celebrate the event, when he broached the subject over a cup of coffee in my room.

'So, be honest now, Robbie; has the lady Caroline allowed you access into her knickers yet? After, what is it now? Three years?'

'Jesus Christ, Cracker, what the hell business is it of yours?' The fact was that Caroline had proven remarkably adept at defending her honour. Coming, as she did, from a strict Catholic background, she held opinions concerning pre-marital sex similar to those of the Pope, and my attempts to convert her to a more liberal point of view had met with nothing but failure.

'Oh, bloody hell! She hasn't has she? Jesus Christ, Robbie, you're nineteen already, and you're telling me you haven't dipped your wick yet? For Christ's sake, what happens if you get run over by a bus tomorrow? You've got to get a grip here, Robbie. This is the fucking swinging sixties and the only thing you're swinging is the lead. Who are you bringing to the party? And please don't tell me Caroline's coming down.'

'No, she thinks it's too far for one night, and a hotel room – '

'A hotel room? For fuck's sake! Okay, so who have you got?'

For the first time in my life, I knew I was about to trump Cracker, for two weeks previously I'd been approached by Sally Fleming, a member of my drama group who had unexpectedly volunteered her services as my date for the party. I was casual as I dropped her name. 'Well, actually, I'm bringing Sally Fleming.'

'Fuck-ing hell! Sally Fleming? How did you? I mean, when? Je-sus H. Christ, Robbie! You jammy bastard.'

Cracker's reaction was triggered by a number of factors: Sally Fleming was a five foot, four inch monument to sexuality with a perfectly proportioned body; she could take her pick of any man on the College campus; and Sally had been around the block – indeed, she was rumoured to spend more time in the men's Phys. Ed. hall of residence than in her own. Not exactly my type then, so what was a woman with Sally's credentials doing pissing around with someone like me?

Cracker though, shrugged aside the obvious questions, and immediately began to contemplate the possibilities.

'You do understand do you, Robbie, that a goer like Sally will expect a bit more than a snog and a quick feel? I mean, this is it, sunshine. Jesus Christ, Sally Fleming. Cracker's face took on a rapturous look as he visualized the potential scenarios, and then abruptly clouded over. 'Have you got yourself organized for this Robbie?'

'Yeah, 'course I have. I figured I'd cook her – '

'No. No. No. I'm not talking fucking menus here, you pillock. I mean have you got the right kit sorted? Have you got a packet of three? Although, come to think of it, with Sally Fleming you might need more than that . . .' Cracker was thinking hard now. 'And what are you going to wear?'

'Well, I was thinking about my yellow shirt with – '

'Oh, for fuck's sake!' Cracker was clearly agitated. 'Underwear, Robbie, underwear. Jesus Christ, listen to me for a minute.' Cracker paced up and down, hands as if in prayer, the tips of his fingers resting beneath his chin. 'Think about this as preparing a lesson plan,' he began. 'First – '

'A lesson plan? What the fuck are you – '

'Hang on, Robbie,' Cracker put his hand up to silence me. 'Just let me finish. First of all, you have the objective – and we know what that is. Right? Next, you have methodology, and we can go into that later if you like, but after all this time trying to get across Caroline, you must have some ideas there. And then, Robbie,' A large smile split Cracker's face, 'you have materials required – and that's Durex and underwear. And by underwear, we're not talking about those clapped-out, white, Marks and Spencer Y-fronts you wander around in. Fact is, we need to go shopping.'

'Shopping? For underwear? Jesus Christ, Cracker, I don't have money for bloody clothes.'

'Bugger off, Robbie. I reckon you won over five quid last night so don't give me that crap.'

Winning arguments with Cracker being somewhat akin to winning a lottery, it came as no surprise to find myself in downtown Oakham that Friday evening, being urged through the door of one of those cheapish looking places with special offers plastered all over the windows.

It was Cracker who spotted them. They were brown, and orange, and green, and yellow, and white, in a kind of crazy paisley pattern. They were the most expensive briefs I'd ever had (and they *were* brief – none of these long, baggy boxers). They fit well too, sitting low on my hips and, according to Cracker, made my package appear bulkier than it actually was.

Since the condoms I'd been carrying around were more than a few years old, Cracker urged me into a chemist's before we returned to Gables, where he rather optimistically pushed me to purchase two new packets of three. I was prepared, 'well kitted out,' as Cracker put it, but as the evening of the party approached my anxiety level rose, and I found it difficult to concentrate on anything but the party. I was aware that one of life's major rites of passage lay ahead of me and my mood vacillated between lust and apprehension.

The evening started off well enough. Sally drove me from the college campus in her Sunbeam Talbot to Gables where she was to shower and change, while I made tea. It was going to be a big party – around a hundred people – so the whole hall was buzzing when we arrived. I was known as a bit of a dab hand with a chip pan at the time, so I was planning a nice, cozy egg, chips and peas job in my room before we went over to the hall bar prior to the commencement of the evening's activities.

Having rustled up what I thought was a fairly stylish supper in the kitchen, I carried the two plates over to my room where I edged open the door ready to exhibit, with more than a little pride, my culinary accomplishments. The picture that greeted me as I made my chef's entrance was one that every male has carried in his deepest fantasies since lingerie was first invented. Framed by the window behind her, my bedside lamp throwing a soft glow onto a body every bit as promising as I'd imagined, Sally, in black and turquoise matching bra, panties and garter belt, was slowly pulling a sheer, black stocking up one very perfect leg. 'Hello,' she said, with a provocative smile and more than a hint of the old film noir huskiness in her voice.

Here it was, the moment I'd been waiting for. Hell, it was more than that, it was out of the pages of a bloody magazine for God's sake: raw, sexual energy simmering away in front of me, in my own room. Obviously, this was the moment to dispense with the eggs and chips and progress through the script I'd been imagining for years – the slow walk across the room, the long passionate kiss, the cool, almost incidental unclasping and peeling . . . It was then I blurted out the less than romantic words, 'Oh shit!' rushed past her, almost pushing her over in the process, and pulled the curtains to. The reason for this apparently insane reaction was my view over Sally's soft, curved shoulder of Miss Richfield, a senior lecturer at the college, staring up from the quadrangle below, at the picture Sally presented.

It was a somewhat quiet tea, during which my efforts to restore the previous romantic atmosphere fell on less than receptive ears. I can't say I was surprised when, shortly into the party, I found myself alone at the bar, watching Sally shaking her body suggestively as she danced with Johnny Henderson, a handsome, rugged, rugby player from the College's First Fifteen. The fact that they were dancing to Elvis's 'Such a Night' was not lost on me and I'm sure it was definitely not lost on Sally.

The truth was, however, that apart from feeling a bit of a prat – everyone knew Sally was to have been my escort for the night – I wasn't too upset. I knew Sally wasn't my type and I was more than happy to get quietly pissed. It was just unfortunate for Sally and Henderson that Cracker was more than upset: he was furious. In his eyes, despite my woeful performance in the seduction department (on which I'd briefly filled him in), Sally's public desertion of me amounted to treachery. As the evening wore on, he took pains along with his current girlfriend, Jill, to spend time with me, but his eyes constantly focused on the antics of Sally and Henderson who were becoming increasingly exhibitionist on the dance floor.

Perhaps if they'd kept their distance, nothing would have happened, but as Roy Orbison's 'In Dreams' washed over the darkened room, Sally and Henderson, groins grinding, almost bumped into a group of us by the bar. It was too much for Cracker.

'Oy! You!' he said, tapping Sally's bare shoulder none too gently; 'I think we've seen enough of you tonight. Why don't you piss off home?'

'What the fuck did you just say?' Henderson put his arm in front of Sally and moved her to his side.

While the music continued, dancers gradually came to a halt as everyone's attention was drawn to the confrontation.

'I told this little tart here to piss off home,' said Cracker. 'And you know what? You can fuck off with the cow as well.'

Henderson's face darkened, and pushing Sally behind him, he moved his fifteen stone bulk forward and pushed his head within inches of Cracker's. It was a stupid thing to do, born no doubt of some noble concept of fair play learned on the rugby and cricket fields of his youth. Unfortunately for Henderson, Cracker's childhood had been lived in harder places, and fair play was not an ideal he'd ever readily embraced: before Henderson had opened his mouth, his nose broke with a sickening crunch as Cracker's forehead thudded into it. Taekwondo tactics clearly not being part of Cracker's thinking, I knew instinctively what was coming next. As Henderson's eyes closed involuntarily against the pain, and his hands came up to his nose, Cracker's right foot thudded into the rugby player's testicles, sending him to the floor. It was enough, but that too was an alien concept to Cracker when the red mist descended, and he had drilled Henderson's head into the floor three times before four of us managed to pull him away.

The room was quiet now: the music had stopped, someone had turned up the lights, and over a hundred student teachers stared at Cracker with a mixture of shock and disgust. Cracker, who had scarcely broken a sweat, ignored the stares, turned to Sally who was hovering over the moaning Henderson, and said, 'As I was saying, why don't you piss off home?' and, turning his back on the assembled throng, including the muttering rugby mates of Henderson who were coaxing him to his feet, he calmly ordered another pint.

Although that party went down in the history of Gables, the dramatic events of the evening caused no significant stir in the College population as a whole. Henderson spent the rest of that night in the Oakham General Hospital emergency room and, despite rumours of threatened retribution by the rugby team on behalf of their injured teammate, no one ever confronted Cracker over the affair. As for me, I stored my new underwear away, along with the condoms, and continued to carry the burden of my virginity. I also retained the conviction born so long ago, that one day, Cracker's proclivity for violence would land him in serious trouble.

I'd always known that Cracker was a serious hard case when circumstances dictated, but during that period of our relationship, I was particularly fascinated by his chameleonic persona. How, I wondered, could someone who so valued loyalty toward friends be so cavalier with fidelity toward women? How could he on the one hand, be driven to put his body in harm's way wherever he perceived injustice, and yet wield the power his van brought him so cynically on the other? How could he be so empathetic toward children and yet betray such a total lack of compassion toward people like George Aloysius? During a presentation of some type to my drama group that year, I used a quotation from Mr. Brown's Letters in which he pondered the mystery of women. 'When I say that I know women,' he wrote, 'I mean to say that I know that I don't know them, for every one I have ever known has been a puzzle to me as I am sure she has been to herself.' I remember thinking at the time that Mr. Brown's sentiments regarding women echoed exactly those of mine concerning Cracker.

Cracker and I had always had differing tastes in women: I was attracted to shy, quiet, thoughtful types, while Cracker was a devotee of the busty, bawdy variety. Thus, with the very early exception of Janet Maybury, we'd never found ourselves competing over the same woman – until that is, I met Catherine, at the beginning of my second year at Lady Mac.

I first made the acquaintance of Catherine Maria Ruggiero on a drama trip to the Nottingham Playhouse that autumn. She was the last to board the college bus, and as she bustled down the aisle offering profuse apologies for her tardiness, my heart was lost. It was her face that captured me: high cheek bones; brown eyes; flared nostrils; even, white teeth; and lustrous dark hair with a fringe. She was to me a vision of perfection. The fact that she was only five feet two inches tall and small breasted was irrelevant, I knew I'd found my mate. She sat immediately behind me in the theatre and her proximity, the thought of her legs so close to the back of my head, ensured that the performances of Judi Dench and John Neville on the Playhouse stage were reduced to a vague, dreamlike quality. Although I never so much as said hello to her that night, the fact that I'd seen her, that I'd found her, was enough for me. I was sure in my own mind that everything else: the first date, the ensuing courtship, the engagement, the marriage, the children, was ordained. I could not wait to inform Cracker.

He was writing a history essay when I burst into his room, but he laid aside his pen and listened patiently as I garbled on about the romantic future that lay in store for me. The amusement playing around his eyes as I described Catherine should have warned me of something amiss, but I dismissed it as reflecting his pleasure in my good fortune, and continued to ramble on. Only when he spoke did I understand the meaning of the droll expression on his face.

'This bird,' he said. 'Wearing a fancy, black mackintosh was she? Kind of a cape thing round the shoulders?'

'Yeah. How – '

'Little, dark-haired party, right? Fringe over her eyes?' Cracker was visibly enjoying himself and, as his evident glee mounted, an awful presentiment settled over me.

'Yeah, but – '

'You're too late, Robbie. Chatted her up this morning in the junior common room. Taking her out Saturday night.'

I was confused, bewildered: how could this be? This woman was the diametric opposite of the type of woman Cracker went for. He'd always been attracted to women anxious to open their legs for him. Oh, Christ; the thought of him luring this innocent girl back to Gables . . .

'You're full of shit, Cracker; you're having me on right?'

'No, straight up, old son. Her name's Catherine Ruggiero, first year dance student from London.'

I was deflated, miserable, devastated: worse, I knew that if I didn't leave in that moment, I'd be shedding real tears of frustration, sorrow, or both.

'Yeah, well, fuck you, Cracker,' I said, and turned to leave.

'What? Aw, come on, Robbie, don't be a prat. She's just a – '

I didn't hear the rest: I was gone – as was the future I'd been contemplating only minutes before.

The next time I saw Catherine was on the following Sunday morning, leaving the bathroom on our corridor at the Gables. Bleary eyed women were a common sight on weekend mornings in our hall where George was such a liberal warden, but seeing Catherine in a men's hall was somehow obscene to me, and it was all I could do to respond to her smiling hello before hurrying back to my room. What was she doing there? Had she been caught out by Cracker's transportation ploy, or had she been a willing overnight guest? Had she . . . ? It didn't bear thinking about, and yet think about it was all I did for the remainder of the day. My misery was compounded by the thought that I could have been so wrong about a woman I'd instinctively assumed belonged on a pedestal. And there, I thought bitterly, lay the heart of my problem. I'd always been a pedestal man when it came to finding the perfect mate. While friends like Cracker searched avidly for loose women who would, I spent my time searching for 'nice girls' who wouldn't. Like most men, I believed there were women you married and women you didn't; unlike most men, I had no interim interest in the latter – Sally Fleming had been an aberration, and one I was unlikely to repeat.

My tortured thoughts continued in the same vein until the following Wednesday evening when Cracker, with whom I'd shared little time and few words over the previous four days, stuck his head into my room and said, 'Oh, by the way, Robbie, you're okay with that little dark haired bird. What's her name? Catherine?'

'What? Hey! Whoa.' Cracker had gone. I dashed out of my room after him. He was standing waiting for me in the corridor with that damned lop-sided grin of his splitting his face.

'Thought that would get your attention,' he said.

'Well, what? I mean, why?'

'Chatted up somebody else, Robbie: bleeding knockout. Another one from The Smoke. Jacqui Bancroft; legs all the way up to her neck, tits like Jayne Mansfield and a mouth like a docker. My kind of girl Robbie, my kind of girl. And by the way, in case you're still interested, that bird, Catherine whatever – she will definitely not come across. Just your type.' Cracker laughed loudly as he ambled back to his room.

She was unsullied by Cracker and she was free; those two facts reverberated in my mind as I sank on to my bed and reconstructed the blissful future I'd envisioned prior to Cracker's brief interference. I had no idea my best friend had handed me a poisoned chalice.

12.

Temptation

Had he and Jean been of a covetous nature, they would have coveted the hell out of the Kosinsky home, McDermott mused, as he maneuvered the Jaguar up the winding driveway to the circle in front of the house. Built atop the high ridge to the west of Westwood, the imposing French-country residence was situated to take full advantage of Lake Michigan's spectacular sunsets to the west, and the rolling countryside around the town to the east. All in all, with its thick, gray stone walls, its vaulted roofs and copper finials, the place resembled nothing so much as a French chateau, and at that moment with the exterior lanterns lit and soft lights showing through the windows, it crossed McDermott's mind that he could be in Provence rather than Western Michigan.

He turned off the Jag's engine and took a deep breath, exhaling slowly. He was nervous; no point denying it. This would be his first social evening with a family for a long time, and while he was looking forward to seeing Holly and her girls, the reticence to expose himself to such occasions was still there. Well, best get on with it, he thought. He took another deep breath, grabbed the bottle of wine he'd brought and walked up to the front door. It was the evening of Day 264.

The door opened as he approached, and Holly Freeman stood before him, arms spread wide, eyes dancing in the light and those improbably white teeth flashing that smile. She had him in a bear hug before he had time to say a word.

'Robbie, how nice to see you,' she said, leaning back to look at him.

'You too, Holly. Nice of you to invite me.' All too aware of her body against his, he reminded himself that not only was this woman young enough to be his daughter; she was also the recently separated mother of two teenage girls. That being said, it wasn't easy. Holly's perfume, something musky and sensuous, was definitely not maternal in nature, and neither was her outfit: a low-cut, loose fitting gray and black striped dress, short enough to have passed muster in the London of the late sixties.

'Come through, Robbie. I thought we'd have drinks in the porch before dinner.'

Thank Christ the girls are here, he thought, as he watched the sway of her ass, accentuated by the floating movement of her dress, precede him through the house. Except the girls were not there: that fact became clear as he followed a chattering Holly by the dining room, and saw the candlelit table laid for two. It was as if Holly had read his mind.

'The girls couldn't make it,' she said. 'Loren's out on a date and Mandy's at a sleepover with her volleyball team.' She led him into the porch where a fire blazed in the grate, and shadows played around the room courtesy of the candles flickering on almost every surface. 'I hardly see those kids these days; mind you, considering what's happened in this house over the last couple of months, I'm not surprised. Now, what can I get you, Robbie? It's Scotch isn't it?'

'Um . . . yeah, thanks,' McDermott said, sitting in one of the two overstuffed armchairs facing the fire. Her knowledge of his preferred tipple, allied to the familiar surroundings, disoriented him for a moment and it was then it struck him: He'd ceased to view Holly as the old friend she'd hitherto been: a wife and mother in a family at the heart of the community, and was now seeing her more as a hot babe. And he could not go there, he warned himself: screwing a high-priced call girl in Chicago was one thing, getting sexually involved with the mother of two teenage girls in Westwood was something else altogether.

'You okay, Robbie?' Holly was standing over him with his drink.

'Oh, sure . . . Yeah . . . Thanks, Holly,' he said. 'Sorry, I was kind of out of it there for a moment.'

'Well, not surprising, Robbie, after what you've been through, and it's early days yet. Here, get this down you,' and Holly leaned forward offering him the drink.

It was not the only time McDermott would find himself peering down Holly's cleavage that evening – indeed, it appeared to him, in retrospect, that his whole night was spent admiring those small, taut breasts that neither required nor appeared to benefit from, the wearing of a bra — but that first look, including, as it did, a hint of brown nipple, caused him to almost spill his drink, and his thoughts flashed back to Chicago. For some insane reason, at the ripe old age of sixty-seven, attractive young women had become capable of reducing him to a klutzy teenager.

If Holly noticed his clumsiness she gave no sign, and engaged him in chatty conversation about the town, local politics, the colleges Loren was considering: the same kind of light hearted conversation they might have shared one year previously when each of them had a spouse. It was only later, after a couple of cocktails and a bottle of wine over dinner, that Holly appeared to change, and while the transformation was not exactly Jekyll and Hyde, it was close enough to throw McDermott. It began with a change in Holly's language which, not surprisingly, perhaps, coincided with a vitriolic attack on her adulterous husband.

'I suppose it's all around town, is it?' she asked.

'What's that, Holly?' said McDermott, knowing the answer but reluctant to give it.

'Steve; fucking that whore down in Traverse. Come on, Robbie, you can tell me, I'm a big girl.'

McDermott tried to get his head around the word 'fucking' coming out of Holly's mouth. In all the years he'd known her he couldn't recall her using any word more colorful than 'damn.'

'Erm, well, yeah, I guess it probably is. I'm rarely in town these days, but you know what this place is like.'

'Can you believe that bastard? Can you, Robbie? Not only was he fucking her, but he was using me as the silly bitch to drive him down there so he could do it! And it's not like she's Britney Spears or something. I mean, have you seen her? She's built like Thomas the fucking Tank Engine for Christ's sake.'

'Um . . . No, no, I wouldn't know her if . . .' Where the hell was her language coming from? Suddenly the strict Episcopalian he'd thought her to be had turned into a fishwife. He'd only ever known two women use that kind of language on a regular basis: Bridie Donovan and Cracker's wife, Jacqui – and he'd regarded that as a remarkable coincidence.

'I mean, look at me, Robbie. Am I so fucking ugly?' Holly stood up, arms akimbo and twirled around on her toes before regarding him with those ice-blue eyes.

'Don't be crazy, Holly. You're a beautiful woman. What Steve's problem is, I don't know, but it's sure as hell nothing to do with your looks.'

'You think?' Holly moved round the table toward him.

Oh shit, thought McDermott, I just said the wrong damned thing. He glanced at his watch and said, 'My God, look at the time. I ought to – '

Holly put a hand on his shoulder as he began to get up. 'Oh, come on, Robbie, don't run off: one more glass of wine won't kill you. Let's have it back out in the porch. But first,' she kissed him softly on the cheek. 'Thanks for the nice words.'

Breathing a silent sigh of relief, McDermott followed her back out to the porch where the fire was dying. With glasses replenished, Holly appeared to revert to her old self. Indeed it suddenly appeared that all she wanted to do was talk about the importance of *moral* rectitude, and he almost dozed off as she railed against the loose *morals* of the younger generation, and what she saw as a breakdown in the workings of society's *moral* compass. He considered whether she might be on something, because she really was all over the place.

'. . . So what I think,' she intoned, as McDermott struggled to follow her line of thinking, 'is that two people should know and understand each other really well: you know, be certain that a genuine relationship exists, before they jump into bed together. Don't you think?'

'Um . . . absolutely, Holly: couldn't put it better myself,' said a relieved, but slightly bored McDermott.

'Good; so if you want to fuck me you'll let me know so I have my diaphragm handy, won't you? Or have you been . . . you know . . . ?'

It was unfortunate that McDermott's mouth was full of wine at the exact moment Holly delivered the invitation. It was even more regrettable that his shock was such as to rule out any possibility of denying the autonomic response her words triggered, and he apologized profusely as the red liquid splattered the carpet at his feet. Holly simply laughed as he leaped up.

'Oh, don't worry about it, Robbie. But you will, though, won't you? Let me know?'

'Yeah – Well – Right – Yes – Definitely.' Jesus H. Christ, he sounded like John Cleese in a Monty Python sketch for Christ's sake. 'Erm, look . . . I'm sorry, Holly, it's just that I'm not used to – '

McDermott's attempt at speech was halted as Holly's arms slipped around him and her mouth closed over his. He couldn't help himself; her darting tongue and thrusting pelvis hardened his cock even within the few seconds he took to contemplate restraint, and his hands slipped beneath the hem of her dress and cupped her tight buttocks.

'Hello! Hello! Mom?' Loren's voice from the hallway shattered the moment and, as if in a carefully choreographed ballet, McDermott and Holly adjusted their clothing, slipped back into their chairs, and were both smiling at the door when Holly's eldest daughter entered.

McDermott remembered little of the ensuing conversation and left a few minutes later, pleading Connor's need of him, but as he drove the Jag carefully below the speed limit out to his cabin, he recalled all too clearly Holly's parting words, accompanied by a brief flick of her tongue into his ear. 'Don't forget, Robbie. Let me know,' she'd whispered.

It was in a pensive mood that McDermott ran with Connor the following morning. The more he replayed the events of the evening, the more convinced he became, that thanks to the timely intervention of Loren, he had dodged a bullet. There was no doubt that Holly Freeman was an attractive woman, and he knew himself well enough to know that despite the considerable negatives, he would have screwed her right there on the porch had her daughter not made a timely entrance. But he'd been bitten in the ass by similar negatives in the past, before Jean had come on the scene, and in this particular case, the negatives were substantial: Holly was twenty-two years younger than him, she was on the bounce from a broken marriage, there were the complex emotions of her two daughters to consider, his own current emotional state was certainly suspect, and there was also the issue of town gossip. Put those ingredients together, he thought, and dodging a bullet wasn't in it – he'd narrowly avoided a fucking train wreck.

There were other issues too that told him messing around with Holly Freeman would be a very bad idea indeed. To begin with, there was the matter of his guilt. There was no getting away from it: when he'd woken that morning, he'd felt as guilty as if he'd cheated on Jean while she'd been alive. Why that should be, he had no idea: after all, he'd felt no such compunction following his tryst with 'Princess' Grisha and he'd fucked her three ways from Sunday. Was it because she was a professional thus making the sex a straightforward business transaction? Was it that Holly was an old friend? His guilt was not the only thing bothering him. There was something else, something about Holly's behavior that wasn't right. Where had her language come from? Neither he nor Jean had been paragons of virtue when it came to the old 'vulgar slang,' and Bridie and Jacqui, knew words the average docker from his days in Kingstown would have been ignorant of, but to hear such words spouted by someone who'd never before uttered a swear word in his hearing. . . And what was it with the seduction stuff? And why him? He was an old man for Christ's sake, and she'd not shown any interest in him in the past. Was it possible she'd always had this other side to her, or was her behavior the simple result of Steve leaving her for another woman? Surely she couldn't think that seducing him would in any way prove something to Steve. Could she? He went back over the previous evening. Was the absence of the girls a coincidence, or had

Holly already known when she'd invited him, that Loren and Mandy would be gone? Finally, as he and Connor approached the SUV in the beach parking lot, he tried to decide what the hell his next step should be, for like it or not, he knew the thing wasn't finished: wasn't finished at all. Holly, with her parting words the previous evening, had laid down the gauntlet, and whilst he'd not taken it up, he'd not refused it either. He owed it to her and to himself to graciously return it, and something told him it had better be done carefully. In the meantime he had some writing to do. It was Day 265.

Paradoxically, he enjoyed an excellent day's work, and he celebrated his labors that evening by opening an expensive Zinfandel to accompany his dinner. Thus he was in a mellow mood when the phone rang. His immediate thought was that it might be Holly Freeman, and he allowed the answering machine to pick up. (What did that say about his resolve?) When he heard Bridie Donovan's voice, he hurried over and grabbed the receiver.

'Hi, Bridie! Sorry about that. I was in the – '

'Don't bullshit a bullshitter, Robbie,' 'you're monitoring your calls, you crafty bastard. So anyway, here's the thing: you doing anything Thursday?'

'Um . . . Thursday?'

'Yeah, Robbie, Thursday. It's Thanksgiving for Christ's sake. You know that holiday thing we do over here, where we stuff all the turkeys then do the same to ourselves?'

'Oh, yeah. Wow, I guess I'd forgotten.' McDermott was playing for time. It sounded to him as if another invitation to a family dinner was on the way, and after last night . . .

'Look, Robbie, this is no big deal, but there's gonna be a houseful here, and one more will make no difference, and I just figured if you had no plans, you know, you might wanna join us. But no pressure okay? If you'd rather not, that's fine too.'

McDermott weighed up the pros and cons even as Bridie was speaking. Pros: He liked Bridie a lot and her family too; he had nothing but good memories of nights at Bridie's, memories that invariably included a lot of laughter, laughter that he could use at the moment. Cons: The memories themselves could set him off again, and his grief, he knew from experience, did not respond well to seeing others' happiness. His fondness for Bridie won out.

'No, no, really, I'd like to. It's good of you to think of me Bridie. What can I bring?'

'How about a stuffed turkey with all the trimmings and a nice dessert? No – only kidding. Just bring yourself, Robbie: oh, and Connor as well. No reason he shouldn't have a good time too. Say around four o'clock. Okay?'

'Sure, fine. Four it is. Thanks Bridie.'

'Okay, hon. See you then.' Bridie rang off.

'You hear that Connor?' McDermott said. 'We're going to a party.'

Connor's only response was a puzzled look followed by a sideways glance at the cookie jar by the telephone.

Despite being able to summon neither the will nor the energy to clean up the cabin – which was beginning to resemble the interior of a consignment store in a bad part of Detroit – McDermott wrote well again the next day and by the time he set out for Greta VanDamm's office on the Tuesday, he was actually entertaining thoughts of agents and publishers.

He arrived almost twenty minutes early for his appointment, and since it was a bracing day with a bright sun, he left Connor in the SUV and went for a short walk, thinking to collect his thoughts before his session. It was, he knew, Day 267. He'd brought his old microcassette recorder with him, hoping Greta would allow him to tape their dialogue. She'd come up with some helpful stuff during his first appointment, much of which he'd forgotten, so he thought recording the session to be a good idea. That way, he reasoned, when the old black pools returned, he could replay her words to keep his darker thoughts at bay.

If he'd not been paying attention, he would've missed her, but as he rounded the corner of the Professional Plaza, there was no mistaking the figure he saw leaving Greta VanDamm's building. Her baseball cap and dark glasses may have gone some way toward concealing her facial features, but there was no disguising the figure or the walk. He paused and watched as Holly Freeman hurried to her car. Why he didn't acknowledge her, he wasn't sure. Awkwardness over their last meeting? Trepidation relating to the last words she'd said to him? Her almost comical attempt at a disguise? His own reticence concerning his presence at Greta VanDamm's building? All bullshit, he decided. The fact was he didn't have the balls to tell her what he needed to tell her, and he remained in the shadow of the building's archway as she drove out on to 31.

If his previous meeting with Greta VanDamm had gone some way toward revising his views concerning the efficacy of therapy, his second session made him a true believer, and by the time he arrived back at the cabin he was anxious to play back the therapist's words on his recorder. Greta had acquiesced to his use of the device, and of particular importance to McDermott, she'd also agreed to see him as a regular paying patient rather than as a 'freebie from the church' as he'd put it. Since he was no longer a member of the church, he'd pointed out, it was hardly proper for him to benefit from one of its volunteer programs.

Greta had used the issue of his anger at the church in general, and at God in particular, to move smoothly into the session, and as he replayed the tape that evening, he marveled at how easily the woman had made him feel comfortable in sharing his innermost thoughts. She'd proved herself a masterful listener as he'd recounted the dark moments he'd gone through during his clearing of Jean's possessions, and his feeling that he was balancing on a precipice. And she'd treated his sexual fantasies as if they were the most common thing in the world. He manipulated the recorder until he found the dialogue relating to sex and the whole guilt thing.

'So, let me see if I have this correct, Robbie,' Greta said. 'You've been having sexual fantasies and you've felt some guilt about that. Is that right?'

'Yes, I have.'

'Do you have any ideas as to what might be causing your guilt?'

'Quite honestly, other than a feeling of being unfaithful in some way to Jean, I don't. And Jean is gone, so –' McDermott had stopped there.

'Okay, so answer me this then, Robbie. Don't you think it's normal that someone grieving, missing their partner and not having that physical connection might have fantasies and thoughts of being with someone else? Think about that, Robbie. I mean, how long is it since you had sex?'

McDermott paused the recorder there, because it was then he'd told her about Chicago and his 'Princess.' That he'd been so frank had amazed him. He fast forwarded through his own words and found Greta's response.

'Well, you're nothing if not interesting, Robbie. So you went all the way to Chicago to pay for sex, felt no guilt whatsoever, and yet you feel guilty about having sexual fantasies. And you have no thoughts at all as to any underlying reasons for that?'

'None at all,' McDermott said, hoping she wouldn't pick up on the lie.

'Do these fantasies involve people you've known in the past? Celebrities? People you know now? Where do these women in your fantasies come from, Robbie?'

'Well . . .' McDermott fast forwarded the tape. Again he had no desire to hear himself spilling everything out. Because that was what he'd done – spilled his guts: his lascivious thoughts about Greta; the dream he'd had of screwing a much younger version of her; and without mentioning Holly's name, the thoughts he'd had in that direction. He finally located the therapist's reaction.

'Whew. Well, I guess that answers my question. But what you should know, Robbie, is that as far as your dream about me is concerned, that's a simple case of transference and is a normal reaction for people in therapy. Transference is what happens when the patient and the therapist have connected sufficiently for the patient to feel safe – safe enough with the therapist, to explore those hidden, unconscious thoughts that might be holding the patient back. Your other fantasies too are perfectly normal under the circumstances. Your Chicago outing and how you reacted to it, indicates to me that the guilt you feel over your fantasies is tied up in some way with the people involved having known Jean. Maybe you should visit Chicago more often.'

McDermott stopped the tape. Greta had arched her eyebrows with that remark. Well, at least he knew he wasn't abnormal or some kind of a pervert. He did feel as if he might have been guilty of dissembling in not mentioning the Holly Freeman episode, but there were way too many intangibles involved in that situation, including the issue of Holly's identity and the very real possibility, based on his sighting that morning, that she too was a patient of Greta's. That was what he told himself anyway.

He went back through the recording until he found the discussion they'd had about his depression episode following his emptying of Jean's bedside table. Once again he skipped through his own words and concentrated on the therapist's remarks.

'How long were you and Jean married, Robbie?' Greta said.

'Almost thirty years.'

'So does it surprise you that after what? Eight months? you should be experiencing these periods of intense anger and depression? That some days are good and others bad? That confronting Jean's absence by packaging up her things, and reliving the fact of her illness, through handling her medications, should drag you down?'

McDermott caught the emotion in his voice as he replied. 'No, I don't suppose it does. Not when you think about it logically.'

'Well, I want you to hold that thought, Robbie, and come back to it whenever the days get dark – and they will probably continue to do that for some time. Will you do that for me?'

'Sure.'

'Thank you. Now, as a professional, I need to ask you a very serious question, and it's important that you be very candid in your answer. You mentioned earlier in our conversation that you saw no future without Jean, so I need to ask you: if you don't see a future, have you thought of bringing about your own demise? Has that thought occurred to you, Robbie?'

McDermott's response was almost a whisper. 'Yeah, yeah. I have, to be honest. If it wasn't for Connor . . .' His voice faded away.

'Have you thought of a plan as to how you might go about it?'

'No, no. I've not got as far as that.'

'So you have not acquired any pills or anything that you believe might help you in that regard?' Greta had been looking straight into his eyes at that point, he remembered.

'No, I haven't.'

'Thank you for being honest with me, Robbie. Now, although I know we've only just started to connect, I need to ask you to make a commitment to me. I need to ask you to promise me that should you entertain any more ideas of your own demise, and it becomes more than entertainment in your mind, you will call me immediately on my emergency number. I really need you to promise me that. I may not be able to respond at once if I'm in a session, but I will call you back within an hour.'

'Okay, I'll do that.' McDermott heard again the break in his voice as he answered. He'd not been far away from the Kleenex option at that point, he thought.

'Thank you: I believe you're a man of your word and you'll keep that promise.'

McDermott paused the recorder again. Would he? Keep that promise? If push came to shove? He'd thought so at the time – looking into those eyes of hers, it was difficult not to promise her anything – but would he? And why hadn't he told her about the book he'd got from Amazon after Jean's death? 'The Peaceful Pill' by the Australian doctors, Philip Nitschke and Fiona Stewart, laid out everything you needed to know about euthanasia and he'd . . . Aw, fuck it, he thought, I'm not there yet. He fast forwarded again to find that part of the session he thought had been responsible for him leaving Greta's office on such a high note. Where the hell was it? Somewhere near the end. She'd been asking him about what he wanted . . . He found the spot and listened, impressed once more by how calm and reassuring that throaty voice of hers was.

'So what is it you'd like to take from these sessions, Robbie?' Greta said. 'What is it you really need? You don't need me to tell you that feelings of anger and depression are normal aspects of grieving. You're an intelligent man, you know all that, so what is it you really want to take from this experience?'

There was the faint hiss of background noise from the tape as McDermott considered her question and then his voice, sounding, he thought, almost like Oliver Twist asking for more. 'Hope, I guess. I'd like to feel as if there's some hope.'

'Well, you know,' Greta said, 'for someone who has thought about hopelessness and not being able to see a future, that's a good answer. You haven't given up yet. You're not ready to leave. So right now, what our time together can be about, is hope. We'll see how far hope takes us. When you leave here I always want you to have things to think about, and today when you leave, I want you to concentrate on the subject of hope. Think of hope as a city: at the moment you may only be on the outskirts of that city, but

I'm confident you can make it all the way in. I also suspect a lot of other thoughts will occur to you as we go along, and if you're willing I'd like you bring them into this room. The one thing, Robbie, that makes therapy different from talking to a friend, is that everything stays in this room, and everything you bring here you can leave here. You can pick it up when you come back in if you want to. If not, we'll dispose of it. That's what makes therapy different. Therapy is about a relationship too, and you've lost a very important one. I also suspect you're running from new relationships because you need to stay safe. So, always remember, Robbie, this is the safest place I know to look at relationships.'

McDermott turned off the recorder and looked out at the dark marsh. Was there hope for him? He'd certainly thought so as he left Traverse for the drive back north. At least he had someone – even if she was a doctor – who understood him: seemed to anyway. And apart from the thing with Holly Freeman, he'd been able to lay himself wide open to Greta: the anger, the guilt, the mood swings, and the sex stuff. She provided, perhaps, the anchor that could keep him steady over the months ahead. After all, she must have seen all of this before. He thought about what she'd said about relationships and running away from new ones. Well, Holly Freeman was one relationship he'd damned well better run away from, and he needed to take care of that *tout de suite*. Other than that, he had to admit he felt as good as he'd felt for some time. He'd spend tomorrow editing, maybe do a little more planning, and then he'd steel himself for Thursday and Thanksgiving at Bridie's.

By lunchtime of the following day, McDermott was feeling pleased with himself. He'd risen early, finished his run with Connor and breakfasted by nine, and had four good hours under his belt of reading and editing. He was, he believed, becoming more adept at weaving together the real and the fabricated, of taking a biographical seed and growing it into a story that worked. He'd had to labor over the chronology which, in his haste to just write, he'd neglected, and he'd remonstrated with himself – again – over his repetitious use of certain words and phrases. Nevertheless, he'd enjoyed the exercise, and there was no doubt he'd found it cathartic. Was it the journey down memory lane? The concentration involved? The humor it brought to mind? And did it really matter? The fact was, he'd always been one for the memories, and Jean had warned him more than once as he'd aged and become more prone to nostalgia, that while the past could be a nice place to visit, it was not somewhere you should attempt to live. Still . . .

He considered the inhabitants of his early life he'd just spent the morning with, especially some of the kids he'd taught at Dagger Lane. What had life offered them? In one class of nine-year-olds he'd had twin girls who stunk so badly, he'd had to breathe through his nose when close to them. During a regularly scheduled inspection, the school nurse had pronounced their heads home to more head lice than she'd encountered in her thirty year career. McDermott had itched for weeks afterwards. The same class had contained a couple of precocious girls who were in the habit of acting as runners for prostitutes on the nearby docks until the early hours of each morning. When they fell asleep – which was almost daily – he'd simply let them slumber, thinking they needed the sleep more than any education they were likely to pick up. Poor, little bastards, he thought, what the hell had the future held for them?

Then there was the poor soul at college he'd based the character, George Aloysius upon. God only knew what he'd done following graduation. What the hell had his name been? Whatever it was, his surname was Bates, and of course he'd been dubbed 'Master' immediately by some wag. The poor lad really did have an odor problem – some foot fungus or other – but, more sadly, he was friendless and was given to prowling the corridors of the residence hall at night hoping to find someone who'd talk to him.

McDermott roused himself from his reverie and began to clean up his lunch dishes. It was as he faced the almost hopeless task of finding a place for his plate and coffee cup among the detritus of God only knew how many meals, that he spontaneously began to clean the cabin. He'd not planned the operation: had not thought to do anything at all of that nature, but a critical level of disgust at the slovenliness he'd slipped into was reached at that moment, and triggered the requisite desire and energy. He began with the dishes, the pots, the pans; moved on to cleaning up surfaces;

putting things away where they belonged; went on to organizing the boxes of Jean's belongings into one room; and thence to vacuuming, dusting, and polishing. Four hours later, tired but content, he walked through each room and decided that the place was in the kind of shape that even Jean, with her high standards, would have approved of. It was Day 268.

Whether it was the euphoria he felt over his rediscovered appreciation of order, or some deep-seated need to get out into the world, he decided to reward his efforts by going out to dinner, something he hadn't done since Jean left. He took a long, satisfying shower, dressed himself up a bit – sports coat, crew-necked sweater and black slacks – and left a disgusted Connor to his own devices.

Reversing the Jag out of the garage, he realized he had no idea where he was going. In the old days – just a matter of months ago, really – it would have been a no-brainer: going out to dinner would have meant the Belvedere. Now, his need to avoid local folks and their sympathy – as well as Holly – sent him north toward Petoskey where he figured he could eat in splendid isolation at the Allegro, the only other fine-dining establishment in the area. It was a forty mile drive, but for a fine meal enjoyed in private, he judged it worthwhile.

Driving up 31 he thought about the whole issue of the Belvedere. Prior to purchasing the place, a rustic roadhouse at the time, Steve Kosinsky, a graduate of the Culinary Institute of America, had been the chef at the internationally acclaimed Le Caveau des Ducs in Chicago, one of the top restaurants in the U.S. and modeled on the restaurant of the same name in Fontainebleau outside of Paris. He and Holly had purchased the Belvedere with the sizable inheritance Holly had received upon the deaths of her parents, and turned it into what was almost certainly the best fine-dining establishment in Michigan. McDermott considered the effect the separation of the couple might have, not only upon the restaurant, but upon the tourism industry of Westwood as a whole. A perennial finalist for the prestigious award, 'Best Restaurant in the Midwest,' the Belvedere drew regular clientele to the town's numerous bed and breakfast establishments from the tonier suburbs of both Detroit and Chicago. Its loss to the area, should that be the outcome of Steve and Holly's separation, would, he thought, be substantial.

He stopped off at Oliver's wine store in Charlevoix en-route to the restaurant, to pick up wine for Bridie's Thanksgiving dinner the following day. Knowing that Bridie shared his and Jean's predilection for big reds and the same disdain for the received wisdom that white meat should always be accompanied by white wine, he selected two bottles of Stags Leap Petite Syrah, before wandering over to the counter in the center of the store. Oliver was attending to a young man of haughty good looks who was avidly speaking to someone on his cell phone. Although well acquainted with the inordinate bad manners of cell phone-toting shoppers, McDermott watched, disgusted, as the man conducted his entire purchase while completely ignoring Oliver. The man swiped his credit card, signed the receipt and moved toward the exit, continuing his phone conversation without so much as a glance or a thank you in Oliver's direction. It was as if Oliver was merely another device like the one he held to his ear.

'Jesus Christ, Ollie,' said McDermott. 'You get many in here like that do you?'

'Robbie, you wouldn't believe what I see from behind this counter. I had a woman in the other day doing the same thing. Not a word to me, chattering away on her phone while she was searching for her credit card, and then when I turned to talk to old Doc Huzzard who was next in line, what do you think she said?'

'Go ahead, Ollie; surprise me.'

'She said: "Would you people mind keeping it down? I'm on the phone here."'

'You're not serious?'

'I kid you not, Robbie.'

'I hope you told her where she should put her phone.'

'Would love to have done, but she's one of the big-spenders from Bay Harbor. I just smiled, said, "Sorry Madam," and reminded myself it's my job to relieve her of her money. First rule of salesmanship when you have to deal with assholes, Robbie; you know that.'

Robbie nodded as they both chorused, 'Keep on smiling and charge the bastards more.' They both laughed.

Still, McDermott thought, as he left the store, what a bloody world where people converse on the phone while ignoring the person in front of them.

Surprisingly for a November evening, the Allegro was busy, but after exchanging pleasantries with Stuart and Michelle, the owners, McDermott was shown to his favorite table in the corner of the dining room, overlooking Little Traverse Bay. Although darkness had fallen long before and there was nothing to see but the flashing of the Petoskey lighthouse, and the lights of Harbor Springs across the bay, he sat, out of habit, with his back to the dining room facing the water.

'Evening, Mr. McDermott. The Glenrothes? One cube of ice?'

'Please, Roger. Thank you.' As the waiter left to get him his drink, McDermott marveled at the man's professionalism. It was over a year since he'd been in the restaurant because of Jean's illness and his subsequent isolation, and yet the man still remembered his favorite tipple. He studied the menu, and when the waiter returned with his Scotch, he ordered the Caesar salad with Stuart's signature whitefish dressing, and the restaurant's famous potato-encrusted whitefish. He was alone with his thoughts again when the interruption came.

'Compliments of Mr. Kosinsky, Mr. McDermott.'

What? McDermott returned to the present as Roger placed a large Scotch beside the one he already had. Compliments of whom? Oh, shit! McDermott's eyes shifted from the drink, to Roger, and then, turning in his chair, to a grinning Steve Kosinsky sitting at a table across the room with a heavy-set brunette woman. McDermott made a quick decision: ignoring

Kosinsky's smiled greeting, he turned back to his table, picked up the drink and handed it back to the waiter.

'Thank you, Roger, but would you please return this to Mr. Kosinsky? Oh, and tell him would you, "Thanks, but no thanks?"'

As the puzzled and clearly embarrassed waiter turned away from his table, McDermott grimaced at the blackness beyond the restaurant's window. His heart, he noticed was racing, its usual reaction to sudden stress, and he felt a thin sheen of sweat over his upper lip. Of all the people he most definitely did not wish to see, it was Holly's husband. A large shadow fell over him at that moment, and Steve Kosinsky, who, judging from his facial expression, was significantly agitated, grabbed the spare seat at McDermott's table and, favoring his right knee, lowered himself into it.

'What's this then, Robbie? A friend sends you a drink over and you turn it down? Is that some strange English tradition, or are you just trying to embarrass me?' Kosinsky's eyes surveyed the other diners, the majority of whom were attempting to eavesdrop on the conversation while affecting disinterest.

'What this is Steve, is me simply telling you I do not wish to accept your offer of a drink. Now, if you'd leave me alone, I'd appreciate it.'

Kosinsky refused to back off. 'No, you know what this really is, Robbie? This is a case of somebody choosing sides in a marital breakdown without bothering to check out the full story. I'm disappointed in you, Robbie. I had you down as a decent human being with a strong sense of justice, instead of which I'm finding you to be just like everyone else. If you knew – '

'Look, Steve, let me tell you what I do know and you tell me if I've got anything wrong. You had an extramarital affair. True or false?'

'True, but – '

McDermott held up his hand. 'No, let me finish Steve. And then, when your wife discovered you were playing away from home – behavior, which as the father of two young, impressionable daughters is reprehensible in itself – you really ground her under your heel by telling her you should never have married her in the first place. That was – '

'Telling her what? She discovered? Let me tell you something, Robbie, I don't know who told you this shit, but I can tell you somebody's been feeding you a line. The fact is – '

'Steve,' McDermott held up his hand again. 'None of it is any of my business, but let me just tell you this. People fall out of love; I understand that, but to tell your wife of twenty years – '

'Goddamnit! I told her no such thing!' Steve Kosinsky's hand slapped the table causing the silverware to jump. 'If you'd just listen – '

'I'm sorry, guys, but if you have a problem, you need to take it outside.' Stuart leaned between the two of them, his arm around each chair back. Michelle hovered anxiously in the background, regarding the rest of the guests almost all of whom were focused upon McDermott's table.

'Yeah, I'm sorry, Stuart. No problem: I'll leave Mr. McDermott here to himself, since that seems to be what he wants.' Kosinsky got up gingerly from his seat, but as he left, he leaned over and whispered into McDermott's ear, 'I've always enjoyed our friendship, Robbie, and I shall miss it. I'm also aware of how you must still be struggling with Jean and everything, but I want you to know you are in receipt of some serious disinformation.' With that, Steve limped back to his table and the brunette, who was, presumably, the 'other' woman.

Thus was McDermott's 'reward' of an evening out, effectively ruined. He hated confrontation, always had, and the incident with Steve left him emotionally battered and with little appetite for fine food. He picked at his meal which he accompanied with another Scotch and left hurriedly, averting his eyes from Steve and his partner as he left the dining room. The drive home was no less devoid of satisfaction than his dinner. He'd always taken great pleasure in driving the big Jaguar, but his thoughts were anywhere but on the finer points of his car. The truth was, he felt uneasy. He really didn't know all the facts relating to the Kosinsky separation. He knew Holly's version, but he'd not bothered to listen to Steve's, and more than that, no matter how much he tried to ignore it, there was the nagging issue of his own transgression in the area of marital fidelity. His mind rolled back the years to his twenties and the intense affair he'd had with the married mother of two young children.

Veronica Jones was a teachers' aide he'd met at a training course shortly after the breakup of his marriage. A large woman but with an hour-glass figure, she was a natural blond with blue eyes and a ready smile. Like many young mothers during the heady times of the late sixties, she did not allow the fact of her motherhood to interfere with her love of the latest fashion, and she was given to wearing leather mini skirts or short smocks which served to exhibit her shapely thighs to full effect. At the conclusion of the course she'd invited him to a party at her home the following Saturday evening. McDermott, full of gloom over the separation from his wife, had reluctantly agreed and gone along, expecting to have a couple of drinks before making an early exit. One drink had followed another, however, and he'd eventually finished up alone in the house's back garden watching the dying flames of a bonfire, as shouts and hoots of laughter reached him from the open kitchen windows. He was definitely the worse for wear both physically (the effects of too much beer), and emotionally (the effects of too much self-examination), when he'd first felt Veronica's hands kneading the muscles of his upper back. A little bit of touchy-feely stuff had followed, but when she'd insisted he stay the night because of his inability to drive safely, he'd thought nothing of it – especially since her husband, Jack, a mountain of a man who owned his own construction company, heartily supported his wife's suggestion.

Once the guests had left, Jack had retired to bed and McDermott had helped Veronica clear things away before she'd shown him to one of the kid's bedrooms where he would be sleeping – the kids having been dispatched to Grandma's for the night. It was as he'd left the bathroom that it became obvious Veronica had more on her mind than mere hospitality. She'd met him on the small landing wearing a very short, white terry-cloth robe. Putting her hands on his shoulders, she'd propelled him backwards with a grin into his room and on to the bed. Pausing only to turn and close the door, she'd divested herself of her robe, and proceeded to acquaint him with the warm and welcoming crevices of her impressive body.

McDermott shook his head at the memory as he drove slowly south through Charlevoix. It had been a small, semi-detached house with the thin walls indigenous to post-war English housing, and her husband had been snoring a matter of only a few feet away in the adjacent bedroom as she'd screwed the living daylights out of him. That had been the beginning of it. Assignations at his house, in parking lots, hotels and even public parks had followed, before he'd bumped into Veronica with her kids in Sainsbury's one Saturday morning. The kids: a five-year-old boy and a seven-year-old girl had the same blond hair as their mother and were cute enough to have featured in soap commercials. The sight of them finished the affair for McDermott who, for the first time, had given some thought to the recklessness of his behavior and the gravity of its potential consequences.

Extricating himself from the situation had been more difficult than he'd thought possible: indeed there'd been times when McDermott had seriously entertained the view that Veronica might have been a nymphomaniac. He'd been reduced on more than one occasion to hiding in the house while her MGB idled in the driveway, and she walked the perimeter peering in the windows. She'd finally accepted the inevitable, but the episode, as thrilling as it had been at the beginning, had left McDermott with an element of self-loathing and he'd never forgotten the faces of those kids. So yes, in the matter of the Kosinskys he could certainly be said to be guilty of hypocrisy. He should, at least, have given Steve the chance to have his say.

McDermott's mind was in turmoil as he tried to sleep that night and he eventually rose, went through to his den, and poured himself a Glenrothes. He knew the confrontation with Steve was at the heart of his agitation. Steve had been a longtime friend and McDermott hated to see friendships end in acrimony. There were also the issues of his behavior with Holly, and the uneasiness he felt over Steve's protestations. Jesus, it was a complicated world – even in Westwood with its population of four hundred plus. Perhaps his old friend, Jim Burroughs, had been right. Jim was an ex-navy guy who'd sailed the seven seas and reached a conclusion that he loved to reiterate at every opportunity: 'Whole world's just one big fucking Westwood,' he would say. McDermott was inclined to believe him now.

Maybe he should revert to his position of the previous eight months and stay the hell out of it. That thought took him to the next day and Thanksgiving, from there to happy families and thence to Jean. Jesus Christ, but he missed her. He poured himself more Scotch.

Day 269, Thanksgiving Day, was into its ninth hour by the time he awoke and it was Connor who alerted him to the fact, pawing his shoulder and breathing bad breath into his face. The dog's bladder was as full as its stomach was empty: pretty much the same as him, McDermott thought, as he struggled out of bed. He watched flocks of sandhill cranes out on the bayous as Connor peed, and listened to the sounds of the marsh. It was Thanksgiving and still the winter felt far away. The sky was blue and although the current temperature felt like the forties, there was a high of sixty degrees forecast. Thanksgiving – another calendrical event serving to remind him of Jean's absence. Once he'd fed Connor, he drove over to the beach where he ran the two of them to exhaustion. The combination of the exercise and fresh air revived his spirits and back at the cabin, after a shower and a big breakfast, he spent a few hours revising the macro outline of his book before setting off with Connor for Bridie's.

The occasion was, McDermott would reflect later, the most enjoyable he'd attended since Jean's diagnosis. From the moment Bridie hugged him hello, and ushered him into the house, he was enveloped in a feeling of warmth and friendship he had, for too long, been a stranger to. Bridie's twin sons, Bob and Frank and their respective wives, Samantha and Cindy, welcomed him as if he were a member of the family, while Bob and Sam's ten-year-old daughter, Sarah, and Frank and Cindy's nine-year-old son, Jack, vied for his attention until told by their parents to cease and desist. Meanwhile, Connor and Bridie's shepherds chased each others' tails throughout the house.

Conversation, like the wine, flowed freely during the big sit-down dinner with healthy portions of laughter thrown in, and as McDermott inhaled the aromas of food and perfume, wood smoke and cedar candles, he was put in mind of Dickens. What would he have made of this great

American feast? How many pages would the great master of description have devoted to this festive occasion that was fast replacing Christmas in the eyes of many Americans?

He watched Bridie as she chatted, laughed, passed plates, urged more food upon her grandchildren and generally played the role of the matriarch. Not that matriarchal was a word one would use, McDermott thought, to describe the attractive woman, decked out in a black, sleeveless, clinging sweater and her fanciest jeans. Bridie was a good looking woman who, with her well cared for body, big blue eyes and short, frosted hair looked much younger than the fifty-four year-old grandmother she was. He found it difficult to believe she was gay. How could a woman who'd given birth and raised such a family have suddenly determined she was a lesbian? Still, when he thought about it, he'd had a male client who'd had six children with his wife of forty years before he'd decided to join the other team, so what the hell did he know? It was a pity though, he thought, as he surreptitiously eyed Bridie's straining sweater. He imagined the course he might take with her were he younger and she straight. Stupid, wishful thinking, he decided: brought on by the heady mix of wine and easy companionship.

Following dinner, McDermott was banished from the kitchen to the living room, where he joined Bob and Frank in demolishing the best part of a bottle of Jack Daniels as they watched the San Francisco Forty-Niners play the Baltimore Ravens. At some point in the conversation, as the mayhem on the television screen provided its own singular contrast to the concept of Thanksgiving, it was agreed that the following day, Bob and Frank would drive over to McDermott's cabin and take away the boxes of Jean's belongings to the Salvation Army collection center in Traverse City. The gesture by Bob and Frank almost reduced the well-lubricated McDermott to tears. What a fine pair of sons, he thought; in fact, what a bloody marvelous family.

When he awoke it was to find the boys and their families gone, the house quiet, and the fire burning low in the grate. As he focused his eyes, rapidly coming to terms with the fact that he'd had the bad manners to fall asleep at a social gathering, he saw Bridie, a drink clutched in both hands on her lap, watching the dying flames of the fire, all three dogs around her feet. His movement startled her and she swung her head round to face him.

'Hey, sleepy head. How were the dreams?' she said.

'Oh, shit, Bridie, I'm sorry . . . I just . . . Jesus, I – '

'Oh, for fuck's sake, Robbie, put a lid on it will you? You got tired, you fell asleep. It's what you're supposed to do after a good dinner for Christ's sake. Don't sweat it. Question is, are you okay to drive?'

'Yeah, yeah, I'm fine. Oh, man, Jean would kill me for doing that.'

'Nah, she wouldn't. She might have had your balls for earrings, but she wouldn't kill you,'

McDermott smiled. 'Yeah, well, whatever, but one way or the other she would have let me know.' McDermott glanced at his watch. 'Jesus Christ, is that the time? I've got Bob and Frank coming over at eight to take – '

'Yeah, I know, they told me. Are you okay with that? I mean, are you sure?'

'Yeah: I'm finally there, I think, Bridie. No point hanging onto that stuff when there are people struggling to put something on their backs. Better off at the Sally Army in Traverse than in Jean's . . . my closet.'

Bridie looked at him and nodded. 'Okay, McDermott. Well, let's get you outta here. I have to open up at seven – though why the fuck people want a big breakfast the morning after Thanksgiving beats the hell out of me.'

They were almost at the front door when Bridie asked if he'd heard about the brouhaha at the Kosinsky house.

'No. What was that?' said McDermott.

'Well, it was Tuesday night, I guess. I'm not sure what the hell happened exactly, but according to Tiffany, my own private ear to the world, there was a whole bunch of wailing and hollering that finished up with Holly lying down in front of Steve's car and screaming at him to go ahead and run her over. Hell of a carry-on according to Tiff who got it from Loren who is really struggling with the whole thing of course. God knows how Mandy is handling it all.'

'Jesus Christ,' said McDermott.' What a bloody tragedy.'

'Yeah: still, if she's —' Bridie stopped.

'If she's what?' said McDermott.

'Nothing, nothing,' said Bridie, 'Here, gimme a hug and get the fuck outta here: like I said I gotta work in the morning.'

McDermott held her tightly, acutely aware of her breasts through his coat. 'Thanks for everything, Bridie: bloody great dinner, great company, and a great time. If — '

Bridie pulled away and looked at him, 'If? If what?'

'Aw, nothing, nothing,' said McDermott. 'See? My turn,' he laughed, and turned toward his car, where Connor, impatient to be home, was wagging his tail furiously by the rear door.

'You sonofabitch McDermott,' Bridie called as he got into the cold car. Her laughter followed him as he pulled away.

Bob and Frank arrived promptly at eight the next morning, and their youth and easy natures, were of immense help to McDermott as the three of them loaded up their vehicles with the boxes of Jean's possessions. Because it wasn't easy: even though the dresses, the bags, the shoes and all the rest of it were hidden away in their cardboard containers, McDermott was still very much aware of Jean's presence receding further into the past. At one point he had a sudden urge to stop everything and go rooting through the boxes to see if he could locate that rust dress she'd worn when they'd met. Just one dress, he thought, just one. That wouldn't be so bad would it? But he knew it would, and he threw himself back into the practicalities of carrying and loading.

After making the delivery, McDermott bought lunch for the boys at Hannah's before driving back home. His feelings were mixed as he made his way north. He knew he'd accomplished something important in the grieving process, but there was a finality associated with the day's operation that niggled away at him. He needed to get back to work on his book and he resolved to do exactly that as soon as he and Connor had had a run.

It was a good decision, for although there were not too many hours left in the day by the time he returned to the cabin – and his tendency was to write better in the morning hours – he found losing himself in the quasi-fictional world he was creating, an intellectual emollient for the harsh realities of the world in which he was dwelling.

Situated at the end of a half mile driveway surrounded by ten acres of woods, and five miles away from any habitation worthy of the name, McDermott's cabin could accurately be described as remote. Unscheduled visitors not surprisingly then, were rare: visitors in the middle of the night were unheard of. Thus when Connor's barking at two o'clock the following morning awoke McDermott to a knocking on the French door of his bedroom, he was justifiably cautious in responding to the summons. Tying his old paisley robe around him, he picked up the length of heavy electric cable from beneath the bed where Jean had always insisted it remain, and approached the door. Snapping up the door's wooden blinds, he was nonplussed to find Holly Freeman grinning at him.

When he opened the door, Holly, wrapped in a fur coat, drifted into his bedroom in a cloud of musky perfume mingled with a sweet smell of something he'd smelled before but couldn't place. It was when he heard her slightly slurred speech and registered the uncoordinated nature of her movements, that he realized she was high, and the faintly familiar smell was marijuana.

'You didn't call me, Robbie,' she slurred as she wobbled past him to his bed.

'Holly? What the hell? Do you know what time it is? What the hell are you doing here? Where are the girls?'

'Aw, girls, whirls,' she giggled, waving her arm dismissively from the bed where she'd curled up. 'They're with their pr-pr-precious daddy.' And just like that she was asleep.

Jesus Christ, what was he supposed to do now? McDermott peered down at her. She was out cold, her knees drawn up beneath the mink coat. It was just gone two in the morning and here he was a sixty-seven year-old widower with an intoxicated, beautiful, soon-to-be divorced woman twenty-two years his junior, curled up on his bed: a woman who had already made sexual overtures toward him and who, if the story concerning her behavior with Steve's car was correct, had some serious issues. Serious enough, he reminded himself, to have made her, in all likelihood, a patient of Greta VanDamm's. Well, first things first: he'd brew some coffee. He had no idea whether people high on grass should be treated the same as drunks, never having been involved in the drug culture, but he would proceed on that principle.

Once the coffee was brewing, he moved back through to the bedroom where Holly was making soft noises in her sleep, and went into the master bathroom and closet where he discarded his robe for his blue tracksuit. Returning to the kitchen, he took a cup of coffee into his den and Googled 'symptoms of marijuana usage,' and discovered that increased appetite often came with a high. Well, he could do something about that, and he went to work. Twenty minutes later the prepared ingredients for a large omelet were ready and waiting in his refrigerator. It was then almost three o'clock, and McDermott walked back to the marsh-side guest bedroom, laid down with Connor beside him, and within a few minutes fell asleep.

He thought he was dreaming at first. Something soft and warm was tickling his cheeks, and he was attempting to figure out how Connor's fur could be against both sides of his face, when the dog licked him in the middle of the forehead. It was then he registered, that the weight on top of him was not Connor, and the tongue was not the long, flat, lapping organ of a dog. McDermott opened his eyes to find himself looking into those of Holly who was straddling him, her fur coat brushing his cheeks as her busy tongue flicked over his face.

'Hello, handsome,' she said. Her voice was much clearer, although her blue eyes were still a little bloodshot.

He would like to have been able to say later that he'd done everything possible to withstand Holly's advances; would have been proud if he could have trumpeted his resolve in the face of her onslaught, but although McDermott had excelled in many areas throughout his life, brushing aside the flattering attentions of young, attractive women was not one of them. He knew what he was about to do was wrong, was shameful, but as pathetic as he knew it to be, he could do nothing but submit to his baser instincts.

'Hello, yourself,' he said, feeling himself hardening.

'Mmm,' said Holly, wriggling her spread crotch over his erection, 'You are growing in my estimation even as we speak. Give me a minute,' and she disappeared into the bathroom.

She was nude when she reappeared, and wasted no time in resuming her earlier position, teasing his lips with her lively tongue. She has the body of a gymnast, he thought, before Holly suddenly swiveled around presenting first her muscled back and then a heart-shaped ass to his eyes as she bent over him and worked his tracksuit bottoms off. Seconds later she had him in her mouth and he was teasing her labia with his lips. It was not long before the approaching point of no return forced him to prize away her mouth and flip her onto her back. There was a brief moment before he entered her when doubts sped across the surface of his mind: What might the consequences be? How old did his body look to her? How would he stack up against Steve? They were all reasonable questions for a man in that particular position, but reason has a short life span in the mind of a fully aroused male, and the questions were dismissed, along with his inhibitions, as he slipped into her. Her hard body was arched, and her thighs were pulsating as they joined. He'd heard of spasms in women's thighs occurring prior to penetration, but he'd never experienced them before and the erotic sensation they provided was almost too much for him, forcing him to grit his teeth and hang on, as her legs closed around his waist and her heels drummed against his ass.

After the first time there was a lull which he took advantage of, God help him, to swallow a fifty milligram Viagra. The second and third couplings featured enough changes in position to cause McDermott to wonder whether her gymnastic body was the result of professional training, and by the time he left her, sprawled face down on the bed, he was feeling his age.

Connor was outside the door of the room when he emerged, and was all over McDermott immediately. Perhaps it was the dog's innocence, the warm feel of his golden fur, or simply the cold logic that post-coital reasoning lent his brain, that brought home to McDermott the magnitude of his stupidity. He had just screwed a woman young enough to be his daughter, a woman who was emotionally fragile at best and unstable at worst. Had he taken advantage of her? Of course he had. She'd arrived at his door giggling, high as a kite, childlike even. Breakers of guilt washed over him. Instead of caring for this vulnerable young woman as he should have done, he'd screwed the ass off her. That she'd seduced him was inadmissible as a defense. He'd been a predatory asshole, plain and simple. Troubled by his thoughts, McDermott began to put together the omelet he'd prepped earlier. He'd give her a good breakfast and get her out of the cabin, but first he had to let her know that this could not go on: neither he nor she was ready for any kind of a relationship. He'd tell her gently so –

'Mmm, smells good. If you cook as well as you fuck we're gonna have a great breakfast.' Holly's arms slipped around McDermott's waist and her body pressed into his back. Her voice was sultry despite the surfeit of sex over the previous few hours, and her hands drifted downwards.

'Jesus Christ, Holly,' He turned to face her. She was still nude but held her eyes wide in mock innocence. 'Listen, Holly, we need to –' His words died in his throat as her clever fingers worked their way down the front of his tracksuit bottoms.

'Yeah?' she said. 'What do we need?'

By the time Holly Freeman left his cabin shortly after noon, McDermott knew himself to be in deep trouble. Not only had he compounded his moral and ethical transgressions, he'd failed to say anything to her regarding the impossibility of a relationship. To make matters worse she'd whispered in his ear as she left, that she loved him and would ring that evening. He felt guilty, depressed and afraid. He had been a willing party to the birth of an affair that could end in nothing but disaster. He was a weak, pathetic sonofabitch: living proof of Jean's oft-voiced opinion that males were always more likely to think with their cocks than their brains. Jean – what would she have made of his behavior? A mixture of guilt, disgust, and despair overcame him then and he crumpled into the chair in his den, loose papers of his manuscript scattered around him. Those feelings turned out to be temporary.

Holly Freeman did not call him that evening: rather she simply arrived at the cabin. It was nine-thirty when she turned up, wrapped this time in a red North Face jacket and wearing a matching wool hat pulled down over her ears. Perhaps if McDermott had not partaken of The Glenrothes after his dinner; perhaps if he'd not been so lonely; perhaps, he admonished himself afterwards, if he'd had any balls at all, he might have stopped the thing in its tracks. In the event, the evening passed much as the previous one, and so it went on, night after night for the next two weeks until it stopped. In the worst possible way. In the meantime, despite his nocturnal excesses, McDermott completed the next chapter of his book and revised much of what he'd already written.

13.

Revelation

Given Cracker's succinct and sexist description of Jacqui Bancroft, I thought it reasonable to assume the ensuing relationship would have a limited lifespan. In common with many of the assumptions I made through the years, relating to Cracker, it turned out to be manifestly false. I met Jacqui for the first time shortly after Cracker told me about her, and it was a meeting that was as eye-opening as it was memorable. It had always been Cracker's policy, when on the nest, to lock the door of his room, so when the handle gave freely one Saturday morning, I walked in fully expecting to have to roust him from his pit. No rousting was necessary. Cracker was washing at his sink while Jacqui was sitting up in Cracker's bed, displaying her magnificent chest in all its glory. Evenly tanned despite the time of year, her honeyed orbs were offset by large plum-colored areoles surrounding rosy nipples. I don't recall who spoke first, what was said, or at which point we all laughed. I do know Jacqui made only the most superficial attempt to cover herself, and once Cracker had introduced me, engaged me in conversation as naturally as if we were chatting in the junior common room.

Of all the girls and young women Cracker had met down the years, I found Jacqui by far the most enchanting. Although not as attractive as Jen Topliss – she was a little on the heavyset side with less than perfect teeth – she had a round pretty face with big blue eyes, a perky nose and cheeky grin, all framed by long, straight, blond hair. Were it not for her heavy use of eye shadow and mascara, and her colourful language, she could have been mistaken for a wide-eyed milkmaid from the Cotswolds. As it was, she hailed from London's East end where, as the streetwise daughter of a fish porter and his wife, she'd had a childhood similar to that of Cracker and me. The minimum five O levels and a distinction in Art as her one A-level had gained her admission to Lady Mac where, like me, she was engaged in the infant-junior program. Her relationship with Cracker matured quickly and the two of them soon became inseparable.

In the meantime, the progress of my courtship of Catherine Maria Ruggiero, featuring stuttering starts, abrupt stalls, and bone-jarring jerks in both forward and reverse directions, bore a marked similarity to that of a learner-driver in an old car attempting a hill start for the first time. A sensible man would have heeded the warning signs, perceived persistence as foolish, accepted defeat and resumed his normal life. I ignored a plethora of ominous signals, raised the flag of perseverance, and rejected failure as an option. Cracker tried to warn me. He screamed about the weekends when she was 'unavailable,' railed against her refusals to travel back to Kingstown with me, and swore on more than one occasion she'd been seen leaving a men's hall of residence on campus late at night. I ignored him and doggedly pursued my chosen course – a course that included the termination of my relationship with Caroline. That I'd not already taken the step, was a typical manifestation of my cowardice in ending romantic liaisons, but my reticence in this case was all the more reprehensible in that she'd invested so much of her young life in our future. Moreover, I'd known for some time that no such future existed, for as much as I enjoyed her company, the intensity of the feelings I had for Catherine was absent. Ironically it was during one of the frequent breaks in my relationship with Catherine that I returned to Kingstown, a few weeks before the Easter holiday, to break the news.

The disbelief, the disappointment, and ultimately the fury displayed by Caroline were to be expected, and were matched by the sorrow and disapproval that Mam and Dad felt. Although it had never occurred to me, they too, had a great deal invested in the relationship, and they felt the loss of Caroline in their lives deeply. Had they been aware of the precarious and tumultuous nature of my relationship with Catherine, they'd have been even more perturbed. The letter I received from Mr. and Mrs. Dunham a week later, reflected the bitterness and disgust I'd expected them to feel at my perceived betrayal, and its receipt, along with the virtual absence of both Catherine and Cracker from my life at the time, made for a miserable end to the winter term of my second year. I saw both Catherine and Cracker around college, but Catherine showed only the faintest interest in my existence, and Cracker's preoccupation with Jacqui was all-consuming. I was relieved when the Easter vacation arrived and I could return home for a break.

The summer term of that year, the final term at Lady Mac for both Cracker and Jacqui, began on a high note with a rapprochement between Catherine and me, and ended on a low with a bitter argument that separated Cracker and me for two years.

Catherine's acceptance of my invitation to the first Gables party of the new term was as gratifying as it was unexpected, and heralded a period during which I became convinced my original happy-ever-after dreams would come to fruition. During that summer, I also landed the lead part of John Proctor in the College Dramatic Society's production of Arthur Miller's 'The Crucible,' and was elected college tennis captain. I saw little of Cracker and Jacqui: just brief meetings at Gables and in the junior common room during breaks. We did try a couple of double dates, but although Cracker affected uncommon civility on those occasions, it was clear that the mutual antipathy between he and Catherine and Catherine's less than warm acceptance of Jacqui, precluded the development of any genuine relationship among the four of us. It was a disappointing state of affairs, but soon became irrelevant in the light of the events at the tail end of the term.

The college physical education department had long offered membership in a gymnastics club to the children of the town's residents. Each Thursday evening the children learned the basics of gymnastics, and the college's P.E. students had the opportunity to practise their teaching skills. The club had always been an integral element of the college's relationship with the town, and was frequently touted as a shining example of cooperation between the academic and civic communities. Until the evening of June 24th, 1965. On that night, a final year P.E. student, James Butterwick, was accused of fondling a nine-year-old boy while teaching him to do a headstand. The boy's mother immediately reported the incident to Dr. Simon de Montfort, the college principal who, following an admission of guilt by the student concerned, elected to call on the services of a top psychiatrist. It was the doctor's opinion that Butterwick's behaviour was an aberration and would never be repeated. That verdict was enough for Dr.

de Montfort who decided to allow the student to graduate and pursue his teaching career.

How the details leaked out to the student population was a matter of some conjecture, but leak they did, and the effect was cataclysmic. Within hours the student body was split asunder with one half screaming for the expulsion of the student, and the other half defending Dr de Montfort's decision. An extraordinary general meeting of the student union was called to debate the motion, moving that the college principal be censured for his failure to take action against the accused.

When the issue first came to my attention, I was as concerned as anyone – primarily for the potential effect upon the child, but also for the college's reputation and the ruination of a young man's career. Nevertheless, after reading Dr. de Montfort's reasoned opinion in a letter delivered to each college student, I respected the opinion of the prominent psychiatrist, understood his assertion that there were extenuating circumstances that owing to privacy concerns could not be revealed, and agreed with our principal's decision. I fully expected my friends to do the same; I was wrong.

It was during dinner at Gables the night before the union meeting that I discovered how reactionary the stances of people I'd regarded as like-minded liberals were. The views of Martin LeGrys, an ex-public schoolboy, I found particularly distasteful, and I was engaged in a heated exchange with him when Cracker rolled up at the table with his dinner. Thank God, I thought, reinforcements.

'Jesus,' said Cracker, 'you can hear you two half way down the hallway. Has he been tapping up your bird, Robbie?'

I ignored the flip comment. 'This pillock thinks Butterwick should be chucked out,' I said, leveling a finger at LeGrys.

'And he bloody well should be,' said Cracker. 'Fucking bum bandit.'

I was stunned. Was this really my closest friend talking? Where was the champion of the underdog, the man with an abiding hatred of injustice? Then I understood: the bugger was joking.

'It's no bloody joke, Cracker,' I said. 'He –'

'You're right there, Robbie old son. It is no joke. That fucking pervert's been living among us for three years; he's shared our showers, used our toilets, who fucking knows – '

My God, I thought, he's serious. 'Cracker, what the fuck are you talking about?' I said. 'The psychiatrist says he's an ordinary bloke like you and me, and if he gets the shaft now, his college years will go down the toilet, and his career with them.'

Everyone else at the table, indeed most of the men in the refectory were silent now, focused upon the two of us.

'No, Robbie, he's not ordinary, he's certainly not like you and me, and as for his career, I don't give a shit. As far as I'm concerned there's no place in schools for perverts.'

'There you are,' put in LeGrys, 'that's what – '

'You shut your plum-filled gob,' I said, and turned back to Cracker.

'So let me see if I've got this right,' I said. 'The great Alastair James McCracken, lifetime crusader for justice, and defender of the oppressed, wants a good, young teacher dropped on the scrap heap despite a medical opinion from one of the top psychiatrists in the country. Is that about the size of it?'

'For fuck's sake, Robbie! Think about it. You can't have paedos as teachers. It's like, like, putting a cat in a cage of mice for Christ's sake.'

'What? What?' I could not believe what I was hearing. 'So I suppose the psychiatrist doesn't know what he's talking about then?'

'Oh, don't be so bloody stupid, man. Fuck the trick-cyclist. Would you trust Butterwick with your son?' It wasn't so much what Cracker said as the way he said it that put my back up. The words were spit out through clenched teeth and his eyes blazed with a fervor that was new to me.

'Yeah,' I said, 'since you ask, I would. But then, I'm not a bigoted bastard like you.'

'What did you just call me?' Cracker's voice had gone quiet, but I completely missed the warning sign, the sign I, more than anyone, should have recognized.

'I called you a bigoted bastard,' I said.

It was then that Cracker came over the table at me. I felt his powerful hands grip my shirt front and found myself staring into those dead eyes I'd seen so often in the past.

'Go ahead, big boy,' I whispered, 'hit me. That's how you usually win arguments isn't it?'

Cracker relaxed his hands. 'Fuck you, Robbie, we're finished,' he said, and walked out of the room.

The union meeting the following day proved to be as contentious as that dinner debate at Gables. The same arguments raged back and forth, scuffles broke out on the floor of the hall, and I suspect more than one friendship crashed and burned during the exchanges. I didn't see Cracker in the audience, but if he was there, like me, he kept his own counsel. I viewed the entire event with a profound sadness, as I watched the so-called union of one of the most liberal colleges in the country, tear itself apart over what I perceived to be a basic human rights issue.

When it was over, the motion was passed, and one of the finest men I'd ever met was censured by his own student body for championing the rights of one of its own members. Dr. Simon de Montfort was not only a great educationist and humanitarian: he was, we all knew, a genuine war hero, having served in the French Resistance for the entire length of the war. The censure ended his tenure at Lady Mac: four weeks later, following the end-of-year Board of Governors meeting, Dr. de Montfort tendered his resignation and retired to the south coast. He was replaced by an officious disciplinarian of the old-school type, who was not fit to walk in his shadow, as either an educator or a man. Butterwick survived the scandal. He was allowed to graduate by Lady Mac's academic board and the last I heard of him, he'd changed his name and was teaching in North Wales.

Cracker and I saw little of each other during the final weeks of the term, studiously ignored each other when we did, and travelled back to Kingstown separately for the first time. It was only through the good graces of Jacqui, who tried in vain to broker a truce, that I discovered both she and Cracker had found teaching positions with Kingstown Education Authority. Such was my antipathy toward Cracker at the time, his future held little interest for me, but the news did carry an element of surprise. Cracker's final grades had been such as to guarantee him a job with any one of the more prestigious authorities in England: Wyvernshire, Hertfordshire, Oxfordshire, Bristol, the West Riding of Yorkshire – and yet he had opted for the educational backwater of our home town. I was also surprised to learn he'd decided upon Junior rather than Secondary education. But then, who knew with Cracker? It had become patently clear that I didn't, and what is more, at that moment, I didn't wish to.

Despite a pleasurable summer term together culminating in the summer ball, after which we finally consummated our relationship, Catherine and I once again went our separate ways over the summer holidays: she to London as a waitress in one of London's classier hotel dining rooms; me to Kingstown to spend the summer pumping petrol. As usual she rebuffed my invitations to visit me and my requests to visit her, and as always, I meekly acquiesced to her wishes.

I returned to Lady Mac for my final year in an old Morris Minor that mam and dad had found for my birthday, and was thus able to enjoy both the freedom of movement and the cachet that car ownership brought as a resident of Gables. Although the car made little impression on Catherine, and the autumn term saw a return to the rocky road we'd previously travelled, in many other ways that final year went well. I produced the first annual college pantomime to good reviews, starred in

Jean Anouilh's 'Waltz of the Toreadors,' and Willis Hall's 'Billy Liar,' played a lot of football and tennis, and finished my college career with distinctions in drama, education and practical teaching. I should have felt exhilarated, but the constant fights with Catherine took the gloss off my accomplishments, while I felt the absence of Cracker acutely. I'd neither seen nor heard from him since his graduation, and after living cheek by jowl with him for twenty of our twenty-two years, I did miss him. Jacqui wrote once, telling me she and Cracker had found a flat together and were both enjoying their respective jobs, but while she mentioned Doris's continued battle with diabetes, new baby boys for both Brenda and Janice, and Audrey's intention to go to college, there was little information about my old friend.

Even in his absence, Cracker's influence upon my life resumed in earnest in June of that year, during my search for a teaching post. I'd been told by my tutors that thanks to my high grades I could pretty well write my own ticket, and thus I'd applied only to Wyvernshire, the most progressive education authority in the country. I was interviewed by the two famous primary advisors to the County who suggested I should apply for a specific position in a school where the headmaster was looking for someone with my background in drama and dance. I accepted their suggestion, and was duly dispatched to interview with the headmaster, a Mr. Dunmore.

Wigginford County Primary School proved to be an excellent building in an affluent neighbourhood. It also boasted outstanding facilities, including a state of the art, fully sprung wooden floor in the assembly hall. It was upon that floor, the head informed me, he wished to see me introduce modern dance into his school, while also assuming responsibility for one of the four top junior classes of ten-year-olds.

There was no doubt this was a plum job: great catchment area; a dedicated staff, handpicked by the headmaster (a first in County history, he told me); superb facilities; a class in the top junior age-range I preferred; and a head who was clearly one of the County's educational stars. Byron Dunmore exuded enthusiasm for kids. A craggy, dark haired Welshman, his clear blue eyes regarded the world from beneath bushy eyebrows, with the same intensity they must have gazed from the bridge of the destroyer he'd commanded during the war. He was a man who inspired respect and admiration, and I desperately wished to work for him. There was just one minor fly in the ointment. Although my teaching certificate clearly stated dance as one of my subjects, it really wasn't. I'd dropped modern dance at the end of my first year in favour of pure drama, had never been any good at it, knew absolutely nothing about teaching it, and had no real conviction that it had any educational value whatsoever. Details, details, details, I could hear Cracker saying; I embraced Mr. Dunmore's concept with all the enthusiasm of a young Rudolph Laban, and when he offered me the job, I accepted immediately.

My first port of call upon returning to college from my interview, was the office of my personal tutor, Harry Wilson who had also been one of my first year dance tutors. I'd always got on well with Harry. He was a small man, heavily set for a dancer, with a great sense of humour and an abiding interest in the lives of his students. His initial response, after listening to the story of my interview and my dance predicament was to dissolve into laughter.

'Well,' he said, when he'd recovered enough to speak, 'you'd better get down the bookstore and buy a bloody book hadn't you?' He was still laughing when I left him.

As I drove back to Gables with a copy of Val Preston's 'Handbook of Modern Dance' on the passenger seat beside me, I too found myself laughing: not at my cavalier acceptance of the job, or Harry's reaction, but at Cracker's continued influence in my life. I thought back to Bricknall and the dramatic society he'd pushed me into, his advice on Lady Mac, how those school plays had gained me admission, and now my first job – a long winding chain of critical life-altering events behind which lay the ubiquitous hand of Cracker. And although I didn't know it then, those were but the first links in a chain that would stretch throughout most of my life.

Should the propinquity of humankind to unite in the face of adversity be regarded as a triumph of the human spirit, or should the frequent requirement of misfortune to effect unity be considered a sad commentary on the human condition? It's an interesting proposition, and one I never had more reason to ponder than in the period between the autumn of 1967 and May of 1968, when the bond between Cracker and me was re-forged in the blast-furnace of devastating loss. Prior to then, from a professional viewpoint, our separate lives were filled with success and satisfaction. In Kingstown, Cracker discovered a penchant for the teaching of reading and creative writing, his success in which drew attention from educators from around the world. In the meantime, thanks to the support of Byron Dunmore, the continued interest and advice of Harry Wilson, and some very creative children, I managed, to my amazement, to elicit similar interest for my work in dance-drama. (It was a measure of fame that Catherine could never come to terms with – born I suspect of her infinite superiority to me in dance performance – and the maggot of her envy would rear its head throughout our time together.)

When I was called to Byron's office to take Jacqui's phone call in late September of 1967, Cracker and I had been estranged for over two years and although the possibility of reconciliation had often occurred to me, I had not thought its agent might be death. Doris had died. Cracker's mam, and the Earth Mother of my childhood, had succumbed to a heart attack at the age of fifty, and Jacqui was direct in letting me know what was required of me.

'Cracker needs you, Robbie. He's hurting. It's time to put all that crap behind you and patch things up. He can't even talk right now or he'd be on this phone. Funeral's on Friday, Robbie. Please say you'll come.'

'If I can get the time off, I'll be there tonight,' I said. 'And tell Cracker what's past is past. We'll sort things out, but first we have to say goodbye to Doris. What's your number? I'll call when I get there.'

Byron's attitude toward any personal time requested by members of staff was simply one of quid pro quo. You put the time in for him and he covered for you.

'Just go,' he said. 'Call and let me know if you'll need Monday as well.'

Things were hectic at Doris's house when I arrived that night, with relatives spilling out into the back garden. It was a family time and so I put in only a brief appearance. Jacqui met me at the door with a big hug. She was as effusive as ever despite the stress of all that was happening.

'Oh, you have no fucking idea how good it is to see you,' she said with her customary East end turn of phrase. 'Come on,' and she took my hand and led me through the house to find Cracker.

Our first meeting, after by far the longest separation of our lives, began with a solemn handshake, progressed to a tight hug, and climaxed with shared tears of raw emotion. We said few words – those would come later, but I knew in that moment, that wherever Doris was, she was smiling. Her only son and his closest friend were reunited.

It was a cold day for September when Doris went into the ground. The north-east winds whipped in from the estuary, heavy blankets of grey clouds rolling in behind them, and the mourners shared red noses and ears as well as their black attire, as they huddled in the spartan, cemetery church. The service, like the facility, was nothing fancy: a couple of hymns; a prayer; and a short eulogy, delivered by a minister (to whom Doris was unknown until he'd made his hurried notes with the family the day before); and it was done.

After the interment, I stood and watched as the mourners left. I registered the closeness of Cracker and Jacqui, the moving sight of my mam and dad still holding hands after almost forty years of marriage, and I gave myself a few minutes to think about Doris. She'd had a short, hard life. She'd grown up in poverty, spent her married life beaten and abused by a thug of a husband, and passed the remainder of her days battling obesity and diabetes while trying to exist on public assistance. Not much of a life, I reflected as I watched the gravediggers begin to heap earth on to her coffin, but then again, she'd produced four great kids despite everything, and I knew she'd been proud of that.

The wake had progressed to the raucous, singing stage by the time Cracker and I found some private time together out in the back garden later that afternoon. The wind had dropped, and that strange inversion layer, redolent with the smell of fish peculiar to Kingstown, had settled over the city warming the air. We sat on a couple of deck chairs, lit cigarettes and listened to the muted strains of 'Danny Boy' coming from the house. Over Cracker's shoulder, I saw Jacqui peering out of the kitchen window at us.

Our conversation was a little stilted at first, but as the number of empty beer cans mounted around us, and one cigarette followed another, we gradually found our way back to the easy camaraderie that had marked our friendship. Cracker spoke passionately of his love for Jacqui and their impending marriage, while I filled him in on Catherine's ambivalence toward me. The comparisons between our respective love lives were striking: while Jacqui embraced Cracker's success in the teaching of reading, Catherine scorned my progress in the world of dance; whereas Jacqui craved Cracker's company, Catherine had taken a teaching post in London following graduation, and was quite happy seeing me only on weekends. As I might have expected, Cracker reiterated his reservations about Catherine, but we both knew it was neither the time nor the place, and we passed quickly on to other issues.

'Listen, Robbie,' said Cracker eventually, 'thanks for – '

'Hey, hey,' I said. 'This is me, remember; you don't need to – '

'Yeah, yeah, I do. It's been a long time, Robbie. You could have – '

'No, no, I couldn't,' I said, noticing that despite the years we still had the facility to converse without finishing our sentences. 'Your mam was a second mother to me as a kid; no way would I not say goodbye to her –' I choked a little and we lapsed into silence. I thought of the countless stories we shared together from childhood and then laughed.

'Remember when she had to go and see old Chatsworth after you'd been caught smoking in the toilets?' I said.

'Yeah; what did she say? "I'm sorry, Mr. Chatsworth, I've tried to get him to cut down, but he can't seem to bloody manage it." I was thirteen. That was the only time I ever saw Chatsworth speechless.'

Silence again fell between us as we thought back over the years. After a while, Cracker went inside for more beer, and I could see from the way he settled himself in his chair on his return, that we were about to have the conversation we needed to have. Before we could really bury the hatchet, we had to dig up the damage the hatchet had done.

'Robbie, what I said that day about Butterwick. There was a reason, and you need to know what it is. The thing is though, Robbie, only Brenda and Janice know what I'm about to tell you: nobody else – not Audrey, not even Jacqui – and it has to stay that way. Okay?'

'Okay,' I said.

'I'm serious man. I need your word that you'll never mention this shit to anybody. Ever.'

'You have my word,' I said.

Cracker lit another cigarette, leaned toward me on his chair, and lowered his voice. 'Remember my old man falling down the stairs and killing himself?'

'You're joking, right? Bloody hell, Cracker, it was the biggest thing to ever happen on our street. And not only that, I thought it was you that was dead. Remember? That was a bad night. Mind you, in retrospect, it was probably the best thing for Doris and you and the girls wasn't it? Apart from Jim's lost wages, I mean.'

'No bloody retrospect about it. Fuck the bastard's wages. We managed on the old public assistance. Fact was, the old sod was a bully, a wife-beater and, worst of all, he was a . . .' he hesitated.

'A what?' I said.

'He was a fucking paedo, wasn't he?' he blurted. 'He'd been messing around with Janice and Brenda for years, but when he started on Audrey –' He stopped, before continuing in a whisper, 'She was only six years old. What kind of a sick pervert does that to his baby daughter?'

His outrage against Butterwick all made sense now, but before I could say anything, Cracker continued.

'Anyway, we fixed the bastard.'

'Fixed him? What do you mean, fixed him?' I said. 'Who fixed him? I thought he fell down the stairs.'

'Well, he did,' said Cracker, 'but he had a bit of help from me and mam and Brenda and Janice. We removed a few extra steps during the week to loosen the nails, and then put them back down. We waited for the Saturday night to get the fucker, because that was the night he'd always have twelve pints instead of his usual eight, and he was always well pissed by the time he got home. Anyway, once the old git had fallen asleep, we removed the loose steps and just waited. He always had to go out for a piss in the middle of the night.'

'But, Jesus Christ,' I said, 'what if he'd just smashed his leg and realized what you'd done? He'd have – '

'Well,' said Cracker, a thin smile on his face, 'the thing is, once he'd got to the bottom, we kind of made sure his injuries were a little more serious.'

'What? You mean you – '

'Yeah, we took turns with those steps, the three of us. We beat the old bastard's head on the right, the front, the left, the back.' He paused and laughed. 'The ambulance men said they were amazed at how much damage he'd got from a fall down the stairs. Said his head must have bounced off just about every step there was left. Well, they were almost right – fact is, the steps bounced off him.'

'But what about the cops?' I said. 'Didn't they – '

'Aw, those prats,' said Cracker. 'They'd seen so many drunks fucked up from falling down stairs missing a few steps, they didn't give us more than a second look. 'Course, we hid the steps with the rest of the missing ones under the coal in the coal house and burned the buggers later.'

'Fucking hell,' I said, staring at him. 'How old were you? Nine? And the girls? Audrey? Oh shit, man, are they okay? I mean – '

'Well, I reckon you can tell from the number of kids Brenda and Janice are producing that they're okay. I mean, two each already,' he paused. 'Audrey though, I'm not sure, Robbie. I think she's okay. We talk about it sometimes, but I think she still struggles now and then. I've suggested maybe she should see someone, but round here . . .' he gestured with his cigarette at the garden. 'Well, you know.' He didn't have to say more. In this part of the world, you mentioned a psychiatrist, or any kind of therapist, and the neighbours would consider you ready for the asylum.

'I think she'll be alright,' Cracker continued, as if talking to himself, and then he looked up at me. 'She says she wants to be a teacher like me and teach poor kids. I don't know, maybe that's why I went this route after college. Anyway,' he stubbed out his cigarette, 'I think she'll make it.'

'What about you?' I said.

'Well, that's the thing Robbie: I'm okay. I mean, I don't have any regrets or anything, but –' He stopped for a moment, searching for words and then blurted out, 'That stuff with Butterwick. I mean . . . I know up here,' he tapped the side of his head, 'that maybe that psychiatrist could have been right, but there's no way I . . .' he started gesticulating with his hands again. 'Aw, Jesus . . . I just saw that bastard . . . Anyway, I just lost it didn't I? I'm sorry, old son, I mean – '

I put my hand on his shoulder. 'Forget it, sunshine. I understand; I'd have reacted the same as you in the circumstances.'

'Yeah, maybe, but I should have still had the balls to pick up the phone and call sometime in the past couple of years.'

'Yeah, well, we have that in common,' I said, 'but the main thing is, it's over Cracker. Let's forget it, I –.' I stopped, realizing that for him, there were some things that would never be over and never forgotten. 'Well, you know what I mean. And you and me? Let's not lose it again eh?'

We both got up as if by some unspoken assent and, for the second time in twenty-four hours, embraced each other.

Although I stayed with mam and dad, I spent most of the weekend with Cracker and Jacqui. We chatted about college days, caught up with each other's news, laughed a lot – especially about my budding reputation as 'Twinkletoes McDermott' – and drank far too much beer.

Watching them during those two days, I was struck by how easy they were with one another. They touched at every opportunity and had developed an almost clairvoyant ability to read each other's thoughts. I couldn't help but compare their situation with that of Catherine and me, and felt envious. The subject of Catherine arose more than once, but since it was clear any discussion in that area would result only in discord, we agreed to disagree, and concentrated on more amenable issues, not the least of which was the wedding they were planning for the following year. It was at some point during the discussion about their plans, it occurred to me that the bond between Cracker and me had broadened to include Jacqui.

Driving back down the new M1 Motorway to Wyvernshire, I thought of how far the three of us had come in such a short time, and how Jacqui had changed in Cracker's eyes. She'd progressed from being a bird with 'legs all the way up to her neck, tits like Jayne Mansfield and a mouth like a docker's' to being the extraordinary woman with whom he intended to spend the rest of his life. There was no doubt she still possessed the attributes that had first attracted him, but he obviously perceived her in a different light from those college days. On a more somber note, it was clear there remained one major potential for friction between the two of them and me: Cracker and Jacqui were united in their belief I should end my relationship with Catherine. If only I'd listened.

While the finality of death drew me north in the early autumn of 1967, it was the promise of life that sent me south in December of the same year. Catherine was pregnant, and while the announcement over the telephone of her condition lacked the unalloyed joy I might have desired or even expected, I reasoned that once I got to London and we were together again, she would feel much better about the situation. How wrong I was. Anger over my failure to use condoms (her refusal to take the pill never came up); dejection over a career that would be put on hold; a lack of any excitement in her pregnancy; and (the final slap in the face) the accusation that I was trapping her into marriage – all of these made for a miserable weekend, and provided a clear indication of the negative attitude Catherine would carry into our wedding.

The photographs of our hastily arranged marriage vividly capture the fog and snow, but close examination of those stark black and white prints reveals too, a tell-tale absence of smiles, an almost visible tension in the air, and a collective hunching of shoulders among those present that had nothing to do with the abnormally low April temperatures. Knowledgeable observers will also note the absence of any family on the bride's side – understandable considering their total ignorance of the event – and read the concerned looks caught between mam and dad for what they were: a silent conviction that their son was making a gigantic mistake. (This was a point of view shared wholeheartedly by Cracker, whose contribution to the official record of the day was a number of snaps taken of the wedding principals, in which the snow covered gravestones in the churchyard featured prominently.) Cracker and Jacqui were the last to leave after the small 'reception' held at our small flat. Catherine was locked in the bathroom sobbing at the time, so I walked them to their car alone.

'I'm sorry Robbie, old lad,' Cracker said, 'but I think you're fucked.'

Jacqui gave me a sympathetic look and nodded her agreement with my friend's assessment, before giving me a hug and whispering, 'Take care, Robbie, love, and don't forget where we are.'

It was not an auspicious beginning to a marriage. The mood of the wedding night reflected that of the day, with few smiles, more tears, and little of anything else. We snatched a long weekend of a honeymoon in one of the cheaper bed and breakfast establishments near Russell Square in London, where the bathroom was down the hall, and the old Victorian radiators hissed and gurgled throughout the nights.

Catherine had applied for, and captured, a post in the English department at Braunstone Secondary School for Girls in the City of Wyvern. The school was not in an area conducive to the development of an enthusiasm for drama and dance on the part of its students, but she clearly enjoyed the challenge, and the satisfaction she found in her job, translated into a happier outlook on life in general. I worked hard in attempting to shape our small flat into a home, and for a few weeks of the summer term we achieved a semblance of happiness.

It ended – all of it, in retrospect – on the third Friday in May. It was the first warm day of the year; I was in the middle of a dance lesson with my class of ten-year-olds in the school hall, the windows open to let in the warm breeze, when Byron interrupted the lesson to give me the news. Catherine had suffered a miscarriage and I was to go to Wyvern Royal Infirmary immediately.

I recall little of the drive to the hospital, or indeed of the following days. To miscarry a child at any stage of a pregnancy is devastating, to have it occur almost at the end of the second trimester is earth-shattering. Concern for my wife and grief for our child sucked the appetite for life from me, and it was all I could do to drag myself to work each day. For Catherine the event was emotionally crippling. Post-partum depression is an insidious condition for any woman to bear: for one who has lost her child it can quickly metamorphose into full psychosis, and such proved to be the case with Catherine. Feelings of worthlessness and guilt, constant involuntary crying, and disinterest in almost everything around her, soon escalated into violent mood swings and delusions. Doctors and psychiatrists could do little to help beyond the usual prescribing of drugs, none of which were effective, and as her depression spiraled out of control, so did our marriage.

Initially I was the ultimate, caring husband. When Catherine suddenly burst into tears in a pub, a restaurant, or other public place, I would quietly escort her out, away from the frowns and stares, and take her home. When she broke into a screaming, crying jag in the middle of Cracker and Jacqui's wedding that June, I put my arms around her and led her quietly down the aisle and out of the church. When I came home after long hours at school to find her crying or staring aimlessly into space, I would hold her tight, cook her dinner, and put her to bed. I became accustomed to her kisses bearing the salty taste of tears, the sight of her reddened nose, and the complete absence of any light in her hollowed eyes. As her condition deteriorated however, so did my ability to cope.

The only positive occurrence of that summer term was Cracker's success in winning the deputy headship of Battling Creek County Primary School in Wyvernshire, very close to Wigginford. At the unheard of age of twenty-four and after only three years in the classroom, Cracker would become a deputy headmaster: such had been his phenomenal success in the teaching of reading and creative writing. Of more immediate importance to me, was the fact that he and Jacqui were coming to live in Wyvern. At last, I would have close friends nearby. Their help would be invaluable to Catherine and me as we fought to escape the cul-de-sac of misery our marriage had become. Or so I thought.

14.

Conflict

It was December 7th, Day 282, when he received the call from Bridie. (In the weeks to come he would consider its being Pearl Harbor Day as an omen.) Normally he unplugged the phone when he was working, but he'd forgotten that morning, having awoken with words in his head that had hurled him back into Cracker's world before he'd even arisen. When the ring startled him back to the present, he begrudgingly picked up the receiver.

'Yes?'

'Holy shit! Is it just the one hair you have up your ass, or you got a whole clump up there?' Bridie Donovan said.

'Hey, Bridie! Sorry, I was . . . erm . . . I was just – '

'Yeah, yeah. Forget it, grumpy. Listen, the reason I'm calling is that, well, old Willie and Elvis are in Traverse tonight and I've got a couple of tickets, and I just wondered if, well, whether you'd wanna go? No big deal, if you're busy – '

'No, no, I'm not busy, Bridie, but Willie? Elvis?'

'Oh for fuck's sake, Robbie: Willie Nelson? Elvis Costello? You heard of them?'

'Oh, yeah. Right. Great. Well, yeah, I'd like that. What er, when – '

'Well if you don't mind driving – my eyes are for shit anymore at night – why don't you pick me up around six? And bring Connor why don't you? He can have a run with the boys while we're gone.'

'Okay, great; thanks Bridie. I'll look forward to that.'

'Good. Well, I've gotta run. That fucking George is about to set the kitchen on fire from the looks of it. George!' Bridie's shout almost deafened

McDermott. 'Sorry, Robbie. See you tonight around six then.' She was gone.

After McDermott hung up, he stood with his hand on the receiver for a moment. Had he just been asked out on a date, or was it just a friendly gesture by Bridie to a sad old fart grieving for his lost wife? He kind of hoped it was the former, but then, if she was gay . . . Oh, sod it, he thought, just go and have a good time. He unplugged the phone and went back to his den. Picking up his pen to continue writing, the thought crossed his mind that he should, perhaps, call Holly to let her know he'd be gone that evening. She'd been dropping in every damned night without any prearrangement, just assuming he'd be there, ready and willing. Then again, if he did call her, would that not imply some kind of assumption on his own part? He determined silence to be the best policy. If she did arrive and questioned his absence he could use the opportunity to bring a closure to the thing, for that was something he most assuredly had to do.

To use the common parlance of the day, Willie and Elvis rocked, as did the accompanying bands: The Sugarcanes and the Imposters opening for Elvis; Attwater and The Pipes supporting Willie. Bridie got so carried away with the music, McDermott believed she may have spent more time out of her seat than in it. Watching her standing and swaying, arms in the air, all kitted out in her tightest jeans and fanciest denim jacket topped off by a black cowboy hat, he'd found it easy to visualize her on the stage, singing along with old Willie himself. Even he had been on his feet a couple of times when Willie's 'On the Road Again,' and Elvis's 'High Fidelity,' had galvanized the audience. A bonus for McDermott too, had been the performance of Elvis's wife, Diana Krall who'd always been a big favorite of his.

There was one tough moment when Willie's gravelly voice sent the evocative lyrics of 'You Were Always on my Mind' washing over the audience. It was a song that had been special to him and Jean and evoked myriad pictures of times, and places. Sensing the tears he had difficulty in holding back, Bridie reached out and gripped his hand. It was a comforting gesture, but had the opposite effect to that she'd intended, for as he felt the touch of her fingers, the implicit compassion compounded his emotion, and despite his best efforts, the tears flowed: tears for his loss, tears of gratitude for Bridie's friendship, and tears of remorse for the dangerous game he'd got himself into with Holly Freeman.

A rousing finale banished his melancholy mood in short order, however, and the drive back to Westwood featured plenty of laughter and even some raucous singing as the two of them attempted to relive the wilder moments of the concert. 'Companionable' was, perhaps, the best way to describe the feeling between them, McDermott thought, the relaxed atmosphere that settles over two people who like each other and are at ease in one another's company. Thus when Bridie invited him in for a nightcap, there was nothing on his mind but a continuation of the evening's easy-going conversation and a welcome glass of Scotch. And that was all it was – until he was at the front door with Connor beside him, preparing to leave. He expected the usual farewell hug, and perhaps Bridie did too, but as their bodies came together, they somehow found themselves eye to eye instead of cheek to cheek. Unspoken questions and answers flew between them in the milliseconds it took for their mouths to join when, as Bridie would express it later, spontaneous combustion occurred.

Such was the helter-skelter frenzy of their initial coupling, they never made it to the bedroom, opting instead for the living room sofa, all three dogs barking around them. Afterwards they climbed the stairs slowly, and spent a long night gently exploring one another, the tenderness of their lovemaking providing McDermott a welcome contrast to the primeval fucking he'd been engaged in with Holly Freeman. He found Bridie's body to be as inviting in the flesh as it was in her figure-hugging sweaters and jeans. Her body defined the word, voluptuous. With its generous yet firm curves, it moved over and beneath him with the same easy eroticism he'd experienced with Jean. They had a lot of laughs too especially over McDermott's Chicago visit which for some reason he saw fit to fill her in on.

'You crafty bastard. I knew you were lying with all that bullshit about banking. I just figured you had something going there with somebody.'

'Yeah, I kind of knew that,' said McDermott, and they both laughed.

'So tell me. Why a whore in Chicago?' Bridie asked him.

'Well to put it bluntly, I felt the need for sex without a relationship, so I figured a hooker. Then if I was going to go that route, I wanted somewhere first class. I wasn't interested in some street walker, or amateur off the internet, so I found this escort agency in Chicago.'

Bridie was quiet for a while and when she did speak it was in a serious tone. 'This relationship thing,' she said. 'I'm not pushing you here am I? I mean, I really like you, Robbie, always have, but I'm not interested in one night stands. That said, I don't want to crowd you either. If you're not ready yet, you need to tell me; I can wait. I know Jean – '

McDermott quieted her with a kiss. 'No, you're fine Bridie. If there's one thing I've discovered tonight, you're good for me. Is it too soon after Jean? I honestly don't know, but at the moment it just feels right with you somehow.'

'So, apart from this Princess broad, I'm the first since . . .?'

McDermott could have, should have, told her then; got the whole Holly Freeman thing off his chest, but he lied. 'Yeah, the one and only,' he said.

'Robbie?' Bridie turned on her side, wrapped a thigh over his legs and laid her head on his chest.

'Yeah?' She had great thighs, he thought: a bit on the large side maybe, but firm, with the muscles bearing testimony to the Pilates regimen he knew she followed.

'Remember Thanksgiving night, when you said "If" as you were leaving and then shut up and wouldn't tell me what you were going to say? What was that about?'

He knew exactly the moment to which she was referring. 'Oh shit, I don't know whether you want to hear that,' McDermott said.

'Why? What?' Bridie was leaning on her elbow looking down at him now.

'Well, er – It's just that I thought – Maybe – Well, that you might be gay and if you weren't – '

'What? What? Me? Gay? Jesus Christ, McDermott, do I look like I'm fucking gay?' Bridie was clearly not impressed by this turn in the conversation.

'Well, shit, I don't know. I don't think anybody looks gay do they? I mean, I've known lots of women who were gay and I'd no idea until they told me.'

'So if I don't look gay, what made you think I might be? I mean what about my kids for Christ's sake?'

'Well, lots of people get married and have kids before they change sides, and there's been this rumor ever since you lived with – '

'Chantal Morrissey? Jesus H. Christ! Are you serious? Just because Chantal lodged at my place, people thought . . . ? And you believed that shit?'

'Hell, I don't know, Bridie. I didn't want to, but then, here you are, the best looking woman for miles, and I've never seen you with a guy, and from what I hear, you get lots of offers down at the Nugget.'

'The Nugget? Robbie, have you seen the characters that go in the Nugget? Holy shit! I'd go to Chicago myself before I took up with any one of them.'

There was more laughter at that point followed by gossip about the various characters in the town, the current rumours about who was screwing who, and McDermott's attempt to write a novel – a subject on which he refused to elaborate – before McDermott brought the conversation back to Thanksgiving.

'Getting back to Thanksgiving, Bridie: you were going to tell me something that night too. What was that?'

'Don't know. What did I say exactly?'

'We were talking about the Kosinskys and that commotion with the car and I said how sad it was, and you said something like, "Yeah, but if," and then you stopped and wouldn't tell me what you were going to say. Remember? What was that all about?'

'Aw shit, Robbie, not now. Let's not spoil a great night.'

'Hey, come on, fair's fair,' said McDermott. 'Let's have it.'

'Shit! I hate passing on rumors, but if you must know, the word I got is that Holly suffers from bipolar disorder, and she's been making life hell for Steve and the girls for years. Supposedly she's got it pretty bad: has depression big time, delusions, hallucinations, and the whole thing. Even had to spend time in some sort of institution when she was a kid. Not her fault of course, but it lends a bit of perspective to Steve's situation doesn't it? If it's all true that is.'

Later, McDermott had a hard time sleeping, his mind working overtime in an attempt to absorb the implications of what Bridie had told him. If Holly did have bipolar disorder – and it would certainly explain some of her strange behavior – he was in much deeper trouble than he'd thought. He was no stranger to the condition, having come upon it more than once during his teaching career. Moreover, if Holly had been institutionalized in the past, she'd probably presented psychotic symptoms, placing her in the most severe range of the bipolar spectrum. . . .

When McDermott finally succumbed to sleep shortly before dawn, Bridie's ass comfortably tucked into his stomach, his dreams were troubled.

When he awoke, it was already gone nine and Bridie was gone. She'd left a note on his pillow.

Morning Lazyass. Connor fed. Help yourself to fridge. Leave door unlocked. Good luck with the writing, See you Wednesday.

Bridie xxx

P.S. Thanks for a great night. Loved it - Hope you did too!

Wednesday? Wednesday? What was that about? And then he remembered. He'd offered to cook her dinner – over her protestations they should take things slowly.

'Bridie, I'm talking dinner for Christ's sake, not a bloody marriage proposal,' he'd said.

'Yeah, well, just as long as you know we need to just take this thing one day at a time. It's early days for you still, Robbie. You've been through a fucking awful time and I don't want you thinking –'

He'd quietened her with a finger to her lips and shared his own thoughts. 'Bridie, I don't think anything – except you're a good friend, the only real one I have right now, and a big part of what makes you special is that kind of concern. So no, you're right, we won't rush into things, but my giving you dinner doesn't seem to me to constitute a mad dash to the altar.'

They'd had a sensible, adult conversation about the whole thing, and driving Connor back to the cabin, he felt comfortable they were on the same page. He knew he wasn't there yet: probably had a lot more peaks and valleys to negotiate before he was, and he was sure too, he still had plenty of tears left in him. His behavior too had been erratic to say the least: Chicago, Holly Freeman, and now Bridie. And what had happened to his conviction that a relationship was not something he wanted yet? It seemed that his convictions, like his behavior, were about as stable as his moods. And then there was the guilt. He'd been honest with Bridie about believing them to be good together, but that whole thing about the proximity to Jean's death was still there. He recalled a couple he and Jean had been friendly with on the east side of the state. The wife had died suddenly and he and Jean had been horrified to discover that within one month, the bereaved husband had been trolling for a replacement. One month? Nine months? Was there seriously that much difference? What would Jean think? She'd always said he would, and should, find someone else, but they'd never spoken of suitable grieving periods. His eyes began to fill and he pulled over north of Torch Lake to get a tissue from the box in the trunk.

The road was deserted beneath a flat, gray sky; the air was clear and cold. McDermott breathed deeply, savoring the scent of pine in his nostrils. Local business owners, most of who catered to the tourist industry, called this the dead time of year: too late for warm sunshine, too early for the skiers or the numerous snowmobilers who would pour into the area once the winter snows were deep enough. Even the deer hunting season was over now, although there was some kind of musket shooting still allowed. Beginning to feel the cold, he got back into the warm car, and pulled back out onto 31.

The worrisome side of the previous evening preoccupied him as he neared his turnoff. He needed to sort out his situation with Holly Freeman sooner rather than later. He'd lied to Bridie about her being the first, and the potential fallout from that lie did not bear thinking about. The night he'd just spent had been the most fulfilling of the past nine months and he'd have said the same had there been no sex involved. The last time he'd experienced the feeling of being so at home with a woman had been with Jean. He believed it to be a rare phenomenon and wanted to hang on to it. What Bridie saw in him he couldn't comprehend. He was twelve years older, emotionally damaged, and certainly no matinee idol. He was comparatively wealthy, he supposed, but Bridie was no gold digger and in fact, based upon the size of her home and the flourishing diner, could not be short of money herself.

As he turned off 31 and approached the beginning of the long winding driveway to his cabin, he focused on the pressing issue of Holly Freeman. Perhaps a meeting with Greta VanDamm might be in order. If the rumors about Holly were correct, he was going to have to put his embarrassment over the affair to one side and seek some professional advice. In fact, he decided, he'd call Greta as soon as he was in the house.

Except it was too late, for as he negotiated the last bend in the driveway he saw Holly's BMW sitting in front of his garage. He was still rolling to a stop when the door of the big Seven Series sedan opened and a disheveled and irate Holly started toward him. He turned off his engine, and leaving Connor in the car, emerged to meet her.

'Holly, what are you doing here? It's –' McDermott got no further.

'Where the fuck have you been, you sonofabitch?' Holly snarled. 'I've been out here all fucking night.' Her face was contorted with rage, and her blue eyes blazed from beneath hair that bore all the signs of her having slept in the car.

'Jesus. Why, Holly? I mean, I'm sorry, I – '

'Don't you fucking "sorry" me, you prick,' she said, jabbing his chest with her forefinger to punctuate her speech. 'You've been whoring around behind my back haven't you? Who the fuck is it? Come on: I want to know, you asshole, I want to know.' She grabbed the lapels of his coat pulling his face toward her.

'Come on, Holly; let's go inside,' said McDermott covering her hands with his own. 'You're upset. Let's get some coffee going and – '

'NO!' Her scream reverberated around the surrounding woods, and she sank to the ground in tears before him. 'I want to know,' she wailed. 'I want to know. I love you, Robbie. I want to know.'

She sounded like a spoiled child, and coaxing her up from the cold driveway was every bit as difficult as it might have been with a stubborn five-year-old. He eventually managed it, however, and once inside the cabin, while she was in the bathroom, he put on some coffee and went out to get Connor from the car. He had no idea what to do. He knew only that he was treading on dangerous emotional ground and would have to be cautious. Somehow he had to disabuse her of this 'love' notion, had to let her know the whole thing had to stop. Perhaps if he could somehow buy some time until he could get in touch with Greta . . .

As it transpired, there was no time to buy, for when he reentered the kitchen, Holly was standing by his overcoat studying the concert program she must have taken from his pocket. Two torn ticket stubs lay on the floor. She brandished the program and glared at him from across the table.

'You motherfucker! You took somebody to this fucking concert didn't you? And then what? You went back to her place and fucked her? How many times did you manage, Robbie? Did you have your pills with you? And what about her? As good as me was she? I'll bet – '

'Holly, stop it, and just listen to me a minute. You've – '

'NO!' Another scream rent the air, sending Connor into a barking frenzy. 'You listen to me, you motherfucker. Your ass is mine. I don't know who this cunt is, but I'll find out and God help her when I do.'

McDermott was simultaneously frightened and affronted, and he was struggling to remain calm. 'Holly, what I do and who I – '

'Shut the fuck up, Robbie,' she said, snatching her coat. 'Don't say one more fucking word. I get the picture, but I don't think you do. Just don't say I didn't warn you.' And with those parting words, Holly stormed out of the cabin.

McDermott slumped into a chair at the kitchen table as the sounds of Holly's car burning rubber set Connor barking again. What to do? He now knew one thing for sure: bipolar disorder or not, Holly Freeman did have a serious problem of some kind, and his behavior was almost certainly a contributing factor to her current state of mind. He had a responsibility to do something, but what? He went through the options and came to a decision. He'd been less than honorable with two different women and he had to set things straight with both of them, but first with Holly, because serious mental issues were clearly involved. He picked up the phone and called Greta's emergency number. He swore as he listened to a recording telling him she would respond within the hour. Shit! What was the point of an 'emergency' number if she didn't answer? He left a message asking for a call back as soon as possible, and emphasized the urgency of the call. She'd probably think he was on the edge of suicide, but what the hell: he needed to talk to her, and fast.

As soon as he replaced the receiver, he grabbed the local phone book, found the number of Bridie's diner and dialed. It took at least thirty seconds before the phone was snatched up at the other end

'Bridie's Diner.' It was Tiffany.

'Hi, Tiff, it's Robbie McDermott. Could I have a quick word with Bridie?'

'Aah, let me see if I can get her, Mr. McDermott.' There was a clunk as the phone was laid down, and he tapped the kitchen counter impatiently as he listened to the background babble of voices over the phone.

'Mr. McDermott?' It was Tiffany again.

'Yeah, Tiff.'

'Bridie says she'll call you in a few minutes. We're kinda backed up here right now and – '

'Okay, thanks Tiff, that's fine. Oh, Tiff –' He'd been about to stress the need for speed, but she'd hung up.

He'd done what he could for the moment. He could do nothing now but wait. He poured himself a cup of coffee and took it through to the den. What a clusterfuck, and it was all down to him. He should have acted upon the earliest suspicions he'd had about Holly at their lunch in Traverse and left her the hell alone. He attempted to analyze why he hadn't. Had it been his loneliness, or flattery from her attentions, or both? Had he subconsciously thought there might be some sex in his future with her, or had he simply been trying to be empathetic? And where did his grief fit in? Then there was Bridie: he should have made a clean breast of the whole affair to her when he'd had the chance the previous evening. And Steve: he should have given him the opportunity to speak at the Allegro. Jesus – shoulda, woulda, coulda.

He considered for a moment how the course of events might have been altered had Bridie told him on Thanksgiving night of the rumors she'd heard about Holly. It would be comforting to think he would have been sensible enough to have resisted Holly's early morning seduction of him had that been the case, but the fact was he'd known there was something wrong based upon her behavior, so who was he kidding? He shook his head in amazement at how fast he'd managed to screw up his attempt to re-enter the outside world. A mere couple of weeks ago he'd been a grieving widower attempting to write a book – a bit of a poor bloody specimen maybe, but at least the misery had been his own. How the hell had it all happened? He retraced the events of the previous few weeks and almost laughed at the irony. It had all started with Pastor Dan's efforts to help him, and had gathered steam from there: Dan to Greta, to feeling good, to Westwood, to Bridie's diner, to – The phone rang. Thank God! Greta? Bridie? He snatched up the receiver involuntarily clearing his throat.

'Hello,' he said, feeling the tension in his voice.

'Robbie?' She only said the one word, but the old cockney accent was still evident.

'Jacqui?' His mind was whirling: he was overjoyed to hear her voice, but the sudden collision between the past and the present in the midst of his current troubles, interfered with his ability to speak.

'Cor blimey, who else do you know, talks like this then?' she said.

Despite his situation, McDermott laughed, 'Yeah, you've got a good point there love, not too many cockneys around here. How the hell are you Jacqui?'

'Fit as a butcher's dog, Robbie, fit as a butcher's dog. Tits hanging a bit lower these days, but that's gravity for you. What about you, flower? How are things with you and Jean?'

'Um . . . Jean died, Jacqui. February. Cancer.'

'Oh my God, Robbie. Jesus Christ, what – '

'She was diagnosed last September, died February twenty-eighth. Six months beginning to end.'

'Oh shit, Robbie, I'm so sorry love. 'Course, I only met her the once, but I could tell she was special. And what about you darlin? You coping alright? And why the hell didn't you let me know?'

'Well, I'm a bit of a mess, one way or the other, Jacqui, to be honest. The whole thing was a nightmare. I don't think I personally notified anyone. As far as I can remember, the people at the church kind of took care of everything, and I haven't spoken to anyone in England except you since mam's funeral. And Christ, when was the last time we talked? Two years? Three?'

'Yeah – fucking ridiculous the way you lose touch with people isn't it? Still, what was it Cracker used to say about letters and phone calls? "We don't need to?" I'd like to think that's still true with you and me.'

McDermott laughed and nodded, even though Jacqui couldn't see him. 'Yeah, that's still true, Jacqui, and I can't tell you how bloody great it is to hear your voice right now. But, never mind me, what's going on in with you? You retired yet?'

'Yeah, did that a couple of years ago, but the real news with me is that I'm getting wed again, and that's why I'm calling really. I'd like you to give me away. I know it's a long fucking way and everything, but dad's long gone, and I can't think of anyone better than you to take me down the aisle. There'd be that link with Cracker, you know? I know it's an expensive proposition for you and everything, and if you can't – '

'No, no, Jacqui, no money issue involved, but when are you talking about? You're not thinking about doing one of those snow and fog things like I did are you?'

'Well, I'm hoping not, love, but it's a definite possibility. It's going to be on January eleventh and I know it's not – '

'Holy shit, Jacqui! That's only a month from now.'

'I know, I know. I know it's short notice and I should have called as soon as we decided this thing, but at first, with you being Cracker's bloody alter ego or something, I didn't know if Bill would approve, and then with you, I didn't know if . . . Well, you know, it's been so long and I thought you might think . . . Shit, I don't know, that maybe I was being a bit bloody cheeky or – '

'You silly cow, Jacqui McCracken. Don't you know me better than that? Anyway, you said, "Bill." Somebody I know is he?'

'No, you don't know him, Robbie. He's a retired headmaster. From Ferryhill in County Durham. Nice chap, you'll like him, and I know he'll like you.'

'Well, I'm chuffed to death for you, love. How'd you meet him?'

'Well, I er – Look no fucking laughing, okay?'

'Jacqui, why the hell would I laugh?'

'Because I know you, you bugger. Anyway, I met him through the Guardian Personals on the internet.'

McDermott couldn't help himself; he roared with laughter. 'Through the what?'

'Fuck you, McDermott. I knew you'd bloody laugh. It was the Guardian Personals and listen, they work. I've got a couple of friends done the same thing and they . . . Well, anyway, I found Bill and we're pretty good together. And I'm happy, Robbie, I'm really happy for the first time since Cracker.' McDermott could hear the emotion in her voice. 'So, you going to help me out or what?'

'Jacqui, I am seriously happy as a pig in shit for you, and as long as I can find a flight I will be there. Let me get on the phone with my travel agent and I'll call you back. You at the same number?'

After he'd hung up, McDermott wandered through to his den and looked out over the marsh. Amazing, he thought, how that conversation, that voice had restored some hope to his life, and some perspective to his sorry situation. And the thought of returning to England for a while, even though the country had long since lost its allure, he found strangely exhilarating. He'd have to get on the phone to call his – Shit! The phone! How long had he been talking to Jacqui? Had he missed Greta? Bridie? He moved fast and dialed Greta's number.

'Greta VanDamm,'

'Hi, Greta. It's Robbie McDermott.'

'Oh, hi, Robbie. I just tried calling.'

'Yeah? I'm sorry, I got an unexpected call. But listen, Greta: I've got a big problem and I don't think it can wait until I see you.'

'Robbie, you're not contemplating – '

'No, no, it's not about me. Well, it is, but it isn't. To begin with, I have to ask you whether Holly Kosinsky – or Freeman as she is now – is a patient of yours.'

'Robbie, I'm sorry, I can't – '

'Okay, client confidentiality. Right? I thought that might be the case, so why don't we do this. I'll tell you the problem, and if she is a patient of yours maybe you can help her, and in the meantime, you can give me, as your patient, some advice on what I should do. How's that? That way you don't have to compromise anything.'

VanDamm was a little hesitant. 'Well, okay, Robbie, as long as you understand I can't – '

'Fine, sure.' McDermott went on to relate the whole story as succinctly as he could: told her of the rumours of Holly's condition, his past experience with kids suffering from bipolar disorder, and finally his concern for Holly's current state of mind in light of the morning's events.

There was a brief silence when he'd finished, and then Greta spoke. 'Well, first of all, Robbie, you need to understand that even if Holly were my patient I could not act on your say-so which, in professional terms, is simply hearsay, no matter how grave you feel the situation to be. Holly or a family member needs to contact someone directly before anything can be done to help her. However, let me say this, leave the situation with me. Do not attempt to do anything yourself; I'll see what I can do. And then I think it might be helpful if you and I had a chat, don't you?'

'I was going to ask for that very thing, Greta. I'm kinda . . . Well, yes. I'd like to see you soonest.'

'Okay, you call my office today and make an appointment, but right now I need to go. And Robbie?'

'Yeah?'

'You did the right thing. See you soon.'

As soon as the therapist rang off, McDermott tried Bridie's diner. Tiffany answered again.

'Tiff? It's Robbie McDermott. Is Bridie available yet?'

'Um . . . She's gone home, Mr. McDermott.'

'Gone home? I thought you guys were getting slammed?'

'Well, there was kind of a big problem here, Mr. McDermott – '

'Problem? What kind of problem, Tiff?' But McDermott knew the answer before it came.

'Well, Mrs. Kosinsky came crashing in, and – '

McDermott didn't wait for the rest: he hung up, grabbed his coat and ran from the cabin.

When he arrived at Bridie's house, her Suburban was in the driveway. Parking the Jag behind it, he ran to the front entrance and rang the doorbell. He tried four times before he moved round the side of the house to the back, where he peered into the kitchen window. Bridie was at the table sobbing, her dogs at her feet. Sensing his presence they looked up and growled. McDermott walked to the kitchen door, and finding it unlocked, walked in. Fending off the attentions of the dogs, he sat down opposite Bridie. He was shocked by the sight of her face. The previous evening it had been glowing, vibrant, full of life, and now it was pale, drawn, haggard even, and glistening with tears. When she spoke her tone was dead, flat, a mere imitation of the powerful voice he'd always known.

'So, I'm the "one and only" huh?' she said, her eyes reduced to slits within their reddened sockets.

'Look, Bridie, I'm – '

'You know, it wouldn't have been so bad if you'd told me you just wanted to fuck me, but all that other shit, Robbie – I had you down as better than that.' The slow and lifeless intonation frightened McDermott: it suggested something beyond anger, beyond caring.

'Bridie, you've got to – '

'And it isn't just me is it? How could you be so low as to take advantage of somebody with Holly's problems? You know, Robbie, everybody, and I mean everybody, was devastated by what happened to Jean, and I don't know one single person who hasn't been hurting for you – even though you shut yourself away – but grief is no excuse for what you've done, Robbie. There's no excuse for that.' Bridie shook her head slowly from side to side in a movement that managed to convey both disbelief and loathing.

'Please, Bridie, at least let me try to explain – '

'Oh, I think Holly's already done a pretty good job of that, thanks. And not just to me, but to everybody in the diner this morning. Yep, she explained alright. Pretty blunt and to the point she was: lots of words with just four letters. Even tried to add a little punctuation with a carving knife; would have done too if old George hadn't taken it off her. Never knew the old guy had it in him.' She stopped and blew her nose into a Kleenex, adding the crumpled tissue to the already cluttered table top.

'Bridie, I know it looks bad, but honestly – '

She looked up and smiled sardonically at him. 'Honestly? Did you say, "Honestly?" I know you're a writer and know a lot of words, but I don't think you have a clue about the meaning of that one. Now, why don't you please just leave, Mr. McDermott?'

'Bridie, I – '

'PLEASE   LEAVE   NOW,' she spat out the words in a staccato fashion, her voice suddenly powerful again.

McDermott knew that if there was ever going to be an opportunity to explain, this was not it, and with slumped shoulders, he turned to go. As he opened the door, Bridie delivered a withering final shot: 'Oh, and you know what? Suggestion for you. Why don't you just do all your fucking in Chicago? Whores couldn't give a shit whether you lie to them or not.'

By the time he arrived home, McDermott felt as low as he'd ever felt, but the day was not done with him yet. There was a message for him on the answering machine from Steve Kosinsky.

'Just thought you'd like to know, Mr. Integrity. Holly was admitted to the Stephens Psychiatric Clinic this afternoon. She was in restraints when they took her in. Since you seem to have been "taking care" of her, I thought you'd be interested in knowing what your "care" has accomplished. Oh, and one final thing, what was that word you used? Reprehensible was it?'

McDermott went through to his den and sat facing the marsh. Steve was right. His behavior had been reprehensible and not only toward

Holly, but Bridie too. He reviewed his options before reaching for the phone. First, he made an appointment to see Greta VanDamm the following day, and then spent considerable time planning an itinerary for his UK trip before calling his travel agent in Chicago. Afterwards, as a powerful nor'wester hurled sleet against the windows, McDermott reacquainted himself with the anaesthetizing powers of The Glenrothes. It was the evening of Day 283.

15.

Counteroffensive

When McDermott left Greta VanDamm's office the next afternoon, he reckoned his condition to be analogous to that of a once drowning man, spent and resigned to death, having been pulled from the water by an expert lifeguard. He was by no means fully recovered from his ordeal, but he was still drawing breath and felt, given time, he could regain some measure of self respect. That a therapist had effected this change in his outlook, in his belief, in his resolve, he would once have found extraordinary, but in merely three sessions, Greta had elevated his opinion of therapy from passive acceptance to enthusiastic embrace. She'd listened patiently to his story before serving the same scenario back to him from a different perspective: one that afforded him the latitude to see everything in a different light and perceive the possibility of redemption.

He'd taped the entire session as before, and once back home he listened to it attentively. He believed Greta's analysis of his behavior to be the most important element of their session and it was upon that he concentrated his attention.

'Why don't we begin, Robbie, by analyzing everything in the light of your own situation? Yes, it's true that the two women you feel yourself to have wronged were both vulnerable, but you too, Robbie: are you not in a similar position?'

'Well, yes, I suppose.'

'You suppose. Let's think about that. Would it not be correct to say that you are a lonely, grieving widower in need of human companionship?'

'Yeah, no doubt about that.'

'And is it fair to say that you'd prefer that companionship to include sex?'

'Um . . . I guess. Yeah.'

'You hesitated, Robbie. Why is that do you think?'

'I don't know. It's just that with Jean only having been gone –'

'Robbie, Jean's been gone now for, what? Eight months? And for several months previously you were unable to enjoy that aspect of your relationship. You might be sixty-seven, but you remain a healthy male with a strong libido. It's not only natural for bereaved people to desire sex, there's even a case to be made that promiscuity can, in certain situations, be viewed as a symptom of grief. Now, I don't believe that to be true in your case, but I want you to put your needs and behavior in perspective. I mean, there's even one case in the literature, Robbie, in which a young woman had sex with twenty-seven different men during the first thirteen months following her husband's death. You haven't felt the urge to try anything like that have you, Robbie?'

'Well, no, but Holly – '

'Okay. Well, if you accept there's nothing wrong with your desire for sex, we'll move on to your relationship with that particular lady – who I understand is currently in the care of the Stephens Clinic. Are you aware of that?'

'Yeah, and that's a big part of why – '

'Whoa, let me stop you there, Robbie. One thing at a time. First of all, you said you should have known there was something wrong with Holly's behavior when she hugged you at your lunch in Traverse City. A little too much contact perhaps. Is that right?'

'Yeah.'

'Tell me, Robbie, has that never happened to you before? In other social situations? Other women hugging you a little too tightly? Holding you a bit too closely? Following parties; after celebrations perhaps?'

'Well, I suppose. Yeah.'

'Of course it has. So there was really nothing in that behavior indicative of any illness on her part. Indeed, since as far as you knew, her husband had simply deserted her for another woman, you could say her behavior was perfectly normal, could you not?'

'Well, I guess so.'

'Okay. Now, let's move on to the night of the dinner. Is it reasonable to assume you were maneuvered into that situation? Were you not led to believe, for example, that Holly's children would be present?'

'That's true, yeah.'

'So you did not drive to Holly's house with anything other than dinner on your mind?'

'Absolutely not.'

'Okay, Robbie. Now, think about the candles, the missing children, the fire, the drinks, everything as you described it to me. Does that not strike you as an obvious attempt at creating a seductive atmosphere?'

'Well, sure, but with her language and her blunt offer; I mean, she's been a friend of Jean and me for years. I should have known –'

'What, Robbie? What should you have known? Think about this for a moment. A much younger, attractive woman uses explicit language about a husband who has abandoned her and her two daughters and then offers you sex. That was all there was to know at that point. You're examining everything with the benefit of hindsight. If you stay within the context of that moment, everything about her behavior and your reaction to it was totally logical based upon your knowledge and situation at the time. Deserted woman, angry, attempts to seduce old friend. Old friend, lonely, vulnerable too, and with a healthy sexual appetite, almost succumbs. What's not to understand? Was her language shocking? Sure, you'd never heard it from her before. Was her blunt offer of sex surprising? Of course – coming from someone you'd never previously thought of sexually. But was there anything to indicate any mental instability in any of that? I don't think so. Do you?'

'Well, when you put it like that, I guess not.'

'Remember what I said about perspective, Robbie. The same logic applies to your confrontation with Steve. It all comes down to the information you had at the time. As far as you were concerned, he was a louse and you treated him accordingly.'

'Okay, I guess I can buy that. But, Greta, that business with Holly and Steve's car: that should have told me something surely?'

'Well, I'll grant you that incident did indicate some sort of problem, but it might simply have been a manifestation of rage, frustration, any number of things. Read the newspapers, Robbie. People commit bizarre acts every day but those acts don't necessarily signify mental illness.'

'Okay, okay, but what about her nocturnal visits? Jesus, surely they should have tipped me off there was something not quite right?'

'Robbie, I could be moralistic, put on my church-lady persona and tell you that you should have sent her away, but once again, you have to look at it in perspective and not in hindsight. You didn't know she was suffering from anything but loneliness. A beautiful young woman offered you sex and you, a lonely man with a need, accepted the offer.

'You still look doubtful. Is this not making sense to you?'

'It is, yeah, although I still believe I was naïve, and the fact does remain I'm as guilty of sin as far as my behavior toward Bridie is concerned.'

'Ah yes, Bridie. Well, you lied to her, Robbie, that's a fact. And based upon what you've told me, she's a sensitive lady with her own vulnerabilities, despite her tough exterior. I could make a couple of suggestions, although since I only know Bridie superficially, they will be merely those of a woman rather than a therapist.

'Greta, absolutely anything you can suggest will be helpful, because right now, I see no future there at all.'

'Well, I would suggest a couple of things. First, you might want to lay everything out in a letter to her, but give her a little time before you mail it. You said you're leaving for the UK in a couple of weeks: you might want to mail it just before you leave. Secondly, if the letter gets you nowhere, you might want to suggest she accompany you on your next visit here, or even make a private appointment. Personally I think you may have difficulty there. From what you say, Bridie does not come across as a big believer in therapy. Then again, neither were you, were you, Robbie?'

'That's true. But I think you're right: having her come here would be a tough sell. I like the idea of a letter though: after all, what have I got to lose?'

McDermott stopped the tape and contemplated Bridie's potential reaction to a letter. Was there any hope there? Was it worth a try? Would she read it? Can it? Burn it? Well, what the hell, he'd give it a try. He'd write that night.

It was gone ten o'clock by the time he'd finished a draft he was happy with. He poured himself a glass of wine, sat down before the fire in his den, and read what he'd written.

Dear Bridie,

By the time you read this I shall be four thousand miles away in Northern England which, based upon our last meeting, you may not feel is far enough - and who could blame you? I lied to you and there is no excuse for that, especially when one considers the circumstances. Nevertheless, although I am guilty as charged, I cannot give you up without some sort of attempt to gain a second chance. The only way I can think of to mount such an attempt, is to lay the whole story before you. I hope you will forgive my use of the bullet points, but old habits die hard, and I always found the form best suited to the delineation of facts.

- *I first saw Holly, following her separation from Steve, at lunch in Traverse where I invited her as an old friend in trouble. This occurred after you told me of the break-up.*

- *After lunch, Holly invited me to have dinner with her and the girls on the following Saturday evening. When I arrived, the girls were absent, and after dinner Holly offered herself to me. In all honesty, only Loren's arrival home prevented my acceptance of that offer.*

- *Holly arrived at my cabin in the small hours of the Saturday morning following Thanksgiving. She was high on grass. I intended to sober her up, and send her home, but in fact made love to her — mea culpa.*

- *Holly continued to visit me for sex for the next couple of weeks — including the evening you and I went to the concert. She was at the cabin when I returned from your place, having spent the night in her car waiting for me. She became extremely angry when she discovered I'd been to the concert in Traverse with someone. I did not tell her it was you who accompanied me and have no idea how she found out.*

- *Until you informed me of her rumored illness that night, I had no idea Holly was sick in any way. I did find her behavior bizarre and did question for a moment, her emotional state - and yes, I was guilty of ignoring those concerns in the interests of my own needs.*

- *Following the very special night I spent with you after our trip to Traverse, I intended to tell Holly the affair was over. This I would have done even had you not informed me of her possible disorder, for I believed you and I were at the beginning of something special.*

Those, Bridie, are the bald facts. I'm not proud of my behavior and would do anything to take back the lie I told you. Since I cannot do that I can only ask for your forgiveness and understanding. I've been stupid, naïve, and immature in my dealings with Holly, and disingenuous with you, but do please believe me, Bridie, when I say I'm deeply sorry for the hurt and embarrassment I've caused you. During the hours we spent together I felt for the first time since Jean's death, that there might be a future, and that I'd found in you, someone I could share it with. The destruction of such a dream seems a steep price to pay for mendacity but I fully understand your viewpoint.

Whatever you decide after reading these words, I do want you to know that I'll always respect and admire you as a very special person. I expect to return to Westwood on January 13th when I shall call you. Until then, I shall think of you often and hope for your forgiveness. Do have an enjoyable Christmas with your family and wish everyone all the best from me.

With my deepest apologies,

Robbie

McDermott closed his eyes. Was it too long? Too businesslike? Too rambling? 'With my deepest apologies?' Shouldn't he use 'love' in there somewhere, or would that be too presumptuous? In the end he left it as it was, and raising Connor from a deep sleep, took the dog out for his evening whizz before retiring. Tomorrow he would need to sort out accommodation for Connor while he was in the UK since Bridie was no longer an option. Perhaps he'd ask Rory at the Nugget. The bar's owner had two Bernese mountain dogs, Harley, and Davidson, that Connor had stayed with before.

The next morning, the morning of Day 285, McDermott awoke to six inches of snow, and took Connor for a one hour walk through the white stuff before he breakfasted. Afterwards he spent a reflective hour on the events of the previous couple of weeks, re-read again his letter to Bridie and, realizing there was little he could do for the moment, attempted to focus his attention back upon his writing. After all, wasn't survival the reason he'd started his book in the first place? He began by reading the previous chapter. When he'd finished, he put the manuscript to one side, took off his glasses and closed his eyes. It had been the most difficult chapter to date and he'd chosen one of the most difficult times of his life to write it. Not content to be fucking up his present, he was reliving his screwed-up past. He thought back to his first wife on whom a part of Catherine had been based. If only she'd had a miscarriage, he thought, perhaps they could have salvaged something, but she hadn't. No, she'd gone the abortion route and the whole sorry affair was branded into his memory so clearly he could replay every moment at will as if it had been recorded.

McDermott gazed out at the snow covered marsh and brooded over the irony involved in his first wife opting for an abortion and the inability of Jean to safely conceive. He thought of the son he should have had. (He'd always been convinced it would have been a boy.) How would he have looked? He would have been in his late thirties now. Would he have gone to university? What would he have become? He wondered how the baby had been disposed of and how any doctor could take a living being at that stage of life and kill it.

He shook off the memories of that nightmarish period and forced himself to concentrate on his writing. Was the style uniquely his own? Were the characters alive? Did they have body? Whether it was the tumult in his personal life, or simply a writer's normal moment of doubt, he worried the issue. He'd been re-reading Waugh's 'Brideshead Revisited,' and had been mesmerized again by the masterful prose. He'd hoped to approach Waugh's easy flowing, evocative, style, but judged himself, at that moment, to be more in line with an apprentice writer of children's comics. Feeling the need for some motivation, he determined to go back to the CDs that had inspired him to start this project initially. It was almost two and a half hours later when he listened to Maureen Duffy's voice bring the discs to an end.

'. . . but if you are any sort of an artist then that is your reason for being. It's that line from Hopkins, "What I do is me; for this I came."'

McDermott turned off the machine. Was he any sort of an artist? He thought not. He needed to clear his head, and calling for Connor, he bundled himself up against the frigid air, and went back out with his dog into the snow. The CDs had not only failed to motivate him, they'd had the opposite effect. What the hell had he been thinking? Those people were all accomplished, published authors: of course they could prattle on about 'writing for yourself' and all the rest of it. Bloody easy to be idealistic when your work has been blessed by agents, publishers and critics; a piece of cake to lock yourself away with nothing but blank pages staring at you, when you know the next book tour is just around the corner. . .

It was Jean who kick-started him. It had been a while since he'd seen her, but as he and Connor turned at the end of the driveway on their final lap back to the cabin, he saw her ambling along, hands in the pockets of her full length shearling coat, big faux fur hat pulled down over her ears. He wanted to shout to her, to run and catch her. But he knew it was pointless and so he stood, his tears freezing almost before they fell, as she disappeared around the driveway's bend. And then her voice was inside his head, insistent, urging: 'You can do it, Robbie,' she whispered, 'You can do it.' When he and Connor turned the bend she was gone – as he'd known she would be – but her voice remained, the words the same she'd used throughout his career when doubts had loomed large and problems had seemed insurmountable: 'You can do it, Robbie, you can do it.' And by God, he would. He followed Connor into the cabin.

16.

Desolation

Had I not been beset by marital problems, the arrival of Cracker and Jacqui in Wyvernshire would have been a happy event filled with laughter, parties and idealistic discussions of the direction in which education was headed. As it was, their return acted as the catalyst for a widening of the gulf between Catherine and me, and our eventual separation. I don't know why I'd thought my friends could play any part in resuscitating our moribund marriage. Cracker had, after all, never liked Catherine – largely as a result of her cavalier attitude toward me at college – and both he and Jacqi had been always constant in their belief that Catherine was not right for me. Nevertheless, they did try their damnedest to embrace her. They recognized her depression for what it was, expressed genuine sympathy during her breakdowns, and endeavoured to offer her some measure of friendship.

It was all a little too late. Wherever Catherine's mind was at that time, it was a place that allowed neither light nor hope to enter, and which remained impervious to any intrusion from my friends. Catherine loathed Cracker, regarded Jacqui as common, and spurned their attempts to befriend her. It was also clear she was jealous of the unique bond Cracker and I had shared since birth. Perhaps that jealousy resulted from her low self-esteem, the delusory aspects of her condition, or a simple need to have me to herself; whatever the cause, I saw it as merely another symptom of her sorry state of mind, a state from which I increasingly sought escape.

Cracker and Jacqui had purchased a small bungalow in a new housing development close to Desford, a village only three or four miles from our flat, with an excellent pub, The Flying Halifax, on its outskirts. It was not long before I was spending evening after evening in the pub with the two of them, before repairing to their house for supper prior to returning home. It was an avoidance mechanism; I understood that, as I did its selfish motives and its destructive effects, but even so I compounded my neglectful behavior by also leaving Catherine alone on weekends.

During his second year of teaching, Cracker, who had long pursued his hobby of refereeing football games, had become a linesman at the professional level, and later, in the same year he became a deputy head, he'd been promoted to the Football League List of accredited referees. Soon I was accompanying him on Saturdays to professional football league grounds where I enjoyed complimentary seats in directors' boxes, and access to the players' lounges after the games.

Thus within a few weeks of my reunion with Cracker, the amount of time I was spending with Catherine had diminished to breakfasts, Sundays and the odd late night coupling, employed as a futile attempt to solve our problems. Catherine tried to rein me in, but the more she railed over my absences, the more determined I became to go my own way. I was, in short, the worst kind of husband for someone suffering as she was, and her condition and that of our marriage deteriorated accordingly.

The first indication that Catherine was rapidly disassociating from reality occurred on a Friday evening close to Halloween. I was working with the kids at school on a major dance concert, and for the first time I was featuring an adult dancer. Valerie Lee was a new addition to our infant staff, and as a dance graduate of Wyvern College of Education, she'd already shown a natural talent for making dance an integral part of the infant curriculum. Val and I had hatched the concept of her performing in the concert during a lunch time chat in the staffroom and had received Byron's blessing. On the night in question, I'd been rehearsing Val after school, prior to a party at Byron's house to celebrate the engagement of a member of staff. Our absorption in the work resulted in us having to call our spouses and arrange to meet them at Byron's house. Catherine was upset and initially refused to go without me, but I managed to persuade her, and thought nothing more about it. Until Val and I arrived at the party.

It was Cracker who answered the door. He and Jacqui had been adopted as honorary members of the Wigginford staff very quickly, and their presence at our gatherings had soon become the norm. The look on my friend's face told me immediately something was wrong. He ushered Val inside and closed the door leaving the two of us on the doorstep in the cold October air.

'Sorry, Robbie,' he said, 'but you've got a bit of a problem.'

'Catherine?' I said.

'Afraid so: she's having one of her things, a bad one. She's in a guest bedroom with Byron's wife right now, but I think you're going to have to take her home. I'll drive her car back later on or tomorrow if you like,'

'Thanks, old son,' I said, and followed Cracker into the house where, registering the sympathetic looks from my colleagues, I walked smartly up the stairs. It was a large house but I had no difficulty locating the room Catherine occupied: I could hear her. I'd been listening to her sobs for almost a year and was adept at judging the depth of her heartache from the sounds she made. Cracker was right. This was a bad one. I knocked on the door and Byron's wife, Helen, opened it. She came out on to the landing closing the door behind her.

'A quick word, Robbie. She's worse than I've ever seen her. She's got some bee in her bonnet about you and Val.'

'What? Me and Val? What about me and Val?'

I was speaking too loud, and glancing at the door, Helen held a finger to her lips in a shushing gesture. 'Well, to put it bluntly, Robbie, she's convinced you and Val are having an affair.'

'An affair? Me and Val?' My incredulity sent my voice several decibels higher again. 'Oh my God. Okay, Helen; thanks. I'll get her home.' I entered the bedroom.

Catherine was lying on the bed in her coat in a foetal position, sobs wracking her body, a tissue held to her nose. I knelt down beside her and put a hand to her wet cheek.

'What's wrong, Cath? What is it?' I said.

It was as if I'd placed a hot iron against her face. She sprang up, swung her legs off the bed and glared at me through eyes running with mascara. 'Don't you "Cath" me you slimy sod. You've been getting your leg over with her haven't you?'

'I've been what? What the hell are you talking about?'

'You know damned well what I'm talking about. That Val. All that shit about rehearsing is a bunch of crap isn't it? You've been shagging her haven't you? Come on, Robbie, admit it. You must think I'm bloody stupid.'

There'd been a shift in her perspective I found frightening, and was at a loss to understand. I could also see that she was beyond the point of reason and there was no point in arguing, especially in my boss's house. 'There's nothing to admit, Cath. I've done nothing wrong, but if you want to talk, this isn't the place. Come on, I'll take you home.'

'Home? Home? What, so you can give me a quick shag and make everything better, just like you always do?'

'Come on, Cath,' I said. 'Let's go.'

'Oh, don't you bloody worry, I'm going,' she said, and stalked out of the room.

I tried to catch her on the stairs because I had a terrible foreboding of what was about to occur. I was too late. Shoving people aside, Catherine strode up to Val and slapped her across the face sending her specs flying. The room wasn't simply stilled: it was frozen.

'You keep your bloody hands off my husband, you bitch,' Catherine said, and turned and walked out.

Cracker told me later that my attempts to apologize to Val, her husband, Byron, Helen, and everyone else, while trying to catch up with my wife, would have gone down well in a Woody Allen movie, so hilarious had they appeared to him. Only Cracker, with his zany sense of humour, could have found anything remotely comical in that terrible scene, but even he would have found nothing remotely amusing in the remainder of my evening.

I like to think now that had I more fully understood Catherine's condition, I could have withstood the depression, the mood swings, the emotional blitzkriegs, even the delusions. I'd like to believe too, that such understanding would have guided my language that night when we arrived home, but I doubt it. Such was my frustration, embarrassment and rage that her illness, its cause and all the empathy I'd endeavored to feel for her, evaporated as I rushed to exact retribution. I shouted, screamed and thundered; she replied in kind. I pleaded and attempted to reason; she spewed out more venom. I threatened to leave; she threatened suicide. On and on, round and round we went, until, shortly before dawn, we collapsed exhausted into sleep.

We did not know it, but we wrote the beginning of the last chapter of our relationship that night. I could see no way forward. We'd tried a succession of doctors, psychologists and psychiatrists, and any number of drugs, all to no avail. As for Catherine, I cannot imagine now, nor could I then, the depth of her despair, or her proximity to genuine mental instability – a condition that in retrospect was perhaps indicated by her suggestion the following day, that trying for another baby might help our situation. It was at that point I determined to appeal one more time to the medical community for help and, concealing my horror at the thought of another pregnancy, I proposed we seek psychological counseling prior to such a move. It was the only issue on which we'd agreed for months. I saw our doctor on my own to bring him up to date on our situation and Catherine's status, and he referred us to a staff psychiatrist at Wyvern Royal Infirmary.

It was a miserable, November day when we arrived for our appointment, but despite the absence of sunlight, dust motes were visible in the dry air of the scruffy waiting room. While I was surprised to be called in alone prior to Catherine, I was stunned by the attitude of the psychiatrist. A tired-looking individual with wispy grey hair, he listened to my story of Catherine's battle with post partum depression, consulted our doctor's notes and pronounced that, in his opinion, I should never have married her. He further prescribed electric shock therapy and suggested she give up work immediately.

'But you haven't seen her yet,' I said.

'I will do so if you would like, but I've listened to you and read her notes and I can assure you those are the steps I will recommend.'

'Then you, sir, are an idiot and your licence to practise should be revoked.' I left his office, told Catherine we were leaving, and ushered her down the Infirmary steps to the street. She shared my opinion of the psychiatrist when I related what had transpired in his office, and also my disappointment in our failing to find any help. She didn't raise the idea of a baby during the journey home, but I knew it was merely a matter of time before she would broach the subject again. I also understood that as far as any help for her was concerned, I was on my own. I was equally sure there was no way in hell I was going to impregnate my wife again.

There are moments in any life which can be identified unequivocally as defining moments: moments which, for better or worse, propel one into a course of action that will alter one's life forever. Such a moment occurred for me with a phone call on a blustery morning a few days later, and with it the endgame of my brief marriage began. The Grandmaster maneuvering the pieces was, as one would expect, Cracker, and it was his voice I heard when I picked up the phone in Byron's office.

'This is Robbie McDermott.'

'Robbie, Cracker. Listen, can you put on a good dance lesson this afternoon, say around three?'

'Jesus, Cracker, I don't know. I'd have to ask Byron. I'm supposed to be in the classroom all afternoon. Why?'

'Well, I've got this woman here from some university in the States. She's a big shooter over there in what they call language arts – reading and writing to us. Anyway, she's been here all morning looking at what we're doing and she's pretty adamant she'd like me to go over there next summer, and – '

'Well, that's great,' I said, looking at my watch as the end of lunch time approached. 'That's great, but what the hell does that have to do with me putting on a dance lesson?'

'Patience, Robbie, patience. The thing is, she's on a tour of schools over here looking for outstanding primary school practices, and I asked her where she was going to look at dance-drama. Robbie, she had no idea what I was talking about. I kid you not. Anyway, I got her pretty excited about it, told her about you, and she'd like to see what you're doing. But it's got to be this afternoon. She leaves the county tonight. Can you do it?'

'Give me a couple of minutes. I'll talk to Byron and call you back.'

Having visitors observe our teaching methods was nothing new: Wyvernshire was a magnet for the world educational community. Not surprisingly, Byron was enthusiastic about the visit, moved a few things around and cleared the way for me to have the hall at 3.00p.m. I called Cracker back, and he told me to expect a Miss Kate Patterson from the Institute of Advanced Studies in Education at the University of Bismark in North Dakota.

The dance lesson went well. Kate, as she insisted I call her, was a charming lady of late, middle age who was clearly an expert in her field, and who professed great enthusiasm for my work in dance, an art form she'd not previously seen. Nevertheless, when she expressed her interest in having me teach at her university's summer school, and told me she'd get back with me, I thought nothing of it. I'd lost count of the number of visiting educators who'd made similar promises and never followed up. This time, however, things proved to be different.

Cracker and I received our letters from the Institute on the same day, shortly before the Christmas holidays. We were offered eight-week contracts for the following summer to teach graduate students, all of whom were practicing teachers. The fee amounted to almost a third of my annual salary – plus expenses. I was reading my letter for the third or fourth time in a state of mixed shock and euphoria, when Cracker called. I passed Byron the letter as I took the phone and he left the office.

'Did you get one?' Cracker sounded as exhilarated as I was.

'Yeah, bloody amazing, huh? Listen, are you taking Jacqui?'

'No way, old love: first of all, the airfare would be a big slice out of the fee, and there's another reason. We just found out this morning we're having a baby. In fact I'll be pushing it to be back before it's due.'

'Jesus Christ, that's great, man; congratulations. I didn't know you two had been – '

'Trying? Yeah, been doing that for a few months. But listen, you're not thinking about taking Cath are you?'

'Well, I don't see how I could leave her: I mean – '

'Aw, come on, Robbie. Don't be so bloody daft. You can't – '

The bell for morning school went at that point and I had to cut him off. 'Sorry, Cracker, got to go. Call you lunchtime okay?'

Byron was effusive in his congratulations when he handed my letter back as I left his office. 'Bloody great, Robbie. You deserve it, all the hours you've put in. You'll need a leave of absence, but we'll fix that up. Well done. This'll be good for your career and for the school. Oh, one more thing . . .' He beckoned me back into his office and closed the door. 'What about Cath?'

'How do you mean?' I said.

'Are you thinking of taking her with you?'

'Um . . . Well, to be honest, Byron, I don't think – '

'Well, my advice, Robbie, for what it's worth, is that you should go on your own. I'm no psychologist but you can't go on like you are doing, son. You need a break, and this would be a good way to get one. Has Cracker been invited too?'

'Yeah, he has, but – '

'Is he taking Jacqui?'

'No: they've just found out they're pregnant.'

'Oh, that's wonderful news. Well then, you go with Cracker and get away from the stress for a while. That's my advice.'

Crossing the hall to my classroom, I was in a daze. Jacqui was pregnant, I was going to America, and two close friends had already told me to leave Cath behind. I thought about what Cath's reactions would be to all this. Learning of Jacqui's pregnancy alone would, I knew, knock her sideways; if I told her I was going to America alone to teach dance . . . As I entered my classroom and quietened the kids, I wasn't sure whether the morning had brought good news or bad.

Since our abortive visit to the psychiatrist, Catherine and I had been limping along under the unwritten terms of a kind of truce. I'd spent more time at home, albeit begrudgingly and she, with a similar reticence, had written an apology to Val. It was a cold existence in which the only warmth emanated from the infrequent sex we had. And even that was a source of stress to me. Catherine had not raised the idea of another child since her original suggestion, and I lived in fear that she might take matters into her own hands. She'd been on the pill since her miscarriage, and I surreptitiously checked the numbered wheel of tablets in the medicine cabinet each day, even though I knew it was a simple matter for her to remove the pills and flush them down the toilet. Ours had become a poor excuse for a marriage at the heart of which was mutual distrust. It was a state of affairs that could not continue, and yet her threat of suicide if I should leave her, was omnipresent as I agonized over possible solutions. And now there was the fact of Jacqui's pregnancy and the North Dakota situation – the latter demanding a two month absence and promising yet more recognition for me in dance, an area in which she continued to view me as a fraud.

As Christmas approached, Catherine was heavily engaged in rehearsals for a concert at her school, and I was able to spend a couple of evenings a week with Cracker and Jacqui at the Flying Halifax, without incurring her wrath. It was there, a couple of days after we'd received our letter from the States that the two of them chose to have a serious conversation with me.

'You told Cath about our baby yet, Robbie?' Jacqui said.

'Um . . . No. To be honest, I'm worried what it'll do to her, what with the miscarriage and everything. I just, well . . .'

'What about the States? You mentioned that yet?' Cracker said.

'No, I haven't: you know how she is about all the attention I've had for dance, and I haven't decided yet whether I should have her come.'

'Have you thought about leaving her?' Jacqui said.

Hearing the words, despite (or, perhaps, because of) everything I was going through on the home front, choked me up and it was I all could do to nod my assent.

Jacqui put her hand over mine and squeezed. 'You have nothing to feel bad about, Robbie. You've done everything you can. Fact is, you fucked up but now it's time to move on. It's you or her. You can't go on like this. You're going to have to take a risk on the suicide threat. And frankly that's all I think it is: once she gets the picture, she'll get on with her life.'

I nodded as I looked down glumly into my pint. 'Yeah, you're probably right, Jacqui, it's just that . . . Hell, I don't know.'

Glancing at Cracker who nodded to her, Jacqui cut in. 'Okay. Listen, love, Cracker and I have talked about this: we reckon you're in need of some serious help and we're going to supply it whether you like it or not. Okay?'

I shrugged. I'd take any advice I could get: after all, I'd been searching for solutions for months.

'Right,' said Cracker. 'Let's look at the facts, and no discussion here, Robbie. We're just talking facts. First, is Catherine showing any signs of getting better?'

'Well, she's – '

'Yes, or no, Robbie,' Jacqui said.

'No.'

'Okay,' said Cracker. 'Have you, the doctors, the psychologists and the psychiatrists done everything possible to help her?'

'Yeah, I think so,' I said.

On and on they went, shooting questions at me until they'd established my position: Catherine was mentally sick; I'd done everything possible; I was on my way down emotionally too, and unless something was done, I'd soon be in the same boat. Moreover, Jacqui's pregnancy and the States trip, neither of which I could expect to keep from Catherine for long, would, in all likelihood, make matters worse unless I took preemptive action. It was all logical, but the solution Cracker and Jacqui proposed that night, threw me for a loop. It was Jacqui who laid it out.

'We finish for Christmas in ten days, Robbie, and unless you're thinking about going to any of the school staff parties – which I assume you're not, considering what happened at the last one – we reckon you can keep the baby thing and the States trip away from her at least until next term. In the meantime, as soon as Christmas is over, you tell her you're leaving and filing for divorce. When she does finally learn about the baby and the States they'll be less important: you'll be gone.

'Jesus Christ, Jacqui, I know what you're saying but – '

'Listen a minute, Robbie, let her finish,' said Cracker.

'We figured it out, Robbie,' Jacqui was leaning forward now and covering both of my hands with her own. 'You use the next few days to get organized. Talk to your mam and dad, talk to Byron, let your doctor know, and find a solicitor. Oh, and one more thing: when you leave, you move in with us until you can find somewhere of your own.'

I looked at them both, not sure whether to laugh or cry, but with a profound sense of relief, emanating, I believe, from my conviction that they were right. I had no illusions that what lay ahead was going to be easy. I dreaded the moment I would tell Catherine of my decision, was filled with apprehension over the scene that would follow, and feared most of all for her sanity and what she might do. All of these thoughts crowded my mind as I looked at the expectant faces of my two friends: Cracker who had always been an extended member of my own family, and his wife, who was clearly intent upon adopting me as a member of theirs.

My eyes were full as I choked out my gratitude; I remember that, but the words I used are lost, perhaps as a result of the amount of post-resolution beer consumed. There was, I recall, a good deal of hugging and talk of brighter days ahead, but as I climbed behind the wheel of my frigid mini, the chill I felt was not simply due to the low temperature of the December evening.

17.

Discovery

The practical aspects of my planned marital getaway were easily accomplished. Mam and dad were relieved by my decision, and Byron too was supportive, having observed more closely than most, the debilitating effects of my unhappiness. My doctor, who I shared with Catherine, while not surprised, was as concerned as me at the potential ramifications for my wife's state of mind, and asked me to consider marriage counseling prior to my making the break. I told him things were beyond that stage, but did promise to try to persuade Catherine to see him immediately following our separation. Finding a solicitor was as simple as receiving a recommendation from Byron who had a friend in the profession. The man laid out the relatively new, no-fault divorce law, involving the irretrievable breakdown of the marriage, and suggested the name of someone Catherine might use on her own account.

It was the subterfuge that was so difficult, for while waiting until after Christmas was, I believed, the decent and compassionate thing to do, it required me to live a lie I found excruciating to execute. I watched Catherine's face as we did the Christmas shopping, listened to her chatter about Christmases past, and laughed with her as we dressed the Christmas tree, all with the full knowledge of how I was about to destroy her world. It was ironic that during those two weeks and four days, Catherine appeared as close to normal as I'd seen her since our college days; she seemed to be actually happy. It was a happiness I knew would make my news all the more devastating.

It was two days after Boxing Day when I broke it to her, and the ensuing hours were every bit as harrowing as I'd expected. Shock, rage, and disbelief provided the initial fuel for the conflagration, and they were soon joined by accusation and counter-accusation, threats and counter-threats, hatred and despair. While experience had taught me to expect the direction in which the drama would play out, I was not prepared for the final act that occurred as I was packing my last suitcase. Catherine shuffled into the bedroom, her hair, her face, her very stature, testament to the tumult of what had gone on for almost six hours.

'Please,' she said, 'please don't leave me.' And she knelt down before me, laid her head against my thighs, and wrapped her arms around my legs.

The sight of the woman I'd once pursued so avidly, on her knees in supplication, was too much for me, and as I left the flat, her cries following me out to the car, my own tears fell freely.

I kept my eye on her during the following weeks. I remained concerned over her threats of suicide, and drove by the flat each night to check the lights were burning. I called her school each day too, and although she refused to speak to me I was at least able to confirm she was at work. In the meantime, as the divorce legal work proceeded, I settled in with Cracker and Jacqui. As the weeks passed, the stress and anxiety that had been my companions for so long receded, as did my fears that Catherine would do herself harm. Cracker and I, in regular contact via phone with Kate Patterson, made careful plans for our American visit, and Jacqui took on the rosy bloom of a contented pregnant woman. We made a happy threesome, but I felt it incumbent upon me to allow them space and privacy in which to enjoy their first pregnancy, and moved out to a small bedsit on the fringes of the city shortly before Easter. Evenings in the Flying Halifax remained a staple of our weeks, however, and weekend football trips to watch Cracker referee also afforded welcome relaxation.

The County's Director of Education had granted both Cracker and me the leave of absence we required to fulfill our summer school contracts, and at the end of June, 1969, the two of us left England for the USA. It was not only the first time either of us had left the country, it was the first time either of us had flown, and as the big Boeing 707 lifted off from London, we grinned at each other like a couple of kids on Christmas Eve.

1969 was a tumultuous year for the world in general and for the USA in particular. In January, as Richard Milhouse Nixon became the 37th

President, the American death toll in Vietnam reached 34,000, while May saw the launch of Apollo10, a dress rehearsal for the Apollo 11 flight. War protests involving candlelit vigils and campus sit-ins were happening all over the country. During our brief stay, Cracker and I watched news footage covering Neil Armstrong's walk on the Moon; the murder of actress, Sharon Tate and four friends by the Manson cult; the Ted Kennedy scandal, and the deaths of 248 people when Hurricane Camille slammed into the Mississippi gulf coast. And yet, to Cracker and me, as triumph and tragedy alike unfolded, it was all but a backdrop to our own adventure, such was the level of our intoxication as we absorbed a new culture.

It began with our walk toward the exit of the arrivals hall at Kennedy International airport and the sight of our first real gun. It was in the holster of a cop standing by the doors, and he regarded us suspiciously as we gawked at the weapon and handcuffs on his belt. Exiting the building, the shock of the hot, humid air hit us with the same force as our first sight of a limousine, lots of them in fact, and as we attempted to take in the size of those monsters, somebody called our name.

'Hey, Mac! Wanna cab?'

Each of us had often been called 'Mac' owing to our surnames, but who the hell did we know in New York? The attendant didn't think it funny when we told him of our confusion, but he did whistle us up a cab and with our luggage loaded, we set off for the International Hotel at which we were to spend the night before heading out the next morning to North Dakota.

Cracker and I had stayed in bed and breakfast lodging houses in the past and even the shabby 'Grand Hotel de France' in Annemonde, but none of our experiences in those establishments prepared us for that first American hotel stay. From the size of our room, the presence of its own phone, and the number of table lamps, through to the private bath and shower, television set and fitted carpets, the place reeked to us of luxury at an obscene level. And it didn't stop there. Feeling hungry, we figured out how to call room service, and ordered a hamburger each. Being English, we assumed a tray would be brought up with two hamburgers similar to the slim meat patties known as Wimpy Burgers we were accustomed to in the

UK. When the two trolleys, each bearing a huge, silver covered platter arrived, we informed the uniformed waiters they must have the wrong room, since we'd ordered only hamburgers.

'And that is what we have brought you, sir,' said one of the men as, in unison, the two of them lifted the domed lids from the silver platters to reveal the largest hamburgers we'd ever seen, accompanied by an array of garnishments including lettuce, tomato, onions, pickles, French fries, onion rings, mustard and tomato ketchup. From the limousines to the hotel room, to the food – we'd already discovered within a mere couple of hours, the veracity of that old saw, 'Everything's bigger in America.'

Our inexperience and ignorance of international travel, was further underlined as we prepared for bed and attempted to lock the door of the hotel room. It was Cracker who made the first attempt.

'Fucking lock!' I heard him say as I exited the bathroom.

'What's up?' I said.

'It's this fucking lock: the key won't go in.'

'Let me have look.' I took the key and tried inserting it into the keyhole. He was right.

'I'll call room service; they'll send somebody up,' I said.

Room service politely informed me they didn't do repairs, but if I cared to look in the book of hotel services on the bedside table, I would find a number for 'maintenance' that might be helpful. I called maintenance, and ten minutes later, there was a loud rap at the door. I opened it to be confronted by a tall, gangly man in dark blue overalls, wearing a baseball cap and chewing a wad of gum.

'You guys gotta problem?' he said.

'Yeah,' said Cracker from behind me. 'We can't get the key in the keyhole.'

The man, whose nametag proclaimed him to be 'Gus,' squinted at us quizzically and said, 'Why'd you wanna do that?'

Cracker and I glanced at each other, wondering just how low this man's I.Q. could be, before I said slowly, as if explaining to a small child, 'Well, it's late, we're tired, we want to go to sleep, and so we'd like to lock the door.'

Gus, chewing his gum methodically, tipped the peak of his cap back a little and said, with a kind of tired resignation, 'Come out here.'

Cracker and I edged by him into the corridor without a moment's thought while Gus stepped past us into our room and closed the door. The thought that we'd just been conned by a thief who would now empty our wallets had already sped through our minds when Gus's voice called, 'Try and get in.'

Cracker and I both tried the handle and confirmed the door was locked, before Gus opened up and gestured us back into the room.

'How the hell did you fix it as fast as that?' I said.

'Bloody amazing,' added Cracker.

'Just a minute,' said Gus.

Closing the door and taking up a position to its side like a teacher next to a blackboard, he pushed his cap even further back on his head, pointed at the door handle and said, speaking very slowly, 'You see, this is what you call an automatic locking door. When you close it from the inside, it's automatically locked from the outside.'

'Wow,' I said.

'Clever,' said Cracker.

'Say,' said Gus, 'you guys from England?'

'Yeah,' I said.

'Well, can you tell me something?' Gus said.

'Sure,' Cracker said.

'You guys got electricity over there yet?'

So began our first visit to the United States of America, a visit that proved what Cracker and I both believed: discovery learning is the most effective form of education. As Confucius said, 'I hear and I forget. I see and I remember. I do and I understand.' By 'doing' in America, we came to understand America. For two months we lived in America with Americans. We taught Americans and learned from them. We drank with Americans, laughed with them and absorbed their culture like sponges. We learned about, and shared their pain over, the Vietnam War; we visited Indian reservations and cried over the level of poverty and alcoholism; we were appalled at our ignorance of the Civil Rights Movement and indeed the need for it. In essence the experience was not merely one of teaching – the *raison d'être* of our visit – but of learning.

The summer school itself was the most satisfying educational experience either of us had ever had. Cracker, hired as a guru in the areas of reading and creative writing, thrived amid the adulation he received, and his lecture hall was constantly jammed with teachers thirsty for knowledge from this Englishman whose pedigree had been well documented in the summer school's brochure. At the same time, my dancers began to acquire a reputation for creativity and talent, and it was not long before I had to restrict the number of observers in the gym. It could have been such a monumental triumph for us both, had not Cracker's libido intervened.

My dance group had just completed an end-of-summer-school presentation to the whole student body, and I was exiting the auditorium with the applause ringing in my ears, when Cracker grabbed me and ushered me into an empty classroom. I could tell from the drawn look on his face that something was wrong.

'Jesus, Cracker,' I said, 'you look like you've seen a ghost. What's up?'

'I've got a problem, Robbie: a fucking big one.'

'Why? What's wrong?' I'd never in all our years together seen him look so distraught, and I found it unnerving.

'It's that fucking Doctor Yates: she turned me in,' he said.

'Turned you in? What the hell are you talking about?' Paula Yates, Doctor of Divinity and an ex-nun was the wife of the Institute's dean.

'Well, you know she asked me to go and watch that film 'Midnight Cowboy' with her a couple of weeks ago?'

'Yeah?' I still couldn't see where this was going.

'So she suggested we go for a little drive afterwards, and, well, she shagged the arse off me didn't she.'

'You what? You . . .' I was struggling to take everything in: his infidelity to Jacqui, the stupidity of screwing the dean's wife, the idea that an ex-nun would . . . 'You are joking aren't you? I mean, Jesus Christ, Cracker, how could you do that to Jacqui? She's about to have your baby, man. And the dean's wife? An ex-nun? What the fuck is wrong with you? And what's this "turning in" business?'

'Well, she's only gone and told him, hasn't she,' he said.

'Told him? Told who? You mean – you mean – Paula's told John you shagged her?' I was beginning to grasp the enormity of what was happening here.

'Yeah, she just told him an hour or so ago,'

'But why for God's sake?' I was struggling to make sense of it all.

'That's what I said, and she told me they always share everything with each other and she felt duty bound to tell him what we've been doing.'

'Jesus Christ! Here, wait a minute, what do you mean, "been doing?"' I said. 'Oh shit, Cracker, this wasn't a one-off was it? You've been shagging her for a couple of weeks haven't you?'

Cracker looked sheepish. He nodded and handed me a piece of paper. It was a memo on the dean's letterhead, and the message was brief and to the point. 'Dear Mr. McCracken,' it read, 'I wish to see you regarding a private matter of some importance following the conclusion of school activities this afternoon. I shall expect you in my study at 4.30p.m.' It was signed by John Yates. I looked at my watch and saw that Cracker had fifteen minutes left in which to contemplate his fate.

'Bloody hell, Cracker, you silly prat! What are you going to say?'

'Fucked if I know. Not much I can say really. I mean it was all her idea in the first place, but I can't see him buying that.'

'Jesus Christ, old son, if this gets back to the Director you're going to be in deep shit,' I said.

'Yeah, I've thought about that,' he said, and started for the door. I'd never seen those big, broad shoulders of his slumped before, but as he left the room he appeared to have shrunk in some way.

'Good luck,' I called after him, and went back to our shared suite to await his news. I did not have long to wait before he returned. I looked at him expectantly, but he just raised a hand, the index finger held up requesting silence for a moment, poured himself a healthy measure of Jack Daniels, and downed it in one before sinking down into a chair with a sigh.

'Well? Come on then, what's the deal?' I said.

'Jesus H. Christ,' he said, 'it was like being a kid in the headmaster's study. I had to stand there in front of his desk while he told me how disappointed he was; how I'd betrayed his trust; how I'd let down Kate; oh, and what did I think my wife would have to say about it? And on and on and on. He – '

'Bloody hell, he's not going to let Jacqui know is he?'

'No, thank God. That's what I thought, but it was a rhetorical question. Mind you, I'm going to have to do a little dance around the issues when I get back, because Jacqui's going to want to know how come you'll be coming back and I won't.'

'What? What did he say exactly?'

'Well, basically that. You're golden – I reckon you'll have your invite for next year before you leave – but me? He made it very clear that, quote, despite my outstanding ability in the field of language arts, it will be a cold day in hell before I'm seen on the Institute's campus again, end quote. The good news is he's not taking things any further in terms of Wyvernshire. He just wants me to see out the next two days to complete the contract and piss off home.'

The last two days of the summer school should have been full of laughter and bonhomie as the students, many of whom had concluded their Masters or Doctorate requirements during the school's session, swapped addresses, said their goodbyes and prepared to leave for another year in their own classrooms. As it was, for Cracker and me, the days were somewhat less celebratory. Cracker, unsure as to how many people knew of his transgressions, and not wishing any contact with the dean or his wife, kept to our room, and I found the activities of those days to be a mix of joy and melancholia.

I was proud of what my students had achieved, exhilarated by the congratulations continuously offered by other members of staff, and flattered by the approbation received from Kate Patterson. She was effusive in her praise and spoke of a continuing relationship between me and the Institute. On the other hand, the unspoken condemnation, the vague undercurrent of reproach that accompanied any mention of Cracker's name, saddened me. I felt guilt by association, embarrassment over his behaviour, and disgust and anger for his betrayal of Jacqui.

Kate Patterson said nothing to me about Cracker, and since I knew he'd been such a big hit with his students, I took her silence to indicate she was aware of his misconduct. It was a less than satisfactory conclusion to what had been an extraordinary experience.

The ordinariness of England and my life within its confines hit me upon my return like a cold shower after a hot sauna. While four thousand miles to the west I'd been an educational superstar, back in Wyvernshire I was plain Robbie McDermott, teacher. Other teachers were no longer constantly requesting my advice, I was no longer in receipt of invitations to address this or that group, and my English accent, the object of daily veneration in America, attracted no attention whatsoever. Welcome home, Robbie, I thought, as I wandered amongst the screaming kids during my first playground duty following the beginning of the autumn term.

We'd been home only a week before Cracker was obliged, in the middle of the night, to ferry Jacqui to the hospital where she gave surprisingly rapid birth to an eight and a half pound baby girl, Erica Jane McCracken. As I watched Cracker by the side of Jacqui's bed holding his child as if she were some trophy he'd won, I could not help but wonder at man's capacity for duplicity. Only a few weeks before, the loving husband and father I was observing in that hospital room, had been undressing an ex-nun in the back of a car. I too was no paragon of virtue: I had, as a matter of course, sat at the McCracken table eating dinner and drinking wine, while regaling Jacqui with stories of our American sojourn, and taking great care to portray my friend as a model of moral rectitude throughout our trip. Sadly, my skill in concealing Cracker's extra-marital forays would be one I would be required to hone in the months and years ahead. Since, by this time, I regarded Jacqui as family, it was not a talent from which I derived any satisfaction.

As Cracker's married life followed its natural course after the birth of a baby – at least for a while – the break up of my own marriage continued apace. The six month separation period required to satisfy the law's definition of an irretrievable breakdown of marriage was completed during my stay in America, and in November I received notice of our divorce hearing at Wyvern Crown Court. Cracker accompanied me to the court where within a matter of minutes my marriage of nineteen months was dissolved. Catherine did not attend the proceedings, but we met at the flat a couple of weeks later for the division of our marital possessions.

It was a civil reunion and not as cold as I'd envisioned it might be. Catherine appeared to have accepted the inevitable and was moving on with her life. She'd heard of my trip to the States and grilled me about the summer school: what I'd done, and how the school had reacted to dance. There was still the cynicism there over my ability to teach the subject, however, and as usual she could not resist a sly dig.

'But how did you do it?' she said.

'How do you mean?' I said, knowing full well what she meant since we'd been through the same argument dozens of times before.

'You know what I mean, Robbie: actually teach them to dance? Getting away with it at primary school level is one thing, but wasn't it a lot more difficult with adults?'

'Hey, less of the "getting away with it,"' I said. 'My kids have been attracting all kinds of – '

'Oh, bugger off, Robbie. You can't dance to save your bloody life. How did you hide that from those American teachers?'

'I just did the same thing I do with the kids, Catherine: I taught them the basics, provided the stimuli and, when necessary, demonstrated ways to improve certain movements. I can do that even if I can't perform like you. When are you going to understand teaching and performing are different things?'

She shook her head: she would never understand the difference. Despite that little contretemps, however, we did manage to navigate our way through a difficult meeting that featured moments of both pathos and humour, as we divided up such items as rubbish bins, knives and forks, coffee mugs, washing pegs, coat hangers and all the rest of the cheap, relatively insignificant, household items that are nevertheless a part of a life shared.

When we parted with a brief hug, I was surprised to feel a sexual stirring. Not a normal reaction to bidding a divorced wife goodbye, I thought: especially since during the months following our separation, I'd felt as if I'd emerged from the wreckage of a nasty car crash and, thankful to be unscathed, had determined never to drive again. And yet, there was no denying what I felt as I bade Catherine farewell.

My life at Wigginford was enhanced, prior to the Christmas of 1969, by my promotion to head of department status, thanks to my work in dance. Still, although I had plenty to occupy me at school and Cracker and Jacqui continued to treat me as an adopted family member – despite the addition of Erica Jane – there was a void in my life that was almost tangible. It was Cracker who determined to fill it, although in light of what transpired I could be forgiven for suspecting his motives were not entirely altruistic.

Cracker and I were well aware of the work and sterling reputation of the Newbold Mallory Dramatic Society, having attended a number of their productions and knowing more than a few of their leading lights. I had, in the past, in fact, resisted a few overtures from the Society arising from their knowledge of my college experience. Nevertheless, when Cracker called me one foggy winter's evening at the beginning of 1970, I was ready to get involved. As always he got straight to the point.

'Listen, Robbie, I've just had Tony Barnes on the phone and the NMDS are struggling for some one to produce a one act play to accompany Pinter's 'A Night Out' that Sam Hughes is putting on at Easter. I said I'd give you a call.'

'Why the hell didn't he call me himself?'

'Well, you know, Robbie: he knows we're mates and – '

'Yeah, yeah; so why don't you do it?'

'Don't be bloody daft, Robbie. I don't mind the odd bit of acting, but you're the producer here.'

'Do I get the chance to choose the play?'

'Haven't got a clue. Sounded like it to me. You interested?'

'Yeah, maybe,' I said. 'On a couple of conditions though.'

'Yeah?' He sounded both heartened and surprised.

'Yeah,' I said. 'We do Pinter's 'The Lover' – make it a night with Pinter or something – and you play the male lead.'

'Aw, come on, Robbie, I'm not the leading man type. I'm more your basic spear carrier; you know that. What's this Lover thing about anyway?'

'Trust me, Cracker, you'll love it and it's not that big a part. Do we have a deal or not?'

'I suppose so, you bastard. Let me call Tony, see what he thinks and get back with you.'

'The Lover' by Harold Pinter, is an erotic play full of sexual tension, and I had my doubts as to whether even the relatively liberal board of the NMDS would give the green light to the idea, but they did and I was cleared to go ahead and cast. There are only three characters in the play and once I'd decided who should play the milkman, I was left with the two main parts of Richard and Sarah to fill. In the interests of fair play, I auditioned a half dozen potential Richards, but there was never any doubt in my mind that Cracker should play the part. His good looks and easy stage presence made him a natural. It was in the casting of Sarah that I encountered the most difficulty. I was new to the Society and received significant pressure to cast one of the four or more perennial leading ladies in what was perceived – correctly – as a 'juicy' part. In a controversial move I chose a newcomer in the shape of Faith Williams, a colleague of mine at Wigginford. Although not called for in the script, I also drafted in Val Lee to perform a sensuous dance to simulate an orgasm that the main characters were to have on stage. With the cast complete, rehearsals began and I believed, within a short period of time, that between the play and the cast we had the chemistry to rock the village of Newbold Mallory to its core.

Faith Williams was a revelation. Like Val, a graduate of Wyvern College of Education, she was a statuesque woman with straight, dark hair and a face that, except for the telltale signs of an adolescent struggle with acne would have been that of a Hollywood film star of the Thirties. The edgy tension Faith created with Cracker was evident from the moment rehearsals began. How I failed to realize that the highly charged sexual energy they created was not confined to the stage, I'm at a loss to explain, but it was not until the night of the dress rehearsal that I discovered the truth.

One of the few moments in the play when Faith was not on stage, called for her to change her costume in the wings. The skin-tight outfits I'd called for her to wear permitted no underwear and thus, for a few moments, when everyone backstage knew that one part of the wings was out of bounds, Faith was nude. I'd called a halt to the rehearsal while she was changing to confer with the wardrobe mistress, and it was as I made my way backstage, that I saw Cracker slip into that part of the wings he had no business entering. Would I have snooped had he not left the curtain ajar? The question is moot for leave it ajar he did, and as I passed, I saw the two of them entwined in a passionate embrace. The look on my face must have betrayed my feelings, for as I bumped into Val at the rear of the stage she arched her eyebrows at me. Speechless, I merely gestured over my shoulder and she nodded. She knew, and as I was soon to discover, so did everyone else connected with the production. Only the omnipresent producer had managed to miss it.

Neither Cracker nor Faith had noticed my passing glance as they embraced, and I said nothing until the week's run of the play concluded and I confronted Cracker in the bar of the Flying Halifax.

'What the hell are you playing at, Cracker?' I said.

'Come again?'

'Oh, come on, Cracker, don't be a pillock all your life, take a day off.'

'Robbie, will you please tell me what the fuck you're on about?'

'Faith Williams, Cracker, that's what I'm on about. More accurately, your shagging of the aforesaid lady – who by the way, has been married less than a year. That's what I'm on about.'

Cracker took a long draught of his pint, wiped the foam from his lips, and looked me squarely in the eye. 'And just what does that have to do with you, Robbie? Or am I missing something and you've become my maiden aunt when I wasn't looking?'

'Listen, you silly prat,' I said. 'In the past ten months you've shagged a married ex-nun, disgracing yourself and me in the process, and commenced fucking a young, newly married colleague of mine who, incidentally, I was responsible for introducing you to. And that's leaving aside your betrayal of Jacqui and your daughter: that's what business it is of mine. Any questions?'

Cracker drained his pint, pushed his chair back, and got up to go to the bar. 'You want another?' he said.

We may as well have been discussing the fortunes of Wyvern City football club. 'You don't give a shit, do you?' I said.

'Keep it, Robbie, I'll be back. Another pint or what?'

I nodded and he was gone.

'Now,' he said, when he returned, placing two foaming pints on the table between us, 'what's your point?'

'Since you ask, I've got a few,' I said, 'but for now try this on for size. You are supposed to be creative, right? Possessed of a little imagination? Have you imagined for one solitary minute what happens to your life if all this extra-curricular shit gets out? Your marriage? Your career? Jesus Christ, Cracker, you've already buggered up your chances of returning to North Dakota. Where do you think your career will be over here if it gets out you've been committing adultery with another county employee?'

'Just how is it going to get out, Robbie?' he said.

'Cracker, for fuck's sake, has your brain gone entirely to your balls or what? Don't you understand? Everybody at NMDS knows you're knocking Faith. How secret do you think that is for Christ's sake?'

'Well, that's finished now,' he said. 'That was just a quick fling, so you don't need to worry about that.'

'Oh yeah? And how long before the next one, Cracker? I mean, what about Erica Jane, man? Have you thought about her at all? How you could screw up her life? Jesus Christ, look at what your old man did to Audrey.'

'Don't you even mention that,' said Cracker, his eyes going dark. 'That's totally fucking different.'

'Well, the method might be, but the end result is still a fatherless child isn't it? For God's sake, man, think about it.'

Cracker let out a long sigh and said, 'Yeah, you're right, but Jesus – the thing is, Robbie, I just can't say no when it's offered. I love Jacqui, I really do, and I worship Erica, but bloody hell – I don't know, it's hard, man, that's all.'

'No, I'll tell you what's hard, Cracker,' I said. 'What's hard is going through tears and depression and Christ knows what else before a divorce. What's hard is going home to an empty bedsit every fucking night. What's hard is watching people you love who have everything, getting ready to piss it all away. That's what's hard.'

There was an embarrassed silence. I'd used the word, 'love' for the first time in our relationship – not a word men used with one another at that time – and we both knew it. Cracker studied my face. 'You're right,' he said. 'I need to get a grip and I'll try, Robbie – honest.'

I looked back at him and shook my head slowly. 'I hope so, you randy bugger, I hope so, because I'll tell you what: as close as we've always been, if you hurt Jacqui, I will fucking hurt you – as big and hard as you are.'

Cracker grinned. 'You reckon?'

'I'm serious, man: your wife is one of the best people who ever walked the face of the earth. You hurt her and Erica because you can't keep your cock in your pants, you'll lose me too – and for good this time. Understand?'

'Yeah, yeah, I've got it, and it's your round – just time for one more.'

Whether I'd got through to him, I didn't know, but I knew his promise to try the idea of fidelity was as much as I could expect and for a while, as far as I knew, he stopped playing away from home.

Unknown to Cracker, while he was exhibiting stupidity of the highest order in one way, I was doing the same thing in another. It all began innocuously enough when I discovered I'd left a dance text at what was now Catherine's flat. I called her and arranged to go round and pick the book up.

She was getting ready to go out when I arrived and looked sexy as hell. Sporting a tight, sleeveless blouse and a pair of the new 'hot pants' with knee length boots, she looked the epitome of early 70s English fashion, and despite everything we'd been through, and all the alarm bells jangling in my head, I fell for her all over again. Within a few minutes of my entering the flat, we were back in the marital bed making love with all the hunger of our earliest days. No promises were sought or exacted: there was an unspoken agreement it was simply about sex. It was convenient, it was safe (we thought), and it was good – as it had always been. What was wrong with that? There followed regular meetings at the flat or my bedsit, and who knows for how long it might have continued had it not been for a traumatic event that occurred in the early summer.

When Catherine arrived at my door on that June evening I was in an ebullient mood. I'd received a letter that morning confirming my return to the Institute in North Dakota where I would be lecturing in educational methodology as well as in dance. On the home front, Byron was pushing me to apply for deputy headships, and our school had recently had a personal visit from the Director of Education during which he'd extolled our reputation in education in general and dance in particular. The future, in short, looked rosy – which was more than could be said of Catherine. During the previous weeks she'd appeared young again: her hair had recovered its shine, her eyes their sparkle, and she'd weaned herself off her antidepressants. Now, as she entered my bedsit, her face was grave, as was her news.

'Looks as if I might be pregnant again,' she said in response to my concern.

With those six words she took me back to Byron's office two and a half years earlier and thence to a fast replay of all that had followed.

'But how?' I said. 'I mean – the pill? How could – '

'Don't know – I've never missed one – I know that. But I'm late, which as you know is not like me. I just wonder. . .' She looked at me with hope in her eyes.

'What?' I said, attempting to repress my dread over what she might be about to say.

' I have a doctor's appointment on Monday to find out. Will you come with me? It's just that I'd feel . . .'

The relief I felt on that Monday evening when Catherine emerged from the doctor's office with the news that it had been a false alarm was all encompassing, and we decamped to the Greyhound pub at Botcheston where we celebrated until closing time. Our post marital affair continued for a few weeks after that scare, but despite the supposed 99% protection of the birth control pill, I always used a condom. Our final lovemaking occurred the evening before I returned to Bismark that July.

While I was gone, Catherine met an actor through her work at the Little Theatre in Wyvern, and when I returned she was as content as I'd seen her. I told her I was happy for her and I was. Our relationship following the divorce had been better than it had been prior to it, and yet there was something not quite right about that continuing sexual relationship. I was pleased we were moving on.

If anything, my teaching workshops at the Institute in Bismark that summer were even more successful than the previous year, and once again I returned with plaudits ringing in my ears. I'd missed Cracker's company, of course, though not the notoriety that came with it. He'd spent the summer at a liberal arts college in Connecticut where, if he could be believed, he'd managed to navigate his way through any number of proposals from admiring students, and remain faithful to his wife. His invitation had been especially fortuitous in relieving him of any obligation to explain to Jacqui why he wasn't returning to Bismark.

Jacqui held a welcome home dinner for us on our return, and Cracker and I regaled each other with stories of our summer exploits. Both he and Jacqui were especially interested to learn that I'd had a summer romance with a young teacher in my dance group.

'Cor blimey, Robbie,' said Jacqui. 'That mean you've been getting your leg over with somebody other than Catherine?' They'd both been privy to my post-divorce shenanigans with my ex – wife, and had breathed a collective sigh of relief when they'd learned that particular chapter in my life was over.

'Jesus, Jacqui,' I said, 'let's have a bit of decorum here: you're talking about my private life.'

'Piss off, Robbie,' said Cracker. 'Since when did you have a life private from us? Come on, out with it.'

I relayed my story in enough detail to satisfy their prurient interest while retaining a modicum of privacy. The truth was I really had enjoyed my first relationship since Catherine. Katarina Nowak was an excellent dancer with a gymnast's background from Grand Forks, where she taught in the public school system. We'd hit it off immediately and thanks to an upfront agreement that a summer relationship was all we were interested in, we'd enjoyed two months of great friendship augmented by frequent and athletic sex. Whether letters or phone calls would follow, who knew – I suspected not – but what was important to me was the return of my interest in pursuing members of the opposite sex other than Catherine. I was not alone in my thinking.

'Holy shit, Robbie,' Jacqui said, when I'd finished my story. 'Sounds like you've become a right randy little bastard. We're going to have to find you somebody quick aren't we Cracker? Don't want the poor sod straining his wrist do we?' And, of course, find me someone they did.

Danielle Arnaud was to me, what Jen Topliss had been to Cracker. Born to an aristocratic Frenchman and an English mother who had moved in royal circles, the only knowledge Dani had of the working class came from what she'd read in books. That those books had been read for the most part at the University of Cambridge placed her even further away from me in the scheme of things. If her pedigree and intellectual capability were not enough, she was also the recipient of her mother's good looks. With a height of only five feet three inches before she donned the monstrously high platform-heeled shoes she favoured, she had close-cropped black hair with a widow's peak, a small snub nose and brown eyes I could drown in. A pixie on stilts was how Cracker described her, but to me she was nothing less than a fairy queen, and from the moment I saw her, I desired nothing more than to be her Oberon. Our meeting was craftily engineered by Jacqui and Cracker who contrived to arrange a dinner party when Dani's boyfriend of the moment, the son of an Earl, was out of the country on business.

My friends had come to know Dani and her boyfriend (a pretentious prat, according to Cracker) through Jacqui's volunteer work with a children's charity to which Dani's parents were major financial donors. When, at the conclusion of the dinner party, it was patently obvious that Dani's wine intake precluded her driving, I offered my services as chauffeur and drove her home. Her invitation to a cup of coffee at her sumptuous home on the outskirts of Wyvern, led to more intimate invitations, and by the time I left the following morning I'd become an acolyte of the upper classes and Dani a champion of Britain's oppressed masses.

Dani represented a first for me in a number of ways: she was the first member of the aristocracy I'd ever met; she was the first woman I actually slept with on a first date (an admission treated with hilarity by Jacqui and Cracker); and the first woman outside the world of education with whom I'd formed a relationship since Caroline. Although the recipient each month of a generous allowance from her father who was 'Something in the Foreign Office', she was a hardworking, senior account executive for Malcolm Stanley and Associates, the largest corporate travel planning company in Britain. She spent much of her time selling spectacular and complex vacation tours to corporations wishing to reward their most successful achievers, and I had no doubt her looks, allied to her Mary Quant-inspired wardrobe, were effective secondary assets to her intellect in achieving her success. Of all the gifts in my life bestowed upon me in some way by Cracker, Dani was the jewel in the crown, and my personal life entered a golden age in which I perceived everything through the eyes of someone freshly awakened to the wonder of life.

It was not long after I met Dani that a seismic shift in Cracker's career occurred when Dr. Brynmor Evans, Wyvernshire's charismatic Director of Education, called Cracker into his office in April of 1971, and made him an offer he couldn't refuse. A new, purpose-built primary school was under construction at Barlington in the southwest of the county, and Evans wanted Cracker to take the headship. The Director, who routinely skirted around rules pertaining to job postings and interviews in order to put his own people in place, envisioned the school as the flagship of the county's primary educational system. It was an incredible opportunity for someone of such relatively limited experience, and one which, Cracker confided on the following weekend, he wished to share with me. We were standing at the time on a low ridge overlooking the bulldozed fields on which stood the school's foundations and the beginnings of construction.

'I want you to be my deputy, Robbie,' he said. 'What do you think?'

The thought had already crossed my mind; I could not deny that. It was certainly time for me to make the jump to deputy head, based upon my success to that point. The question was: would becoming Cracker's deputy be the right move, even were I to be successful in the interviewing process?

'Well, it's certainly going to be one hell of a building,' I said. 'But I don't know, Cracker, I don't know.'

'Don't know? Don't know? Don't know what? For God's sake, Robbie, what's to know, as our American cousins say? You and me, running our own school? It's a fucking dream, man. We'll have the best primary school in the country before we're done.'

'Yeah, but think about it,' I said. 'Just because we're close mates and share the same philosophy, doesn't necessarily mean we'd make a good team. I mean: I love Dani to bits, but we're so much alike we'd probably kill each other if we worked together. Think about Jacqui: could she take orders from you or you from her in a workplace situation?'

'Yeah, but that's different, Robbie, it – '

'No it's not and you know it. Somebody has to be the boss and that means giving directions to people. I just think we might be too close for that to work.'

'Well, the interviewing won't happen until after Easter: will you at least think about applying?'

'Oh, I'll think about it. And you think on about those interviews too: you deciding you want someone and getting them are two separate things. Last I heard, interviewing committees comprised half a dozen folk. Has that changed?'

'No, but Jesus Christ, Robbie, think about who they are: a couple of suits from County Hall, a member of the board of governors, some "leader of the community," and probably some old fart from the church. If I can't maneuver them around a bit, I shouldn't have the job for fuck's sake.'

As we left the site and walked back to Cracker's car, I mulled over the possibilities. On the one hand there was the opportunity to be in on the ground floor of a great educational adventure with a significant increase in salary, while on the other there was the issue of Cracker. As talented as he was, I knew the loose cannon side of him better than anyone – with the possible exception of Jacqui – and although the Director was famous for his infallibility in defining quality in people, I had doubts as to whether Cracker was the right choice for such a project. In the end I opted to leave the matter in the hands of the gods and the interviewing committee. I applied, was granted an interview, and turned up at County Hall at the appointed hour on a spring day at the beginning of May.

The entire interview was directed by Cracker who steered me through the hotchpotch of questions, and it came as no surprise when I won the job. Polite conversation over celebratory tea and biscuits ensued with the members of the committee, and as I watched Cracker act the part of the respectable headmaster for the first time, I thought that perhaps I'd been wrong to doubt his suitability for the job.

That night Dani and I, Jacqui and Cracker celebrated my appointment and 'The Coming of Cracker and Robbie,' as Jacqui put it, until the early hours of the morning. Beforehand I called Byron and thanked him for everything he'd done for me, and most important of all, I called mam and dad. I didn't know it at the time, but that call back to Kingstown, despite all the future success I would enjoy, would always remain the proudest moment of my life. My parents had sacrificed much for me, and I'd finally repaid their faith in my abilities.

Despite those special telephone calls, all the congratulations and the celebrations, however, there was a moment of doubt. It came as Dani and I slipped into bed that night.

'You happy with it all?' she said.

'Couldn't be happier,' I replied.

But I wondered, just for a moment: had I done the right thing?

18.

Return

Day 300. Christmas Day: US 31 South, Torch Lake, Elk Lake, Acme, Cherry Capital Airport, Long Term Parking, Check-in, Security . . . McDermott went through the familiar ritual on automatic pilot, devoid of any Christmas spirit. But then, why not? Immediately after dropping Connor off at Rory's the previous evening, he'd begun to feel the world locking him out of its festivities. The perception had grown as he'd passed the lighted windows of rural houses on his way back to the cabin, Connor's hurt expression still with him as he drove the deserted roads. There were no Christmas lights in his house, no trimmings, no tree: no nod to the season at all. Christmas with its strange mixture of pagan and Christian rites had no meaning for him anymore – other than one: it was one more fucking first.

The flight from Traverse to Chicago was uneventful, and once within his terminal at O'Hare, he wandered down the muted concourse to the Admiral's Club. He had three hours before his flight, three hours in which to wallow in his festive funk, and relive the dozens of similar journeys he'd made in happier times. He ordered a Panini from the Club's small kitchen, and found a seat at the bar where the underemployed barman supplied him with a Bloody Mary with unusual alacrity.

Although he'd completed only the first four hours of a journey that would take the majority of a day, he felt exhausted. His fatigue, he judged, was less the result of his sleepless night and the journey from home, than it was the weight of nostalgia he carried, the stone of grief that continued to bow him down, and the self-loathing resulting from his behavior during the previous few weeks. He turned on his barstool and surveyed his fellow Christmas travelers: A few were gazing at talking heads holding forth on TV sets arranged around the lounge; others were engrossed in the previous day's newspapers; and the rest were engaged in laptop computer work, or cell phone chat, or both. What was evident to McDermott was that, with the exception of a young couple laughing on an adjacent couple of barstools, there was little sign of happiness anywhere. Was such communal misery the result of the rigours of modern day travel, or a contributing factor? He recalled the excitement and sense of adventure that had accompanied his initial flights between England and the States: flights made all the more enjoyable by the sparsely populated airplanes, reasonable food on real china, and exemplary in-flight service provided by attentive flight attendants. He sighed, finished his drink, and ordered a Scotch: what the hell, it was Christmas.

He thought about what Bridie might be doing. He imagined her and the entire family gathered round a festooned tree exchanging gifts, a great fire crackling in the hearth, the kids' delighted yells as paper was ripped off more presents, the smells wafting in from the kitchen . . . Had she thought of him at all since she'd sent him packing? She should receive his letter the next day or the day following. How would she react? Would she consign it to the bin or would it, at least, give her pause for thought?

Once his flight was called, the choreography of his journey resumed: the walk to the gate, the smug satisfaction of boarding first, the glass of cheap champagne, the take off, the warm, mixed nuts, the pre-prandial drinks, the third rate food, a couple of glasses of Chateau American, a sleeping pill, oblivion.

The Boeing 767 was off the coast of Lancashire when he awoke, the early morning street lamps defining the shape of the coastline. Spurning the breakfast offerings, he used the bathroom to freshen up, and resumed his seat in time to see the warmth of the twinkling street lights give way to a wintry drizzle over fields that, despite the limited visibility and time of year, still appeared to him to be the essence of green.

There had been a time when the sight of those fields, whether shrouded by rain or not, had filled him with love for England: when he'd looked forward to the chatter of old friends, the first pint, the taste of a 'full English' served up by his mother, the welcoming smell of fish and chips in newspaper from the chippy. Now the friends were mostly gone, beer gave him painful wind, and the fat and cholesterol of fried food – English or otherwise – were strictly off-limits. Still, that wasn't the whole story: at some point in time, England had lost its allure. When had that happened? When exactly had he lost his affinity for the country of his birth and all things English? He could remember precisely the moment he'd realized America had become home. Jean was merging on to the interstate after picking him up from one of his visits to see his parents, and as they'd passed beneath the green and white road signs with their blue and white shields spelling out I-94 and I-96, he'd felt an overwhelming happiness at 'being home.' That was when it had hit him: when he'd understood those once unfamiliar green and white road signs had become his, that driving on the right had become his norm, the dollar not the pound was his currency, the President not the Queen was his head of state, the Stars and Stripes not the Union Jack was his flag. . . Of course, realizing America had become his home and his loss of appetite for England were different issues, the first having occurred so abruptly, whilst the latter . . . just what the hell was it that had soured his taste for England?

He supposed it had begun with the Thatcher years, a period with which he'd had no direct contact, but which he'd observed horrified from afar, as the Iron Lady destroyed the fabric of a society (the existence of which she'd denied), and promoted the fortunes of the few at the expense of the many. He believed her systematic emasculating of the unions had broken his father's heart – what bit he'd had left of it – while on a national level her policies had ushered in a period of resignation on the part of the working classes: resignation to a never-ending loop of poverty and a loss of hope. It was a period he saw as having been responsible for the loss of the nation's soul. Certainly the England he'd known and loved had begun to disappear during those times. That period had been the catalyst for his disaffection, and since then subsequent visits had revealed further erosion of the edifice that had once been the heart of an empire.

As the plane taxied, he stared out at the approaching terminal building and considered the England that awaited him. Road traffic had increased exponentially since his emigration which, allied to a largely antiquated road system, threatened daily gridlock in the larger cities. Now, drivers paid fees to enter London and the concept of charges based on individual road usage had been mooted. No longer was it possible to calculate the length of a journey in time, and families with small children routinely left for holiday destinations in the small hours of the morning to avoid vast traffic-jams. The BBC and the broadsheet newspapers had been dumbed down, while the educational system . . . Well, it was almost impossible to catalogue the damage that had been wrought upon that in the previous twenty years or so: the advent of the national curriculum; the establishment of the Office for Standards in Education (OFSTED), with its interminable inspections and reports; and the publication of 'league tables,' had all accompanied an alarming drop in standards at university entrance level. It broke McDermott's heart to think of the destruction of what had once been the envy of the world. And society as a whole was, naturally, paying the price. He and Jean had observed first-hand the growth of binge drinking by the country's disenfranchised youth; the fouled pavements, and the increase in litter left by louts who knew no better; and the growth of a culture of violence that had more in common with the inner city of Detroit than the England he'd grown up in.

Ironically, one of the most negative aspects of twenty-first century Britain was its unalloyed admiration for, and importation of, the worst America had to offer. The enthusiastic embracing of fast food restaurant chains (and the obesity that came with it), and impersonal box stores along with the shabby architecture that housed them, had bequeathed the country a plasticity totally at odds with the class and style with which England's name had once been synonymous. It was also a fact that the tackiest offerings of American network television were increasingly drawing the largest British audience ratings.

Despite his depressing thoughts, McDermott smiled as he approached the immigration hall and re-read the sign that had incensed him when he'd first seen it: the official notice directing him to a line for 'EU Nationals.' British citizens, it seemed, had been consigned to history. Was that when he'd said his real farewell to the country of his birth: that moment when he'd perceived the loss of Britain's independence?

'Something funny, sir?' The immigration official was clearly intrigued by McDermott's smile.

'No, just remembering when British people had British passports,' said McDermott.

'Aye, well; I can remember when British people were mostly white an' all,' said the officer, handing him back his passport. 'Next!'

The chill engendered by those words stayed with McDermott as he followed the signs for baggage retrieval, and remained with him all the way through customs and to his airport hotel. He'd known, of course he had, that England had acquired a significant immigrant problem since he'd left, and he remembered the shock he'd felt when the British National Party, with its loathsome fascist beliefs, had won two seats to the European Parliament in 2009, but to hear the type of racist comment that could have come from a Klansman in Mississippi uttered by a British immigration officer staggered him.

The Radisson Blu remained the same – right down to its steady rate of slow decline, as evidenced by its lack of sufficient check-in personnel, the scuffed appointments and worn carpets. Fortunately his stay was short, and showing its age or not, the hotel offered the break in his journey he needed, and when he boarded his train for Leicester the next day, he felt reasonably rested.

The previous day's rain had moved off to the east, but the temperature had dipped, and the winter fields were hard-furrowed and frost-rimed, as he watched them slip by his window. Strange, he thought, but from a train, carried as it was by tracks originally laid down over a century before, England must appear largely unchanged from that Larkin had observed in July of 1955, when he wrote the first notes for his Whitsun Weddings. There was none of the late afternoon heat of Larkin's London trip on this journey, but he guessed that the farms, the canals and the houses the poet had written of were probably much the same (other than the intrusion of the odd conservatory). There was, of course, no steam from the engine sweeping past his carriage; his train was moving a good deal faster; and his first class carriage bore little resemblance to that in which Larkin had travelled. Nevertheless, he found comfort in the thought that perhaps, as long as rail travel survived, some of old England would survive with it.

It was shortly before noon when he arrived in Leicester, the city on which he'd based Wyvern in his book, and by the time he'd picked up his rental Jag and negotiated the unfamiliar streets to his hotel, he had only five hours to kill before his dinner with Jacqui. After unpacking, he availed himself of the hotel swimming pool, and during his swim he allowed his mind to play over the next couple of weeks. He was hoping to finish his book, and to that end he'd rented the top floor apartment of 'Stoker Lodge,' part of the Royal Crescent in Whitby. Once a hotel, the place had been home to Bram Stoker during the summer of 1890 when the writer had discovered the name, Dracula, in the town's public library. McDermott was hoping the famous author's talent might in some way rub off on him, but be that as it may, it looked from the photographs and description his travel agent had acquired, as if the location should prove ideal. Apart from the views of the North Sea and the excellent beach washed by the daily tides, a seaside resort in Northern England in January, he knew, would provide the ultimate isolated location in which to write.

Although McDermott was in excellent shape thanks to his strictly observed fitness regimen, it had been a long time since he'd swum, and he was pleasantly exhausted by the time he finished a metric mile and a ten minute cool-down. A long nap following a room service sandwich, served to restore him, and he felt rejuvenated when he left his hotel and made his way to The Gaslight Room where he and Jacqui had arranged to meet.

It was the first time he'd walked the streets of the city in over thirty years, a period during which not only the streets but the people upon them had changed dramatically. Saris, turbans, hijabs and all manner of colorful South Asian fashions swirled around him as he attempted to follow the street signs to his destination. When he'd left Leicester, there'd been a few ghettos providing homes to migrants from India – indeed he'd lived in one of them – but now a visitor from another planet could be forgiven for thinking he'd been put down in Mumbai itself. McDermott thought back to his youth. He'd been born and bred in one of the largest ports in the country, but he'd been eighteen and a college student before he'd seen anyone who was not Caucasian. Now, here he was, fifty years later in a major industrial city in Central England, where white people were apparently in the minority. He looked forward to hearing from Jacqui what the local, white populace thought of these changes, although based upon the comment made by the immigration official in Manchester, he thought he had a good idea.

The restaurant was busy despite the sluggish economy, and as he followed the maître d' on a meandering route to the corner of the L-shaped dining room, he marveled again at the cosmopolitan nature of those around him – until the maitre d' stopped and stepped aside to reveal Jacqui staring up at him from her seat against the wall.

'Now then, darlin,' she said, scrambling to get out from behind the table. 'How the hell are you?'

It was all still there, McDermott thought, succumbing to her enthusiastic hug: the cockney accent, the impressive chest, the irrepressible grin. Perhaps there was a little more of her, and the laugh lines on her face had deepened and been joined by a few extra ridges and furrows, but he could still discern the pretty woman who had first attracted Cracker.

'I'm fine, Jacqui, I'm fine, love,' McDermott said against her cheek. 'And what about you? You look great.'

'Yeah, and you're still full of it, Robbie McDermott, but thanks anyway. Now, let's have a good look at you.' Jacqui pulled back, gripped him by the upper arms and examined him. 'Fucking hell, Robbie,' she said, 'you're Bob Hoskins to a bleeding T.'

'What?' He was confused for a moment and then laughed as he realized the last time he'd seen her at his mother's funeral, he'd still have been wearing his hairpiece. 'Cheeky cow,' he said, and just like that, the intervening years fled and it was as if they were back in the Flying Halifax and Cracker would walk through the door at any moment.

'How you doing really, love?' Jacqui's face took on a concerned look as, once seated, they gazed across the table at one another. 'It was such a shock to hear about Jean.' She reached across and took McDermott's hand. 'You didn't have to do this you know: I could have managed.'

He smiled at her. 'Seems to me I recall someone giving me a lot of help once when she had some big problems of her own,' he said. 'And anyway, to be honest, you couldn't have called at a better time.'

'Oh yeah? Why's that, then?'

'Oh, usual kind of McDermott clusterfuck,' he said. 'I'll fill you in later, but I wanna hear about you first. Tell me about this Daily Mirror guy you've found yourself.'

'It was the Guardian you cheeky bugger,' she said, hurling her napkin at him. 'And that's how you meet people these days. It's all part of the social networking thing and it works: well, most of the time anyway.'

'Most of the time? What? You mean, what's his name, Bill? He isn't the first?'

'Jesus Christ, Robbie, do I look like that much of an old fart? No, Bill isn't the first, and to be honest, I've had some real losers, but seriously, this computer matching thing makes sense when you think about it. It's a helluva lot better than hanging around pubs and clubs hoping somebody'll tap you up. You should try it, I –' She stopped dead. 'Sorry, what I mean is – When you get over –' She was rescued by the arrival of their waiter who waited patiently as they mulled over the menu.

As soon as the waiter had left, McDermott changed the tack of the conversation. 'Well, methodologies aside, tell me about Bill. He must be pretty special to tie you down after, what? Thirty-something years? And what does he think about you having a date with an old mate a couple of weeks before the big day?'

'Oh, shit, he knows all about you and Cracker, Robbie, and he knows me well enough to know he can trust me. Believe me, if he didn't have that much gumption marriage wouldn't be on the agenda. Christ, you know that. So anyway, like I told you, he's one of us: left-leaning, progressive, a headmaster from Ferryhill, County Durham: retired, likes to fly fish, a big reader . . .'

McDermott watched Jacqui's face as she extolled the virtues of the man who after so many years would be replacing Cracker. She'd waited three decades to find someone else he mused, and he'd managed only a few months, before he'd started entertaining thoughts of replacement therapy with Bridie.

'Robbie? Robbie!' Jacqui's calls brought him back to the present.

'Sorry, Jacqui, sorry,' he said. 'I seem to have this habit lately of drifting off. I don't know, I – '

Jacqui took his hand again. 'You don't have to explain, Robbie. I know what you're going through, remember. I'm just gobsmacked you're doing this for me considering – Oh, Jesus, Robbie, what is it?'

McDermott's shoulders convulsed as the tears sprang from his eyes, and he covered his face with his napkin. It all came out then: the details of Jean's illness, the anger, the depression, Holly, Bridie, the whole bloody mess he'd left behind.

'One gigantic fuck-up really, aren't I?' he finished, wiping his eyes.

'Don't be so bloody daft, Robbie. You think you're the only poor sod left on their own who needs some loving from another human being to alleviate the pain? Jesus Christ, a year after Cracker had gone, I was like a bleeding rabbit in springtime. I'd have fucked old George Aloysius if I could have got my hands on him!'

McDermott started laughing at that and as Jacqui joined in, both of them visualizing the picture the idea threw up, the waiter arrived with their order.

'So,' Jacqui said, as they settled in to eat, and she stripped lobster from a gigantic claw, 'this, what's her name? Bridie? You think your letter will do any good?'

'Shit, I don't know. First of all she has to read it and then, well, who knows? What about you? You think I did the right thing?'

'Don't see what else you could have done, love. If the lady wouldn't talk to you, I guess a letter was the only option. Hey, what about if I give her a call? You think the 'one woman to another' thing might work?'

McDermott laughed, 'Not with this lady, Jacqui, no. Best thing, I think, is for me to just wait and see. Anyway, enough about me let's hear more about you.'

As course followed course and drink followed drink, Jacqui filled McDermott in on the intervening years. Erica Jane had been twenty-one the last time he'd seen her at his mother's funeral; now she was the forty-two-year-old mother of eighteen-year-old twin girls, Poppy and Daisy, who were about to go up to Cambridge together. Erica Jane had made a name for herself in the rag trade as a designer (her mother's artistic genes, Jacqui insisted), and her designs were to be found in only the most up-market stores in Britain. As for Jacqui, little had changed in the three years since he'd last spoken to her except for her retirement – which, considering the way education had been going, had not come soon enough for her. She passed on a number of horror stories of nervous breakdowns and even suicides on the part of teachers haunted by the spectre of OFSTED inspections, and the news that everyone they'd known had left the profession. From a personal point of view, despite a number of affairs, she'd never felt the need to remarry until now, and she was enthusiastic over her husband-to-be.

'So where are you living at the moment?' McDermott said as they sipped coffee.

'We're in a big old place by the castle in Kirby Muxloe right now, but it's on the market, and as soon as it's sold we're gonna look for something on the South Coast, maybe Brighton: somewhere where a quick train ride can get us into London.'

McDermott grinned, 'Once a Londoner always a Londoner eh?'

'Well, I wouldn't say that exactly, love: I mean I've been gone most of my bleeding life haven't I? It's just Bill and I both love the theatre and, well, you know.'

'Yeah,' McDermott said, although he really didn't. He was still attempting to come to terms with the cosmopolitan entity of twenty-first century Leicester in comparison to rural America, and the thought of what London might be like was too much for him.

'What about you, Robbie?' Jacqui said. 'You ever think of coming back?'

'No, I don't think so, love: too much of a Yank now, and too much of a country boy. Besides, based on what I've read and seen over the last couple of days, I think I'd be a stranger in England now.'

'Yeah, well, you're probably right about that. What do you think of our new Leicester?'

'Well,' McDermott cast his eyes around the room at the colorful saris, turbans and hijabs that were much in evidence, 'it's certainly changed.'

'Oh, you've no idea, Robbie,' Jacqui said, following the line his eyes had taken. 'In fact this year, Leicester will become the first city in the country where whites will be in the minority. Think about that.'

'Yeah, but – '

Jacqui held up her hand, 'I know what you're going to say – who gives a shit? Black, brown, white, it doesn't matter. Right? And I agree, except the entire culture of the city is changing: there are fireworks almost every week in celebration of one religious festival or another, there's a constant debate about appropriate clothing for school, demands for faith-based schools, and even for halal food in hospitals. But more important than all of that is that this city, over the past ten years, has produced a whole bunch of arseholes who preach the evils of Western culture, hatred against Christians and Jews, and disgust for females who want an education.'

'Jesus Christ,' McDermott said, 'sounds like a recipe for disaster.

'Too bloody right, Robbie, and it won't be long. It's a long way from the Leicester you knew. It seems like there's stuff on the news every night, about forced marriages, 'honour based' violence, kidnappings and abuse of women. If you don't live here it's difficult to imagine how fucking bad it's become.'

'But wasn't there some immigration act or something round about the time we left college that was supposed to stop all this happening?'

'Yeah, sixty-eight, I think that was, but it didn't bleeding work I can tell you that. According to Bill who's studied all this stuff, during the last Labour government, immigrants landed in Britain at the rate of almost one a minute and a hell of a lot of them came to Leicester.'

McDermott shook his head in astonishment. The States was struggling with its own immigration problems, but nothing on this kind of scale. In any event it was time to move on and change the subject. 'Well, enough of the changes in Leicester, let's get back to you. Tell me a bit more about what you've been doing since retirement – other than checking out the eye-candy on your computer, I mean.'

'Fuck you, McDermott; knock that shit off will you? And anyway, you bugger, if this Bridie thing doesn't work out, I bet you'll soon be all over the personals in the Westwood fucking Gazette or whatever.'

McDermott laughed. 'No way, Jacqui, no way. But seriously, what have you been doing with your freedom?'

'Well, you'll be surprised. I started painting again – oils mostly – opened a little gallery in Hinckley, and I've been doing okay. Well enough to pay the rent and put a bit in the bank, anyway. What about you? You got into photography after making your millions didn't you? You still snapping away?'

McDermott told her about the book then. He hadn't been sure whether he should, not knowing how she might take it, but any misgivings he'd had disappeared when he saw the immediate fascination in her eyes.

'That's fucking brilliant, Robbie. Good for you: I always knew you had a book in you. And you're right: Cracker's story needs telling.' She paused for a moment and McDermott saw in her eyes that she was back there living it all. 'Are you – Will you – Have you – Jesus Christ! Listen to me! What I mean to say is: how are you treating it? You telling it exactly like it was or what?'

'Well, mostly like it was. I've embroidered a few things here and there, omitted the odd episode and changed the names of course, but generally, yeah: I'd say it's around eighty-five, ninety percent as it was.'

'Does that mean – Have you – Well, what about his women, Robbie? You got all them in there?'

'Ah jeez, Jacqui,'

'Oh, come on, love, I know all about them you know: including the ex-nun in North Dakota – that was a bit over the top even for Cracker.' She laughed. 'And then the piece from the Dramatic Society. Cracker had more than one 'Come to Jesus' moment with me after he . . . Well, you know. Anyway, I forgave him – just like he knew I would – the randy bastard. Let's face it, I always knew he had a problem keeping it in his trousers even before we got together at college. It was just part of who he was, wasn't it? I sure as hell knew it was no reflection on me. There might have been a few wifely things I wasn't too good at, but shagging was never one of them. I gave him everything he could handle in that department so I know those odd games he played away from home never really threatened our marriage. But tell me, what about – what about – '

'The end?'

'Yeah,' Jacqui looked him directly in the eyes. 'The end.'

'Well, I'm not there yet, but I will be by the time I leave, and right now I'm planning to tell that part exactly as it played out, because that whole thing was a national fucking disgrace. In fact –' McDermott stopped abruptly because something had occurred to him he'd not thought of before.

'What?' What's up, Robbie?'

'The kids, Erica Jane and the girls, do they – '

'Hell, yeah, they know everything, don't worry about that. I brought Erica Jane up to be proud of her father and what he did, and she made the girls understand exactly who their granddad was and what he stood for.'

'Not that this thing's ever likely to be published or anything, but if it was I wouldn't want to hurt the girls.'

'No worries, Robbie. If this book does see the light of day, and knowing you, I believe it will, those girls of mine will be proud as punch. They know who Cracker was, warts and all, so don't give it a thought. But you said you'll finish it before you leave. Where are you gonna write? Not in your hotel, surely?'

'No, I've actually rented a place in Whitby. I'm figuring on spending the next couple of weeks before the wedding up there. I reckon I've got one, maybe two chapters left, and I can't believe there'll be too many distractions in Whitby in January.'

Jacqui laughed. 'Yeah, that's a reasonable assumption.' Her face took on a more serious look. 'I think it's kind of fitting you'll be finishing it on the shores of the North Sea since you and Cracker damned near grew up on it – don't you?'

'Yeah, I guess you're right; I'd not thought about that.' Or had he? Had there been some unconscious desire to finish Cracker's story so close to where it had started? Whatever: it would, he realized, be particularly satisfying to complete the work amid the sounds and smells of the ocean that had always represented such magic to him and Cracker.

'You have any other plans while you're over here?' Jacqui said.

'Well, I thought I'd stop tomorrow on my way out and check out the Flying Halifax and the school. I just thought –'

Jacqui held up both hands, palms out, signaling him to stop. 'Don't even think about it. The old Halifax was boarded up a couple of years ago and you do *not* want to see the school.'

McDermott stared at her. 'The Flying Halifax? Our Flying Halifax? Boarded up? How come?'

'Jesus Christ, Robbie, where have you been? The decline of the English pub's been going on for years. Shit, they're still closing at the rate of fifty a week if the papers are to be believed.'

'Bloody hell, Jacqui, what happened? I know the "Don't Drink and Drive" campaign and the introduction of the breathalyzer hurt, but that happened before I left, and the smoking ban can't have helped, but fifty a week? Holy shit! Why?'

'Long story, Robbie, but mostly greed: on the part of the government hiking the tax on beer every chance they get, and the pub chains who've become more interested in property portfolios and rents than beer sales. Bottom line: pub ownership no longer makes sense for small business men and women.' McDermott's mouth tightened as he digested this latest loss to England's ancient identity. 'But what about the school? Don't tell me that's boarded up?'

'Oh no, it's still functioning, but you won't want to see it. It's around three times the size – most of the additions being "temporary" classrooms standing on what used to be the playing fields – and all the countryside behind the school has long been given over to housing. And as for the philosophy, well, let's just say it's best described as traditional – just like every other school in the country thanks to the national bleeding curriculum and OFSTED.

McDermott was numb. He sat, flashing back over the work they'd all done in those early days: the countless hours of planning, the hard graft put in by the initial staff to ensure the place would be something special, the model of parent-teacher cooperation they'd created, the international reputation they'd had for Christ's sake. How could it all have disappeared? And how would this news impact his writing about one of the most important parts of his and Cracker's lives – writing that still lay before him?

'Robbie? Robbie! Jesus H. Christ, you're doing it again!' Jacqui waved her hands in front of McDermott's face.

'Sorry, love: another senior moment there I guess.' He looked round at the deserted restaurant and the hovering waiters. 'I suppose we oughtta leave and let these folk get to bed, huh? Christ, well into our sixties and still closing places down, Jacqui; Cracker would be proud wouldn't he?'

'No doubt about that,' she said as he pulled the table out to allow her to get to her feet. 'But listen, you are gonna be at the dinner the night before the wedding. Right?'

'Sure, I'll be there.'

'Seven o'clock, Sunnyside Lodge by the castle in Kirby. You can't miss it – it's right where that old farm used to be. Same place we're having the reception. I want you to meet Bill and spend some time with Erica Jane and the girls, and the vicar is going to go over the logistics of the thing – not that that's a big deal.'

The bill paid and apologies for the late exit made, Jacqui and McDermott emerged into a brittle, cold night, and as they walked toward Jacqui's car, McDermott recalled how Jean used to refer to this type of temperature as 'English cold' – the type of damp, bone-chilling cold that no amount of thermal clothing seemed capable of protecting one from.

'Robbie,' Jacqui's voice, apart from their steps, was the only sound on the deserted street and McDermott immediately picked up the anxiety in her tone.

'Yeah?'

'There is one thing about the wedding I haven't told you.'

'Oh yeah? What's that then?'

'Andi's going to be there.'

'Ah,' McDermott stopped walking and then commenced to laugh.

'Fucking hell, McDermott, you're a bugger, you are. Here I was worrying myself to death you might go off half – cocked or something, and you're bloody laughing. You weren't laughing the last time you saw her.'

'That's true. But listen, Jacqui, Andi's a long way behind me now. It was fantastic while it lasted, and maybe the pain at the end was the quid pro quo for the happiness we had. Anyway, the whole thing was my fault wasn't it? And don't forget, if it hadn't have been for what she put in motion I'd never have gone to the States, never have met Jean and never have become a fucking millionaire.'

'Well, there is that, I suppose,' said Jacqui. 'So, you put her in your book, or what?'

'Yes and no,'

'Yes and no? What the hell does that mean?'

'It means you have to read the book to find out,' said McDermott, and walked on laughing as Jacqui ran to catch up.

'You really are a dickhead, McDermott, you know that?' she said, hooking her arm through his.

McDermott replied with more laughter.

He left early the following morning hoping to beat the rush hour. It was a forlorn hope, and as his car crawled the tortuous route that would take him to the A50 and thence to the M1 motorway, he marveled anew at the volume of traffic. Once on the motorway he had time for nothing but concentration on staying alive. After living for so long in a country where eighty miles an hour was regarded as fast, he was petrified by the speed with which traffic bore down upon him, even when in the 'slow' lane. It looked as if a hundred miles an hour was the norm on British motorways now, while he gauged a number of cars to be topping a hundred and twenty as they sped past him. Even when he left the A1M for the A64 he couldn't relax, as aggressive drivers roared up behind to sit on his tail before swinging out to overtake him – often in the most improbable places. He reckoned the six and a half hours it took him to reach his destination to be among the most fraught of his driving life, but as he struggled out of the Jag in front of Stoker Lodge, heard the screeching of the gulls and smelled the raw salt and seaweed in the air, he knew instinctively it had been worth it. Here, was peace; here, was the past; here, he could write; and here, he would finish the story. He carried his bags up to the entrance, his mind already on an opening sentence for the next chapter.

19.

Birth

Enthusiasm invariably trumps apprehension, and as we huddled around Cracker's kitchen table night after night during the spring and early summer of 1971, my misgivings over his suitability for the headship of Barlington gave way to exhilaration, as we planned to give Brynmor Evans the flagship primary school he desired. Our core educational philosophy would revolve around a belief that *how* to learn was more important than *what* and that the child's individual interests were central to the learning paths he or she would follow. Augmenting our child-centred approach would be a focus upon parents that would turn the idea of the old parent teacher organization on its head. We intended to establish the school as the centre of the community, providing parents with the same opportunities for learning and socializing as their children. Further, we adopted as part of our philosophy, the concept that parents should be partners with their children's teachers in the educational process, rather than mere mixers of paints for art lessons, and chaperones on school field trips.

In common with all organizations, schools succeed or fail based upon the calibre of people they employ. That was Cracker's bailiwick, and as I worked out my last term at Wigginford, he spent hours upon hours wading through applications and conducting interviews. Although I helped with the short listing process, in the end it was Cracker who hired the men and women upon whom our success would depend. With one exception, Cracker did an outstanding job. In Linda Stone and Sandra Bruce we acquired two highly regarded graduates in the area of dance, while in Charles Baldwin we found ourselves a charismatic teacher who could play almost any musical instrument and was an excellent orchestral conductor. Valerie Small and Yvonne Lyons in reading and Pauline Green in mathematics joined Linda Stone on the infant staff. In the junior department, Charles and Sandra were joined by John Cromer, a calligrapher, Pam Livingstone a talented choir director, Sheila Reynolds an artist in her own right, Margaret Hornesby, a reading specialist, Patricia Harrison a wizard in stimulating creative writing and Frances Lane, an avid mathematician. In addition to identifying the teachers, Cracker hired an excellent secretary in Marion Rosenthal and a superb cleaning staff headed by Harry Barnes, the school caretaker.

With the exception of Frances Lane, the staff Cracker assembled would, within the course of a few years, be instrumental in establishing our school as a paragon of primary education in England and around the world. From the beginning, however, Frances Lane was our Achilles heel. The level of dissemblance in which she had to have engaged during her interview must have been impressive, for Cracker totally missed those aspects of her character that would blight our lives during our first year of operation. In her late forties with twenty-five years of experience, she was a reactionary. She believed in children sitting in rows, speaking only when spoken to, and had no time for what she disdainfully dismissed as the 'new-fangled' approaches to education. She also made it clear she expected to put in no more time than the five and a half hours per day for which she was contracted. Mrs. Lane clearly functioned on the opposite side of the educational spectrum from that of ourselves and it did not take us long to discover the fact.

We had been open for only a month when Cracker stormed into my office one Friday, slammed the door and started pacing in front of my desk. 'That fucking woman!' he said. 'That stupid, fucking cow!'

'Jesus Christ, Cracker,' I said, 'sit down; you'll have a heart attack. What's up?'

'I've just had Mrs. Jagger in my office.'

'Oh yeah?' Mrs. Jagger was one of our most involved parents and a big booster of what we were trying to do in the school. Her son, Simon was in Frances Lane's class.

'Yeah, seems Simon got home yesterday with wet trousers.'

'Wet trousers?' I said. 'What do you mean wet trousers? How come?'

'Remember old Kenworth?'

Cracker's use of that hated name brought instant comprehension and a level of rage to rival Cracker's own. 'You mean . . . ?'

'That's right, Robbie: seems our Mrs. Lane has the same idea about kids pissing on demand as Kenworth had, and treats those who can't with the same disdain. Simon's been struggling for weeks: in pain during the day, bad dreams at night and finally, yesterday afternoon – '

I was up and almost out of the door before Cracker grabbed me. 'Not now, Robbie, not now. We'll do this by the book. I'm as pissed as you are, but the two of us will meet our Mrs. Lane formally after school in my office. In the meantime you and I need to talk about the way forward.'

Later that afternoon, following an emergency meeting with the Director and an agreement with me to take over Frances's class, Cracker ushered Frances Lane into his office, where I already occupied the visitor's chair by the window. When she was seated he took his seat behind his desk. The grim expression on Cracker's face should have served as a warning to Mrs. Lane to choose her words carefully, but her ability to read mood and body language was, it seemed, on a par with her teaching skills.

'I hope this isn't going to take long, Mr. McCracken: as you know, I – '

'Like to be the first out of the school gates at the end of the day; yes, I'm aware of that, Mrs. Lane. Nevertheless, on this occasion, you'll be here as long as I deem necessary.'

'Well, I don't think – '

'Shut up, Mrs. Lane, and listen. I'm about to speak to you on a very serious matter and thus the presence here of Mr. McDermott.'

'Well! I have never – '

'Will you shut up, woman, and listen!' Cracker's sharp command caused Frances Lane's eyes behind her horn-rimmed glasses to narrow, and her mouth to purse. She was a plain woman with prematurely graying hair swept back in a severe bun, and her very appearance: that stern face atop a square dumpy body, begged the question as to why Cracker had not seen her for what she was during the interviewing process.

'Now,' Cracker said. 'You and I both know that I made a mistake in hiring you. You don't belong here; I personally don't believe you belong in a classroom at all. Be that as it may, I have, until now, been prepared to put up with your lack of commitment, your antiquated teaching methods, and the disdain with which you treat your colleagues. But what I will not tolerate under the roof of this school is your cruelty toward children. I – '

'I beg your pardon?' Francis Lane said. 'Be very careful, Mr. McCracken, you're making a serious accusation. I've never been cruel to – '

'Mrs. Lane,' Cracker said, glaring at the woman across his desk, 'I have been obliged today, to listen to Mrs. Jagger describe Simon's life of hell in your classroom resulting from your Dickensian belief that children should relieve themselves at a time of your choosing rather than their own. Simon's mother also intimated that you enforce this stupid concept through the use of intimidating sarcasm. Now, is that true or is it not?'

'Mr. McCracken, it is, and always has been, my understanding that the correct time for children to visit the lavatory is during playtime breaks and at lunchtime. If children fail to do that, it's part of my responsibility as a teacher to point out the error of their ways. I can, in no way, see – '

Cracker had heard enough. 'Mrs. Lane, as of now, I'm relieving you of your current responsibilities. Commencing Monday of next week, Mr. McDermott will assume your regular teaching duties; you'll be employed as a remedial teacher of reading and mathematics working out of the library. You and I will go over your duties on Monday when – '

Francis Lane was on her feet, her eyes blazing. 'You can't do that! You have no right to – '

'On the contrary, Mrs. Lane,' Cracker said, 'I have every right to reassign you as I see fit. If you will consult your contract, with which I know you are so well acquainted, you'll see that the only agreement between you and the county is that you have a teaching position. What that position entails, and where it is to be conducted, is at the discretion of the county.'

'We'll see what County Hall has to say about this,' Mrs. Lane said as she got up to leave.

'County Hall, in the person of the Director himself, has already spoken,' said Cracker. 'Dr. Evans is aware of the situation and has approved your reassignment. Should you wish to speak with him further, I'm sure he'd be happy to accommodate you, although based upon his reaction to Mrs. Jagger's complaint, I'm not sure I'd recommend you pursue that course of action.'

It was at this point that Francis Lane lost the plot. 'You think you're clever don't you? Coming here with your half baked ideas and fancy "philosophies." The fact is you know nothing. I've almost as many years in the classroom as you have on the face of the Earth. Why, I've forgotten more about teaching than you'll ever know, you jumped up – '

'Thank you, Mrs. Lane; I think you should leave now before you say something you might regret later. Frankly, were I, or even the Director, able to legally dismiss you, you would be fired on the spot. As it is, you may be assured he and I will work diligently to find you an alternative position as quickly as possible: one in which, hopefully, the damage to children might be kept to a minimum. Good day to you.'

Frances Lane stormed out of Cracker's office almost taking the door off its hinges as she slammed it behind her.

That weekend, as Cracker laboured over the details of Frances Lane's new role, Dani and I spent our time reorganizing the classroom that would become mine. When the kids arrived on Monday morning, they found a new, more inviting environment. Desks were arranged in groups not rows, the blackboard was no longer the focal point of the room and the 'teacher's desk' was shunted off to the side. More importantly, I believe – especially to Simon Jagger – the kids were relieved to find a new teacher in charge of their education.

The catchment area for Barlington was both interesting and challenging in that it provided us with pupils from two opposing ends of the social spectrum. On our side of the main road – brand new and still smelling of new paint and wet plaster – was an expanding estate of private homes quickly being snapped up by the families of young professionals: business executives, architects, doctors, dentists and the like. On the opposite side of the road was an old postwar council estate similar in its working class culture to that from which Cracker and I had escaped, and which fed us the children of labourers, factory workers and the unemployed.

Despite the challenges presented by such a diverse community, by the end of our first year, we'd made tremendous progress in our parental agenda. During the school day the sight of parents in classrooms working with kids in reading corners, and with mathematical apparatus, became commonplace, while in the evenings the school fast became a destination for our adult community. Monday evening was the preserve of the Monday Club, a club for women organized by Jacqui. On Tuesday and Wednesday evenings, our school was the destination for those wishing to avail themselves of the Workers Education Association classes: woodworking, pottery, men's and women's keep fit classes, embroidery and so on. Whatever our parents expressed an interest in, we endeavoured to provide.

As I watched Cracker during that first year, I marveled at his development. He'd always had the natural attributes of leadership – albeit with a few weaknesses – but now he was hitting his stride as a leader in the world of education. He was by no means perfect and he would remain the consummate chameleon, but by virtue of his advocacy for children he inspired us all. There was nothing he would not do, no professional risk he would not take, no rule he would not break, to obtain the best for our kids. Other than completely ignoring the concept of staying within the school's budget from the start ('What are they going to do?' he'd say after purchasing some more equipment we couldn't afford, 'Ask for it back?'), Cracker's first real foray into the rule breaking business involved carpeting. As beautiful as our facility was, there were no carpets in the classrooms: an omission of importance to all of us on the staff who believed children needed carpets to stretch out on to read, to sit on in groups around the teacher at story time and so on. The infant teachers saw this as being especially important and Cracker and I agreed. None of us could have dreamed of the lengths to which Cracker was prepared to go to get them.

Paradoxically, the County had provided carpets for Cracker's office and the staffroom and it was this provision that gave him his idea. When he brought up his brainwave at a staff meeting we all laughed and told him he had no chance of pulling it off. We reckoned without his brass balls.

The following day, Harry Barnes and Cracker rolled up the carpet in Cracker's office and carried it down to Val Small's classroom where it became the focus of the reading corner. Immediately afterwards, Cracker got on the phone to Lennie Simpson, our school's purchasing officer at County Hall. Lennie was a good lad of some fifty years, and was a big fan of Cracker's who, through his refereeing connections had managed on numerous occasions to get free tickets for Lennie to watch his beloved Wyvern City.

Cracker replayed the conversation to me over a pint at the Crooked Billet, our local watering hole close to the school, that lunchtime.

'Lennie? Alastair McCracken here,'

'Now then, Alastair, me duck,' said Lennie. 'How's things?'

'Champion, Lennie, champion, but I've got a question for you.'

'What's that then, Alastair?'

'Well, I was over at Stratford Leys Primary yesterday to see Gordon Jones, and he had a carpet in his office.'

'Well, 'course he did,' said Lennie. 'All heads get a carpet; eight by ten, rubber backed – just like yours.'

'But I don't have a carpet, Lennie. That's my question: where the hell is it?'

'You don't have a carpet? What? Are you sure? I could have sworn . . .' Lennie was in total confusion. 'Look, let me call you back, Alastair, okay?'

'Thanks Lennie,' said Cracker.

In the end, although Lennie's records clearly showed the delivery of a carpet for Cracker's office, Cracker's assertion that he'd never received one did the trick, and within a couple of weeks a new carpet arrived which was promptly installed in Yvonne Lyons's classroom.

For the majority of even seasoned con men, such a coup would have been sufficient, but Cracker wasn't finished. The next carpet to disappear from the school's administrative block was that belonging to the staffroom which found a home in Linda Stone's room. Three out of four infant rooms now had a carpet. A few weeks later, when he had a free Saturday from refereeing, Cracker acquired three tickets for Wyvern City's game against Leeds, and invited Lennie Simpson to join us. It was before the game, in a pub close to the ground, that Cracker broached the subject.

'By the way, Lennie: remember that cock-up over my office carpet?'

Lennie, who had a mouthful of Mitchell and Butler's best bitter at that moment, nodded and swallowed. 'Yeah. Never did sort that bugger out, you know. Every bit of paperwork I had said you got it. Why?' His round face suddenly clouded. 'Don't tell me you didn't get the new one.'

'No, no, we got that okay, Lennie: very nice it is too. It's just that I was at Countesthorpe recently having a coffee in the staffroom and I noticed they have a carpet in there, as well as in Brian Hall's office.'

Lennie's face went pale and he seemed to have difficulty closing his mouth. 'No. No,' he said. 'Come on, Alastair, you're not telling me you never got a staffroom carpet either? That's not possible.'

Lennie's bewildered expression, made all the more comical by his combed over hair and mutton chop sideburns, had me struggling to keep a straight face, and I buried my face in my pint glass.

'Straight up Lennie. We can go over to the school after the game if you like and you can see for yourself, but no, we don't have a staffroom carpet; never had one. Right, Robbie?' Cracker was enjoying himself.

I nodded vigorously and choked out a sound indicative of assent.

'Well, I'll be buggered,' said Lennie. 'I've been in supply for thirty years and I've never known one carpet go missing never mind two. Leave it with me, Alastair and I'll get on to it first thing Monday.'

'Thanks, Lennie,' said Cracker, slapping the purchasing man on the back. 'Knew I could count on you.'

It was around six weeks later, following a number of phone calls between Lennie and Alastair concerning paperwork mysteriously missing from our files, that Pauline Green's classroom received its carpet.

While the acquisition of carpets for our infant department resulted from a carefully planned campaign, the transformation of the octagonal assembly hall into a professionally lit drama studio at the beginning of our second year was occasioned by an act of sheer vandalism. The whole thing started innocently enough. Cracker and I were enjoying a coffee and a cig in his office one day, when our conversation turned to our state of the art facilities and what, if anything, we might have done differently had we been in on the planning.

'I'll tell you one thing I'd have done,' I said, exhaling smoke.

'What's that?' said Cracker.

'I'd have nixed that chandelier, as beautiful as it is, and put in a lighting system for dance and drama that would help stimulate creativity.' The chandelier to which I was referring was a magnificent lighting fixture that was a piece of artwork in itself. Featuring fifty plus lamps in concentric circles, it hung from the apex of the vaulted hall ceiling and lit the entire room.

'Well, why don't we do it?' said Cracker. 'Get together with Linda and Sandra, come up with a concept, and then we'll have a go at Lennie – see what he can do.'

Within a few weeks, after speaking with a couple of lighting specialists at the Little Theatre in Wyvern, we had a plan, and Cracker designated me to handle the project through Lennie Simpson. As I finished outlining our concept over the phone I could almost see the purchasing man shaking his head.

'Sorry, Robbie, there's no way. The Director will never go for it. That chandelier cost thousands and it was a big deal to him: specially imported – part of his beauty in schools thing.'

'But, Lennie, couldn't some other school use it?'

'Not the point, Robbie, me duck. Barlington is Dr. Evans's big show school, you know that. No, there's only one way that chandelier's ever going away.'

'How's that, Lennie?' I said.

'Well, like I said, it was imported: from Sweden I think. Anyway those cut-glass lampshades are a one-off: can't get replacements. Daft bloody purchasing decision if you ask me, but the point is, if any of them were to get smashed we've no way of replacing them, and the whole fixture would look like hell. *Then* it would be replaced: Dr. Evans does not like anything ugly.'

'Okay, thanks anyway, Lennie,' I said, and hung up

By this point in our relationship I really believed that Cracker was incapable of surprising me. I was wrong: his solution to our lighting dilemma made even my jaw drop.

'Well, that makes it easy then,' he said, when I related my conversation with Lennie.

'Easy? How do you mean, easy? We're fucked: nothing we can do,' I said.

"Course there is,' said Cracker. 'We'll just wreck it.'

'Wreck it? We can't do that: it's worth bloody thousands.'

'Well, it's not our fault is it?' Cracker said. 'We've tried. I mean, I'm all for beauty and all that, but kids come first and that chandelier's in the way of us giving them the best kind of creative environment. Isn't that what you said?'

'Well, yeah, but Jesus Christ, Cracker. A cut glass chandelier?'

'Look, it's simple, old son. John Cromer has his guys in men's keep fit on Tuesdays play five-a-side football. Right?'

'Yeah, so?'

'Well, just tell him to drop the "ball below shoulder level" rule. Wouldn't surprise me if there's some wrecked lampshades by next Wednesday'

As always, things turned out as Cracker foretold, and within a couple of months the chandelier, resembling nothing more than a giant mouthful of broken teeth, was removed from the school and replaced with the theatre lighting we'd planned for.

As we moved on into our second year, the future looked bright. The school was a thriving community for a full twelve hours a day, and our reputation for educational innovation was already well established. Like Wigginford and Battling Creek, we were drawing visitors from around the country and the world, and Dr. Evans was constantly inviting Cracker to County Hall to introduce him to visiting dignitaries. Frances Lane was history, having been banished to a village school on the far side of the County, and we'd found an excellent replacement in Maureen Husthwaite, a young but expert teacher in new mathematical approaches. Maureen replaced me in the classroom and I resumed my office position.

Drawing from a catchment area so split in socio-economic terms, it was inevitable we should experience both educational highs and lows, but thanks to Cracker's indomitable belief that children should come first, the former far exceeded the latter. Even today, almost half a century later, many of our triumphs remain with me: Allan Drummond, the ten-year-old incorrigible thief, who Cracker persuaded to join my dance group, and who went on to star in West Side Story at the high school, and later became a success in the West End; Diane Temple, the skinny asthmatic, who seized upon dance after a lifetime of being denied physical exercise, grew into an athlete and went on to the Royal Ballet School; Sammy Chapman, the stutterer who the County speech therapist pronounced beyond help, who played the lead in numerous school plays thanks to Cracker's personal investment of time, energy, and belief. . . .

The failures we suffered will be familiar to anyone who has taught: the kids who never conquered their inability to decode the mysteries of the written word; those who remained baffled by mathematical concepts; and most of all, those who, through circumstance of birth, found themselves attempting to overcome overwhelming odds in order to merely survive. One of our greatest failures in the latter regard was that of Michael Singleton. His story is worth recounting in order to illustrate Cracker's indefatigable efforts on behalf of challenged children, and the ineptitude of the bureaucratic agencies charged with caring for them – both of which would eventually play a pivotal role in Cracker's demise.

Michael Singleton was a wretched boy: all knees and elbows, he shuffled to school each day in ill-fitting, hand-me-down clothes reeking of urine, and if that were not enough, he was cursed with immense jug ears and a cleft palate. The fifth son of a poverty stricken family on the council estate, he lived with his mother, an obese woman who drank and smoked her way through the family's national assistance money. Michael's father and four brothers were all serving jail time for an assortment of crimes including, in the case of his father, murder. Michael, in short, was one of those unfortunate kids born with nothing but obstacles, almost all of which would prove to be insurmountable.

Cracker went to extraordinary lengths to help Michael. It was not easy: the boy's inability to speak properly, allied to his smell and unkempt appearance, made him the butt of jokes that would invariably ignite his ferocious temper which in turn lent him incredible strength. (It was a strength he demonstrated vividly when he once threatened Cracker on the school playing field with the eight foot stanchion of a goalpost that he whirled around his head.) Later, at the beginning of his final year with us, he flipped over Cracker's desk when the County psychologist annoyed him, and was in the process of attempting to crush the poor man between the desk and the wall, when the psychologist's cries brought Cracker to his rescue.

Cracker's attempts to help Michael went the whole gamut: speech therapy; remedial English and mathematics tutors; psychiatric counseling; anything at all he could cajole from the County, Cracker found for him. He worked with John Cromer, Michael's teacher, to give him the kinds of responsibilities that all the kids yearned for: milk monitor, blackboard monitor, book monitor – whatever he could dream up. He even created a special position, in which Michael became responsible for assisting Harry Barnes with feeding the birds in the school aviary. Cracker's goal was to develop a relationship that would demonstrate to Michael and his peers that not only was he capable of performing the same tasks as other kids, but that he was trusted. Until the traumatic day when Michael did his runner, Cracker thought he had him.

Cracker and I were in his office shortly after lunch when it happened. Mrs. Braithwaite, one of our lunchtime supervisors, burst through the door with the story. Michael was chasing a younger boy round the playground with the expressed intent of 'killing' him. Michael had been climbing up the ladder to the school's tree house behind Sam Nunns, a second year boy, when Sam's foot had slipped and hit Michael in the mouth. The pain had lit the fuse of Michael's temper. The playground was at a standstill – an eerie experience in itself – when we charged out of the school doors. Every child was transfixed by the chase going on around them as the petrified Sam ran for his life.

'Michael!' Cracker shouted. His call did not merit so much as a glance from the boy and so we were obliged to give chase. We gained on him quickly, and when he saw his position was hopeless, he committed the cardinal sin of leaving the school property, and haring off along the street toward the main road. Fearing for his safety from the traffic, but fully cognizant of the fact we couldn't simply let him go, we increased our speed and finally caught him. Wide eyed and breathing heavily with green mucous bubbling from his nose, Michael at that moment resembled nothing more than a cornered wild animal. It was a painful journey back to the school, not only physically – Michael repeatedly kicked our shins as we stumbled along – but emotionally, for it had become clear in just a few minutes that Cracker was nothing more to the boy than any other adult. All the effort, the understanding, the special help he'd put in, had been for naught.

After managing to maneuver Michael into Cracker's office, we laid him on the floor, Cracker holding his arms, and me his legs. At that point we looked across the length of Michael's contorting body trying to decide what the hell we were going to do. School was back in session by this time and Mrs. Braithwaite, hovering by the office door, was the only help available. The raw strength of Michael's writhing as he sought to free himself was extraordinary, and no amount of gentle coaxing from the two of us had any effect.

'You getting tired, Robbie?' Cracker said.

'You could say that, yeah,'

'Same here. Mrs. Braithwaite?' Cracker said over his shoulder to the increasingly distraught woman.

'Yes, Mr. McCracken?'

'Would you please go to the gym store as fast as possible and bring me a couple of skipping ropes?'

Mrs. Braithwaite's eyes widened. 'Are you sure? I mean – '

'Just do it, please Mrs. Braithwaite, and quickly.'

'Yes, sir.' The woman scurried off while Cracker eyed me from above Michael's twisting body. His face was reddening with the effort of holding Michael down and sweat was dripping from me.

'You got any problems with skipping ropes, Robbie?' he said.

'Don't see any alternative,'

When Mrs. Braithwaite returned with the ropes, we managed to bind Michael at his hands and feet and deposit him in an easy chair in the staffroom. I made him a cup of hot, sweet tea, and while Cracker held the cup as the boy sipped, I patiently explained to Michael that once he felt okay again, we'd release him and he could return to his classroom.

John Cromer was more than a little surprised an hour later to find Cracker entering his classroom with a peaceful Michael in tow, and so, judging from their expressions, were Michael's classmates. As Michael took his seat as if nothing had happened – normal after one of his outbursts – John walked with Cracker to the door and muttered in his ear.

'Are you sure about this, Cracker? I mean, is it safe?'

'Absolutely,' Cracker said. 'Otherwise I wouldn't have brought him back. Don't worry, once his rage passes, he's fine.'

Except this time he wasn't – although not through any fault of his own. Mrs. Braithwaite, distressed over what she perceived as the danger Michael posed to other pupils, and our subsequent restraining of the boy, reported the incident to somebody at County Hall that very afternoon. The following day, the County psychologist, accompanied by a couple of the Director's senior advisors, turned up on our doorstep, and following a long session in Cracker's office, Michael was taken from his classroom and led out of the school for the last time. He was to be dispatched to a 'special' school deemed 'more suitable to his needs.'

Cracker was enraged: not only over the usurping of his authority, but at the realization that for all of the County's vaunted progressiveness, it was still in the business of isolating underprivileged and difficult children from their peers. He did try to get the order rescinded of course, but the Director, for once, was intractable.

That evening in the Flying Halifax, I asked Cracker about the thing that had worried us. 'What did the trick-cyclist say about the skipping ropes?'

Cracker took a mouthful of beer from his pint before replying. 'He said we did the right thing to restrain him, or he may well have injured himself. He did give me a little advice though, should a similar situation occur in the future.'

'Oh, yeah? What was that?' I said

'Next time, use towels: they're not as emotive as ropes.'

Three years later, Michael was committed to Her Majesty's Borstal at Ellsworth in Buckinghamshire after grievously wounding a teacher with a pair of scissors. The 'special' school it turned out was not as suited to meeting his needs as had been thought. It was the last we heard of him.

20.

Hope

New Year's Eve. McDermott laid down his pen and wandered over to the bay window looking out over the promenade and beach to the North Sea. He found the view as stimulating as it was spectacular, reviving a plethora of seaside memories. Today, the sea, as if to emphasize its notorious perversity, lay calm and blue, as much at odds with the time of year as the cloudless sky above it. He'd been fortunate in finding the location which, although a touch spartan in its appointments, afforded him the perfect space in which to write. Comprising one bedroom and bathroom, a large kitchen, and the living room that he'd converted into his study, the apartment provided everything he required, and was within easy walking distance of Whitby's pubs and shops. He'd made The White Horse and Dragon in the town center his home away from home for his evening meals, and he'd found the easy camaraderie of the proprietor, Jack Smallings, and his staff, a welcome antidote to the isolation of his days.

Turning from the window he picked up the pages he'd written that day, and read them through as he paced round the room. He'd found recounting the creation of the school difficult in light of what Jacqui had told him of its current condition, but it had to be done and he thought he'd managed it without falling prey to the rose-tinted lenses of nostalgia. Although he'd planned one lengthy, final chapter, it felt to him as if the pathos of Michael's story called for a natural break before he moved on to the story's denouement – the subject matter of which he felt to be of sufficient import to demand its own defined space. It occurred to him that he was going to complete his manuscript well before his deadline of January 10th when he had to return to Leicester for Jacqui's wedding. He stared out at the fine weather beyond the windows of the high-ceilinged, Victorian room, and for the first time, seriously entertained the notion that had lurked in his mind from the moment he'd booked his flight in the States. Hitherto he'd dismissed the idea as being too emotionally taxing for his fragile psyche, but the unseasonably fine weather and the sea air, together with the satisfaction he'd drawn from his writing, had given manna to his spirit and he thought that perhaps . . .

It was later that night, as he observed the clientele of the White Horse celebrate the advent of the New Year that he finally made the decision and resolved that he would indeed visit Hull, the city of his birth – the city on which he'd based Kingstown in his novel. Within the boundaries of that city, lay all the clues to what he'd become. Using the Inn's private phone, while struggling to make himself heard over the celebrations around him, he was able to book a room for the following two nights at the Mercure Hull Royal Hotel. Armed with its address for the Jag's navigational system, he thanked Jack Smallings for the use of the phone and returned to his flat determined to make an early start the following day.

He'd drunk little during his sojourn in Whitby, including that evening, and it was early the following morning when he set off on the sixty mile journey south. It was the first time he'd driven the car since he'd arrived at Stoker Lodge and because it was the New Year's Day holiday – with little traffic around to provide visual clues – he was obliged to concentrate hard on electing the correct side of the road on which to drive. The journey proved uneventful, however, and by noon he'd checked in to his hotel and unpacked.

During a light lunch in the dining room, surrounded by a number of patrons who bore all the signs of having partied too long and hard the previous night, he scribbled an itinerary for the next day and a half. He thought it sensible to begin with a walk around the City centre, since he was already effectively there, and one hour later, well buttoned up against the wind off the Humber, he left the hotel through its rear door and entered Paragon Station – and an alien world.

The old train and bus stations had been combined and now rejoiced under the title of Hull Paragon Interchange. Although he could recognize some of the original elements of the train station, the bus station, with its columns and brick archways bore no relation to the place where he'd waited for buses as a child. The Regal cinema, once the Saturday morning home of ABC Minors, and the Saturday evening meeting place for courting couples, was gone. In its stead he found a new glass and steel monstrosity of a shopping mall going under the name of St. Stephen's Centre, 'Hull's Premier Shopping Experience.' He wandered around in a daze attempting to place exactly where the Regal had been, but gave up and decided to head for the familiar territory of Whitefriargate, the old shopping centre, and the pier. Only there was no familiar territory. Gone was the famous quay at the head of Whitefriargate where huge ships, their bows almost intruding into the city centre had awed him as a boy: in its place was yet another shopping mall (which some developer had had the gall to call 'Princess Quay') rearing up on stilts above the water. Whitefriargate itself was also unrecognizable. Clearly a victim of the mall developments on its doorstep, the famous old shopping venue was now lined with boarded windows bearing 'For Sale' and 'For Rent' signs, with the few shops still functioning, plastered with 'Going Out of Business' messages. Now almost deserted, the street he'd once run down to spend his weekly pocket-money at Woolworths resembled nothing more than a target for demolition.

He did find remnants of the Hull he'd known: The Land of Green Ginger pub, once infamous for refusing to serve women; Holy Trinity church, the destination of Remembrance Day parades when he'd been a Sea Scout; the famous Victorian 'Public Convenience' on the pier. On the whole though, little remained of the city he'd once called home. It was an observation underlined on the way back to his hotel, by the sight of the unfamiliar burgundy and beige livery of the East Yorkshire buses, and the absence of the traditional blue and white Hull Corporation buses apparently supplanted by 'Stagecoach Hull' vehicles.

McDermott was subdued as he dined in the hotel's formal dining room that evening. Such had been the disappointment, and even sorrow, engendered by his afternoon's peregrinations; he had decided to forego his planned visits to old haunts on the following day. He already felt as if part of his childhood had been taken away and feared that if he continued along the itinerary he'd planned, he may lose the remainder. There was, however, one visit he did have to make and he would take care of that the following morning.

He awoke the next day to a fine drizzle – the last thing he wanted to see, considering his destination – but armed with detailed directions from the hotel concierge, he set out as planned, and gingerly maneuvered the Jag through the city's narrow streets toward the city's western suburbs.

Malcolm McDonald

It came as no surprise to McDermott that Mill Lane Cemetery, Kirkella, exhibited little change – cemeteries not being generally noted as targets for modernization. He made his way down the central path to the southeast corner of the small wooded graveyard. The ground was wet from the morning rain and the grass growing above the dead had the unkempt tussocky look that grass acquires in winter. A few graves were headed by fresh flowers, but the majority, many of which represented the final resting places of people gone for over a hundred years, were marked merely by dark, algae-covered headstones.

The ashes of Ian and Annie McDermott were interred side by side beneath the open pages of a book fashioned from black marble, the opposing pages bearing their names and the measured lengths of their lives in faded gold script. He sat on a wooden bench and stared fixedly at the small monument to the two people who had been giants in his life. He should have brought some flowers, he thought, taking in the empty urn: they'd have liked that. Then again, even had the thought occurred, he knew he'd have done no such a thing, his sentiment regarding the decorating of graves having gone the way of his belief in the hereafter.

He raised his eyes and looked across the cemetery, past the bus stop on Mill Lane, and up Kerry Drive to its junction with Kirkway. The small bungalow in which his parents had lived out their last days was clearly visible on that corner. He smiled at the memory of his dad's oft repeated line, 'Well, one thing: tha' won't have far to cart me, lad.'

Big Mac McDermott they'd called him on the docks, and he was big too: big in stature and big in political power among the union hierarchy. Fully six feet two inches tall, and built like a brick shit-house, he'd begun his working life on the docks handing rivets at age fourteen, and steadily progressed up the ranks, eventually becoming a key figure in union and Labour Party politics. His real rise to prominence had occurred in 1954 when he'd been instrumental in leading four thousand Hull dockers out of The Transport and General Worker's Union and into membership of the 'Blue Union,' the National Amalgamated Stevedores and Dockers,' in a move described at the time as 'the biggest prison break in all history.' That movement of the rank and file out from under the bureaucracy of the

TGWU had established Big Mac's reputation as a leader. It signaled the beginning of an inter-union fight that would drag on for years and bring significant hardship to his family, but as difficult as those years had been, they paled in comparison to the fight the big man had waged with Parkinson's disease.

It had begun with the tremor in his left arm when he was in his mid-fifties, a few years prior to McDermott's move to the States, and the subsequent thirteen years saw him reduced from a muscular giant to a frail skeleton of less than nine stone, incapable of wiping his own arse or even walking to the toilet.

He thought back to a visit he'd made when his dad had been in a respite centre for a week, affording his mam a break she'd desperately needed. It was another of those gut-wrenching scenes from his father's struggle he'd never forgotten. Access to the centre had been via heavy security and a succession of locked doors, but nothing could have prepared him for what he saw upon entering the facility's lounge. The windowless room was ringed by a hodge podge of mismatched armchairs from which a collection of slumped physical wrecks stared vacantly at some sort of game being played in the middle of the room. A group of clearly mentally challenged patients was batting around a number of large, brightly coloured balloons amid screams and giggles, as a young man in a blue uniform urged them on. As he watched the activity, his view was abruptly obstructed by middle-aged woman who appeared to be repeatedly miming the locking and unlocking of a door as she mumbled away to herself. There was an old man too, repeatedly pleading to go home, and an old lady constantly chanting the words, 'My son's dead, you know, so he can't come and see me.'

His father had been propped up in a corner chair: head leant to one side, a string of drool hanging from his mouth. As dead as his eyes had been, they'd lit up at the sight of McDermott, and with the help of a couple of attendants and a wheelchair, he'd 'taken' his son to his room. McDermott had been unable to stay for long; such had been the stink of urine pervading the small space. His father had shared the room with another man who had been lying on his bed in what had appeared to be a catatonic state. He shuddered at the memory.

His father had managed a whispered goodbye to him at the end of his next visit home – in spite of his difficulty speaking – and McDermott had known as he'd taken his leave, that it was the last time he'd see his father alive. McDermott's final memory of his dad had been that which he'd related to Pastor Dan: two carers provided by the NHS, using a hoist contraption to lift his father from his bed and carry him to the bathroom.

He bowed his head as he remembered, and stamped his cold feet against the wet ground. He should have known then that the whole God movement was nothing but a bunch of mumbo-jumbo, for what sort of God could allow the kind of horrors that had been visited upon his father? How almighty could he be if he was incapable of protecting the bodies he'd supposedly created in the first place? But, he'd gone blithely along, caught up in the sentiment of the language, the music and the rituals, either too ignorant of, or frightened by, the big questions he should have been asking: the questions Dawkins and Hitchens had finally posed and answered for him.

He thought of his mother: now there was someone worthy of worship. Quietly spoken, gentle and thoughtful, she it was, from whom he'd inherited his sensitivity and love of books and education. His mother had been a petite, brunette beauty with a kiss curl and an eighteen inch waist when she met his father; she was the mortise to his tenon and their union had been correspondingly tight. She'd been bright had his mam, passing her scholarship and attending a fancy school in the city's suburbs. Indeed, had it not been for the deaths of her parents from the TB epidemic that had raged across the city, he had no doubt his mother would have become the teacher she'd always aspired to be. As it was she'd been obliged to live with an aunt and uncle and leave school early to become a shop assistant. She'd met his father as a fifteen-year-old at the local Trades and Labour club where her uncle and aunt were members, although it had been some time before she'd been willing to take a chance on the young firebrand of a dockside worker. She'd died of a stroke just two years after she'd seen Big Mac buried.

McDermott got up from the cold bench and bent to pick up some dead leaves from around the grave, reflecting as he did so that whilst he'd hero-worshipped his dad, he'd loved his mother with an intensity that had sometimes frightened him. Depositing the rotting leaves in a nearby bin, he paused and regarded the last resting place of his parents. What would the two of them have made of his current situation? Certainly they'd have scorned the idea that he was going through a tough time: to them, grieving and sorting out your personal problems were a natural part of life; tough, to them, was battling for survival. His dad had traipsed all over hell and creation with Monty's lot during the war, while his mam had cared for McDermott at home, running to the bomb shelter night after night with him in her arms. And the prize for winning that war had been rationing for almost another ten years and living hand to mouth. McDermott kicked out at clumps of wet leaves on the path. And he had the temerity to feel sorry for himself: how pathetic was that? He straightened up, threw his shoulders back and strode to his car. He'd finish his book, do the wedding, get home and sort his life out. In fact, he thought, why wait? He'd phone Bridie that night. Fuck it, she'd either forgive him or she wouldn't: it was time to move on.

By the time he arrived back at the Mercure, he'd missed lunch and had to wait for afternoon tea. It was worth the wait. A peculiarly English custom still adhered to by establishments fancying themselves a cut above the average, the late afternoon repast on offer appeared the same as it had always been, and McDermott delighted in the old fashioned ritual. Nibbling away at the tiny triangular sandwiches from which the bread crusts had been carefully removed, he attempted to analyze the complexity of his feelings for this city of his birth, and the real reasons for his journey.

True, he'd felt it a duty to visit his parents, but he had thought to spend the best part of two whole days dipping his toes into the past of a city he'd done nothing but excoriate since he'd left it almost half a century previously. Why? Was it sorrow for the passing of a time and place, and the disappearance of the friends and relatives who'd inhabited them? Did he feel regret for the decay of his home town, or smug satisfaction that he'd chosen to leave it? Was he mourning its passing, or celebrating his freedom from it? In the end he came to the realization that despite the greyness of it all, the vulgar attempts at progress, and the missing chunks of its once proud traditions, he did feel something: a certain empathy for the place that had spawned him. It also occurred to him that his appreciation for the big skies and wide open spaces of Northwest Michigan might be less had he not been raised among the claustrophobic streets of Hull's inner city. Would he relish the slow pace of rural Michigan life and the wild beaches of the Big Blue, as much as he did, without his awareness of the scurrying lives led by those living in this urban backwater?

Thinking about those lives, as he eked out the final cup of tea from the pot, McDermott had to admit to an inner anger over the apparent prevailing mindset of England's working class as he'd perceived them during this trip. Their body language evinced a timid willingness to accept the status quo: a readiness to live within the parameters of the limited expectations the class system had thrust upon them.

He glanced around the dining room, taking in the well-dressed women, replete in twin sets and pearls, and the few scattered elderly males poring over the early edition of the Hull Daily Mail while chewing ruminatively on their sandwiches. They were the type of folk, he thought, who had sat on the school stage at Speech Days, gazing down with their superior expressions upon the assembled pupils, slumming it for the day away from the cozy confines of conservative strongholds such as Haltemprice and Tranby Croft. This was the up-market face of the class system: one of affected airs, accents and attitudes and, more often than not, a holier-than-thou opinion of his adopted country. Politicians on both sides of the Atlantic might trumpet the special relationship between the two countries, but he knew from experience that many of the kind of people around him held jaundiced views on all things American, largely because of the States' late entry into the Second World War. The fact that without the eventual intervention of America, the war would have been lost seemed to escape such xenophobes.

'Will that be all, sir?'

McDermott was jolted back to the present by the waiter's question. He signed the bill, and retired to his room where he worked on formulating a conversation with Bridie.

It was midnight when he made the connection, having deemed seven in the evening in Michigan the most likely time to catch her. Despite his earlier resolve, his heart was racing like that of a kid calling for a first date, and his hand clutched a glass of mini-bar Scotch, as he listened to the familiar American ring of Bridie's phone.

'Hello?' The greeting was perfunctory and McDermott almost hung up. He took another swig of Scotch instead.

'Hello!!' Now she sounded pissed, and he'd not yet spoken.

'Bridie?' His voice whilst not quite a croak, was not the assertive male baritone he'd thought to deliver either. 'Um . . . Happy New Year, Bridie, I just – '

'Robbie?'

'Yeah, yeah, it's me,' he swallowed more Scotch. 'I was – '

'What the hell's this Happy New Year horseshit, Robbie? It's almost January the fucking third, and where the hell are you anyway?'

McDermott breathed a sigh of relief. He'd yet to say anything of substance, but at least she hadn't hung up on him, and based on her familiar language, her feelings toward him were somewhat warmer than during their last meeting.

'Um . . . well, I'm still in England, Bridie, I – '

'Well, shit, I know that. You said in your letter. But where in England? Rory told me you were gonna be shut up somewhere finishing your book,'

So she'd read the letter, and she'd talked to Rory about what he was doing; was that any indication –

'And talking of Rory, you oughtta know I've got Connor here.'

'Connor? He's alright isn't he?' McDermott's stomach churned at the thought of his dog being sick in his absence.

'Yeah, he's fine. Rory had to rush over to Detroit for a while: his mother took a fall. So right now I've got five, count 'em, five, dogs round my feet. It's like a goddamned zoo around here.'

'Well, thanks for looking after him, Bridie. God knows, I don't deserve it.'

'What the hell have you got to do with it? This is Connor we're talking about; it's not about you.'

'Right, yeah, sorry. Look, Bridie, about that letter – '

'Oh, shit, my brood's just arrived for dinner. I gotta go. Look, I'll see you when you get back okay? Next week is it?'

'Yeah, Thursday, actually, but what I –' A chorus of barking sounded down the line before it went dead.

He drained the last of his Scotch and hit the mini-bar for another. Sonofabitch, he thought, what did it all mean? Anything? He made a mental list of positives: she hadn't hung up on him; she'd read his letter – that was a biggie; she'd taken Connor, and she'd said she'd see him when he got back. Then again, she'd have to see him when he picked the dog up – unless Rory was back by then – in which case . . . Damn! He looked at his watch. Should he wait up and call her back? No, something told him that wouldn't be a good idea. Best accept that her reading of the letter was a positive sign and leave it at that. He took his Scotch to bed, lay back against the pillows and reflected on his day, Day 308. He thought about the changes he'd seen, his parents, Bridie, and finally, as always before he slept, Jean. He had a strong suspicion that she, like his father, would tell him to pull his finger out, stop worrying and get on with life. As he dozed off, he vowed to do just that. Of course, he'd made that vow before.

Eight days later, thanks to a succession of winter storms keeping him from the beach, and a burst of creative energy, he returned from Whitby to Leicester with the first draft of his book completed. The final chapter had been the most painful to write, but the words had come easily enough, almost pouring out of him at the end. It wasn't a big book – around 80,000 words he reckoned – and he still had no title, but then Mitch Albom's books weren't exactly voluminous, and he had plenty of time to come up with the title.

All he had to do now was get through the family dinner that evening, the wedding the following day, and he'd be on his way home to Connor, his cabin, the Big Blue, and whatever Bridie had in store for him. Holly Freeman he tried not to think about, although he did wonder what had happened to her since he'd left. Generally speaking though, he was a happy camper as he checked back into his Leicester hotel and unpacked for what, he believed, would be his final days in England.

Sunningdale Lodge sounded to McDermott as if it belonged in an Enid Blyton story from his childhood: the name conjured up pictures of a perfect family enjoying the seaside on endless sunny days, or eating toasted muffins by the fire on odd cloudy ones. As it happened, the company he kept that night would have been perfectly at home in such a story, for the same kind of idyllic happiness – with one sad exception – was much in evidence.

Although he was pleased, and even honoured, to be Jacqui's escort down the aisle on her wedding day, thoughts of his attendance at the family dinner – at which he felt he'd be an intruder – and the necessary mingling with strangers at both the dinner and the wedding had been a source of anxiety since Jacqui's invitation. To his relief, the reality proved infinitely more enjoyable than the imaginary, and rather than re-awaken his grief for Jean as he'd feared it might, the experience called to mind the possibility – however slight – of future happiness with Bridie and her family.

Jacqui's fiancé, Bill, turned out to be much more than the affable, pipe smoking, gentle soul he'd imagined. Apart from his love of fly fishing, reading, and a retained interest in the country's educational system, the man had a dry sense of humour, evinced a genuine concern for McDermott's loss of Jean, and clearly idolized his wife to be. Also important to McDermott was Bill's avowed love of dogs in general and his Bernese mountain dog, Max, in particular. You'll do for me, old son, McDermott thought, as he imagined what Cracker might have made of the avuncular guy before him. A squarely built man with a craggy jaw and a mop of unruly silver hair, Bill had clear blue eyes, few wrinkles for his age, and had retained a trim figure. He was undoubtedly, in Yorkshire parlance, 'a good lad.' Cracker would have approved, McDermott decided.

As always with such events, one was allowed little time to socialize with any one individual, and it was not long before McDermott was pulled away from Bill by Erica Jane who grilled him unmercifully about the course his life had taken in the years since she'd last seen him. He was surprised she remembered him as well as she did, and was particularly warmed by the fond memories she carried of her father. He suspected Jacqui would have had a great deal to do with keeping Cracker alive in her daughter's affections, but the revered way in which she spoke of him was undoubtedly genuine, and he suffered a twinge of regret that he had no sons or daughters who might keep his memory alive.

If Erica Jane was pretty, with her mass of blond hair and model's figure, her daughters, Poppy and Daisy were beautiful. It was not often McDermott yearned for his younger years, but the sight of such lovely young women, the sound of their animated conversation, and the easy fun-loving way in which they comported themselves with their equally bright boyfriends, aroused an envy in him that was rare. It was in the middle of an intense conversation with the young people, about the relative merits of Britain's relationships with the European Union, and the potential future of Anglo-American relations, that his sleeve was tugged by Jacqui who excused him from the girls and their escorts.

'There's someone I want you to meet,' she said, taking his arm and moving him out of the bar area into the dining room where dinner would eventually be served.

It was only as he drew close to a table occupied by three women and three men that McDermott recognized those with whom he was about to be reacquainted. 'Jesus Christ,' he said, 'Brenda, Janice, Audrey: what a lovely surprise.'

All three McCracken sisters rose and gave him tearful hugs as he attempted to keep his own tears from his eyes. They were all old now, he thought, as he hugged each in turn and marvelled, as he had so many times before, how people remain the same age in one's memory even as age advances upon oneself. Damn, it was good to see them, and for the next half hour, following introductions to their respective husbands – who were active partners in their own painting and decorating business – life stories were exchanged interspersed with recollections of Cracker's escapades as a kid.

He'd not been aware of Audrey leaving the conversation, but it seemed to him later that it was just prior to someone tapping a glass with a spoon to signal that dinner was about to be served, when she appeared in the doorway with one of the cutest little girls he'd ever seen, albeit with a complete absence of hair. It was the girl, rather than Audrey, who led the way to McDermott's table, and not waiting to be introduced, she said, 'You're Uncle Robbie, aren't you? I'm Melanie and I've got Ewing's Sarcoma. You can call me Mel if you like, everyone else does.'

Staring into her wide, blue eyes while retaining his composure was, McDermott thought, the most difficult thing he'd done in his life. 'Hi, Mel, yes, I'm Robbie and you're a beautiful young lady.'

'Well, I wish I had some hair, but I have to have chemo and radiation and that stuff makes your hair fall out.'

'Robbie, this is my granddaughter, Mel,' put in Audrey, 'Her mum and dad are taking a little break this weekend.'

The little girl's eyes regarded him solemnly, 'My hair could grow back you know: it all depends on how much more treatment I have to have.'

It was then that the second call to be seated was tapped out, and McDermott took hold of Melanie's hands as he left the table and said, 'Well, you know what, Mel? You look beautiful to me just the way you are. I have to go and sit with your great aunt Jacqui, but may I come and talk to you after dinner?'

'Yes, please,' Mel said. 'Do you know any stories about great uncle Alastair? I like hearing those.'

'Lots and lots,' said McDermott, 'I'll see you later, okay?'

'Okay,' said Mel, and with that she sat on her chair and watched as he made his way to the top table and took his place beside Jacqui and Bill.

McDermott had never been any good with sick children, being more likely to cry than to be of comfort to them, and that fact, along with the memories that Mel's baldness evoked of Jean's battle, put him in a somber mood as he took his seat.

'I see you've made the acquaintance of our Mel,' said Jacqui.

'Yeah,' said McDermott, 'she's really beautiful. How long has she been . . . ?'

'She was first diagnosed with Ewing's a couple of years ago, but she's been fighting it like hell. Believe me, Robbie, if you ever think you're having a rough day, just remember that kid. She kinda puts things in perspective – a fucking cliché I know, but no less true for that.'

'Yeah,' said McDermott, looking across at Mel, 'I can see that. What's the –'

'Prognosis? Well, we thought she had a chance until a couple of weeks ago. It looked as if she'd done well with the treatment, and the doctors were pretty upbeat according to Audrey, but then –' Jacqui's voice quavered.

'Don't tell me,' said McDermott. 'It came back,'

'Well, the thinking now is that metastasis may have been present from the beginning, although how the hell all the scans could have missed it is a mystery to me. Anyway, a couple of weeks ago, they discovered she's developed Myelodyplastic syndrome – MDS to you and me. Now they're looking for a bone marrow match so she can have a transplant, but the chances aren't good'.

'Does she understand all this?' said McDermott.

'She's really very bright and understands about the Ewing's thing, but they haven't told about this latest development.'

'Jesus,' McDermott said. 'How are her parents doing?'

'Struggling: don't know if the marriage will survive this to be honest. The pain's been ripping them apart since the first diagnosis. They're just emotionally and physically exhausted. I told them to forget about the wedding and piss off and spend some downtime together. And Audrey's great with Mel: works with special needs kids and has that touch, you know?'

'Shit,' McDermott said. 'And there I was crying to you about my troubles the other night. Why didn't you tell me about Mel then?'

'There's a time for everything, Robbie and that wasn't it. You had your own stuff to get off your chest. I knew you'd meet Mel today, and I knew the effect she'd have on you too. So, now you've met one of the bravest little lasses you'll ever meet, you can think on can't you? The next time the odd dark cloud appears on the horizon, remember we owe it to kids like Mel to honour their bravery by pulling our finger out and facing up to life.'

'You're right, goddamn it, Jacqui. My first reaction to Mel was sorrow when it should have been admiration. I – '

There was a sudden clatter of cutlery accompanied by the sound of china breaking and Audrey hurried out of the room carrying Mel, her husband close behind.

'Ah, Jesus,' said McDermott.

'Don't panic, Robbie. Happens all the time: she has sudden bouts of nausea. All part of what she's going through.'

The remainder of the party went as planned. The food was excellent, numerous bottles of wine were consumed, and a variety of people got up and made speeches about the benefits of matrimony the second time around. Nevertheless the night for McDermott had already been claimed by Mel. Before the evening was over, the vicar of St. Margaret's, the village church where the wedding was to take place the following afternoon, spent ten minutes or so with the members of the wedding party. He took them briskly through the choreography of the thing, and McDermott found the informal session refreshing after the complex planning and over-the-top rehearsal dinners so common in the States.

As he drove back to his hotel, he thought again of Mel. As uplifting as it had been to see Cracker's sisters after so long, and to share in the obvious happiness of Jacqui and Bill, he knew that meeting Mel was a defining moment in his life. He could not envision a future crisis with which he would not be able to cope, as long as he carried the face and the story of Mel with him. He fulminated once more against the religious establishment, its insistence upon the existence of a loving, caring God, and its total inability to explain the agony of the Mels of the world. It was the night of Day 316.

Whether it was the result of too much alcohol, anxiety over the wedding, Mel's illness, his imminent return home, or a combination of everything, McDermott had a restless night, and when he arrived at the church an hour before the service, he felt less than his usual self. A couple of nips from Bill's hip flask revived him, however, and he carried out his duties with aplomb.

As the wedding party made its way to Sunnyside following the ubiquitous photography session, he was looking forward to a relaxed evening at the reception and a relatively early night, allowing him time to pack before leaving for the airport the following morning. It had been a pleasant ceremony, the kind of understated affair he and Jean had enjoyed so many years previously. The day was made all the brighter for him by the presence of Mel who, recovered from her setback of the previous evening, had brought to the proceedings the innocent beauty of a child, in her role as Jacqui's flower girl.

It was at the reception that things began to go downhill. Initially, the event promised to be every bit as enjoyable as the dinner the previous evening. As the 'father of the bride' he delivered a speech that was well received, while Bill's younger brother, Ray, as Best Man, delivered an hilarious discourse on the pitfalls of matrimony entered into later in life. McDermott's enjoyment of the event was increased considerably too, when Mel suddenly materialized in a vacant chair beside him, as the room was being readied for the post dinner dancing, and laid a piece of paper before him.

'I drew you a picture,' she said.

McDermott picked up the sheet of paper and stared. The scene was rendered in crayon but was no less accomplished for that. It depicted a brown road stretching into the middle distance where it eventually disappeared, lost in the enveloping foliage of the trees that lined the edges of the road. Someone must have taught Mel perspective, for the way in which the trees decreased in size from the foreground into the distance was damned near perfect. On the bottom right of the picture was a yellow butterfly pulling a streamer on which was drawn a heart and the word, 'Mel.'

'Mel, this is really good,' he said. 'When did you learn to draw like this?'

'We have this lady in the children's center at the hospital: she's one of the volunteers and used to be an artist. She says maybe I could be an artist when I grow up.'

McDermott swallowed hard, and masking his emotions as best he could, he passed her comment by and said, 'Tell me about the butterfly, Mel.'

'It's kind of like, my signature. I love butterflies.'

'Yeah, so do I,' said McDermott. 'But tell me, what is it you like about them so much?

'Well, I like them because they're so free and pretty,' she said, and then thought for a moment before adding, 'and they're always hopeful: they never give up.'

'That's a beautiful thought, Mel,' McDermott said, 'but what exactly do you mean?'

'Well,' Mel screwed up her eyes as if in heavy concentration. 'They just fly through life hoping the next flower will bring more of what they love, and if it doesn't, they just fly on to the next one.'

'Wow! You know what, Mel?'

'What?'

'I think that's one of the most beautiful things I've ever heard.'

Mel regarded him shyly from her big, blue eyes, 'Thanks. I sometimes dream about flying with butterflies. Wouldn't that be cool?' She smiled inquiringly up at his face. 'Gran said you might dance with me later. Will you?'

'I'd love to, Mel. Thank you for asking.'

'Okay, see you later. Bye.' She skipped away.

He was so entranced with his new friend and the words she'd spoken, he almost missed Andi's entrance. It occurred after the tables had been cleared and the small band had commenced to play. The reason for her late arrival became all too clear as she made her way across the room toward Jacqui. She was on the arm of a tall, broad-shouldered man carrying a sizeable paunch before him, and who was clearly the worse for wear – a condition, based upon his bulbous nose and mottled cheeks, with which he was not unfamiliar. Andi, herself, was still a pixie, still attractive, but her once jet black hair was now frosted, and the laugh lines he'd once known so well had deepened around her brown eyes.

McDermott observed her progress across the room with the man he presumed to be his successor as her husband, a man not averse to elbowing people roughly aside, he noticed. As the pair engaged Jacqui and Bill in conversation, he looked at the woman who had been his wife, and remembered.

It had seemed a marriage made in heaven, his union with Andi – who had provided the inspiration for his fictional Dani – and then the depression had come. He'd had a previous bout during his first wife's abortion when the cause had been obvious, but when the black periods had returned in the fourth year of his marriage to Andi, there'd been no discernible cause that anyone could fathom. He'd spurned the idea of a psychiatrist, opting instead for prescribed doses of Librium. The drug had given him bouts of dizziness and painful headaches but no relief from the dark places to which his mind continually led him, and when during one particularly bad stretch, he'd accused Andi of stealing from their joint bank account, her patience had snapped. She'd tried, God bless her, she really had, but he'd been beyond help. He harbored no hard feelings toward her: indeed he could still recall with fondness the great times they'd had together. As he'd remarked to Jacqui too, he was fully cognizant of the fact that divorce from Andi had led unerringly to divorce from Britain, and thence to Jean. Emigration had seemed a logical move at the time, especially when the offer from Kate Patterson to open a satellite campus of the Institute in Michigan had arrived. Barlington by then was as fine a school as it was ever going to be in his judgement, and a new challenge in a new country had held a lot of appeal.

Andi's husband had now disappeared from the head table, and McDermott observed Andi and Jacqui as they laughed and chatted, before they abruptly halted and started looking around the room. He knew what was coming as soon as they pushed their chairs back, and he watched as they made their way toward him.

'What are you doing? Dodging the limelight, Robbie?' Jacqui said. 'There's an old friend here who'd like to say hello. You'll have to excuse me a minute, I can see Bill looking stricken over something: probably lost his pipe again. See you in a few,' and with that she left them alone.

'Hello, Robbie, how are you? I was so sorry to hear about your wife.' Andi's voice had changed little over the years: a little hoarser perhaps, but that would be the cigarettes.

'Hello, Andi, and thanks. Yeah, it was an ordeal. What about you? How have you been?'

'Oh, fine, you know. Got married again. He's here somewhere, probably at the bar.' She looked around uncertainly.

'Well, please, have a seat,' McDermott gestured to an empty chair beside him. 'Can I get you a drink?'

'Not right now thanks, Robbie, but you go ahead if you'd like.'

'No, no, I'm fine.'

'So, why don't you tell me what you've been up to? Jacqui told me how successful you've been in the States.'

'Yeah, well,' Robbie began a brief explanation of his life since they'd parted and was recounting his move from education to the business world when a slurred voice brayed over his shoulder.

'I say, darling, it's a bloody cash bar. Who'd have thought of such a thing at a wedding? Damned cheap, what? Who's this then?' Andi's husband slumped down beside his wife, partly spilling what appeared to McDermott to be a quintuple Scotch.

'This is my former husband, Robbie McDermott, Charles, and I think you may have had enough.' Andi appeared less than thrilled with her husband's condition. 'Robbie, this is Charles Welwyn-Hurst, my husband.'

'Oh, so you're the chappie who got to Andi before me?' said Charles, ignoring Robbie's outstretched hand. 'Pissed orf to Yankeeland didn't you old boy? Bit bloody extreme wasn't it, leaving the Old Country for the Colonies? What?'

'Charles,' Andi said.

'No, no, no, I'm interested, I truly am. So what are you doing back here, Bobbie? Figured it out, I'll be bound: no place like Old Blighty eh?' Charles took a loud slurp of his Scotch.

McDermott was cold in his response. He well understood the dangers of engaging in conversation with drunken boors, but this guy was seriously pissing him off. 'Actually, I'm just visiting. I return home tomorrow.'

'Home? Home? But you're an Englishman, old boy. Good God, man, what are you playing at? Your home's here.'

'No, my home is in Michigan and I happen to be an American citizen.'

'What? You mean you converted?'

'Charles,' Andi rose with the clear indication of wishing to leave, but McDermott's blood was up now. Old Charles's plum-in-the-mouth accent alone was sufficient to raise the small hairs on the back of his neck, and the man's uncouth behaviour had further stoked his fire.

'I think you're confusing citizenship with religion: one doesn't convert to another country, one swears one's allegiance – in my case, to the United States of America.'

'Good God, old chap. You must be sicker than old Andi told me you were. Surely – '

'Charles,' Andi was plainly agitated.

'Be quiet, Andi, there's a good girl.' Charles turned his attention back to McDermott. 'Now, Bobbie, tell me. Why on earth would you do such a thing?'

'Why wouldn't I?' McDermott said.

'Why wouldn't – '

'Charles,' Andi put her hand on her husband's shoulder.

'Andi,' Charles snapped at her, 'will you please shut the fuck up! I'm trying to make sense of this wannabe Yank. Now, come on, Bobbie; really, why the hell would you want to live in a place like America?'

'The name is Robbie,' McDermott said deliberately, 'and I repeat: why should I not wish to live in the United States?'

'Well, figure it out old chap: I mean, they're just not as smart as us are they?''

'I'm sorry? What did you just say?'

'The Yanks, Bobbie, the Yanks: they've not quite got it all together in the old brains department, have they?'

'And just how have you arrived at that conclusion?'

'Well, think about it, old boy. I mean look at London, St. Paul's, all of that. I mean, the Yanks couldn't have done that could they?'

'I'm sorry, Robbie. Perhaps I'll see you later.' Andi gave a contemptuous glance at her husband, and left the table.

'What? What?' George swiveled his body and watched his wife stride away.

Feeling freer now to speak his mind, McDermott leaned forward toward the clearly inebriated Charles and said, 'Tell me, Charles,' McDermott put a mock emphasis on the "ar," 'have you ever been to Manhattan?'

'Good God, no. Ghastly place. New York isn't it? Lots of, what do the Yanks call them? Skyscrapers?

'But you have seen photographs or seen it on the telly?'

'Well, yes, of course, but – '

'Well,' McDermott put his face very close to Charles's, 'the next time you see it Chucky, I want you to examine the size of those buildings, and when you do, I want you to remember a couple of things: One, every one of them is built on solid granite; and two, most of those buildings were not even there a hundred and fifty years ago. And then, when your xenophobic mind has managed to absorb that information, I want you to remember this. It's around two and a half thousand miles between New York and San Francisco; roughly the same between LA and Washington D.C.; and close to three thousand, between Seattle and Miami; and that entire country was crisscrossed with highways before the fucking M1 was built. So, the next time you find yourself thinking how dumb Americans are, you – '

'Everything okay?' Bill, obviously dispatched by Jacqui and Andi who were hovering behind him, looked enquiringly at McDermott.

'Absolutely, Bill,' McDermott said. 'I was just giving Charles here, a wee geography lesson. Isn't that right, Charles?'

'Now, you listen to me, you – '

'Charles!' Andi appeared at his shoulder. 'We're leaving: get your coat.'

'Who the fuck asked your opinion, woman? If – '

'Would you like some assistance, Mister Welwyn Hurst?' Audrey's husband, Larry, a giant of a man flanked by his brothers-in – law, looked down upon the purple-faced Charles. 'Up we get then,' Larry said, not deigning to wait for a response, and over his protestations, the drunken Charles Welwyn-Hurst was raised to his feet and escorted from the room.

'I'm so sorry, Robbie,' said Andi. 'He's . . . Well, he's . . . I'm sorry.' And she turned and hurried off after her husband and his escorts.

'So, now you've made the acquaintance of the Right Honorable Charles Welwyn-Hurst,' said Jacqui, pulling a chair up.

'Honorable? Not much honorable about that prick,' said McDermott, 'How the hell did Andi finish up with a dickhead like that?'

'Actually he was okay when she first met him: tall, handsome, ex-Eton and Oxford, with a promising career in politics. He was polite, funny and a good guy to have at a party then.'

'So what the hell happened?'

'Money, Robbie, money. His parents were something big in South African gold mines and when they died he inherited a fortune. Everything was wonderful at first: he and Andi moved into the ancestral home in Rutland and it was all Rolls-Royces, servants, and long holidays in the Bahamas. But the fact was, he couldn't handle it – the sudden wealth I mean. He started drinking and – Robbie! What is it?'

The tight feeling in McDermott's chest came out of nowhere as it had with his first heart attack, but this was different. His chest felt as if it had been wrapped in steel bands that were slowly being tightened, and he was struggling to breathe. His left arm suddenly lost all feeling and as he felt consciousness slipping away, fear overcame him.

When he came round, he was aware of being propelled on a cart toward the open doors of an ambulance and of breathing through an oxygen mask. The pain in his chest was more bearable, but his left arm remained numb, and the top of his head felt as if it was going to explode – probably the effects of nitroglycerine, he thought, as his eyes watched the roof of the ambulance appear to slide over him. Suddenly he was aware of a commotion. People were shouting for some reason, and then he felt a small hand slip into his, and something was placed on his stomach. He couldn't raise his head, but he glanced down and saw Mel over the top of his oxygen mask.

'You forgot your picture, Uncle Robbie,' she said.

He reached out his hand to her, but a burly ambulance man wearing a Day-Glo yellow jacket was pulling her gently away, and his fingers closed on thin air. Just before the ambulance door was slammed he heard Mel's voice. 'Remember the butterflies, Uncle Robbie! Fly with the butterflies!'

He knew it was serious before the consultant in the Intensive Care Unit at Leicester's Glenfield Hospital spoke to him later that afternoon, and he understood too, the need for an angiogram and the associated risks. What the consultant did not know was that McDermott had no intention, if he could possibly avoid it, of placing himself at the mercy of the National Health Service, and when Jacqui and Bill were allowed to visit, he asked them to take his wallet and follow the instructions on the back of his MedjetAssist card. Twenty-four hours later, being deemed medically stable for transfer, McDermott was airborne on an intensive-care-equipped Learjet bound for Munson Medical Centre in Traverse City. During their travelling years he and Jean had religiously renewed their membership in the medical evacuation company, and once installed in his private room at Munson, McDermott privately congratulated himself on their prescience.

As the Glenfield consultant had suspected, based upon the use of his stethoscope alone, the blood flow to McDermott's heart had been severely curtailed by blockages in three arteries. That was the bad news revealed by the angiogram taken at Munson; the good news was that the left anterior descending artery, the 'widow maker,' was only fifty percent occluded. Nevertheless, the chief cardiologist, while extremely positive, took pains to point out that the triple by-pass surgery he faced, although a common procedure was not without risk.

It was a full forty-eight hours after his arrival at the hospital, and following his movement from the ICU to the High Dependency Unit, that he was allowed visitors, but he thought it well worth the wait when he awoke to find Bridie sitting beside his bed.

'Jesus Christ, McDermott, I've heard of being wired, but this is fucking ridiculous,' she said, eyeing the various wires and tubes attaching McDermott to an array of fluid bags and machines.

McDermott smiled up at her, 'You always did have a subtle way of breaking the ice,' he said. 'How the hell are you, Bridie, and how's my boy?'

'Connor is fine, and I'm a damned sight better than you from the looks of it. What's the story, Robbie? Those bastards refused to tell me jackshit because I'm not a relative or something. Took an act of Congress for me to get in here.'

McDermott explained the situation and Bridie grew pensive.

'It's not that big a deal, you know,' he said. 'They do this stuff every day. To them it's like your diner frying up a breakfast.'

'Well, in that case, let's hope they're more careful than that fucking George is with the eggs,' she said. 'No, seriously, Robbie, I'm not worried; it's just that . . . Well, if you don't come out of it, can I have that desk of yours?'

McDermott stared at her. And then she laughed that glorious belly laugh of hers. 'Got you going there for a minute didn't I, McDermott? Had you thinking what a callous bitch I am for a moment. Right? She laughed again.

'Not for a minute, Bridie,' he said with a smile, 'not even a second: well, not the callous bit anyway.'

She stabbed a forefinger at him and raised her eyebrows to acknowledge his sharp response, and then looked serious again. 'So, when will –'

'Tomorrow morning: seven-thirty.'

Bridie nodded and looked thoughtful.

'Bridie, listen, thanks for coming. I'm not looking for sympathy or anything, but this shit is kind of crappy when you're on your own, and you being here has helped a lot. There is one more thing I want to ask you, though.'

'If it's about that letter and all that shit, let's just leave it for now, Robbie. Okay?'

'No, it's not the letter, love, it's,' he swallowed. 'It's Connor. If anything gets fucked up and I – Well, you know – Will you – '

'Jesus H. Christ, McDermott, what the hell do you think I am? You, I have my doubts about, but Connor? Don't even think about that. I'm not even sure I'm gonna let you have him back when you get outta here.'

At that point, the Unit's very own version of Nurse Ratchett entered the room, curtly informed Bridie her time was up, and left, pointedly leaving the door open.

Bridie rose to go and as she did, her eyes fell on the picture tacked up on the wall by McDermott's bed. 'Nice picture,' she said. 'Who did it?'

McDermott turned his head and looked at the piece of art. 'That was done by a new friend of mine,' he said. 'A little girl who taught me in a few minutes what I've spent a lifetime trying to learn.'

'Oh, yeah? What's that then?'

'That, we should go through life with the same abiding hope that butterflies demonstrate – or, as my friend put it – we should fly with the butterflies.'

'That's nice,' said Bridie, studying the picture closely. 'The kid can draw too.' She gathered up her bag off the bed. 'Listen, Robbie: all the best for tomorrow. I'll be thinking of you, and I'll call and see how you're doing tomorrow – always supposing I can get one of these fucking Nazis to tell me anything.'

'Thanks, Bridie. Just one more thing before I forget though.' He reached out his hand toward the bedside table. 'Would you take that binder with you? It's the manuscript of my book and I'd hate it to go missing.'

'Oh, wow; so this is it, huh? Well, no problem, Robbie – might even give it a bit of a read if that's okay.'

'No, don't do that, love,' McDermott said. 'I do want you to read it eventually: in fact I'd like you to be the first, but there are still a couple of revisions ahead of me before it'll be ready for consumption. Do you mind waiting a bit? 'Course if anything goes pear-shaped with this operation –'

'Don't you even go there: you're going to be fine. As for the book, sure I can wait. You just concentrate on getting yourself back in shape to finish it.' She kissed him on the forehead and turned to leave.

'Bridie, about that letter.' There, he'd said it.

She paused with her back to him for a moment before turning.

'Robbie, I won't pretend I haven't thought about that and here's the deal: I'm not the kind of broad to come out with a bunch of happy-clappy horseshit just because you're sick and facing surgery. You hurt me and you hurt me bad, but your letter was much appreciated, even though I almost threw it in the garbage before I read it. So, I'll just say one thing.'

'What's that, Bridie?'

'She glanced at Mel's picture on the wall. 'Why don't we get you outta here and then follow your friend's advice and fly with the butterflies for a while. Take it one flower at a time and see what happens?'

McDermott was so struck by her use of metaphor that Bridie was out of the door before he could respond.

The following day, at precisely seven-thirty-five in the morning, as he succumbed to the anaesthetic, McDermott watched thousands of yellow butterflies fluttering against a jet black background. Their myriad paths appeared to be completely haphazard until they settled for a moment, as if choreographed, into a formation which proceeded to spell out a flickering yellow word. He almost figured it out before the background became the foreground.

Malcolm McDonald

Epilogue

She sank down into the sofa with a glass of wine and opened the manuscript to the last chapter. She'd spent the whole day reading and was anxious to discover the denouement: adjusting her reading glasses she picked up where she'd left off.

As Cracker and I entered the third year of operation at Barlington, the period I would come to see as the golden years of our relationship continued to unfold. More and more parents became involved in their children's education, and we broke ground on a custom designed community centre on the school grounds – the Director's reward for our pioneering efforts in parental involvement. That year was memorable too for providing yet more examples of achievement on the part of both teachers and children, but as I look back it is perhaps more to the plain, everyday life of the school that my thoughts stray. So many stories, so many magical moments; who remembers them now? Does the county auditor who discovered Cracker had never made an entry in the school's 'Daily Logbook' during the first three years of the school's existence, recall his astonishment at such audacity? How many of John Cromer's pupils remember his first attempt at teaching sex when little Jimmy Harland asked the question, 'What if you get it wrong and go to the toilet instead?' Does Brendan O'Neill's mother recall standing in my office, blood dripping from her left wrist as I prised the Stanley knife from her right hand? Is Megan O'Neill still around to remember? And what of Jack Wilton? Does he recall his father finding him reading 'The Godfather' beneath his bedclothes? Does his father have any memory of the threats he made against our school because, Jack had borrowed the book from a classmate in Maureen Husthwaite's room? And the Jehovah's Witnesses, the parents of Jimmy Appleton, who were so upset with Pauline Green for teaching that the animals went into the Ark two by two – rather than three by three – what became of them? And Jimmy?

That the fund of tales and the breadth of our educational success are forever clouded by Cracker's downfall, is something I'm sure still

332

haunts so many of the parents, kids and staff who witnessed it. Maybe it was inevitable, simply a matter of time: almost certainly it had its genesis in Big Jim's violent and predatory nature, but even I, as well as I knew Cracker, was totally unprepared for the events of early 1975.

By the time eight-year-old Tracy Nichols arrived at our school in the autumn of 1974, she'd already been the subject of screening by four social services departments, three child protection police teams, three hospitals, two NSPCC centres and a number of volunteer organizations. That she remained in the care of her mother and stepfather beggared belief. The school records we received described her as 'small and frail.' A more accurate description would have been diminutive and skeletal: with staring, hollow eyes and sunken cheeks, she brought to mind pictures of Holocaust survivors. Her stepbrother, Barry, on the other hand, while dirty and unkempt, was the correct weight and height for his age, and exhibited the typical boundless energy of a nine-year-old. (This clear indicator that the two children were being treated differently – resulting, as subsequent inquires would ascertain, from his father's preferential treatment of his natural son – should have raised red flags at the beginning of their stay with us. That it did not continues to trouble me.)   Although their school attendance was sporadic at best, that was the least of our worries, for during the entire length of their brief stay with us, we were engaged in a war with the agencies charged with the protection of children. Each week it seemed, Margaret Hornesby, Tracy's teacher, would arrive in Cracker's office or my own with Tracy in tow, to show us the suspicious bruises, cuts and scars that Tracy swore were self-inflicted, but were clearly the results of child abuse.

Cracker was constantly in a state of incandescent rage during this period, and restraining him from making a personal visit to see Tracy's stepfather became an integral part of my job description. I'd met both parents when Tracy and her brother were enrolled, and I knew Cracker's opinions would not be enhanced through personal contact. Trudy Nichols, the mother, was a heavyset woman with bleached blond hair, and an acne scarred face who regarded school as nothing more than a free babysitting service. Fred Norris, her second husband, was a brute of a man with muscular, tattooed arms and a ponytail, whose contribution to the State was to extract as much as possible from it in the form of child support and unemployment claims, while remaining steadfastly unemployed.

Our battle for Tracy's life — for that is how we viewed it — ran through the autumn term of 1974 and the first few weeks of 1975. During that time, Cracker spent countless hours swimming against the tide of bureaucracy administered by social services. He was passed from 'customer service' officers to various persons in the children's social work department, to 'intake duty team managers' to actual social workers who appeared ill-trained and ineffective. And the National Health Service was not far behind in its level of incompetence. During one hospital stay alone, Tracy passed from an 'emergency room admitting doctor' to a 'senior house officer,' to a 'paediatric registrar,' to a 'senior paediatrician,' while a seventy-two hour police protection order was first placed, and then withdrawn. There was nothing Cracker could do to convince the responsible authorities that Tracy should be taken into care.

That all of this was happening less than two years after the infamous Maria Colwell case, made the chain of events even more incredible, for the similarities were chilling: Maria, like Tracy, had a history of abuse at the hands of her stepfather; Maria was seven when she died from severe internal injuries and brain damage resulting from child abuse, while the child we were attempting to help was just eight; with Maria, the relevant child protection agencies failed repeatedly in their duty, and we were experiencing similar incompetence in Tracy's case.

The tipping point came just two weeks into the spring term of 1975. It was a Friday morning and I was looking forward to a relaxing weekend with Dani, when Margaret Hornesby walked into my office and put into motion the chain of events that would tilt Cracker's world on its axis.

'Robbie, it's Tracy: we have a problem,' she said.

'What is it this time?'

'She won't speak, Robbie and she refuses to sit down. I've got her in Marion's office. Can you have a word? My kids –'

'Of course,' I said. 'You get back to your classroom.'

I alerted Cracker and we went to see Tracy in Marion's office. Marion was more than a school secretary: she loved kids, and took a full part in the school's activities. She was quietly attempting to coax Tracy to speak when Cracker and I entered her room. It was no good: whatever the three of us tried, Tracy merely stared at us, biting relentlessly on her fingernails, and refused to talk or sit. Eventually, Cracker called me outside.

'You stay in there for a minute, Robbie, I'm going to talk to her stepbrother; see if he knows anything.'

It was ten minutes later when Cracker motioned me into his own office. He was pale and wasted no time filling me in. 'Barry tells me he doesn't know what's wrong, but Tracy slept with his dad last night while his mother slept in Tracy's bed.'

I stared at him, understanding all too well the implications. 'We need to call – '

'No! Fuck that! We're not calling anybody. This time we're going to act. Go and get Margaret, quick as you can: we need to have her take a look at Tracy.'

Margaret examined Tracy in the Ladies room, returned her to Marion's care, and rejoined Cracker and me in his office. As soon as she'd closed the door, she slumped into a chair and began sobbing.

'Oh, God, I'm sorry,' she said, blowing her nose.

'No need, just tell us,' said Cracker, his face tight.

'Oh, Jesus Christ, Cracker, she's – she's –' It took a little more time before she could continue. 'She's split open!'

As much as we'd been expecting evidence of sodomy, Margaret's blunt description of the damage to Tracy, and the primitive wail that accompanied it, brought tears to the eyes of both Cracker and me. Cracker recovered himself and got us moving.

'Okay. The hell with the procedures: here's what we're going to do. Robbie, you get your car round the front. Margaret, you grab Tracy's coat and take her out to Robbie's car. We're going to the hospital. I'll follow you in my car after I've had a word with Bill Cousins. We need the police meeting us at the hospital. Go!'

Bill Cousins was the local bobby attached to our school, and although this type of thing was beyond his remit, I understood Cracker's motives. Bill would get things moving on the police side of things, but we'd be at the hospital well before his colleagues, thus foiling any ideas they may have about calling social services.

Cracker upset an awful lot of people at Wyvern Royal Infirmary that morning, but he got things done fast. By the time the police arrived, Tracy had been through emergency admitting, sodomy had been confirmed, and she was safely in a children's ward. When the two police constables approached us making noises about social services, Cracker identified Margaret and me as being the people to whom they should speak, and muttering something about having a school to run, he left us to it.

I should have known, of course I should have known, and yet I watched him leave and believed, like Margaret and the policemen, he was returning to Barlington. I find it difficult to comprehend, even now, that with everything I knew of Cracker's past, I could have been so gullible. It's possible I couldn't have stopped him anyway, but there are still nights when I lie awake and think of alternative scenarios that could, perhaps, have saved him.

When the police arrived at the Hopkins house that afternoon, Fred Norris was dead. While the autopsy showed death was attributable to cardiac arrest, it was determined that the injuries sustained by Tracy's stepfather prior to death, were 'significant contributing factors.' According to the chief pathologist, Fred Norris had been subjected to a savage yet methodical beating. His face was barely recognizable: the nose was totally collapsed, both lips were split and most of his teeth had been broken. In addition the bones of both arms and legs had been shattered and six ribs and both kidneys had sustained serious damage. All of this, the pathologist adjudged to have occurred prior to the systematic destruction of Norris's testicles and penis which appeared to have been beaten repeatedly by a heavy object. (That 'object' it would later be revealed, was Cracker's lethal, Taekwondo-educated, right foot.)

In the world of fiction, Cracker would have carefully planned his assault in order to escape apprehension, or in the event of capture, his actions would be viewed by a sympathetic court as those of an avenging angel. Neither imaginary scenario approximated the reality of what ensued.

Throughout his life, Cracker had been nothing if not spontaneous, and retribution for Tracy rather than evasion of detection had been uppermost in his mind as he drove from the hospital to Tracy's home that day. Even so, since Trudy Nichols was absent when Cracker went calling, he might still have avoided arrest. A practitioner of Taekwondo at the level achieved by Cracker can destroy a human body without the inconvenience of a weapon or any damage to himself, and thus when Cracker left the inert form of Fred Norris, an elevated heart rate and perspiration-soaked clothing, were the only indicators of how he had spent the previous, violent fifteen minutes. In short there was nothing to invite suspicion of his part in the affair. In the event it was the ubiquitous, nosy neighbour who placed Cracker at the scene.

Gladys Potts, the mother of Susan Potts, a pupil at Barlington, spent most of her days watching the comings and goings of her neighbours through her lace curtains, and witnessed Cracker's arrival and departure from Tracy's home. When the police and ambulance arrived at the scene, Mrs. Potts was only too ready to 'do her duty' and assist the police in their inquiries. Once the police arrived on his doorstep, Cracker made no attempt to evade responsibility for his actions, although he vehemently denied knowing that Fred Norris was dead. He'd already told Jacqui what he'd done, and as he was led away, she called Dani for help in finding legal advice.

While Cracker was remanded in custody awaiting trial, at HMP Wyvern, Jacqui was as much a prisoner as he was. Their home was surrounded by a cordon of press and TV reporters, cameramen and gawkers. Finally, Dani and I moved in with her for a few days to help in any way we could. It was a difficult time for all of us. Jacqui's emotions were all over the place: like the majority of the public she understood Cracker's actions, but she had difficulty – as did Dani – in comprehending why he would not put the welfare of Erica Jane and herself before vengeance for Tracy. I made the appropriate sympathetic noises, and was desperate to explain the effect of Big Jim's molestation of Audrey upon my friend's psyche, but until Cracker released me from my vow of silence on that subject, I could say nothing. And that he refused to do. I had thought that perhaps Janice or Brenda might break their silence, but although they moved into Dani's house during the trial, and spent a lot of time with Jacqui, they remained mute on the subject.

According to his barrister, there were three positives for Cracker going into the trial: a charge of manslaughter as opposed to murder, his immediate admission to the police of his attack, and the heroic status conferred on him by the public. The latter was understandable in light of the outcry from the Maria Colwell case and the horrific injuries suffered by Tracy. The press hailed Cracker daily as a just avenger, cloaking him in the mantle of courageous defender of children, and letters to editors throughout the country echoed the sentiments behind the headlines. As Jacqui, Dani and I followed the news in the press and on TV, we could be excused for thinking Cracker would receive a minimal sentence.

In order to fully understand the riots that swept the country following the judge's sentence of ten years, one has to be aware that Maria Colwell's stepfather was given eight years for battering his seven-year-old stepdaughter to death (a sentence that was halved on appeal). One should also take into account that six months prior to Cracker's trial, a judge had given the rapist of a ten-year-old girl a sentence of four months imprisonment on the grounds the girl had dressed provocatively. But the marches, the protests, the overturned cars, the fires: none of them helped

Cracker. Eventually the unrest died down, other stories claimed the front pages, and the social services community resumed business as usual. Cracker's one triumph was that Tracy was taken into foster care. Her stepbrother remained with his mother.

Following the trial, pending the appeal process, Cracker was moved to HMP Attwood, a maximum security prison on the northern edge of the County – another incomprehensible move on the part of the justice system. Attwood was a notorious institution that held some of the most violent criminals in Britain, along with a number of IRA terrorists. Situated approximately fifty miles north of Wyvern, visiting was limited to just two visits of two hours each per month, with a maximum of three visitors allowed at one time. Although Dani and I usually accompanied Jacqui, the two of us spent the majority of our time amusing Erica Jane in the children's play area, and thus my time with Cracker was limited. Nevertheless, I was able to discover and appreciate something of what he was going through. I learned with horror during my first visit, of his Prison Reception: the official opening of his prison file; the receipt of the number he would become; the donning of the uniform he was required to wear; the reading of the endless rules and regulations, including the required addressing of all officers as sir; and the indignity of his strip search.

From my experience of that first visit alone, I knew that imprisonment was as dangerous to Cracker's physical wellbeing as it was destructive to his soul. We'd often joked about our good fortune in avoiding National Service, and how our inability to follow rules would have resulted in us spending most of our time on a charge. Now, if Cracker failed to toe the line, he would be placed in solitary confinement, something he learned quickly was to be avoided at all costs. As visit followed visit, my concerns grew. It appeared to me that Attwood prison had been constructed to specifications designed to guarantee misery, while the prison's policies seemed targeted at dehumanization rather than rehabilitation. The more I learned, the more I doubted Cracker could survive the place. The absence of space, the lack of privacy, the noise, the boredom, the food, were always going to be problematic, but the authoritarian regime based upon a myriad of petty rules was anathema to

Cracker. He described each day as a fight to retain his humanity, his dignity, and his individuality.

Of major concern to me as I sat across the cheap plastic table from him in that hangar of a visiting space, was his assertion, frequently repeated, that it was not from the prisoners he had anything to fear, but from the men in uniform: the screws. Contrary to what we'd always been led to believe, he said, there was little violence among the prisoners, but he'd been horrified at the beatings he'd seen administered by the screws. He told stories of men beaten unmercifully in their cells, and of prisoners dragged by the hair from the cells to solitary. There were tears in his eyes as he related the story of seeing one man treated as a punch bag while senior officers looked the other way. The main concern of medical officers, he said, was that the faces of beaten prisoners remain unmarked. He also told Dani and me that because he was held in such high regard among the prisoners for the crime he'd committed, he was under particular threat from the screws. The screws, he said, hated integrity, and loathed the concept of admiration for a prisoner; they also had an aversion to anyone who was well educated.

The more I heard of prison life, the more convinced I became that eventually Cracker would break, and with disastrous consequences. Jacqui shared the same fear. She lost both colour and weight during those early weeks. In addition to worrying about Cracker, holding down her job, and caring for Erica Jane, she'd been obliged to put the house on the market in order to move somewhere smaller, while her father's deteriorating condition demanded frequent trips to London.

The anxiety I personally felt for my friend as we awaited the appeal process, was assuaged by two people: Dani and Brynmor Evans. Without Dani, *I* may have broken. She was magnificent: she somehow changed her work schedule to be around me whenever I wasn't in school, and worked through her father's contacts in the legal profession, to ensure Cracker's appeal process was handled in the most effective way possible. Dr. Evans spent a lot of time with me too. As deputy head, I automatically assumed control of the school in Cracker's absence: a job which, owing to the publicity and general outcry, was especially sensitive, and I was in real need of the support Dr. Evans supplied. Despite a schedule which I knew to be horrific, he visited Barlington on numerous occasions, offered me full access to every resource at his command and, most significantly, reiterated his support for Cracker. Owing to the crime he'd committed, Cracker would never be able to re-enter the teaching profession – even were his conviction to be quashed on appeal – but Dr. Evans, hinted at possible career paths at County Hall that might offer Cracker possibilities. He also asked me to consider accepting the headship of Barlington, an offer I thanked him for, but one I told him I would have to consider.

Cracker's application for leave to appeal was granted, and his appeal against both his conviction and sentence was heard in the full court in June. He'd already served almost five months in prison by then, but somehow he'd stayed away from trouble, and we were hopeful that with the resurgent publicity surrounding the appeal, and the work of his barrister, Sir Andrew Huntington Q.C., his conviction would be quashed. Sir Andrew had been retained courtesy of Dani's father, and had a history of successfully appealing draconian sentences. It was in him that I saw our greatest hope. Unfortunately, while he was successful in having Cracker's sentence halved, the court upheld the integrity of the conviction, and Cracker was returned to Attwood to serve five years, less time served. With time off for good behavior – if he could manage that in the hell that was Attwood – he would be released in a little over two years.

While Cracker lived out his stark existence, I carried on what I perceived as his work at Barlington. In July I accepted the headship from the Director after countless hours of thought and discussion with Dani. On the surface it looked a straightforward decision: I knew the school, the philosophy, the kids, the parents, and felt a real responsibility to continue to develop what we'd started. On the other hand, I was constantly saddened by Cracker's absence as I moved through the school, resulting in moments when I thought it would be healthier for everyone if I moved on. It was Cracker's argument in the end that convinced me to stay.

'Fucking hell, Robbie, you've got to stay. Think about it, old son: everything we've worked for; everything we've accomplished; it could all go down the toilet if you leave, and you bloody know it. You owe it to the kids, the parents and the staff, Robbie: who else could do what you can do?'

'Well, actually, if I owe it to anyone, I owe –'

Cracker glared at me. 'Don't you fucking say it, Robbie, don't you say it: you owe me nothing.'

If ever he was wrong about anything, he was wrong about that, but I did agree to stay.

That summer was the first since 1969 I did not spend in North Dakota. Instead, Dani and I got married, and after a small reception, followed by a visit to see Cracker, we went on honeymoon to Provence. On our return we moved into a new home – purchased largely with Dani's money – and I threw myself back into work. I found an excellent deputy head in Pauline Green, whose hard work as the head of our infant department, and knowledge of what Cracker and I had always visualized as the ideal school, made her both deserving and qualified to take the position. As we began the new school year, Barlington slowly began to return to normal after the trauma of the previous months.

I was in my office at the end of a long week in October, when I first heard of the riot at Attwood. Dani had picked it up on her car radio and called me immediately. From her initial description it seemed the prisoners had taken over part of the prison in protest against the beatings of prisoners in the segregation unit. Arranging to meet her at Jacqui's house, I drove over there to find Jacqui in an agitated state.

'You just know the silly bugger's involved in this, don't you?' she said.

She knew me too well for me to attempt denial, and we both waited anxiously for the six o'clock news on the BBC. Dani arrived just as the stern-faced news anchor began the report, and we watched the story unfold.

Three of the four wings in the Prison were in the hands of the prisoners who appeared to be systematically demolishing anything they could get their hands on. The prison inmates were protesting not only the beatings in the segregation unit, but the widespread use of 'Rule 43' which allowed for solitary confinement (the brutality of which Cracker had made me privy to), the sadism of a number of screws, and slave labour conditions in the prison workshops.

The TV images of the massing of police officers in riot gear in and around the prison were Orwellian, but it was when a group of prisoners burst out on to the roof of D wing, and unfurled a white sheet bearing their demands, that we had our worst fears confirmed. Cracker looked the consummate revolutionary as he stood there, holding one side of the sheet with his left hand while brandishing his right clenched fist above his head. He was wearing a heavy black coat, a prison officer's hat, and what appeared to be a home made white scarf around his neck. He and the rest of his cohorts were chanting something, but the words were indistinguishable – unlike those on the sheet upon which the cameras zoomed in. The words were concise and undoubtedly the work of Cracker:

> Humane conditions
> Free Speech
> Dignity
> An End to Slave Labour
> A Government Enquiry
> Prosecution of Sadistic Screws

When the news concluded, with an update promised for the ten o'clock broadcast, we sat in silence, except for Erica Jane who, excited over seeing her daddy on TV, was full of questions that Jacqui attempted, through her fear, to answer. The ten o'clock news offered no new information and Dani and I left, promising Jacqui we'd return the following morning, a Saturday.

The police struck in the middle of the night with what the ensuing Commons Inquiry would describe as 'admirable restraint.' Quite how the use of tear gas, stun grenades, and savagely wielded batons, qualified as 'restraint' was asked loudly by the newspapers afterwards, but for Jacqui, Cracker's sisters, Dani, me and the community of Barlington County

Primary School, the issue was of secondary importance. Cracker was dead. How he came to plunge from the roof was never ascertained, but when his body was discovered in the prison yard, his neck and lower spine were broken and his skull was shattered. He was thirty-one years old.

The funeral service, Cracker's views on religion notwithstanding, was held at Wyvern Cathedral, there being no other building in the city or county capable of holding the fifteen hundred mourners. As I listened to the words of 'Abide with Me,' at the end of the service, I wondered what Cracker, the avowed atheist, would have made of it all. I have a suspicion he'd have been more impressed with the wake the parents of Barlington held in his honour that night, at the community center he'd been responsible for building.

It would be a long time before any of us would heal, especially Jacqui who was visibly shrunken by the death of her husband. In the meantime, we took what comfort we could from simply having had the pleasure of his company during his short life. I can see him now in the Flying Halifax, after another sixty hour work week: that great head on those broad shoulders, tipping his pint back; drawing back like a child as Jacqui wipes the foam from his upper lip; and I can hear his laughter splitting the fug in the yellowing lounge. I see him with his arm around Dani's shoulder, telling his tales as Jacqui rolls her eyes at me, but most of all, I see him surrounded by kids, their eyes reflecting the adoration they felt for him. Yes, Alastair James McCracken was a friend of mine. He wasn't perfect, being rather too fond of using his fists and other men's wives for that, but he was special.

Bridie laid the manuscript aside and closed her eyes. So much to reflect upon; so many questions. Why, for instance, had McDermott waited so long to write when he clearly had the ability? Had he seen it as a one-off? A coda to his life? Or had he used the process of writing as a vehicle to deal with Jean's death? And how much was fact and how much fiction? Cracker, for example: was he real or imaginary, or a little of both? She tried to weigh the whole story in her mind. She'd enjoyed it, no doubt about that. It reflected the vicissitudes of life well, she thought: the ups and downs, the laughter and tears, the triumphs and tragedies. . . . Bit of a fucking downer that ending though. She considered the educational backdrop to the story. Had McDermott actually been a teacher? It sure seemed like it, but he'd never spoken to her of that part of his life. Why was that? She tried to imagine a younger version of him teaching kids and found she could do so with little difficulty. She'd watched him with her grandkids and . . . yeah, he'd have been a good teacher, she thought. She poured herself another glass of wine and went outside. The sun was hot on her face despite the late afternoon hour as she made her way to the top of the riverbank. March 20th and eighty degrees in Northern Michigan – how crazy was that?

McDermott sat, sipping his wine, watching the geese coming in as the sun retreated. Their numbers were shrinking daily now, the migration to the north nearing its completion, but latecomers or not, the graceful approach of the birds to the river and bayous drew her eye too, just as the peculiar mix of melancholy and triumph in their honking entertained her ears. Turning from the marsh, she paused for a moment, taking in the picture of McDermott swirling his wine, Lance, Shep and Connor comatose at his feet. The sun bathed his face and she marveled again at the speed with which he'd recovered from the surgery. Ten weeks since his heart attack, nine since his discharge from the hospital, and except for the impressive scar on his chest, he looked as fit as ever. He turned his head and grinned as she sat beside him.

'So? Did you finish it?'

'Yeah. Just.'

'And?'

'Well, I'm up to my ass in questions, but I loved it. Now, you know me; I'm no fucking literary critic, but I think it flows well, keeps you wanting to turn the page. Shit, I think it's entertaining. I do have one suggestion though.'

'Only one eh? What's that?'

Bridie hesitated a moment before she blurted it out. 'Okay, well, you do want to sell it. Right?'

McDermott laughed, 'Well, there's the small question of finding an agent and, or, a publisher first, and it's not *that* important, but I'd be lying if I said otherwise. Why?'

'Well,' Bridie said, looking out at the marsh, 'call me an old fashioned fart, but I figure most people prefer happy endings, triumph of good over evil, and all that happy horseshit. You know? So if I was you, I'd change that ending.'

'Ah.' McDermott leaned back in his chair and took a sip of his wine before he continued, 'Now that's one thing I can't do.'

'You mean – Cracker – he was a real guy – and that prison thing – it really happened?'

'Oh he was real alright, and yeah, it all went down the way I wrote it. Pretty much anyway.'

'Jesus Christ, I'm sorry, Robbie. And had you really known him since birth?'

'Well, since we were old enough to talk.'

'Shit!' And what about Catherine? How real was that? And Dani? What happened there? And while we're at it – '

'Whoa, whoa, whoa. You can't expect an author to give away all his secrets you know. But, maybe if you get me another glass of wine, I might let you in on the odd one.'

'Oh yeah?' Bridie said, taking his wineglass, 'And you know what Mr. fucking Tolstoy, if you don't, your chances of getting lucky tonight might just go away.'

'Now that's not fair, Bridie,' he said to her retreating back. 'We're talking about my professional integrity here.'

'Yeah? And I'm talking about this,' she said, and wriggled her ass provocatively at him as she went into the cabin.

Laughing and exulting in his good fortune at the same time, McDermott closed his eyes and tilted his head back to take in the sun's last rays. He thought over what Bridie had said about the ending to his book. It was true, people did like happy endings, but the fact was, real life rarely delivered them. Cracker had certainly not had one; a happy ending had been the antithesis of what Jean had endured; and there'd been nothing positive about little Mel's death in early February either. And then there was Holly Freeman. Her ending had yet to be determined, but her journey toward it, based upon what Bridie had heard, looked destined to be one of darkness and despair, as she continued to battle her demons within the walls of the Stephens Psychiatric Clinic. He remained troubled by the part he felt himself to have played in that whole business. His continued sessions with Greta VanDamm were helping, and Bridie's eventual grasp and acceptance of the facts behind the affair were integral to his current emotional wellbeing, but thoughts of Holly alone in that place surfaced regularly to the detriment of his own affect.

A couple of sandhill cranes kicked up a commotion on the edge of the river returning him to the present and what Bridie had said about selling his book. He'd been putting off his decision, well aware of the overwhelming odds against success, but he supposed it was time to face up to things on that front too. He had edited and polished to the point where he knew he was in danger of losing his original spontaneity: it was time to either begin the process of finding an agent or a publisher or of publishing the book himself. He rather thought he'd go through the motions of the agent/publisher route simply for the experience, but if, in the end, he simply had a few copies printed for himself and a couple of friends, then that was fine too. Sure, he'd like to see his book professionally published, gracing the shelves of bookstores around the country, but it had always been more about the process than the product, and he could live with the simple success of having had the balls to attempt and complete the –

'Holy shit! You're looking serious; I was only joking you know.' Bridie held out a glass of wine for him.

As always happened when she appeared before him, any thoughts extraneous to her mere presence took flight, and he smiled up at her as he took the glass. It was Day . . . It was Day . . .

Author's Note

I have taken the following liberties in the writing of this book:

- The Upper Peninsula and Canadian species of Canada geese that McDermott would have been familiar with in northwest Michigan, actually begin their southern migration in September a little earlier than I have indicated at the beginning of the book

- The British Library's 'The Writing Life' CDs were released in 2011 rather than in 2010. (I heartily recommend them for anyone interested in the craft of writing.)

- The art of Taekwondo was in its infancy in 1950s England and thus unlikely to have been practiced as a sport in any English school – especially a traditional English grammar school as represented by 'Bricknall'

- The Potawatomi marshes do exist, but in southwest Michigan rather than the northwest where I have placed them in this novel

- The view from Stoker Lodge in Whitby is slightly different from that which I have portrayed, the Pavilion obscuring the view of the beach

Malcolm McDonald

Acknowledgements

My thanks must go first to my wife without whose constant belief in me, this book would not have been written, and without whose shrewd eye, it would probably have been sold by the pound. I also owe a good deal to my readers who braved the choppy waters of the early manuscripts: my dear friends, David Lee, and Jan Garner; and my brother-in-law, Colin Firth. Natives of England all, they set me straight on countless issues. My gratitude too, to Dr. Julie Hutson for her advice on all things medical, and to psychotherapist, Sherry Petro-Surdel for her insights into the world of psychotherapy and the grieving process. Any errors are, of course, my own. Thanks also to my friend and primary editor, Karen Kennedy, who, as always, was not backward in coming forward when it came to suggesting necessary revisions – thanks, Kar.

Short extracts from the double audio CD *The Writing Life: Authors Speak* (British Library publications, 2011) are copyright of the British Library Board and are reproduced with permission. Please note that P. D. James, Ian Rankin and Michael Morpurgo each retain the copyright in their words, but licensed the BL to use these edited extracts from their recordings in the double audio CD. *The Writing Life* audio CD contains short extracts from the wider oral history project *Authors' Lives*, run by National Life Stories at the British Library: http://www.bl.uk/nls/auhors. (Special thanks to: Mary Stewart, Curator, Oral History and Deputy Director, National Life Stories at the British Library for her help and support, and to Sarah O'Reilly, Project Interviewer for the CDs, and Rob Perks, Lead Curator of Oral History.)

Finally I must thank Peter Pouncey whose magnificent novel 'Rules for Old Men Waiting' gave me the original idea. Anyone who has not read his work should hurry down to their nearest bookstore and acquire it at the earliest opportunity.